"DAVID GURR HAS THE SUBTLETY OF A LE CARRÉ . . . TERSE AND ELUSIVE AS DEIGHTON . . . BUT HE HAS A DEPTH AND LYRICAL QUALITY WHICH NEITHER OF THESE MASTERS CAN MATCH."

—*Houston Post*

"A SUPERB THRILLER."

—*Toronto Star*

A WOMAN CALLED SCYLLA
BY
DAVID GURR

A WOMAN CALLED SCYLLA

David Gurr

BANTAM BOOKS
TORONTO · NEW YORK · LONDON · SYDNEY

A WOMAN CALLED SCYLLA

*A Bantam Book / published by arrangement with
The Viking Press*

PRINTING HISTORY

*Viking edition published March 1981
Bantam edition / May 1982*

*Grateful acknowledgment is made to the following for permission
to reprint copyrighted material:*
*Chappell Music Company: Portions of lyrics from "The Old
Soft Shoe" by Morgan Lewis and Nancy Hamilton, Copyright
1946 by Chappell & Co., Inc. Copyright renewed. International
Copyright secured. All rights reserved. Used by permission.*
*Ched Music: Portions of lyrics from "Don't Sit Under The
Apple Tree With Anyone Else But Me" by Lew Brown, Charles
Tobias, and Sam Stept.*
*Mills Music, Inc.: Portions of lyrics from "Run, Rabbit, Run"
by Noel Gay and Ralph Butler. Copyright 1939 by Noel Gay
Music Co., Ltd. Copyright renewed. Exclusively published in the
Western Hemisphere by Mills Music, Inc. Used with permission.
All rights reserved.*
*United Artists Music: Portions of lyrics from "We're Off to See
the Wizard (The Wonderful Wizard of Oz)" by Harold Arlen and
E. Y. Harburg. Copyright 1939, renewed © 1967 by Metro-Goldwyn-
Mayer, Inc. All rights administered and controlled by Leo Feist,
Inc. Used by permission. All rights reserved.*

ISBN 0-553-20691-5

PRINTED IN THE UNITED STATES OF AMERICA

0 9 8 7 6 5 4 3 2 1

*This book about Jane is for
my father*

Contents

Author's Note

This book is a work of fiction. Although its plot is focused on the historic office of Lord Chancellor in the British Government, no resemblance whatever is intended to any past holder of that office: most especially not to its incumbent in 1977, Lord Elwyn-Jones.

For personal observation of life in the Reuter (with no "s"!) world I should like to thank Stuart Underhill. For Montreal, Fleurette. For help with Washington's tricks and jokes, my oldest friend, Frank Mitchell, and Jo. For a balanced South African perspective, Jonathan Franklin and his courageous wife. For a unique opportunity to listen to his fine radio documentary, *Islands of the Jacarandas*, Mr. K.M.J. Perreur-Lloyd. For superlative assistance with the minutiae of life in the country that was Rhodesia, Richard Cooper. For the British Army, Stephen Petzing, John Barnard, and Yeoman Warder J. Chaffer, MM. For an Australian view from the sidelines and a flawlessly typed manuscript, Gwen Anscomb (with no "e"!).

Above and beyond all these helpful people I must thank Christian Bailey in London who went into the labyrinth on my behalf and returned to show that the art of letter writing is not dead. Dolphin Square and the War Rooms belong to her.

With the exception of the selection from Matthew Arnold's poem, the Mackenzie King diary extracts are my own.

And for readers not familiar with the acronyms, past and present, in the text, a small glossary has been included at the end.

Prospect Lake
May, 1980

Glossary

D Notice	Defence Notice (British), an advisory warning that prosecution will follow if disclosure continues.
FANY	First Aid Nursing Yeomanry (British), a cover organization for women working in special operations.
GCHQ	Government Communications Head Quarters (British).
"J"	The initial used to designate General Menzies as wartime Chief of British Intelligence; other office holders have used "C."
LCS	London Controlling Section.
NASA	National Aeronautics and Space Agency.
NSA	National Security Agency (American).
OP	Other Place. Churchill's unlisted country retreat at Ditchley Park.
PATU	Police Anti-Terrorist Unit (Rhodesia); made up of both police and civilian volunteers.
RCMP	Royal Canadian Mounted Police.
SD	*Sicherheitsdienst*, the Nazi Party intelligence apparatus.
SIS	Secret Intelligence Service (British), headquartered in Century House near Westminster Bridge.
SOE	Special Operations Executive.
ULTRA	The cover name for cryptanalysis of German message traffic; originally the name of the Admirals' signal code used at Trafalgar.
WCR	War Cabinet Rooms under Whitehall.
ZANLA	Zimbabwe African National Liberation Army.

A
WOMAN
CALLED
SCYLLA

THE ROAD TO
A DARK LAND

Some talk of Alexander, and some of Hercules;
Of Hector and Lysander, and such great names as these;
But of all the world's brave heroes, there's none that can
*   compare,*
With a tow row row row row row row to the British Grena-
*   dier. . . .*

> —Traditional British Air and Regimental March
> of the Grenadier Guards

London, October 1943

Big Ben stands at six o'clock. A woman stands in the court below it. She remarks to a sleek, black-haired man in a car beside her on the superstitious coincidence of clocks, of the hands of time in line.

She crosses her fingers, pats the black body of the Austin once, twice, climbs in, slams the door. She looks at blacked-out London leaving in the dusk, and from the anonymity of signless wartime Britain she watches for other English towns and places: places with English names known all her life. She watches for Croydon and Redhill, then Reigate, then Dorking, then Holmwood and Coldharbour and Leith Hill and the Roman ghosts of Anstiebury Camp. She watches most for a village called Wellbury St. Mary and an Elizabethan manor called Roone's House.

The manor door, built of timbers from the house before this one, opens. Small feet run crunching across gravel toward the blue-dimmed crosses of the war lights on the car. There are kisses, hugs. Now tears. A terrible moment. The sleek man waits. The car's door closes. The car's wheels swing it in an arc through invisible scented borders of the last late-summer roses and lavender and thyme, then take it south again. South along a road built and christened Stane Street twenty British centuries ago.

In Roone's House, in a nursery bedroom at a nursery window a child waves at a woman she can no longer see. Waves, waves...

Past Codmore Hill and Bignor Hill and into a nameless field with a nameless house and more nameless people. The car stops for the second time. The last time. The woman leaves the backseat. The sleek man with her carries a soft leather satchel—carefully, but easily.

3

At the head of a single flight of stairs, narrow and steep, the sleek man stops, opens a door, unlocks a silver-steel link around his wrist, hands the woman the satchel, the chain, and the key.

"It's armed," says the sleek man. "You will remember?"

She smiles a smile with gray eyes and shuts him out.

A rail-backed chair, a small oak table, a mottled full-length mirror: so familiar, yet so strange. So cold. The bricked-up window and the portable electric fire have all but given in, having surrendered long ago to the damp from the flats at the edge of the sea. She stands naked. Shivers. Looks for a moment at the lines on her stomach from the child in the nursery window.

She takes clothes from the neatly folded pile on the table and dresses once more. A print blouse, serge skirt, darned cotton underpants. No stockings. With each item, she checks by rote for names, for lint, for grass, for gravel: for anything of England's. For this heart-catching photograph of the child playing with her dog beneath an apple tree.

The new-old handbag holds false identity: ration coupons for the Danish Region; ersatz lipstick. A tiny box marked "L."

Downstairs, a woman in a FANY uniform checks clothing and bag meticulously again. "I'm sorry we couldn't let you wear stockings," says the FANY woman. "We're told the Danes have pretty well run out. But you're going to be cold without stockings. Have some tea."

Tea. A last trace of something English. A buzzer sounds twice in the hall.

The woman in the FANY uniform kisses the woman without stockings, holds her hands. The woman without stockings walks across wet, autumn grass toward the aircraft. The satchel with the silver-steel chain bumps against her thigh. Her feet are cold. Her stomach aches.

The aircraft, a Lysander, is a child's toy of wood with stubby dragonfly wings glued to the top of its thorax, black-painted and invisible. The pilot, death's charioteer, black-leather–suited, sits in front.

"Sixpence each way," says the pilot. "Jump in."

The engine spits twice behind its baffles to clear its throat. The black propeller jumps, grabs, catches the night.

Inside the house, the woman in the FANY uniform unplugs the tired fire and packs the discarded clothes and handbag in a cheap black suitcase. She makes a list of the contents and places it with the clothes. She sees the photograph, she picks it up.

"Oh, my dear," says the woman in the FANY uniform. *"My dear."*

Two hours after midnight a short, bald, rather fat and very tired man in a tatty dressing gown embroidered with ragged dragons receives the picture, looks at it, turns it over. On the back sees lines written in a clear, sharp, very English hand.

Wearing flight boots with unzipped tongues that protrude absurdly beneath the dressing gown, the tired man slops to a window, stares at a single searchlight slicing the black sky above Britain. And then a voice graveled by hard times and hard liquor—a voice though imitated, once heard, never forgotten, recites the inscription written as some sort of explanation by a mother for a daughter.

> *In the darkest night of the year*
> *When the stars have all gone out,*
> *Courage is better than fear,*
> *Faith is better than doubt.*

Tears roll down the puffy yet almost childish cheeks and smudge the ink.

Three hundred miles from a prime minister's tears, Scylla, the woman without stockings, descends into hell.

THE
PAPER WAR

1

She woke late with a headache, and did only half her exercises; quitting at the sit-ups which after twenty years had made her abdominal muscles an obstetrical dream. She poked the muscles with a finger that sank in half an inch—she was quitting at the sit-ups too often. Why not? The flatness of the belly was only window dressing anyway, a come-on for the preliminary round in the charade of sex. This close to their fourth fertile decade the muscles must be as aware as she was that they might never hear the bell for childbirth, the main event.

Fuck it! And deep-breathing ten degrees of frost had made her headache worse. The blue smog of cigarette smoke from last night's Bourbon-flagged Parti Québécois rally at the Forum was still locked in behind her eyes. She closed the hotel window and called room service for the foreign correspondent's breakfast: coffee, aspirin, and a fifth of Scotch.

"A fifth, madam?" French Canadian room service was confused. "A mickey?"

"Whatever. A bottle, okay? And send up three cups."

A mickey for three Mouseketeers of the press. How many Poynter's Corners hours of her life had she spent with Disney at Saturday-morning movies with the yo-yo competitions? She could not imagine Roger Alleyn of London's *Sunday Times* at a yo-yo competition. Skinny Tremblay of *Le Devoir*, maybe—if a Depression childhood in Quebec had left cash to spare for Mickey Mouse.

9

The angular Alleyn was someone she could work with, but she was already fond of the rotund Tremblay. "Skinny" was one of those ass-backward, war-zone names: the Canadian's rounded back and sparse hair brushed wetly across the head in a vain march against time reminded her more appropriately of a beaver. The crazy oddball-guy connections she made on war locations . . .

If this battle of linguistics was a war.

She stared out of the window at the frozen heart of Montreal, now newly white. Most of her wars were hot—and in hot climates—although their politics by this time always left her cold. She was here only for the mechanics of separation: if the Canadian nation state wanted to tear itself apart, Reuter wanted background on it for the files in the morgue.

Yesterday, with Tremblay as chauffeur for a trip around town in the snow, she had been certain she was going to join the files in an icebox of her own. All she could remember was being hurled against Alleyn in a succession of miraculous vehicular escapes between endless rows of sooted brick apartments hung with frozen washing. Alleyn had not seemed to mind the hurling.

And lunch, with Irish coffees to mask the fright, had been a ball. But after lunch she had had her first meeting with séparatiste Québec.

The interviewee, a PQ education spokesman trained at Yale, had talked of *Anglophones* and *Francophones* and of half a million immigrants who became in this Orwell's newspeak, *Allophones*. The Allophone children, said the Yale man, would be considered "non-persons, for linguistic purposes, education-wise. . . ."

Anywhere else, she had jotted in her notebook, the use of words like 'non-persons' had eventually led to war.

She looked down on to a snow-shawled statue of Victoria guarding the anglo lines in this white square. Behind the Queen an Allophone newcomer's sign on a tavern—Luigi's—desperate for compromise, offered Smoked Corn Beef et Châteaubriand.

There had been no room for compromise in the hymn-singing fervor at the rally. No room for anyone out of step with a new social order for Quebec. Her education spokesman had been on the platform beside the jug-eared little man with the cigarette who hoped to ride this nationalist tiger.

With tears in his eyes the man from Yale had led the singing. The crowd's favorite song had been sung by nationalists and socialists before.

"*'Tomorrow Belongs to Me!'*" Alleyn had exclaimed to Tremblay. "Good Christ—doesn't Lévesque know where that comes from?"

And Tremblay, A French Canadian with dreams of his own for his country had said sadly, dropping an "h," "He should. 'E was with the U.S. Army when they opened Auschwitz."

She had been spared Auschwitz, but there had been Vietnam, Cambodia, Ireland, and now Quebec. The world of non-persons and tomorrow belongs to me. The human condition. She needed a break from it. A change. When she got back to Washington she must bug the boss.

Which made her sound like any little girl hassled in the office! She did not think of Fadiman as a boss. With a sharp winter bite of introspection she wondered what Fadiman, as he passed out the Reuter marching orders, thought of her.

She pulled on a sweater and jeans, did a bare minimum with lipstick, tried to hide the craters under the eyes with Erace, which only made the wrinkles worse.

"Mrs. Montigny, honey," she said to the mirror, "it's time for something drastic. We're going to have to change that hair."

Once in a decade seemed about right for something drastic.

Cutting the waist-long hair off had certainly changed things last time, in 1967. Freedom from the weight and care of it had sent her out to Saigon with a new man and a new name and a fresh hope of finding Joseph Conrad's meaning up a jungle creek. Her head had never felt so light . . . But this time it couldn't be just a cut or a set—and the ash-blonde rinse was no longer going to make it. This time it would have to be real color. Dramatic streaks. Slashes of gold.

At the end of the next decade would the rinse be blue? . . .

"*Jesus.*" She stared stricken at the mirror and was rescued by room service with Scotch outside the door.

She gulped two aspirins and poured coffee with a spike of booze. By the time the Mouseketeers arrived, and knocked, the pain behind her eyes was gone. Alleyn's head stooped just below the door frame.

"Two lost souls on bloody Sunday, ma'am. May we come in?"

"Make that three," she said. "Roger, you're more like Galbraith every day."

"I'm certainly hopeless about money."

"*The Times* means you won the pot, Jane." Tremblay followed Alleyn across to the bottle. "Goddamn women's intuition!"

"What was the final tally?"

"Seventy," said Tremblay. "Plus or minus one. They're still waiting for Chicoutimi. We could get it on the radio."

"For a couple of bucks, Skinny, there's really no sweat—"

"—Is there, Jane," Alleyn appeared to be occupied with finding his pipe, "might one ask, a Mister Montigny?"

"Covering crime for the *Seattle Post-Intelligencer*. Or he was, eight years ago."

"Ah."

The pipe had found itself. Now it had to be filled and lit.

"I'm safely divorced, Roger."

Eyes free to wander, Alleyn grinned. "*Intelligencer*—what an extraordinary name. I must say I'm surprised the Sisterhood holds a member in good standing—keeping the Mrs."

"Outside home base, it's a man's world, sweetheart. I need a key to the kingdom."

"If it unlocked a chat with the Pope and Uncle Ho—my God, I'd give an arm!"

"Even for a man from *The Times*," Tremblay inserted his needle smoothly, "the operation has to be a little more drastic, eh?"

She turned on the news to head them off. The score had settled at PQ:69 and the CBC was sounding a death rattle for Canadian federalism. Either Trudeau or Lévesque had compared the English voters of Montreal to white Rhodesians. Suggestions had been made that they should go back where they came from. A great line, she thought. The Indians could have used it.

"We continue now," said the announcer, "with our dramatization of the Mackenzie King diaries from 1943. As you will recall, at the Quebec Conference, King was very much the host basking in the reflected glory of his guests. . . ."

"Mackenzie—" an actor doing a good job on Roosevelt's

Hyde Park diction cut in, "Mackenzie—posterity must be told of the *enormously* fine job which you have done."

She reached to shut it off.

"If you don't mind," Alleyn said, "I do a bit of this sort of thing. May we leave it for a moment?"

A pen could be heard scratching across paper, and now a third voice started. A monotonous, self-ingratiating voice. "Later in the evening, Winston said much the same to me. I wished with all my heart that there had been some recorder present who might have been equipped to set down the scene for generations of Canadians yet unborn." Now the pen again, and then the voice: "Upon the conclusion of the dinner we three were left alone. We three who control the destinies of our Free World and thus of all its peoples—for Victory, though still removed, is now assured. And I thought, if she—Mother—could only be with us now in person, as she is with me in spirit..."

"Skinny," she said, "I hate to criticize one of your leaders, but this guy is a fucking fruitcake."

Tremblay turned his sad eyes upward. "Not one of mine, chérie."

The scratching continued. The self-satisfied voice droned on. "I observed the hands of time as Winston spoke. They were aligned at midnight. And at that point—surely the most propitious of *all* positions on the clock—we discussed the future of mankind. It was past two when we concluded, and though I could scarce speak because of my exhaustion, yet there was a vast exhilaration in the knowledge of the force we should arrange. I do believe with all my heart that there is a Divine Presence here—an intervention, if you will—which guides our feet. Yet how much we owe. Franklin and Winston both almost in tears as the latter told us of the grey-eyed young woman, Scylla...."

The pen had stopped. The writer was no longer talking to his paper.

"Arnold's poem, Mother," the voice took on an eagerness, a joy, "do you remember?

> "'In this fair stranger's eyes of grey
> Thine eyes my love I see.
> I falter for the passing day
> Had borne thee far from me....'"

Music swelled in a fade-out. "These excerpts," said the announcer, "are from the segments of the diary recently released by the Public Archives of Canada. Next week we continue with King's thoughts on preparations for the invasion of the Continent."

Scylla.

And mother. Both at once.

"Thanks." Alleyn turned off the set. "Not badly done at all."

"Jane," said Tremblay, "are you okay? You look pale, eh?"

"Weird," she said. "Weird."

Both men looked at her.

"King's coincidences. His 'fair stranger' was my mother. She died in the war. I never knew her. It's okay."

But it was not okay. It was a shock. A chill from a dark land.

"She was a nurse?" asked Tremblay.

"No. One of those agents sent into Europe. And she must have been something. She was awarded a George Cross."

"To an American?" There was no hint of condescension in Alleyn's voice.

"She was British, Roger. My Down-East accent hides it, but I was born over there. My father brought me back right after her death. For me as a kid, she never existed. There were no photos, no scrapbooks. My father had seemed to just wipe her out."

"Not even a picture, Jane?"

"I did dig one up, Skinny—with her medal—but I wasn't a kid. I only found them when I was going through his things."

At the end of that perfect New England April day which began with the message to the Dean, stretched through the uncomprehended miles back to Maine, and finished as she stood alone by the enameled steel strongbox which she had never known he had.

It had not been possible! Surrounded by all the shared familiarity, all the evidence of "father-daughter" fun—his hiking boots, the Icelandic woolen toque she gave him one Christmas, the first editions of Jefferson and Franklin he gave himself in a particularly good year, the *Jane's Fancy* at the dock, which was for both of them—in all that *fun*, this secret parent life was just not possible.

But the open strongbox with its picture and its medal had showed that anything was possible: a man could remember a woman without pictures; a woman could die with the highest gallantry for reasons and in ways and means unquestioned; a girl could grow up and grasp that in the middle of her college finals the masculine support was gone. That life was solo from here on in.

"In the picture my mother's sitting under a tree with me and a little terrier dog and this Mary Poppins nanny in a uniform. But I can't remember any of that. There was some writing on the back of the picture but my father had even inked that out."

"But with the medal, Jane," Tremblay poured another round into the hotel cups, "the George Cross is the big apple for non-combatants, eh? There were no details on the citation?"

"Just her code name, Skinny. That's the only mention I've seen anywhere—until here. And I've looked. Not a crusade, like the adoption thing everyone's so hot on right now—I mean, dead is dead. But you've got to be curious. So if a new war book comes out I pick it up in the store and check the index for Scylla, just in case. All zero."

"Perhaps this really will have been your day for jackpots," said Alleyn. "If you want to try for more about the Scylla thing from our side, I might be able to help. Do you have British relatives? Do you know your mother's maiden name?"

"Arbright."

"Old Dorset? The old Duke?"

"My grandfather."

Alleyn's man's-world English briar dropped.

"I can beat that, Roger, old dear—I have joint citizenship. I registered just before I was eighteen. My act of rebellion against Daddy for settling on Radcliffe." She took a drink. "The registration was typical chauvinism: with a British *father* we could have skipped the formality. I picked up a U.K. passport five years ago to get into Peking. I'll tell you, State sent a shitty 'expatriating act' form letter over that."

"Well, blow me!"

And then Alleyn's astonished English face flushed—very slightly: perhaps just taking color from the booze.

Or perhaps, despite the old adage, the two sides of the Atlantic were beginning to speak the same language.

"Skinny," she said, to fill an awkward lull, "for a follow-up on the Mackenzie King diaries—is getting to Ottawa a big deal?"

"Only for the politicians, darling."

"I'll drink to *that*," said Alleyn. "And to you, Lady Jane—in your search. May all hearts and doors be opened."

2

Ottawa, November 1976

After Washington and Montreal, Ottawa jumped from its surrounding countryside with a village suddenness. They swept down off the ramp of a freeway into a narrow street of dirty old brick houses herded around an auto-repair yard and some sort of museum. The snow that had begun to melt in Montreal was still here and traffic crawled.

"I would have figured they were used to it, Skinny," she said.

"Every year with the first fall it's the same thing. But what else in the nation's capital than wishful thinking, eh?" Tremblay stopped at the bottom of a small incline and watched the beetle scrabble of a Volkswagen stuck ahead of them. He turned off to one side under a sign, *Rue O'Connor Street*. "Welcome to Fun City, Jane. Our bilingual heart."

Which was worn on the sleeve for all to see. Glass. Everywhere glass. Even the elevators exposed their guts to view outside the buildings. The largest mirror wall reared at the last corner.

"No energy crisis, Skinny? The heating must be mega-bucks!"

"It's the Bank of Canada, darling. And when the Bank can't print it fast enough—" Tremblay's melancholy reached rock bottom, "there's Parliament."

The blackly gray Victorian Gothic buildings hiding their skirts behind an iron fence stared scandalized at their inflated reflections across the street. Tremblay parked at a white box building equally incongruous to the west of them. Its tiny square windows were arranged in a cubist's vision of a dovecote.

"This is your archives?"

"We never had your Jefferson. See you later." Tremblay held his few hairs against the wind and pattered east to cover a rally of postal workers working themselves up for a fight at the Peace Tower.

The dovecote's lobby held two white-hatted commission-aires in a marble grotto off to one side. They gave her a half-ignoring, half-suspicious glance.

"Hi," she said.

One of the men got up reluctantly and came across to a counter. She explained what she was after.

"The King diaries?" Another glance. "That's third floor. Miss Palois."

The French name was pronounced grudgingly—with an Anglo-Saxon emphasis on the silent "s."

The third floor was mercifully free of marble and com-missionaires, full of books and deserted. She rang a small bell at an empty desk. A woman about her own age emerged from the stacks. *"Bonjour."*

"Good morning. The Mackenzie King diaries—are they available?"

"Certainly." The archivist switched effortlessly to En-glish. "The originals are in the vaults but we have copies here."

"Are they hard to read—his handwriting?"

"Oh no. Only the early years before 1935 were handwritten. After that, he dictated everything to a private secretary."

"From the selection I heard on the radio she must have been very private."

The woman smiled. "Yes. In any event we have had

them retyped—he used many abbreviations and initials and so on. Not all the diaries are released yet. We work on the thirty-year rule so that we're only up to 1946. And some is restricted beyond that. Personal correspondence mainly. Letters to people who died after King. The rule runs from the date of their death. And the spiritualist series cannot be released until 2001."

"A good year. Where do I start?"

"Register here and I'll take you through." The woman watched as she filled out a card with the reason for request. "Do you mind if I ask how personal?"

"I think my mother's mentioned. Why?"

"If you wish—if you think something's left out in transcription to microfiche you may see the originals. We don't like them handled too much—but, *pour une occasion spéciale, n'est-ce pas?*"

"Quite special. Thank you."

"Not at all." The woman took her across to a bank of microfilm readers. "You know how to run the machines? How to use the index?"

"Yes."

"I'll leave you then. Ask if there is any question. *Au'voir.*"

"*Au'voir.* Oh, one thing—"

"Yes?"

"The Quebec Conference—I know the year was 'forty-three—do you know the date?"

"Not exactly, but it was summer. July or August."

"Okay."

The room was empty. Large, long windows looked across the Ottawa River to the November drabness of Hull on the Quebec side. More new buildings had been thrown up there in the desperate haste to establish a federal foothold—a wall for the *séparatiste* hordes to beat against outside. The buildings looked like a women's prison and blocked the view of the Gatineau Hills. The Peace Tower was to her right. She wondered how Tremblay was doing with his strikers. She took out the first fiche.

> Have told Pearson *must* have blitzed Abbey stone from Westminster by 20th July at latest. Let him use much vaunted charm to this end. If we can convoy one million tons a month east, the Royal

Navy can bring two tons west by warship. *Am
utterly determined* to see it standing at Kingsmere
Ruin. Mother can be seen most clearly when de-
fined in arch or window. Little Pat agrees. Whining
& becoming greatly agitated when I discuss with
him . . .

The voyeuristic pull of the diaries was intense. It required
effort to avoid being trapped into reading everything. She
changed cartridges to August.

> *Aug. 5:* Winston now en route upon high seas
> in the *QM*. . . .
> *Aug. 12:* W to Hyde Park to visit R. . . . Press
> much amused by W's remark that Niagara Falls are
> unchanged since his last visit. "At least the principle
> remains the same," he said. "The water keeps fall-
> ing over. . . ."
> *Aug. 17:* R arrived Citadel seemed tired. . . .
> *Aug. 18:* I sit in "unofficially" but feel at last
> fully in the picture. . . . Tube Alloys incredible . . . our
> agreement for work at Trail & Chalk River may well
> be *vital*. . . .
> *Aug. 24:* W made Privy Counsellor of Domin-
> ion Cabinet & attended meeting of same. . . .
> *Aug. 27:* W to Lake of the Snows for fishing. . . .

She ran through the microfiche again to be sure. Nothing. She even read ahead through September, but by then all
the participants of the conference were long gone; flown off,
as Churchill said, in all directions like fragments of a shell.

She sat back in her chair. Why not let this hunt go, too?
But it was impossible that a scriptwriter had imagined Scylla.
She got up and went out to the desk at the head of the stairs.

The archivist was working at a catalogue. She looked up.
"Hi. Was it interesting?"

"Fascinating. Say, who was little Pat?"

"His dog."

"Why did I ask? Is it a problem to look at those
originals—just a few pages?"

"Not at all. I'll put this away and take you down. Push
the button."

She followed the archivist toward the elevator. As the doors closed, the Peace Tower clock was framed with its hour hand hidden at five minutes to eleven.

Vaults implied mystery. The reality was prosaic: chairs, carpet, equipment were all identical to those upstairs. Only a lock on the door and an absence of windows made the atmosphere confining.

The archivist opened a cabinet. "This is the drawer you want. The other one has the early years—when he went out to look for prostitutes at night."

"To 'reform' them, like Gladstone?"

"From the guilt in his writing, I don't think so." The woman smiled. "Toronto in 1910 was pretty up-tight for a young guy. The entries are looseleaf in binders. The commissionaire will sign you out when you're finished. Take care."

How was it that the difference between a copy and its original could be so extreme? Make such a difference? Make it seem that the peculiar little man with the dull voice and the hidden habits could be beside her? She found the entries for mid-August again. The twelfth, no thirteenth. Unlucky thirteenth—was that deliberate? No, here it was. Then the fourteenth, fifteenth, sixteenth, seventeenth.

The eighteenth. Numbered, page 300/43.

"*I sit in 'unofficially' but feel at last fully in the picture....*" Just as she had read upstairs, "*...work at Trail Chalk River may well be vital.*"

She turned the page.

"*I observed the hands of time—*"

The phrase on the radio. She looked at the heading: again, 300/43. The private secretary—overworked, late at night—for whatever reason, the girl had given two consecutive pages the same number.

The radio extract had not been verbatim. A word or a phrase had been modified here or there to increase dramatic effect, but the sense was the same.

Franklin & Winston both almost in tears as the latter told us of the grey-eyed young woman, Scylla. At news that she must without doubt be lost, I myself succumbed. Can it be believed there are such perfect women?

Later tonight: Through communication with An-

other, Beyond, I think I may understand the necessity for sacrifice—I pray that I do. Certainly if Hitler
is to be misled the involvement of Red Rose in the
Tube Alloys subterfuge must achieve that surprise.
Shall see HRH en route High River. Incredible
Oakes's death part & parcel. I shall dream of that
young woman tonight. . . .

She put away the files, thanked the commissionaire, left
a note to be delivered to the archivist, went up to the lobby.
Tremblay was already waiting.

"You look ready for lunch, Jane."

"A drink," she said. "A goddamn stiff one."

"The Press Club?"

"Skinny, I live in a press club!"

"A choice, then. I can get us in the Parliamentary
Restaurant—excellent food, and cheap. Or The Rideau Club,
rotten food and not cheap but good color for you. A year ago,
a woman, you couldn't have got in, eh? Now—" a Gallic
shrug, "you can see all the wheels sniff each other's arse."

Tremblay's mournful cynicism lifted the gloom of the
past from the vaults. She gave him a quick squeeze of the
hand.

"Let's go with your wheels. And I'll buy!"

"You must have found something, eh?"

"The reference was there all right, but Jesus—that King!
That incredibly bland, suet face—how could you *believe* all
that stuff about his 'Mum' was floating around inside?"

"I believe it!" Tremblay stopped briefly beside two tables
in an alcove and sniffed loudly.

The politicians, groomed by their media Frankensteins
for image, ate with caution. The uniformly tinted, marcelled,
puff-blown hairdos over the fleshy faces with heavy glasses
were grotesque as a row of aging widows at a fat farm.

"But no worse than Washington," she said. "Tell me,
Skinny, what's at Chalk River?"

"Atomic Energy of Canada."

She felt the first flicker of a hunch. "And High River?"

"Joe Clarke—our new Leader of the Opposition."

The hunch went out. "No. This was forty-three. Where
is it?"

"Alberta. But I can't imagine—"

"Could you check it? Give me a call if you find anything?"

"Just hayseeds, darling," Tremblay said with positive relish. "I'm *sure* of that!"

3

Washington, February 1977

She watched the intersection of Pennsylvania and Fourteenth, six floors below her window in the Press Club, change in time-lapse motion from candied icing to wallowing slush as the first stragglers from the suburbs arrived at the parking lots. A poster on the litter basket in front of the trick and joke shop across the road disconsolately urged them all to Pitch in for D.C. Tricks and jokes: an apt summary for Washington. She turned back from the window. The bureau was barely functioning: the night stringers hanging on, punchy after too much coffee. None of the other day people had managed to crawl from their core apartments. Her two-mile hike from Sutter's Lane should qualify her for a bonus from Fadiman. It would not.

She looked distastefully at the copy on her desk describing her visit to Plains, the new Lourdes of the South. Was Plains a joke or a trick? She dropped the story.

Despite the walk, she felt enervated, drained, her life half-frozen like the streets outside. Back to the blahs of Montreal. Blame it on the Pill, the day of the month, the state of the union, too long in the job. Dead ends from Scylla. Nothing helped.

She picked up Tremblay's note. Again.

Jane—sorry to forget so long about High River. We've been busy. Our new Messiah has feet of clay.

You remember the Mission drunks we missed outside the Palais de Justice? Lévesque hit one with his
car. At three in the morning, driving without his
glasses—but with his secretary. Only you won't see
any mention of *that* here! Frantic work at the inquest to keep it from the Anglo press. All of us
inside the hothouse have known for years.

Anyhow, High River's thirty miles south of
Calgary. Remittance men from England had a world
polo team in 1912—since then just farming and Joe
Clarke. The highlight for 1943 was a visit by the
Duke of Windsor to his ranch! Sorry again.

Oh yes—"Luigi's" has switched to Kentucky
Fried and Escargot.

Vive le Québec libre!
Skinny

Free indeed! Dear Skinny.

So High River was a dud. She'd expected it—thirty-four
years was too big a gap. And why should it matter? But like
the initial jolt, it did.

She played idly with a pen. Cover-ups brought back the
Tass man. For her year in Washington he had been invisible.
Today, of all days, the bastard had come to work in the
third-floor office which never gave up a sound or a scrap of
paper. Through the open door the room was spotless, deserted, the single typewriter obviously never used. Why today?
Some Kremlin instruction to show the capitalist effete that
Russians could cope with winter? The Tass man seemed to
have had a cold. The phone rang.

"London," said the switchboard. "Okay?"

"Go ahead." The phone made little switching noises.

"Jane Montigny?"

"Speaking."

"Jane—hullo. Roger Alleyn here. How are you?"

"Roger. I'm fine. Great!" And suddenly she felt it. She
smiled wryly at her own nature for its reversal. "What's new?
Are you coming to Washington?"

"I doubt it. I may be in the Tower tomorrow about you."

"About *me*?"

"Not exactly. Your Scylla. Strictly hands off—"

"Hold it, hold it." The starkness and lack of connection

in British speech was even worse without eye contact. "Start over."

"From the beginning, Lady Jane. As I said I would in Montreal, after I got home I put in a standard request to the PRO—our Public Records Office—for anything on code word Scylla. I got a chit acknowledging the request, but their mailing staff or cleaning women went on a work-to-rule strike and I forgot all about it. And then this morning—boom! Tallish, tweedish Colonel Smythe with a Guards' mustache. All very amiable. Suggests lunch and over it drops the bomb. No talkee. Any further investigation and we'll get a formal D Notice to stop research and publication. 'Of course we all hope,' says Smythe, 'indeed *know*—nothing like that will be required, old boy.'"

"Is that standard operating procedure, Roger? I mean do you get it often?"

"It happens—but I can't recall anything so far back tripping any wires. It's usually to stop some trivial embarrassment like a police payoff to dirty booksellers, or the Government reading all our cables. Your Scylla must be powerful voodoo."

"There's nothing else you can dig out?"

"I might be able to—"

"I hear cold feet."

"My editor's leery. We were burned last year over the Rhodesian oil and it still smarts. It would have to be rather special to make him go around the buoy again."

"I understand. Thanks any—"

"Why not bring your own shovel? I can show you the graves and if you find a worthwhile skeleton we'll put it in the paper, how's that?"

"That's *crap*."

Fadiman, chief correspondent for Reuter in Washington, ate lunch at his desk. He ate like a gigantic squirrel— breaking bits off his sandwich and passing them to his mouth with each hand alternately. He was totally bald, and although she had once seen him wearing a full wig, like a hat, at a White House concert with Pablo Casals before the collapse of Camelot, he was no fool. Thirty years with Reuter had not inured him to change.

"I can't do it, woman. Christ, I'm down two first stringers with goddamn flu, one extra on full time for the changes at State after Kissinger. Goddamn office girls sick and pregnant or vice versa, requests from outside for fillers like that junket to Montreal last fall—and what a waste *that* bastard was—"

"Fadiman, dear, I'm going. If I do it through the firm, I can afford to eat. But you choose. Give me a formal leave of absence, or just kiss me good-bye."

"Janey, honey," setting down the sandwich, "come on! After ten years—"

"Eleven."

"Eleven? Jesus. Anyway, all my children get the itch. You get tired of the pressure, of not having your own by-line. No familiar face mouthing off on the tube and becoming a bore and a household word. Too much time away from home."

"Not in my case. Look, Fad, there's a story. Why else the red light over there?"

"Secrecy's the nature of the bureaucratic beast, Janey— like the Kennedy witnesses, some things just happen. People live and die because of time and chance. It's not *always* a conspiracy. You know that."

And of course he was right.

"I'm going," he said.

"*Bitch!*" The crust was hurled into the wastebasket. Fadiman stared morosely after it. "Okay. Williams is howling for bodies for the Silver Jubilee."

"Thank you."

"Yeah. You're your old man's daughter." But he was pleased by the kiss. "It's going to be a paper war, Janey. It's new for you. You're used to twisting people—I'm the prize example."

"Some prize! Fad, tell me, was sharing a paper route with my father the reason you gave me the job?"

"It got you in the door." Fadiman shrugged. "Two small-town boys—either you throw rocks or you stick together. But don't start your digging with me. Dex and I may have been in the same kind of war business, but it was opposite ends of the pipe—our tracks never crossed again until it was over."

"What business?"

"Processing signal traffic. Dexter was supercool in the U.K. and I was in Bermuda reading love letters."

"Fadiman!"

"I kid you not. Rule one was honeymooners—they got away with murder; no one likes to pry. Bermuda was surprisingly big with honeymooners—even in the war. Service people who could get a flip."

Fadiman scratched absentmindedly at his chest. "Couldn't blame them. My first time I went by ship. I've never forgotten it. If the wind's right you catch it a whole day out—a smell from some kind of trees or flowers, you know—

> *"What thing of sea or land? . . .*
> *Comes this way sailing*
> *Like a stately ship. . . .*
> *Sails filled, and streamers waving,*
> *Courted by all the winds that hold them play;*
> *An amber scent of odorous perfume*
> *Her harbinger?*

And then you see these pink sugar-cube buildings. . . ."

"Not bad for an old man, dear."

"Thank Milton." Fadiman grinned with a mock self-consciousness. "What bits I can remember. All Waikiki by now I guess, and after we got off the boat we didn't see it anyhow. Or smell it. Everything was underground. We were moles—hundreds of us—"

"On love letters?"

"On anything going between North America and Europe. Letters, cables, passenger luggage on the clippers—the old flying boats to you kids. And the air conditioning was always screwed up. With everything in radio being tubes, it made a real Lower East Side sweatshop. One of the goddamn compressors used to drip—" Fadiman stopped.

"Something?"

"The one time I might have met your mother. She had a holdover of half a day going through to the Bahamas and Dex had asked her to stop by, but I was back in the States—my only leave that year." Drops like those from the compressor trickled slowly down outside the window. "I found the note on my desk. Ships in the night, Janey: Cronkite would tell you—that's the way it was."

The Capitol at the end of the avenue was almost obscured by the drops and sleeting snow. "Everything about life then seems so overmagnified," she said. "Did it seem that way when you were living it?"

"It went on too long, hon. We're talking about years! Looking back, everything gets compressed—only the buzz words stand out: Spy, Nazi, Glenn Miller. But most of it was wait, shortage, no mail."

"From the little bit I know, it was *all* buzz words for my parents. Girl courier; trapped in France; neutral all-American brings her through; the last boat from Le Havre. . . ."

"Okay—it's Scarlet Pimpernel. But after that, what? A golden weekend, maybe? Two? Just long enough for you to be here? I don't think they even met after the Bahamas, before she was lost." Fadiman slammed the seat forward and stood up, crushing the lunch bag. "Three weekends in three years? You need a fucking big magnifying glass to pick that out, Janey."

"Maybe the intensity made the short times worth it? I could see that."

"Maybe. But not for me—and I'm goddamn sure not for your father." Which left only her mother, the unknown duke's daughter, who tied herself better and worse to a corner-store boy and a Yankee's belief in never-say-die.

"I know Dex found out her run was compromised—we had a boys' drinking session in forty-six. I think he even got in to see Churchill while she could have turned back." Fadiman stared at his window. "But you've been there, Janey—war never turns back. I'll tell you, Dexter hated Churchill. 'The old fucker *cried*, Fad. The son of a bitch pulled the pin with his own hands, and then he cried. . . .'"

Now the Dome was gone, and the porno stores, and even the old Willard Hotel across the street with the scaffolding up for renovations. "I guess Churchill had to shed a lot of tears," she said finally. "I don't think I could blame him."

"Me neither." Fadiman folded the crumpled lunch bag meticulously and put it in a drawer. "And you'll get a whole lot further with the Brits if you can stay impartial—but I don't have to spell that out. You know your relatives fished through London when I took you on?"

"You never told me!"

"At twenty-five, my pet, you weren't a girl asking directions."

"I guess not. When Dad died there *were* flowers and

they did ask me to visit, but I was wearing all his hostility. I didn't even thank them." Which was another of those adolescent rudenesses that dripped like the rain on one's conscience throughout life. "Working for Reuter though, it's crazy I never got back."

"Crazy."

"Not a fluke?"

"Fleet Street would have loved to get you anytime. Now, they won't know what's hit them." The lock clicked shut on the lunch bag drawer. "I'll tell you—there's a guy at CIA I think was with Dex in the liaison units. The bastard owes me—I'll check him out."

"Thanks." She patted the bald head. "And for London. You know, Fad, it's not *who* she was, really. Nor that she was my mother. More than anything, all my life I've wanted to know *how*—how those women got the guts to jump in there. Buzz words, holy Jesus, just *say* it—*Gestapo....*"

And get all the rest of the night-crawling images that spoke louder than any words.

"Twain had courage as the mastery of fear," said Fadiman. "Not its absence."

"That's an answer?"

"Short of going the route, Janey, I guess it is." A large paw squeezed her shoulder. "I'll give you a last tip for the British—tell the Buggers there's no 's' on Reuter."

4

Langley, Virginia, March 1977

The daffodils beside the bus-stop lean-to building at the gate had not been planted by a gardener's hand. They stood severely ranked in lines of three, space; three, space; three, space until the bed was filled. The side of the building sheltered them, so that they held their heads as still as the guard inside the booth.

"Name and business?"

"Jane Motigny, to see Mr. Selbach."

A computer terminal flashed at the counter. There was a camera lens beside it and a microphone beneath the grille. A message appeared and disappeared on the screen.

"Proceed. Park in visitor allocation one zero one."

The wire gate swung inward.

She was not prepared for the size of the place, or its design: university library—second-rate. The insignia set into the floor and on the facing wall she found impressive.

A young man clean and spruce as a Mormon missionary waited beside the insignia.

"Mrs. Montigny? This way please."

There was no hint of a peg for a cloak—or a dagger. The corridors were wide and unremarkable. A large picture of a missile site in Cuba was exhibited to support future budget requests. There were no pictures of the last days of Saigon or Phnom Penh.

The Mormon opened a door without knocking and closed it behind her without introduction. A man stood inside the room. "Mrs. Montigny, I'm Selbach. This is a pleasure." But how could you tell? Fadiman was right: a faceless bastard. Lawyer, banker, merchant prince? She had never seen such a closed exterior. "I've got coffee," he said. "Please sit down."

There was no desk. In all her time in Washington she had never seen an office without a desk. Or a telephone. The coffee sat on a coffee table beside a vase of daffodils. She counted them. Nine. Like the flower bed: three times three. Mackenzie King might make something of that. There was no ashtray, either.

"I believe you no longer smoke?" Selbach said—to let her feel that they knew each other. "I read your analysis of the Quebec election. Incisive and excellent. We could use you on staff."

The smile lasted for three seconds like the message on the terminal at the gate and then turned off leaving the face blank. She smiled back. "I don't want to waste your time, Mr. Selbach."

"You wouldn't be here, Mrs. Montigny, if it wasted my time. If I can help to put your mind at rest about your mother I'd like to do that."

"I'd prefer to start with my father," she said. "How did you come to know him?"

"The old OSS story. Dex recruited me."

"'Recruiting' sounds like Dow Chemical coming on campus."

Smile on, smile off. "Pretty close. Your father was approached by Bill Donovan directly on graduation—"

"This is as a lawyer?"

"Right. For Number Two Wall Street." Selbach's eyes were narrow and never left her. "That would be thirty-six, thirty-seven. In early thirty-nine Dex made a trip to Germany that had very little to do with law practice." Smile. "He told me about it—I was a couple of years behind him at school— introduced me to 'Wild Bill.' The rest was chance."

Nothing about this man was left to chance. Not only was the bottom button of his vest undone; the buttonhole was sewn shut.

"Fadiman told me you were in some kind of liaison duties?"

"Right." Smile. "'Somewhere in England,' they used to say. Now the lid's off that side of the war I can tell you we worked from a place called Bletchley Park—the main interception center for German crypto traffic. After things began to break out with the Italian landings in forty-three I went with Eisenhower's staff. Dex was called home by Donovan and stayed with The Firm until 1946 when he went back to Maine and a more normal private practice. I guess the rest you know."

If this was not a waste of time, what was it? Next to nothing had been produced. And nothing at all that had not been asked for.

"Were you ever in the Bahamas, Mr. Selbach?"

"The Bahamas?" Her subconscious always asked the best questions. With the narrowing of his left eye, was there just a flicker of a power failure on the terminal? "I've vacationed in the islands. Kind of a backwater in the war. Why would you ask?"

"My mother went there."

"R and R. Any operative who could swing it took a flip to

a warm climate." Selbach shot a sudden glance at the daffodils.

This place was not an office! It was a consulting room—with only Christ knew what eyes and ears participating vicariously like med students inside the curtains at a gynecological examination. Selbach, watching her minutely, had the same apparent frankness in his secret probing.

"I have this feeling I'm not being too helpful, Mrs. Montigny?"

"Starting from zero everything's a help." Selbach accepted the obvious as his due, and nodded. "Did we get details after the war of what happened to people like my mother?"

"The Brits did some follow up. It might not be what you'd want to know."

"Why?"

"Nazi interrogation practices—the Gestapo liked taking photographs for some reason. No, I'm sure you wouldn't want to know."

His bland concern had a goading quality.

"You guys must have copied NASA and brought back a von Braun of your own," she said.

"How was that?" The smile was no longer automatic.

"I came in on the tail of an interrogation by *your* people during Tet. After the montagnards were given the prisoner, your station man had blow-ups made of the results and passed them around the villages—"

"Not many organizations came out of Vietnam with reputations intact, Mrs. Montigny." A large blue stone of a class ring flashed for a moment. "You may not like *this* organization—but contrary to popular belief, we do have the best interests of the country at heart." Another quick glance at the daffodils for moral support. Selbach pitched a little harder for D.C. "Like your birthplace, our Western democratic community is a small island now, Mrs. Montigny. Only a handful of governments are elected by the people, for the people. We need all the help we can get to keep the sea out."

After all the bodies left twisting slowly in the Watergate winds, the son of a bitch was trying to *recruit* her!

"This is the current line on campus, Mr. Selbach? You guys should stick to blackmail."

The daffodils shivered violently. "Mrs. Montigny, don't misunderstand me—this is strictly a hands-off approach—but you're going to be asking questions of the Brits, and newspersons asking questions often get in the way of Intelligence material. If you don't know how to run with it, that's why I'm here."

"News*persons*" and such effort at support deserved some reward from the little woman. "It was good of you to meet me, Mr. Selbach. Thank you again."

"My pleasure. I'll see you out."

They passed the picture of the missiles and came back to the lobby. Selbach pointed at the engraved rows of gilded stars arranged with flower-bed precision. "Like your mother, many of these good people were women, Mrs. Montigny. They believed in our country and our Constitution."

Such heartland simplicity must have arrived at Langley with the bus from Plains. She searched for something adequate. "That's nice," she said.

Selbach seemed satisfied. "Most of the top people in your line of work have cooperated. I don't think they ever—"

"Lived to regret it?"

"I felt that one go in, Mrs. Montigny." Yet Selbach appeared anything but annoyed. "I hear you're flying out at seven—"

"You *do?*"

"The airport does have our name on it—Dulles, right?" With the game a draw Selbach, like Fadiman, volunteered a parting tip with his outstretched hand. "When you visit Saint Margaret's in Westminster tomorrow, Mrs. Montigny, pay my respects."

5

London, March 1977

"From America? We have an American here with us—a Ramsey, steam engines, I think." The pale-pink face of the curate under its pale-straw hair looked earnestly to her for nationalist approval.

"Oh?" she said to be polite. "What part of the States?"

But her guide was patting a hard quartzite slab with a soft hand. "Ah, yes, *Rumsey.* James Rumsey, 1792. And we have our other connections with the New World. Raleigh— and, of course, our glass—" the hand waved gently upward, "our great window for Ferdinand and Isabella—or their daughter actually. Catherine—such a trouble."

"Trouble?" She felt she was sitting in on a family squabble at a Sunday lunch.

"Her marriage to Prince Arthur—Henry the Eighth's brother. Divorce is always *so* disturbing, don't you agree?"

"It can be," she said. But he didn't seem to require answers—his tourist recitation was as routine as liturgy. Probably more rewarding: a collection box was prominently displayed beside the door. An American twenty-dollar bill was visible inside it.

"The Covenant was signed here in 1643—and Milton's marriage a little later in 1656, and Pepys before and Sir Winston and Lord Louis afterward, so you see, we have our history. Which, of course, we should, as Parliament's parish church! Ah, here we are."

Here we are.

At this niche in a wall of white Portland stone with a vase ground from dark granite and a brass plaque with an engraving:

TO MARY

ONLY DAUGHTER OF GEORGE FREDERICK HENRY, DUKE OF DORSET
ON WHOM HAS CONFERRED THE GEORGE CROSS
FOR DUTY WITH HONOUR IN OCCUPIED EUROPE

1912–1943

A rose, once red or crimson, now with its petals cracked and blackened, bent its head across the lip of the vase.

"So someone remembers," she said. "Is it the family?"

"One supposes. I'm afraid our sexton deals with our practical affairs—the watering and changing—"

"Could I ask him."

"Oh, yes, indeed you *could.*" The clerical head bobbed

forward almost dislodging the glasses. "If he were here. Sadly, he's not with us—having an operation. Cancer, I believe."

"I'm sorry," she said. Being "with us" had a long-term ring.

"A heavy cross. And replacements *are* so difficult." A distracted wave toward the vase. "It *should* have been emptied." The man gave a sigh from the heart. A thought occurred to interrupt it. "Our plaque is seldom noticed—off to one side—"

"She was my mother."

"Oh. Oh I *do* see. And of course you wish to meet the donor. *Most* natural. Would you like me to ask our sexton when I next visit?"

"That would be *most* kind." Half a day past jet lag and she was already sounding like an English priest. Thank God Fadiman was absent.

The curate picked up his patter and walked with her to the East door. "The brass on the left to Raleigh, I mentioned—did I not?—a fine portico dedicated to our Canon Farrar, the author of *Eric, or Little by Little*—and, oh yes," stopping to point at a wooden engraving where a hand as graceful as his own had been severed and spitted on a spike, "our William Flower." Gouts of blood poured graphically from William Flower's hand and stump. The rest of the body was about to be engulfed at the stake.

"What for?" she asked.

"Stabbing our rector—on Easter Day. Converts are always *so* unreliable—ah, the plaque to Pym and our parliamentary martyrs, dug up and cast into a pit. . . . Guy Fawkes—but you'll have heard of *him*. 'Remember, remember, the fifth of November. . . .'" He left her and turned to walk back alone into the body of the church, still vaguely chattering the rhyme.

She stood, looking past Cromwell and Richard Lionheart on his horse, looking across old Palace Yard to the Houses of Parliament that Guy Fawkes had tried to send sky-high. *Gunpowder, treason, and plot*.

And one dead rose.

Big Ben crashed a quarter hour into the court. A bitter wind swept in from the river.

Williams, Fadiman's London equivalent, was twenty years his junior, had a full head of hair and a twisted gut.

"Jane—where the Christ!"

"In church," she said.

"*Church!* The Tories spring a Confidence vote, Amin's flying on a broomstick for a showdown at the Palace, the Government announces a new Foreign Secretary—all in one bloody morning—and you're farting around at *church!*"

"Ted, dear, can I get you a glass of milk?"

"Sorry. I'm a bastard. Find anything?"

"An American steam-engine person is still with us. And we married Sir Winston and Lord Louis."

"And all the other social climbers—I could have told you that! Be a love. Cover the Amin circus. Here's a number in Whitehall. They know all the Africans. Oh Christ, bloody phone!"

The Foreign Office spokesman was not aware of the Field Marshal's plans but would "personally shoot the tires off his fucking aircraft—excuse me—if the fat ape tries to land. No," laughing, "not for attribution, Mrs. Montigny."

She wrote the denial and a color paragraph on three schoolgirls weaving a Jubilee mat from the hair of a dog, and went up to the seventh floor, where policy was determined and travel vouchers approved, to see if her reimbursement for the trip across had gone through.

"Sorry, we've been madly busy," said the girl.

"I'd never know it. Gerry Long's director's office is a tomb."

"The Anniversary of the Pigeon Post—they've all gone over to America to celebrate, somewhat belatedly, the 125th. You should have stayed put. But I'll really try and get the check through for you by the end of this week."

"That's be great." A framed Paul Julius Reuter stared down at them with a raised eyebrow. "Why his 125th?"

"Mr. Long says it's for anyone who missed the 100th and might not see the 150th."

"You're right. I should have stayed."

The elevators, recently repaired, no longer shivered with fright but their speed was still sedate. She passed gently by the Press Association floors and the newsroom on the fourth and economics on the second, to the Fleet Street entrance.

Two pigeons were perched on a flagstaff over the door as she came out. Perhaps their ancestors had given Paul Julius the bright idea. She turned north into Chancery Lane and the Public Records Office.

The smell of history, the smell of paper aging in uncountable quantity enveloped her. A girl with horse teeth waited behind a desk positioned on cracked red linoleum. "May I help you?"

"You'll have to. I haven't got a clue where to start."

"Oh, you're American. Academic?"

"With Reuter. I'm a correspondent."

"*Really?* Jolly good. I mean—well, you know."

"Yes," she said, "I do." They smiled at each other. "What's step one?"

"A reader's ticket." The girl produced a form and a pen. "Name, address, occupation."

"This says I should be recommended in writing—"

"Unless you can be otherwise vouched for as to occupation and suitability. I can do that. Would this be for a book, thesis, dissertation, or article in a learned journal?"

"Maybe a book. My mother was an agent during the war. I'm researching the circumstances of her death."

"Really?" the girl said again, and stopped writing. "Do you know which department you'll want to begin with? All our filing is by department you see—not by subject."

"A meeting with the Prime Minister?"

"Then you'll want the logbooks. That would be Treasury: Records, timekeeping. It sounds restrictive I know, but it covers a lot of ground. Our system is a little different—let me show you an example." The girl took out a mimeographed form. "Everything has a three-part reference: Group, class, and piece. To get the first two you have to know the approximate subject. But you may have to try quite a few to get where you want to be. You can check that from our guide. Once you have the group and class you need the piece number which refers to the specific item. For instance: CAB 23/27 would be a Cabinet Minute, page 23, Volume 27. Clear?"

"I'll figure it. Are you computerized?"

"Half and half. We're on the verge of moving the bulk of the collection to a new building at Kew. In fact, some of the sections are there already—although not the ones you want, I think. But bits and pieces go all the time. Kew's full computer—when they get it working. Do you think you want to start with the logs?"

"I have to leap in somehow. Sure, let's go with the logs."

"You'll be West Wing, then, second crypt. B22 is the Reference Room. I'll write it down for you. Normally you draw three requests at a time and take them to a reading room, but some of our crypts are rather a jumble. We'll be much more civilized at Kew."

"But not as romantic, I guess? You've been fantastic."

"Well, a project like yours is a little special, isn't it? My older brother was killed in the war. A bomber sergeant. He was lost in the North Sea and since no one really knew—well, it took my parents a long time—I think it helps to really know. Oh—if you don't mind, just check your handbag here."

All the activity in the building seemed to be upward, seeking the sunlight. As she went lower, people disappeared and the air took on a dead, cellar smell of damp. No wonder they were moving. What priceless things must be tucked away for the ground-water to seep in on. The stone steps to the lowest level were worn in the centers and the balustrades nicked and chipped and not revarnished. Once-yellow paint had browned with a hundred years of dirt.

Room B22 was twenty by thirty feet, with a rounded brick ceiling like a tunnel. Lights hung down from it. The walls were completely hidden by permanent shelving. Free-standing units choked the remaining floor space. Sufficient square feet had been left open for a table and a chair. Guide lists were fastened to the table with a chain. A large sign said emphatically, No Pens! An empty box marked Pencils was provided.

The volume of paper, the weight of material produced the same sensation of momentary panic she'd had leaving the runway's light for darkness on her first night solo.

She picked up the group lists.

Air Min. 1/34; Fisc. 7/35–36, page after page of civil-service jargon.

She searched with increasing frustration for some Rosetta stone. Churchill? Nothing. Winston Churchill? No better. What goddamn initials did he use? WC? Hardly—not in this country. Winston Spencer Churchill—WSC?

Not listed. There was an entry, *WCR—see: Logs—PAA 11/39 ff*. Hopeless. She would have to find a researcher familiar with the system. For the sake of practice she decided to track down WCR. Logs seemed vaguely in the ball park.

The filing system followed quirks of its own and PAA followed SXC. The books were on the bottom row of one of the free-standing units and she had to get down on hands and knees to see them. They were all a fading blue with an anchor, and *Admiralty: Form 12 B* printed on their backs. A date was scratched in ink below each anchor. She reached for one at random: "May–June, 1940."

She selected a page.

PRIME MINISTER WAR LOG.
Date: June 16, 1940:
1030—In the WCR: Meeting of the War Cabinet.
      Present: Mr. Churchill, Mr. Attlee, Mr. Eden...
1130—The WCR: Mr. Churchill, General de Gaulle,
      Major Morton...
1605—The WCR: The War Cabinet, Sir Archibald
      Sinclair, General de Gaulle, Sir Robert Van-
      sittart, Major Morton, M. Corbin...

Here in her hand they met for the fall of France—facing the death agony of freedom while Churchill bears his Cross of Lorraine and proud men weep.

August 15, 1940:
2215—In the WCR: Mr. Churchill, Lord Beaver-
      brook, Mr. Bevin, General Ismay, Air Mar-
      shal Trenchard...

The Battle of Britain. Would the Few be enough? And at the time of writing, who knew the answer?

May 26, 1941:
2030—In the WCR: P.M., Admiral Pound, Admiral
      Fraser...

Sink the *Bismarck!*

December 7, 1941:
2130—The O.P. Present: P.M., Ambassador Winant,

> Mr. Harriman, ... calls to: H.M. the King,
> Mr. Eden, Mr. Roosevelt ...

An infamous day that made the work of men like Donovan and Selbach legal.

> *October 23, 1942:*
> 2000—In the WCR: P.M., Full Defence Committee,
>   General Brooke ... calls to General Alexander,
>   General Montgomery ...

The end of the beginning—Alamein.

Page after page, until the historic names had become a blur, the drama a routine. August with Mackenzie King— What the Christ would Churchill have said if he'd known approval of his decisions was being sought from a dead old woman and a dog! She had missed the beginning of the month. She started again at October the first. The second, the third.

> *October 6, 1943:*
> In the O.P.:
> Present: Mr. Churchill, "J," Capt. Dexter ...

Dexter.

Her father. The grocer's boy from Poynter's Corners, Maine, sitting deep in the earth of his ancestors. Sitting with the warlord, her mirror image, Winston Churchill: who was himself product of an American mother, an English father. The Commons and the Lords.

But what did they say?

"Five minutes to five, miss."

"Huh?" The voice startled her. A commissionaire, impassive as a prison guard, stared through the door. She glanced at her watch; the hands formed a perfect diameter across the face.

"Sorry, miss. We close at five."

"I forgot all about time." She set the log back in the shelf.

"Easy to do that down here, miss. I mean time doesn't really mean much when you can go back to your Domesday Book, does it? Makes you realize they were real people—

never seemed like that at school, did it? If you don't mind, miss?"

She stepped out into the passage. "Is it a problem looking after the Domesday Book?"

"Oh no, miss. I've been here twenty-three years and never a hint. Mind you, at Kew we'll have it all done up with these electric things—lazy beams and what have you. More bells than the blitz if any one tries a pinch there."

"You must really know your way around the collections."

"Well not all—I mean we've got millions here, haven't we? But I know a bit. After twenty-three years you'd pretty well have to know a bit, wouldn't you?"

She agreed that you would. "I got hooked in there with the logs of the war days—who met Churchill, the Cabinet meetings, that kind of thing. But I couldn't find the contents of the meetings—what really went on. What was said."

"Under so many headings, miss. I mean you've got your War Cabinet Record, you've got your Defence Committee Minutes, your Steering Committee, your War Production Council—"

"I get it," she said, to cut off the list.

They were in the main rotunda. An iron grille like a portcullis was being drawn across the arch separating the museum from the rest of the building.

"You've been in, miss?" The commissionaire nodded at the grille.

She shook her head.

"Oh, *my!*" The man was genuinely shocked. "You must see *that*, miss. That's where all your *real* history is. Your Guy Fawkes, your Magna Carta, your Dambusters..."

"I'll go tomorrow—"

"Not tomorrow, miss," a civil servant's satisfaction at delay exceeded even the pride of display. "Closed Saturdays and holidays, miss."

When all the poor bastards footing the bill would have a chance to see what they were getting for it—but she said, mildly, "With the logs—would there be minutes kept? Even for small meetings?"

"That'll be your War Admin. Yes, that'll be right. But tell you what, miss—I've not much else on and it's a long shift between rounds. I'll check it out for you and leave a note at the desk."

"That would be tremendous, Sergeant?—"

Hithertwaite, miss. Just say Hithertwaite. Your registrars all know me."

6

"Who?"

At nine on Monday morning a sour, bespectacled young man had replaced the horse-faced girl at the information desk.

"Sergeant Hithertwaite—he left a note for me, I think? Montigny?"

The sour replacement reached under the counter and pushed an envelope across without looking at her.

She held her tongue.

The note inside, neatly composed in a rounded, fifty-year-old elementary-school script, was addressed to Miss Montain.

> The information which you have requested is to be found in your Special Documents Section of your War Administration Section under Ministerial Secretarial Recording. Either under your Shorthand Writers' Originals (or Clear Copies, if made).
>
> The above records may be found in Room A25 (which is in the crypts but one floor higher than yesterday). I have marked your section.
>
> Hoping that this will be the information which you require,
>
> Yr. Obdt. Servant,
> Henry Hithertwaite.

Room A 25 was indistinguishable from B22. The same shelving, the same endless rows of books with unremarkable appearance and the most remarkable contents. She found the

section Hithertwaite had marked: rows and rows of secretarial
pads. Pads which had once been set on secretarial knees
ogled by officers stuck underground for endless hours, as the
bombs fell and Big Ben chimed and Churchill dictated.
Inside their covers the sheets were immaculate, after initial
recording and transcription, closed up and locked away—
perhaps not seen again until this moment.

On these sheets she was turning it really *had* happened.
With the plain-language headings on the pages, the bombs
were really falling, the ships really sinking. And then a tide
turning, immense armies forming, Allies invading. Politics
intruding.

Yalta.

With a dying man in a wheelchair hanging on, and
another tired old man with a cigar, puffing up an Empire
already broken. Between them, a little man with ferret's eyes
and a brush mustache sniffed the rat holes of Europe. And
after it was over, the red Mercator world of Raj, and cavalry
charges by the Nile, and tea in the Grand Pacific Hotel in
Fiji, all dead and gone. Replaced by a new red order. . . .

If she could only read shorthand.

She must stop dreaming! She began to check rapidly
through the pads for 1943; July, August, September. Then
week by week. September 26 to October 2; October 10 to 17.
A gap. She started again from the beginning and checked the
entire length of three long shelves. Missing. In the course of
a six-year war was that so surprising? Girls must occasionally
have been sick. Perhaps Churchill had been visiting—the
Citadel in Quebec, Teheran. Perhaps there had been weeks
with no meetings.

Or perhaps not.

She checked her notes from the previous week. No.
There was never a day without a meeting, and seldom a
night. Invariably at the later hour the list reduced itself to
one-on-one encounters: at night, when the administrative
load was lighter Churchill found time to talk, needed to
talk—*had to*. Had to get assurance, locker-room support:
"We'll knock 'em dead in the second half, men." So at night
the list showed Churchill and a soldier from Dunkirk; Churchill
and a fighter pilot newly decorated; Churchill and a crony—
Beaverbrook, or Lindemann, or Morton.

Churchill and her father? The missing pages couldn't say.

In the absence of knowledge there must be something she could take from all this work. Some pattern in the pads. She examined a number of them again. They all began in the same way with a heading meticulously set out at the top of each sheet:

MINUTES FOR MR. CHURCHILL:
Date:
Time:
Visitor:
Recorder:

And then the shorthand: The world locked up by the skill of the recorder. *The recorders!* There was the key. Although three or four girls shared the days, at night it was only one, and always the same: Cynthia Dodgeson.

Her enthusiasm waned. Even if Cynthia Dodgeson, this special girl Friday, still existed—if she was anything more than wartime memory—would she remember one stray half hour of a wild-eyed American raging at the Grand Old Man?

She wrote down the name. What else was there to try?

Outside the building, the city was gray but not wet, and she decided to walk to her flat in Dolphin Square. Walking might pump enough blood to the brain to get some rational thought working—or even better, to spring a hunch.

At the Embankment she found herself swept up in a touring crowd of Arabs—robeless junior execs and wives, escaping the veil and the crucible of the Gulf for a blue-jeaned spring in Britain. The crowd stopped opposite Scott's Antarctic ship, *Discovery*. A Royal Marine and a sailor stood doll-like at the gangway surrounded by posters urging kids to join up for a year or two of extra-special high school and then get out again to find a real job. What the hell would Churchill make of it if he came up from his bunker? For that matter, what about Scott? With Amelia Earhart—another lost soul—he had been her childhood hero. She remembered his last words: "God look after our people."

Which He had. The British had muddled through their blitz. And Palestine. And had inherited the Arabs.

One of the Arab shoulders shoved her off the curb. A cab screeched to a halt and she took it home. So much for exercise.

The hall porter had a message for her with the key. "Mr. Alleyn, at *The Times*. If you'd call back?"

She felt a sudden lift at being rescued from the masses outside. Dialing, she even welcomed the prospect of media gossip.

"Lady Jane!" Her rescuer treated her with extravagant respect. "I got your note on the Bahamas. Not arrested yet?"

"I haven't turned any rocks. If you've dug out anything, I could use a bull session."

"Where are you?"

"Reuter keeps an apartment in Dolphin Square for visiting firepersons. In Rodney House."

"I know it. All the comforts: butcher, baker—even a squash court. A slight sense of communal living, perhaps. What's that bloody row?"

"School kids across the street." A coarsely impossible suggestion from one child to another came through the open window. She closed it. "Progressive education," she said, "but with your hotel rates I ain't complaining. Do you know any private eyes?"

"My God, you workingwomen! Is there to be not a moment for harmonious discourse? Why do you need a nark?"

She explained. "If I could find this secretary she might remember the meeting with my father. She might talk."

"And she might not! A woman who worked as a cipher clerk on Ultra refused to go under the knife last year without an absolution from the Foreign Office—afraid she'd blab with the anesthetic. Jane, isn't the obvious starting place with the family? Your mother's people?"

"Sure. But they've had thirty-five goddamn years to get started. First I want to know if I'm being conned. You Brits are Oriental—you can lie with straight faces."

"Albion's perfidy. Our enduring strength." But there was a touch of discomfort in Alleyn's laugh. "I don't think I've heard it expressed quite so baldly. How many of these deceitful relations are there?"

"I only know about two. My grandfather, who's got to be

ninety and spends all his time in the bush, and my uncle. He must have let down the side and 'gone into trade,' as you say. Some kind of small bank. His office is hidden away behind the Corn Exchange. I walked by it the other day. One of your real odd British names."

"Leofric—the ultimate Anglo-Saxon. Means 'Dear Ruler,' I believe. I see it at all the right dinners, but the Harrow–Buck's Club level of the aristocracy's a long way out of my league. Shell just bought my old school for pollution testing. Appropriate, mind you. And speaking of dinner, Mrs. Montigny—I trust you're offering home cooking?"

"There's a place downstairs overlooking the pool—"

"Nothing ventured!" But there was a sharpness in the good-humored masculine acceptance of rejection. "At least there'll be lithe young bodies in nylon wisps."

"If I'm lucky," she said.

The diving board gave an agonized rattle of springs as two of the bodies hurtled by below them. A strong smell of chlorine drifted into the eating area.

"As soon as you asked about the Bahamas," said Alleyn, "I realized it must be Harry Oakes—I mean the murder of Harry Oakes was the only thing that happened in the Bahamas during the war."

"You're ahead of me," she said. "Who was this Harry Oakes?"

"Harry Oakes, my good woman, was the original Goldfinger. All he wanted out of life was the biggest gold mine in the world—and after twenty years of pissing away his family's money, a career at medical school, his American citizenship—he got it. In Ontario. How, is still an open question: Harry himself said he was a mining genius—Hollywood said a squaw threw him out head first onto a nugget. Real life was somewhere in between."

"And once he finds the gold, it's Tombstone for the tough-guy pardners—"

"Harry's partners," said Alleyn, "really *were* called Tough!" The diving board rattled again. A boy in a skintight Speedo suit of green and white jacknifed immediately in front of her. The boy was clearly circumcised. "Jane—are you listening?"

"Just window shopping."

"It's obscene."

"I know, dear." She patted his arm. "So Harry's rich, and Canadian."

"But miserable, because he's got the gold but hates the Canadian taxes. Especially as he's kicked a quarter of a million into the political slop chest and hasn't landed the Senate seat promised by Mackenzie King—"

"King," she said thoughtfully, "he's like a catalyst. . . . I'm sorry—keep going."

"I'm trying, madam. What Oakes *has* landed by this time is an Aussie wife, Eunice, and some kids. First-born, a daughter—Nancy. The shock of family life sends Harry to ponder fate in Florida, where he runs across an island property pusher called Christie."

"Enter the Bahamas?"

"Enter the Bahamas—a land if not of milk and honey, then the next best thing: no income tax and no death duties. Now Oakes really falls in love. He changes citizenship for the umpteenth time to become one of us—British—and through his new friend he buys up the place. The hotel, the airport, the golf course. And outside working hours Harry becomes better than a father to the blacks, with waterworks, schools, hospital. A fund for unwed mothers—"

"A real Daddy Warbucks."

"A man with his heart's desire," said Alleyn. "All the good works, and half a million in the right London pockets, have finally bought him a baronetcy—oh, bloody hell!"

A gout of water had splashed the back of Alleyn's neck. "Let's go," she said. "I make better coffee anyway—if you'll light the burner. Gas scares the hell out of me."

"After Beirut?"

"Okay, okay." She laughed with him. "I can get the damn thing going if I have to—but I'm serious about gas. You know how many deaths there are each year? The nuke freaks should spend some of their energy on that!"

As they stopped outside her door to find the key, the blond boy in the skintight suit ran by leaving frog feet marks behind him. He flicked a quick eye up and down and flashed a smile.

"Christ," said Alleyn. "Have they no shame?"

"Catch his room number. At thirty-six it's good to know there's a God who cares!" Inside the apartment, the burner was subdued without incident. Masculine pride was restored. "Go on about Oakes, Roger."

"Still 'the unsolved crime of the century.' There was a plethora of the motivated—Oakes was cordially disliked by large numbers of persons and from descriptions it's not hard to see why. A fat five feet six, blotched and mottled like a toad, had a filthy tongue, and ate peas off his knife in all the best houses."

"So nobody's all bad!" She set cups on a tray. "But if there was a trial they must have found a fall guy, right?"

"The son-in-law with the eldest daughter, Nancy. A man called Count de Marigny."

"Another good Huguenot name."

"If it was genuine. Oakes never thought so—that was the main point of dispute between them: A phony count after the Oakes's treasure. Which rumor said there really was. Chests of doubloons in caves of the Outer Islands. As to the bad feeling—it was common knowledge. In a tiny world like that, every nuance of family feud gets endlessly dissected. But when it came to the crunch, de Marigny was white as a lily—although the thing followed him the rest of his life. I think he died in Rio about ten years ago—Oh, thanks." Alleyn took a sip of the coffee. "Full marks."

"We little career women—"

Alleyn sighed. "One has to be so bloody *careful*. Anyhow I'm jumping again. Thursday, July the eighth, 1943. Oakes is found on his four-poster—burned, blistered, and bludgeoned— feathers and blood all over the place."

"It sounds more like voodoo than a family fight."

"And the investigation was black comedy not black magic. Pal Christie, who's at Harry's overnight—and sleeping the sleep of the just, of course—finds Harry in the feathers and goes off the deep end. In point of fact, to his friend—and Harry's friend, Edward, HRH."

And now she felt it would be all right, that it was not time wasted, because this piece fitted with a solid click.

"The Duke of Windsor?"

Alleyn nodded. "No less. In exile as governor of the Bahamas for the Duration. And here it's not comic—just damn silly. The Duchess doesn't care—'Never a dull moment in the Bahamas,' as she says—but Edward tries to hush the whole thing. Jams the telegraph, muzzles the press—this is war, chaps! But some press rat's got through to the States and all hell breaks loose. What are we doing? Who are we catching? Where's Scotland Yard?—on the wrong side of the U-boats. So where can we turn for help? Miami—"

"Miami!"

"Lady, you've got it! Messrs. Melchen and Barker—a pair of flat feet straight out of an Edward G. Robinson movie. How the Duke got hold of *them*, God knows! But after that, it was bungled clues, missing evidence, fudged thumb prints on a screen, blood running uphill. The trial was a dud, the goat got off, the Duke looked an idiot, the Allies invaded Italy, close the book."

"And no loose ends?"

"A couple. One theory had Meyer Lansky sniffing for gambling concessions, and being double-crossed by Oakes on the deal. Certainly if the mob was in there, it would have caused Royal shivers on both sides of the Atlantic. And a positive Mafia link did turn up. Barker, the cop, was found to be on Lansky's payroll. He'd become a drug addict and was shot dead with his own police special—by his son."

"If you tried," she said, "you couldn't make this up."

Alleyn finished his coffee. "It's given me a bloody headache."

"Sweetheart, I know the feeling!" She laughed and opened the door. "You need a good night's sleep. I'll tell you how I make out with Uncle Leofric in the morning."

The word, *perfidy*, lingered with a smell of chlorine and pipe tobacco in the hall.

7

This man facing her so calmly across his walnut writing desk was her mother's brother. With a numbing surprise she found herself about to cry to a complete stranger. For five seconds that she could not have said she counted, she forced herself to watch the pendulum of the carriage clock beside him swing back and forth, back and forth.

"Forgive my staring," said Leofric Arbright. "I'm trying to see Mary."

One of her Saturday-morning cartoon sidekicks used to have the same lisping trouble with the "r": as Churchill had. As, Alleyn had told her, any good Harrovian should. And she had been so sure that with the missing letter there would be coldness, an impervious and shining wall of British reserve; because the surroundings—the brass plate on the door, the antique pieces of desk and clock and chairs, the whole attempt to disguise the business function, the tailoring and cuffs so indifferent to fashion—all that was so exactly as she had expected. Only the man behind the marquess's steady gaze and slightly florid face was wrong.

"It's your neck and ears," he said. "That must seem absurd to you, to remember someone from the ears. But brothers and sisters do that, don't they? Pick on silly things other people never think of. And again, you're so close to her age—she was only thirty-one—it's rather as though the time machine had brought her back, d'you see?"

"You needn't apologize. But I've got to tell you that I have no memory at all, not even of her perfume. Family just doesn't play a part in my life."

"Your stepmother had no children?"

So he knew her father had remarried. And what else? What other inquiries had been passed by word of mouth over a lunch with a newly appointed ambassador? *"A reporter, old boy, she works in Washington, you might keep an eye ..."*

"No," she said, "some cousins on the West Coast—we've never met—and you people over here."

"Who must appear inhuman to have ignored so close a tie."

"Why did you?" Asking bluntly restored some sense of control.

"Your father's wish," Leofric said simply. And by God, she thought, we'll respect privacy if we cut off an arm to do it! Leofric was still answering. "But the Duke took it very hard—you're his only granddaughter. I have a boy—the Guards—and he has sons, so the line's assured."

And there's no pot of gold for an interloper sniffing a

dead end for an inheritance. "But why was my father so adamant?"

"I'm not quite used to such directness of attack." The apology in Leofric's smile implied that attack was crass. "I suppose," he said eventually, "that Dexter felt the Duke could have brought more pressure to bear to get Mary's mission stopped. To get her back."

"Was he right?"

"It's true that my father acceded to Churchill's reasoning. But so did the King—my father had spoken to him personally—and if both His Majesty and the Prime Minister were convinced her task was for the good of the country— Her George Cross supports that view, I think."

"But *my* father didn't."

"No. I was damned sorry for him. It must have been very hard to go on without that comfort. To believe that her death was useless: caused by ineptitude, and shielded afterward. What you would call—"

"A cover-up."

"Precisely."

"Perhaps," she said, "it's possible that he was right."

"Anything is possible, Jane." Leofric set his cup carefully upon his saucer. "But it's not our way, is it?"

Our way.

Our way has smothered princes in the Tower, changed churches and wives for Henry the Eighth, hidden Jack the Ripper, and bought peace in our time. She felt without a trace of doubt that if a cover-up was what was needed "for the country," *our way* would produce that too.

"I agree that it would be improbable," she said. "I want to write a book about her—more accurately, about women like her. Would you object?"

"As a testament?" She nodded. "I think it would be marvelous!" said Leofric. "Quite splendid! God knows I can't explain it—how they faced that sort of death."

"Don't martyrs need that?"

"I suppose you're right. Although martyr seems synonymous with nun—and Mary wasn't that!" He looked at her across the table. "I'm so very grateful you don't share your father's feelings."

"A psychiatrist might still find a few scars under my skull—but by now I think that at least I'm impartial."

"I'd like to think, my dear, that perhaps you might end up a little over the line. In our favor. Would you drive down with me this weekend, and meet your grandfather?"

"Fadiman? The line's bad. Is that you?"

"... fucking redundancy." The phone squawked into crude but recognizable speech. "Why not ask if I'm asleep? How the hell are you, Janey?"

"Quite splendid, you foul-mouthed old bastard. My language is being cleaned up rapidly."

"I hear that. Don't stay away too long." Then casually, "How was the family?"

"Uncle's okay. We meet Grandfather tomorrow."

"And dukes still seem kind of overwhelming?"

"Kind of. Listen, Fad—in forty-three, that time when you missed my mother—when you were out of Bermuda—could you put a date on it?"

"Thirty-five years? Come on, Janey!"

"You've got to remember winter or summer?"

A grunt. "Summer. I was home for the Fourth of July. . . . The last one for my mother. And then Washington for a couple of days. Waiting in Norfolk for an air flip and the same in Pensacola. Maybe a day. Two at the most. That's going to be, what? Around the eighth, ninth? Right?"

"Right. Ain't it just amazin', honey, what a good wire man can do?" The line made an impossible suggestion half obscured by noise. She laughed, then asked: "Could you send me over anything you can dig up on the murder of a guy called Harry Oakes?"

"I *could*," said Fadiman. "Which is to say, it's within the physically possible so to do."

"Oh shit! *Would you?*"

"With such charm, how can I refuse?"

She told him.

After she hung up the phone she sent a Telex to Tremblay asking him the same question about Harry Oakes.

8

Her grandfather George Frederick Henry, tenth Duke of Dorset, had lived to ninety-one by living for his garden: he was as gnarled and twisted as one of the sticks in the case made from an elephant foot which stood beside him in the hall of the abbey. Light streaming into the hall from a south window threw a stage spot onto the duke's very wide, and very worn, tweed-trousered legs. And onto his immaculately shined, brogued feet.

"*Mary's girl*." The duke blinked twice.

"Grandfather." She kissed a chamois cheek that smelt slightly of peat moss.

The duke looked at his son.

"Mary's girl, isn't she, Leofric?"

"She is, Father." Her uncle kept a firmly kind control. "But I think we'd better go through to the family's apartments—the weekend crowd can't be far behind us. We open to the public, Jane. To keep our fences mended—in both ways."

A small drawing room had been furnished with mismatching bits and pieces. "My favorites," said the duke. "I'm too old to be uncomfortable. I hope we're going to be allowed a drink, Leofric."

"We are, Father. Jane?"

"Scotch—sorry—whiskey, please." She would have liked it on the rocks but there would be no ice. "And a little water?" Leofric passed her the drink, and another with soda to her grandfather, then opened a small silver bucket, took out three cubes, and poured a stiff gin and tonic over them for himself. Once again—as with the old aristocrat's almost com-

52

mon accent, as with Leofric's kindness—nothing about these people was as she expected.

The duke was continuing to stare at her. Where was his mind wandering behind the watery, circumflex eyes? "To Mary's girl," he said for the third time. A bent brown hand raised the glass. "That which is lost is found."

They drank. To ease the strain, she said, "I've never seen so many kinds of trees."

"Our arboretum?" The old face reflected a young passion. "The third Duke planted the first section. Mine is the *Pranus sinensis*—makes a marvelous show next month. We lost some ground in the early part of the century—the navy took most of our oak for Napoleon. But we've regained a bit since then, haven't we, Leofric?"

"We have, Father." A tale told a thousand times by a tenth duke to the next in a long line. But there was no stiffness between them, no sense that children in waiting for succession must be seen and not heard. There was a definite affection, and she hadn't expected that either.

"Jane want to write a book," said her uncle.

"A *book*?" The thought apparently astonished the duke.

"A kind of memorial," she said. "Like your plaque in the church."

"Jane wondered whether she might ask you questions, Father?"

"Of course she can. Of *course* she can! Ask questions. To Mary. What a wonderful idea. . . ."

The eyelids drooped. The glass tipped. Leofric brought it gently back. "Jane's going to take the tour, Father, while you have your rest."

"Only the buildings!" The old-reed voice woke with a surprising vigor. "I want to show her the garden."

"Only the buildings," said Leofric. "We'll do them before tea."

Behind her, as the door was closing, she heard, "Mary's girl."

The arch to the graveled forecourt was blocked by three buses on a group tour of National Trust gardens. The buses held back a motorized menagerie of campers, mini-cars, mopeds, bicycles.

"I had no idea you'd get so many," she said. "What does it cost them?"

"A pound a head. You're sure you won't mind if I leave you? I should see our estate manager."

"And you *have* heard it before?" She smiled. "No problem."

The guide was a girl about ten years younger than herself, plumply attractive and with the crisp accent she'd expected of her grandfather. "Off we go then! Keep inside the roped walks when we do the ruins—we don't want any beanings, do we?"

The crowd gave a dutiful, collective smile and ambled away to "do" the family Rembrandt, and two Turners, and the lecture on the Dissolution of the Monasteries, and the awarding of the abbey to the family by Henry the Eighth, who seemed to crop up everywhere.

They came back into the courtyard to inspect the ruins. The Gothic points of the arches soared a hundred feet above her head; the beauty of the curves against the sky, timeless and perfect.

High up on a buttress a shadow came away from the wall. She ducked. Recoiled instinctively. Another of old Reuter's pigeons flee from a glassless window.

"Mrs. Motigny?"

He had materialized at her elbow from one of the tour groups. Military back, rough jacket with slanting pockets, greenish-brown felt hat. Mustache. How the hell did he know her name?

"Forgive me, I should have introduced myself. Smythe— Colonel Smythe."

The tallish, tweedish son of a bitch who had tried to muzzle Alleyn with a pocket full of D Notices over lunch.

"Ah, you recognize the name. Good." Smythe fell into step beside her. "Mrs. Montigny, this is always a matter of some delicacy—freedom of speech being, of course, the cornerstone of our two countries."

"With motherhood, Colonel."

Smythe inclined his head. "Hackneyed, I agree. But it *is* a very difficult question, isn't it—drawing the line between freedom to speak, and yet insuring that freedom can exist at all? On your side of the Atlantic, with your ongoing constitutional interpretation by the Supreme Court, things are relatively more clear-cut and exposed—perhaps too exposed if I may say so?"

And fuck you, Jack! Instead she said, "Guys like Ellsberg keep us sane. Nixon would still be there."

"Yes. Mr. Nixon was freely voted in." Smythe said it mildly, to annoy. "By rather an ample majority as I recall. However, I didn't mean to offend, simply to observe that the mass electorate doesn't always know what's best for it, does it? Burke's dictum—the independent mind of an elected representative—really must still apply."

"Someone should tell Parliament. Your party whips haven't got the word."

"There has to be some discipline: frreedom carried to excess breeds chaos. There has to be common sense—"

"'Our way.'"

"I beg your pardon?" Smythe shot a glance, no longer mild. "But, yes, if you like. And 'our way' in this country *is* the supremacy of Parliament. So that the law is, at any time, only what Parliament says it is. And our judges are bound by it."

The girl guide was pointing out memorials. There was another at a church in Westminster. "You've got your job, Colonel. I'm used to the adversary relationship. What's off limits, and why?"

"The 'what' is quite straightforward—and I must stress it's not what *I* wish, at all. We—the Government—are concerned that your investigation of the circumstances of your mother's death—heroic though it was—may lead you into other areas which might affect present-day security."

"How about your thirty-year-disclosure rule?"

"A popular misconception, Mrs. Montigny. Disclosure is at the discretion of the Lord Chancellor's office—which is to say, the Government of the Day. Not all topics fit the same period of quarantine. Roger Casement for example. The inflammatory nature of our situation in Ireland would be greatly exacerbated if we were to release his diaries at this time—even after fifty years."

"For Christ's sake! There's got to be *some* limit."

"Certainly. Not much could be harmed after a century."

"One hundred years!" The old duke with his oak stolen for Napoleon, the Casement diaries: these people batted centuries around like lost weekends.

"Perhaps extreme," Smythe conceded. "However, in your case—your mother's case—I'm afraid thirty-four years is too soon. We cannot allow disclosure."

"Look—nothing is being disclosed! It isn't even really her mission I want to know about. More like a search for her motivation."

"And a laudable search it is. But there are trip wires in the grass, Mrs. Montigny, which you may not see. If you'll take my advice—"

"I'd call it a warning."

"Let us simply consider me the velvet glove. Good day, Mrs. Montigny."

The touch of the hat was just right. The rueful smile, perfect. To anyone watching, a perfect gentleman on the make and rebuffed. Annoyance would please the son of a bitch. She smiled back. Seething.

"You gathered an admirer," said Leofric. "Decent-looking sort."

"Real pleasant," she said. "All this walking's great for the appetite. I've got to tell you again, Grandfather, your gardens are incredible."

"My own idea," said with an old man's satisfaction, "eating here on these tray things. So much more—much more—"

"Comfortable." Leofric was used to the turns in the conversation. "You're too old to be uncomfortable, Father."

"Yes, I am."

There was an element of the absurd to eat off television trays with this rambling old man while a dining room the size of a museum, a museum-piece Sheraton suite and a bank's worth of silver, sat on the other side of the wall.

The butler-handyman removed the trays.

"Brandy, Your Grace?"

"Can we, Leofric? It's rather special, isn't it?"

"Yes, Father. Thank you, Kendall. Leave it on the sideboard."

"Very good, my lord. Your Grace, Madam."

The transition to the eleventh duke was already almost made. Both master and man deferred to Leofric. But how well he did it: How gently allowing an old man his illusion of authority. Illusion again—what Smythe and his anonymous masters suffered from. As though the world would even blink in its sleep over anything that had happened in this has-been little country almost her lifetime ago.

"He said she'll be our Edith Cavell of the Second War didn't he, Leofric?" With the speed of great age the duke had turned another mental corner to gather memories. "Of course, she was ready for it. Trained for it—languages, mathematics. God knows where that came from. D'you remember, Leofric, when that damned Russell came to visit?—had that school of his next door—if you can call running naked in a field all day a *school*. Tried to rope Mary in. A brilliant mind, he said . . . and she could ride, eh, Leofric?" The old eyes turned for a moment to Jane. "The right hands, d'you see, my dear? Gentle, gentle. That's what the Prince always said about her hands. She should never have gone to France. Not once we knew the damned Huns had cracked the line. . . . A close run thing eh, Leofric? Dunkirk. Damn close run."

"Yes, Father." Leofric prodded very gently along a well-worn track, "When you spoke to Mr. Churchill—"

"Churchill. I was in the junior school, you know, when he was just leaving—I never did well at arithmetic either—strange where Mary got it. His secretary girl put me through—middle of the night and still working. Why we won, isn't it? When we have to, we just get on with the job. . . ."

"And Sir Winston, Grandfather?"

"Winston . . ." The pauses were longer, the recall slower from more far away. " 'Duke,' he said. 'I've spoken to the King about your Mary. I'm so awfully sorry.' And I said, 'But look here, Churchill—I'm told the Hun knows already that she's coming over. We've heard them talking. Is that so?' And he said in that gruff way of his, 'I'm afraid that it is, Duke. But they cannot know that *we* know it. Never. *Never!* She'll be our Edith Cavell of the Second War.' . . . She didn't suffer though, did she, Leofric? They told us that she didn't suffer. They had special pills, you see. . . . It was the atomic bomb and Hitler couldn't get that, could he? That's why she went. Our Mary—gentle hands, gentle hands . . ."

Outside her room, Leofric said, "I did write to your father—after the war, when they told us about the bomb. And I'd met Captain Barham, the FANY woman who looked after Mary, and went to Germany in 1945 to track things down. I put all that in the letter—that it was clean and quick. And that whatever Mary—that if anyone died for a *reason* in the bloody war, *she* did. I thought he might settle down if I told him that. Because Mary and I were rather close."

What upper-class emotions were contained in "rather close"?

"I'm sure your father thought we put him beyond the pale, but that's not right. I mean the differences were pretty stark, but if she felt he was her chap—well then, he was. And if it might have been a more normal road in peacetime with someone like Geoffrey Piers—well, thank God she took the man she wanted, because she didn't have him long. And they were happy, not a doubt about that. I visited them after they were married—just once, for a weekend. Only a month before the last I saw you, until the other day. They were happy. Good night."

"Good night," she said.

They ate breakfast without the duke, under the eyes of the Arbrights on the wall of the great dining room. "I rather got the impression that you were disappointed with the surroundings last night," said Leofric. "As you see, we can still do an Edwardian breakfast—although my doctor would throw a fit at the fat."

She laughed. "You're very perceptive. And kind. I'm thoroughly impressed. You must have quite a kitchen staff."

"Just a cook and a girl. And Kendall. I couldn't do without—Speak of the devil—what is it, Kendall?"

"The telephone, my lord. The General, again."

"Damn that man! Excuse me, Jane."

She finished too large a plate of things she would normally never touch, and looked at the tree of her ancestors. The branches must have reached every corner of the earth by now. How many others were there like herself so far from the trunk?

"Coffee, madam?"

"Please." She watched Kendall pouring first coffee, and then hot milk into a large, blue-willow cup. "Do you mind if I ask how long you've worked for the family?"

"Since I was fifteen, madam—with a break for the war. I was under training with the air force in Canada. I visited your country once for a weekend of leave. A place called Buffalo?"

"That's not the greatest piece of the United States to take home as a memory."

"Not prepossessing, physically, madam. But I met a young lady—in what you call a diner, I believe?" His eye caught hers. "I passed a pleasant leave."

They shared a smile. She wondered if there were an up-and-coming short-order cook with a butler's back and a New York accent slinging hash beside Lake Erie.

"If I may say so, madam, we think it wonderful that you've come home. Lady Mary was a very special person. His Grace will have shown you her portrait?"

"No."

Cup in hand she followed Kendall through the private drawing room. An adjacent study held the duke's favorite effects: a worn pair of red rubber kneeling pads; a stuffed Retriever; privately bound gardening books with hand-painted color plates; a tall old chair faced half outward to the garden.

Faced half inward to the picture.

Lady Mary was very young, very blonde, very poised. And yet Lady Mary's hand—a gentle hand—reaching for the floral hat that was going to tear it from the head the instant that the sitting was done. The light in Lady Mary's eye told her that as clearly as though the two of them were speaking. She reached out to stroke the pale-green material of her mother's dress. She touched the hand in the picture. It was hard, varnished. There was no moment of Creation, no spark between them. The life was all in her mother's eyes. . . .

Kendall had left her. At least one prejudice held true—the coffee was undrinkable. Perhaps because it was cold. She put down the cup. And at the same moment made the decision to let it go, the digging and disturbing. To let Harry Oakes and Mackenzie King and Little Pat snooze on with all the other sleeping dogs of war.

"Ah—here you are." Leofric was back. "Sorry to be so long. How that colossal bore got a brass hat! . . . He's running the committee for our county Jubilee celebrations and he's sprung a meeting. I've been putting it off for weeks. I really should stay. Please take the car."

"I couldn't—"

"Driving on the wrong side?"

"No. But you need—"

"I prefer the train to the traffic. Just as long as you're quite sure you'll be all right. There are too many damn people on the roads in this country. I suppose after my saying that, you'll go—hell or high water."

"Yes, Uncle." They both laughed. "But I'll be fine. Really."

"I'm sure you will. Kendall can see that you're packed with something suitable for lunch. Do you like the picture?"

"I've never seen her in color—never at all really." She explained about the solitary orchard photograph.

"That would be Roone's House," said Leofric. "But just one snapshot? I'd say you're traveling through life rather light." With an unexpected intimacy he took her arm and tucked her hand in against his side. "Come along, we'll go upstairs so that you can say good-bye."

In a bedroom as large as the dining room her grandfather was tiny in an enormous bed. A crab-claw hand pointed at French doors to a balcony and a vista of lake and garden. "Capability Brown, they say. Don't believe it, my dear. My great-grandfather's work. Your great-great-great. You *will* come back—now you've found us?"

"Yes."

"So glad. So glad. The *Prunus* are very fine. . . ."

The Daimler was waiting in the courtyard. Leofric closed the door with a barely audible click.

"I've marked the map. Keep to the right at Tidpit and the A354 will take you to Salisbury. You'll be crossing the downs—it's a good day, you may see Clearbury Ring." Leofric smiled. "Dodge the army, they're maneuvering. After Salisbury it's a clear run to town on the A30."

"I'll stay with the map. I hope you're insured."

"To the hilt. God bless."

She drove for a mile through the changing trunks of the arboretum, as pine succeeded beech, and beech became balsam. A pair of yews, vast in age and spread, saw her out of the estate.

She turned east and followed the map, unable to decide whether the names were from Hardy or a Gothic Romance: Twerne Courtney on Shroton; Winterborne Stickland with Winterborne Clenstone and Winterborne Houghton and Winterborne Whitchurch. Were Winterbornes people or places?

Then Tolpuddle of Martyr fame, and a dozen other puddles: Turner's and Aff's and Gallows Hill. No ambiguity there. She crossed Cranborne Common and a bridge with a sign saying Dorset on one side and Hampshire on the other. Too many people, Leofric said, and yet the Daimler drove itself on country roads deserted between their hedges. She slipped the map back into the glove leather of the map case in the door.

Glove leather, and maple burl, and Kendall's light lunch in a hamper on the floor beside her. "Just fowl, madam, with some fruit and cheese." And wines, a red and a white, strapped in beside the cut glass and the Georgian knives and forks with the Arbright crest, in an old reed basket that her mother might have taken through these same small hamlets.

A delivery van pulled into the road ahead of her, Burgate Feed & Seed painted on the tailgate and wisps of hay sticking through the gaps at the sides. The "&" reminded her of King's diary. At the first slight widening in the road the driver pulled over and waved her past. She gave him a honk and a nod of appreciation. A signpost leaning loosely in its hole, its white paint flaking and graying, pointed back at *Whitsbury Upper 3*, and ahead, to *Salisbury 10*. The paving dipped sharply to round a bend.

The detour, a large checkerboard and arrow, was set squarely in the center of the road.

Ministry of Defence. Caution. Follow Arrows.

A lane went up to the right at a one in three gradient only wide enough for a car and a half. Less, for another Daimler. She switched on her headlights as a precaution and slowed to a crawl at the ridge, but all was clear on the other side and she picked up speed. The next arrow turned her east again, almost south, she thought, and the paving changed to hard-packed gravel and dirt. The Daimler's suspension didn't seem to feel the difference but she slowed again to twenty-five. Christ, at this rate it would take all day. She stopped to read the map but the scale was too large for such small tracks.

Another dip in the road. This time to a stream with not even a bridge—just rough fieldstone cobbles for a ford. The Daimler protested a little but got across. The ground was dry on the other side; she must be the first vehicle this morning. Now there were only two ruts, barely visible through last year's dead grass.

One of the downs rose again ahead of her. Why downs? The goddamn things went up just as often. The car changed gear ratios effortlessly. A sudden drop. Something at the back made a scraping sound.

"*Shit!*" A muffler must cost a fortune.

She slowed and pressed a button. The window lowered without a sound. She stuck her head out to look back for damage.

CRACK CRACK CRACK

Black clouds shot up ahead of her. The flaming throats and thunderous roar of the afterburners came and went overhead before she could blink. She jammed the brakes. Clods of dirt dropped on the gleaming body. "Oh, *Christ!*"

The flying figure on the radiator cap lay bent over to one side.

A second wave of aircraft. Duller thumps this time. Gray smoke clouds erupted with a hiss of flame. A whistling railroad scream above the smoke.

She jumped from the car. *And was back at another dirt track with the pyramid-hatted women and children running ahead of her, shrieking and screaming, the stinking black smoke rolling over them, beating with melting hands at the gluey burning filth eating the children's clothes and then their naked bodies.*

Again the whistling. Heavy blasts, close in, .120mm shells. Coughing and gasping, she lay on the ground under the car and pressed her face into the dry grass.

Jesus, to screw up and go like this, in peacetime Britain. How fucking stupid. The ground trembled in a continuous, steady, rocking movement.

Tanks! God, please God, let them see the headlights.

A piece of metal on the Daimler's chassis began vibrating over her head, shivering her hair. The whole road was moving.

"*Trompete, hier Violine. Schiess, Bahn frei. Ende.*"

German words crackling on a radio. *German! I'm crazy.* There was an uncontrollable urge to giggle. Stop it. She bit her finger. *Stop it!*

"*Trompete, hier Violine. Rechts schwenkt! Bestätig!*"

"*Violine, hier Trompete. Okay!*"

Okay in German, and trumpets and violins taking monstrous metal form thirty feet away. She could smell it. Hear the links of its tracks running over its driver wheels, hear the whine of its turret, pitch rising. *Pointing toward her.*

"*Ziel Panzer ein Tausend.*"

"DON'T SH—"

The concussion smashed her head and words into the ground. She heard the turret whining again for one more shot. Sensed the Daimler lifting off two wheels. *It's going over!* But now feeling no more fear: Time running endlessly ahead of her like the nightmare peasant children.

"*FEUER PAUSE! FEUER PAUSE!*"

A muddled steel track was five feet from her hand. But stopped.

"*Trompete, Trompete—was ist los? Dort ist ein Panzer?*"

There was blood on her finger.

"*Nein.*" Boots thudded to the ground beside the track. A blond head, blue eyes ringed with oil in a face shock-white under the dirt, stared at her. A leather-gauntleted hand reached in, touched, held, gripped her own. Dragged her out. Helped her to stand beside a Daimler dwarfed by the monster.

"*Scheisse!*" The radio was incredulous, "*Eine verdammte kleine Frau?—Im Kraftwagen?*"

Her head spun: saw images of a Swastika and a boy in a Speedo swim suit turn to a cross of black and white and this young German with a hand shaking as much as her own.

"You could haff been *killed!*"

9

The story was in the London press before her own arrival in the battered Daimler. The *Evening Standard*, with "Leopard Spots Lost Lady," and *verdammte kleine Frau* clutching her Teutonic knight was bad. The text was worse.

The phone rang its head off. First, Williams at the office

for a column of her side, then Leofric trying not to let concern for his car obscure concern for her, then Alleyn.

"Taking on the Wehrmacht's carrying reenactment a bit far."

"A bit."

"I suppose it wasn't funny. Easy to do though—driving on the wrong—"

"*Jesus Christ!* If I hear that again—"

"Sorry, sorry. What about the rest of the trip to the family tree—how did . . . ?"

"I met your Colonel Smythe."

"I see." The banter faded. "Do you want to talk?"

"Give me a half hour for a bath."

She took the phone off the hook and lay in the tub. Thank God the car was in one piece. She was quite sure she had made no mistakes with signs. Her head still hurt. With its usual gift for timing, her period had arrived.

Alleyn was holding a galley sheet. "Our morning copy. I've cleaned out the little woman stuff."

"Thanks. Help yourself. Give me a double."

Alleyn poured the drinks and lit a pipe. "I still don't understand how you missed the warning," he said. "The army are usually so damned careful. Red flares going up, choppers overhead."

"I should have followed Burgate Feed and Seed," she said absently, reading the copy. "How come you British are so blasé about German tanks in England?"

"The anti-Boche brigade was certainly out in force the first time that NATO sent them over here, I can tell you— What is it?"

"This time. This operation. Catch this quote: 'Units of the 21st German Armored Division are participating in Operation Mailed Fist 1977.'"

"Yes?"

"I asked that bastard Smythe if he was an official warning—he said, 'Consider me the velvet glove.'"

Alleyn shrugged, "If the bloody army and the Foreign Office could fine tune to that degree, we'd sleep like babies, love."

"Yeah? Well, with dirty tricks, I'm a believer!" She emptied her glass. "It's ironic—I was going to drop it. The whole deal. Not now, boy. Screw Smythe. Your fucking

Foreign Office can't D-Notice me—and if you don't like it—"

"Steady." Alleyn put down his pipe. "I'm not the enemy, Jane."

"I know that—you just have a way of looking sometimes. I'm sorry, Roger. Forget it."

"No," said Alleyn. "I won't forget it. It's been a bad day, but you're quite wrong. Let me tell *you*, the working bodies over here don't like them either, the Smythes. We don't like any part of the bloody Press Council or the bloody D Notices. You may not know it, but we're already fighting the bastards over the Thalidomide story all the way to the World Court at The Hague, for abridging the European code on freedom of expression. Get it through your head, Jane, you can't do it alone over here. Not even with your 'Mrs.'" Alleyn stood up and moved over to the door. "And I'll tell you somewhere else you're dead wrong: with your joint passports and your joint citizenships—if the bastards want to, they can nail you as British ten ways to Christmas under the Official Secrets Act. And do it all *in camera*. There'd never even be a peep! Good night."

Leofric's chauffeur arrived at Dolphin Square at eight-fifteen the next morning to collect his charge. From his shell-shocked reaction to the crushed ornament on the hood the man might have been through the battle with her, but he managed to drive her to work without incident.

At the office Williams was still outraged. "Fucking army. Even worse, fucking Germans."

"I didn't see any of that," she said. "Maybe the smokescreen—"

"Funny bitch. But I'm glad you're in one piece."

Alleyn made the first move at mending fences and called her—to arrange a meeting at Saint Margaret's in the lunch hour. By five minutes before noon the article was finished and Fadiman had read the morning wire in Washington. "Jesus, Jane—goddamn Krauts—"

"You must have been speaking to Williams. I'm just fine, for God's sake, Fad. I really am. And I'm busy."

But Fadiman grumbled on. "Hey," he said, as she tried to end the call for the third time, "I got your Harry Oakes. I'm sending it commercial wire. But you just take care—okay?"

"Okay," she said. "*Okay!*"

From Abingdon Street, Saint Margaret's was a small gray sister leaning against the great black shoulders of the mother Abbey. The square beside them was lined six deep. She finally spotted Alleyn next to Oliver Cromwell.

"Hi. Thank God you're so tall. Sorry I'm late. What gives?"

"Church service for the opening of Parliament. When they all ask for a divine pat on the back for Supertax and deficit spending."

"Our guys use Billy Graham at a prayer breakfast."

"And you expect Truth in Government?"

"Not in my lifetime!" They laughed together and she squeezed his hand and was glad they were friends again. The doors of the church opened and an unmilitary procession straggled out. "What is this," she said, "a geriatric Hamelin?"

But should she laugh at these gowned, limping, medaled men, carrying their archaic symbols? Didn't they, in their erratic walk with their maces and embroidered handbags, make the struggle for democracy real too? Make the continuity from Runnymede, to Cromwell, to Jefferson—to Churchill—human?

Two men in black damask gowns edged with gold lace followed the sergeants.

"Speakers of the Lords and Commons," Alleyn said. "One must admit that the thing would lose a bit in cloth caps."

"And the guy with the purse?"

"Lord Piers—the Lord Chancellor—he follows Canterbury in order of precedence at tea parties. The bag wasn't always so ornate. For great occasions it used to be of snow-white kid and carried the Seal of England until some oaf dropped twenty pounds of silver alloy on his foot. At least that's the established joke. Now it just holds the chap's hanky and ends up as a souvenir cushion cover."

"So he's just an ornament?"

"No, I'm joking. He's no longer the monarch's right hand like Thomas More, but he's still one of the busiest men in the Cabinet. And could be one of the most powerful if he wanted to chuck his weight about. His fingers are in all the judicial pies—tribunals no one's ever heard of, but they can carry a lot of clout. What we were wrangling about last night, to be specific. The bookies are laying the present incumbent will chuck his title and be ready for the leadership next time round."

"A lord in the Labour Party?"

"He's surprisingly popular—even with the union die-hards. 'The Piers Touch.' The tabloids like the play on words—and shots like that." Alleyn pointed at a minor royal receiving bows. The wind playing too vigorously with her dress, had exposed too much royal leg, and was being slapped down.

"It was the height of fashion just after the war," Alleyn continued, "to be on the Left. The Mountbatten influence. Picnics for the party faithful in the ancestral grounds. Nothing like being against privilege when your own's unassailable. Before the war of course, and especially in Piers' case, it was the other way: pushing the Nazi line at the family seat at Anstiebury, or at Cliveden with the Astors—and Dawson, our editor at *The Times*."

"Are you serious?"

"I'm sorry to have to admit it. Oh, they didn't all wear brown shirts and shoot themselves for love of Adolf like the Mitford girl—but there were a hell of a lot of hangers-on like his Lordship waiting to see which way the wind would blow. The abdicated Edward among them. I think we can go in now."

Ecclesiastical wrapping up was taking place. A junior curate genuflected to the altar with plates of ready cash. Through a small doorway she saw her man from the previous visit helping an elderly cleric off with a surplice in the vestry. The odd soft word wafted out.

"... attend His Grace, tomorrow... Lambeth?"

"... most certainly, Canon."

"Poor food..."

"... little annoyances, Canon."

Her man came out and closed the door behind him with a sigh.

"Excuse me." The round pink face looked up. "If you remember, I was here a week ago? We talked about the plaque for my mother?"

"I'm so sorry," a vague shrug of rounded shoulders, "we have so many visitors...."

"I'm sure you do. But it was about the flower—the single rose. You were going to ask the custodian."

"Oh yes! Yes. Our Lady Mary Memorial. But I am most terribly sorry—it quite slipped my mind. Our sexton's ill—I think I mentioned? . . ."

"You did. And I don't want to bother you. Maybe I could visit him myself?"

"Possibly," the soft voice was doubtful, "but I really do think I should check with his doctor first. Poor Johnson's very frail. In hospital—Saint Thomas's—he almost left us. Could you come back once more—if you don't mind? Perhaps at the end of the week?"

In the square, the parade had unraveled into knots of M.P.s talking, laughing, pairing for lunch. The illustrious were being skimmed into limousines like Leofric's.

"God bless our humble efforts," said Alleyn. "My turn to buy, Lady Jane."

"Roger," she said, "do me a favor. Don't call me that."

She came back from lunch with one drink too many to make much sense of Fadiman's stack of wire copy waiting on her desk. The facts were interesting but seemed unrelated and had as much to do with the Duke of Windsor as Harry Oakes. That, she realized after a cup of coffee, could *be* the relation.

Harry's money, it was clear, really ruled the islands: the Duke despised them—and their climate and their Government House. He liked Harry's house, Westbourne, scene of the murder, and stayed there with the Duchess while renovations were undertaken down the road to relieve the vice-regal distress.

Halfway through the renovations the Royals removed themselves to the mainland: the Duchess, with her personal hairdresser, went north to New York for the fashions, and the Duke went west to High River in Alberta for the hunting. The Duke's aide—Major the Honourable Geoffrey Piers—accompanied the Duke.

To the surprised annoyance of society tongues, when the absentees returned to the islands, the Duchess, immaculately coiffed, carried out good works with good grace and great style. The tongues, fighting back, flew hairdressers in from Florida. The hairdressers were often airsick. The Duke, who disliked hairdressers, most of island society, and most of all men of color aspiring to office, played golf on Harry Oakes's golf course until Sir Harry climbed aboard a large bulldozer, tore down all the trees around the course and dragged them by their roots across the greens. This was stated at the inquest to have been a reflection of a troubled mind and a support for the Duke's theory of suicide.

The presence of a four-pronged hole in Sir Harry's head was not. Nor were the blisters, which—it was stated by Doctors Quackenbush and Fitzmaurice—had had to form while Sir Harry was alive.

The trial prompted more queries than solutions. Reuter had wanted to know why censorship was being imposed in a civil case. The London office had been asked not to ask the question. The Washington office had asked and got no answer.

After the trial some things changed and some did not. Five hundred Cameron Highlanders, who had arrived to surround Government House with barbed wire for Christmas 1942, departed. The ratio of service grass widows to men in the islands—white men of course—leveled off at fifteen to one.

Harry's daughter Nancy, the wife of the accused, was a great friend of the son of the Nazi ambassador in Lisbon, Baron von Hoyningen-Huene, and subsequently married him—after divorcing the unfortunate de Marigny.

The ambassador had held numerous meetings and discussions with the Duke in Portugal, and with Himmler and von Ribbentrop in Berlin.

The Duke often visited the Outer Islands in his yacht, the *Gemini*.

Axel Wenner-Gren, a Swede almost as rich as Oakes and friend of both Harry and Hermann Göring, removed his yacht *Southern Cross* from the Bahamas after the murder because of unkind comments in the press about his other friendship—with the Duke.

Wenner-Gren kept his canning factory at Bimini.

Fadiman's summation was eclectic but concise:

Dr. Quackenbush's first reaction to the news on Harry had been, "Santa Claus is dead."

Harry had sold the Duke a lot of shares in his smelting business but there was never any conclusive proof of Meyer Lansky's hand, or other Mafia involvement. De Marigny had never seemed guilty. The jury recommended he be deported from the islands—as a cad. He was.

There had been a gap of five hours between the Duke's first knowledge of the crime, and his reporting it to Erskine-Lindop, the District Commissioner of Police.

The British Colonial Hotel made a lot of money from the hairdressers.

Harry Oakes struck gold at an Ontario mining camp called Swastika.

She wrapped it up and put a thank-you note on the night wire to Washington.

In all the mass of names only one stood out: Piers, the man with the funny handbag in the square. The man, her uncle said, who once thought himself a match for her mother.

10

The summons the next morning had Hogarthian echoes of banishment or imprisonment for debt.

> Whereas you, Jane Montigny, have this day been charged before me that you have committed trespass upon property of Her Majesty, this is therefore to command you in Her Majesty's name...

Back to the boonies, there to be dealt with according to law. She looked up at the member of the London Constabulary shifting from the slightly curling, squeaking sole of one black boot to the other.

"*For the Identification of Criminals Act!*" she said. "Jesus Christ, you people have a nerve!"

"It's not really our job, ma'am—only when all the servers are tied up." The constable's helmet was clasped beneath his arm like Anne Boleyn's head. The constable seemed almost as discomfited. "It's always bad after a long weekend, like."

"And I've got to go all the way back to *Salisbury*?"

The constable looked again at the particulars of the charge on the summons. "It's Crown property, they might be able to change the venue." The constable's face brightened. "And you're American. I should think it's all a mistake, then. Not being able to read the signs, like." The constable smiled kindly at the ignorant bloody foreigner before him. "That's it. If I were you, ma'am, I should get a solicitor." The constable recovered his helmet with his composure and squeaked off down the hall.

Williams at the office had his ulcer boiling. "*Trespass!* This fucking country gets more fanatic every day. The bastards should be paying *you*, for Christ's sake—I'll get Legal on it right away."

One arm of the law jogged her thoughts of another: she called the number Alleyn had given her.

"Spoonfield and Coombes. Spoonfield speaking. Major Spoonfield."

"I want to locate a cousin," she said.

"Ah. A cousin." It had already become a conspiracy between them. Slightly sordid.

"All I know is her name, Cynthia Dodgeson, and that she worked in the Government in 1943. Is that enough?"

"Indeed it is, Madam! Most assuredly. One of our associates should have it out in a trice." The voice warbled through morning phlegm. "A trice. I myself, Madam, you understand, am more involved with physical security. Perhaps, as this is a matter of a personal nature I might refer you to our Mr. Coombes?" The line deadened with a hand across the mouthpiece.

"Coombes 'ere." The other half of the team had a thin cockney whine. "Missing person, is it?"

"I just explained. A cousin." She went through it again. "I've tried the phone books and the *Government Directory*. Can you find her?"

"I'd imagine. Terms are twenty quid down and balance with report. Travel costs extra. Weekends double. Miss?"

"Mrs. Montigny."

"It would be foreign," said Coombes. "Send us the cash and call tomorrow about four. Might 'ave something."

She spent the rest of the morning at a trade meeting on Common Market agricultural quotas. An invasion of sheep farmers from Yorkshire made it bearable. After lunch the Reuter lawyer called.

"We've been able to get a stay, Mrs. Montigny—pending clarification of the charge. I had hoped that under the unfortunate circumstances the matter would be dropped altogether. Indeed, I still do—I'm lunching one of the prosecutors in chambers tomorrow. We must keep our fingers crossed."

At three she heard from Spoonfield. The major's voice was now almost drowned beneath the lunchtime gin. "News, Madam! A moment—my associate."

"Mrs. Monteen? Coombes. Not much yet I'm afraid."

She was not surprised: stretching it out to the weekend and double time, the crooked bastard. "Though I do 'ave an address. Can you drop round to the firm? Save our time and your lolly."

The firm, a very pale shadow of its namesake in Virginia, was hidden behind a rippled glass door at the head of a flight of dingy stairs in the East End. The "Coombes" still adhered neatly to the window light but the "Spoonfield" was peeling, sliding down the glass as though heading, like its owner, for a fall.

Major Spoonfield himself, in a tattersall check with a frayed collar and horseshoe cuff links was flushed with enthusiasm for the case. "Most *satisfying*, Madam! *Most* satisfying—"

"I've got it, Jack." Coombes emerged from a back office. A nimble little man with wire-rim glasses and a shirt with broad purple stripes. "Your 'cousin' wasn't working for just any old bloke, eh, Mrs. Monteen?"

"She wasn't?"

"Of course, you wouldn't know." Coombes's wink was shrewd but without malice. "With our Winnie 'imself for five years—almost six. The address is old Mum and Dad—and very old they are! Eighties at least but still going strong—from the postmistress. The daughter's alive. That's all I've got."

"Way more than I figured. Thank you."

"My pleasure. Account's forty-five altogether—"

"And if I *may*, Madam." With a speed from an alcoholic's desperation, Spoonfield's hand was on the bills.

"How do I find the parents?" she asked.

Keeping one eye on the major and the money, Coombes took out a road map. "Little Baldon. The M40 to just past Tetsworth at the junction with A329, then cut west to B480, and that's it. The old boy's a colonel—" Coombes flashed a look at his partner, "the genuine article."

Leaving London in a hired car was unpleasant—Coombes's reminder of road maps and the army almost made her chicken out—but once on the motorway she relaxed and enjoyed the country with its Cotswold cottages of stone and slate, its village greens and ponds: country as it should be for a colonel, retired and rose bowered.

The Post Office said, "Number nineteen, dear—a mile down on the right, can't miss it. You'll see the caravans."

Trailers—hundreds of them, destroying an apple orchard. Next to the ruined orchard and separated from it by a steel-link fence, two equally misplaced raw, red-brick bungalows squatted in a field.

The cement lintels of the building on the left had been painted white to relieve the starkness of the brick. A matching barrack line of small white rocks edged a tiny drive. Boxes of flowering bulbs sat on each side of the front door.

The knocker under the number was a fox-mask head, and feet, in brass. The colonel, as Coombes had said, was very old, very tall at six feet six, and quite definitely the genuine article. His left arm ended in a pinned-up sleeve. One eye was blank. Other watermarks of battle scarred his neck and forehead.

"About Cynthia?" said the colonel. "And the war? What a long time back. You had better come in. From America? Wonderful country. Wonderful. Not popular though. But then we never were either."

The colonel's good shoulder closed the door behind her. "This way," said the colonel as though she might get lost in a hall three paces long. At the end of the hall, all the props for a drawing room, library, and study had been squeezed into a single space, so that carpet covered carpet, and landscapes of highland cattle bumped photographs of officers reclining in matched pairs beside tigers and a bearded George the Fifth. One of the tigers lay now on the topmost carpet. It was not a good skin and the bullet tear was visible across the top of the head. In the manner of the blind, the colonel avoided the head without looking at it and pointed her at a seat next to a ball of wool and a book of knitting patterns resting on a tabletop supported by crossed Gurkha kukris with solid-gold handles. The notches to stop blood dripping down the handles were slightly pitted. Above the table of the knives and the knitting was a case of medals and ribbons. She recognized a Croix de Guerre. One or two others with diagonal bars looked important. Beside the medals was a picture by a *Life* photographer of the colonel playing with his Gurkha children as they cooked a concrete pillbox with a flamethrower and waited for something to crawl out. One of the little brown men also played the bagpipes.

"A great honor." The colonel waved his one hand at the wall. She thought he was referring to the medals—but of course it was the photograph. The cigar stuck out over an inscription toward the picture of the tiger hunt. The inscription said, *To Jumbo and Her Klop—Winston S.C.*

"His name for her, Jumbo. Don't know why."

"And the 'Klop'?"

"Sorry." The colonel sat in his chair beside his *Times*. "It was a tight-lipped show then. One didn't ask too much about things. My wife's shopping with the car or I'd offer you tea. Appalled her when Cynthia went off to learn typewriting." The colonel thought about that for a time. "Odd where things end. But the girl wanted to do something—and the heart murmur wouldn't let her be active. I was in Belgium with Gort—didn't know a thing about it until we got back. And then her training couldn't very well be wasted, and I knew a chap in the War Office who was short-handed. Do you believe things happen for a reason?"

"Sometimes it's hard not to. Did your daughter work closely with Churchill?"

"Like a glove. There were other girls but she was boss-wife you might say, in his harem. Went everywhere with him. Quebec, Yalta, Potsdam. He offered her blood and treasure if she'd stay on after the war. But she had the chance of marriage, and quite right to take it. Children at the end make all the difference." The colonel stared down at the tiger's head. "We lost our boy at Messina—Ah, my wife."

A car door slammed outside and a tiny bird of a woman with snow-white hair flew into the room. "Oh, *hullo*." Despite the accentuated words, she seemed quite unsurprised by anything.

"My dear," said the colonel, "Mrs. Montigny, from Washington—in America."

"How *exciting*. And *what* a time you've had with your Mr. Nixon—thank *goodness* it can't happen *here*."

"Mrs. Montigny's writing a book, my dear. She wants to know about people like Cynthia."

"Oh, what *fun*! Show her the treasures while I put the kettle on." Mrs. Dodgeson flew out of the room.

"Treasures?"

"Cynthia keeps a small trunk here. No room in her flat in town."

"I thought she had a family?"

"She does, but her husband died and the boys are both grown. One in Canada—she's visiting him now as a matter of fact. The other in Brussels, of all places!" Katmandu and Canada were relevant: links of Empire as familiar as the tiger. Across the Channel was a foreign land. "That was a rough show," the colonel said, "Belgium. The trunk is in the cellar."

The building mind that had stuck red brick in a rural field had ignored drainage and the place ran with damp.

"I had a man look at it," said the colonel. "Too damned expensive though. Like everything else now. *I* don't know the answer."

"Do the finance ministers?"

The colonel appeared to laugh. "Damn good!" Then he said, "I have trouble bending—would you mind?"

The trunk sat on two bricks clear of the wet dirt floor. The colonel stooped at the foot of the steps and stared at it. "I have your word that this is not for public consumption?"

"Nothing without your daughter's approval."

"Good. Good."

She dragged the black metal weight up the narrow stairs, puffing at the top. She must find some way to keep exercising. She set the box down on the tiger skin. The trunk was locked but its key hung on a tarred string attached to one of the handles.

"May I?" she asked. The colonel nodded. "When will your daughter be back from Canada?"

"A month, I think. My wife will know. Our grandson

asked her over for their spring. She's always gone in summer before. Appalling heat then—bad as the Frontier. The boy wanted Cynthia to go this time to watch the damned ice melt." The colonel looked at her inquiringly with the one eye. "Do they make something edible from trees?"

"Maple syrup?"

"That was it. Ah. There you are."

The case had been packed with meticulous hands, and the contents wrapped in a double layer of plastic sheeting and cotton quilting. On top, separately wrapped, was a photograph album. "I'll see how my wife's getting on," said the colonel.

All the old familiar faces, all the old familiar places. And all identified by date, location, and occasion. Most were candid shots—the participants unaware that history was wrapping itself around their shoulders. Between the pictures were news clippings; menus signed in Russian, French, American-English... *To a great gal from a fellow keyboard puncher— Harry S. Truman.* Hotel cards, train tickets, each with its annotation. One from the Shoreham, Washington, August 30, 1943.

Under the next layer of wrapping were some separate photographs in frames.

These seemed to be of conferences—formal groupings with none of the spontaneity of the album pictures. But one intrigued her: Nine or ten men sitting around a heavy elliptical table with Chippendale legs, maps of a world at war on the walls behind them, Persian carpets identical to those the trunk was resting on now, under their feet.

They were not all men. The middle figure of the group was a woman wearing a khaki uniform devoid of rank badges or insignia. She looked totally composed. Middle-thirties, attractive. A strong face with high, arching brows. Thick dark hair in a heavy, pageboy cut rolled onto her shoulders. The hair caught the photographer's light.

The group were staring at an object on the polished surface of the table. A Grecian statuette of a prancing satyr reached out of the center foreground toward the camera.

She turned the picture over. It was unbacked and the cardboard was held in place by tiny brads that had rusted and left marks. A rough horseshoe to approximate the table had been drawn in ink of almost the same color as the rust. An

"X" had been marked for the participants' places. In the open center of the horseshoe there was an additional mark and the word *Faun*—presumably the statuette. Some of the places had names: Derek, Noël, Dennis W. The lone woman's name was Violet B.

LCS—In War Rooms. '41–'43 was written underneath.

The picture was puzzling, enigmatic; the statuette and the woman with her rich hair so out of place in that masculine world. She put the frame aside reluctantly.

Under the photographs were files, dozens of them, all a dull buff color with the stock file number on each one: *HM 174: By the King's Printer.*

Inside the first file were transcriptions of official letters. Sandwiched with them were short notes home stating the obvious. *"So incredibly busy . . ."* and stiff-upper-lip references to being bawled at by the great man for losing a copy of something vital for *"action this day"*; having to start again from scratch, the writer sure that she was going to be flung into hell forever. *"I shall never, NEVER, do that again. I have devised my own little system of 'treasures,' to be hidden away against the chance of future catastrophe. . . ."*

Hidden away as well, tucked down the side of the trunk, was a picture of Cynthia Dodgeson. Not pretty, too gauntly like her father, but so radiantly happy beside the young naval sub-lieutenant grinning self-consciously by a gangway, their arms linked. A couple of buddies grinned with them, below a gilt-lettered mahogany nameplate, HMS *Hood*.

Under the photograph was a minute dated May 25, 1941: *". . . Must report to Your Majesty the loss, with two thousand hands . . ."*

The minute was typed as perfectly as all the rest.

"Jeremy's picture." Mrs. Dodgeson had fluttered back. "What a *nice* boy. From South Africa, I think. My father was Bishop of Matabeleland. I remember as a small girl seeing a very *very* bright bird—but do you know I *cannot* recall the name. I shall never visit now, of course, so I shall *never* know. A water biscuit?" Mrs. Dodgeson gave a little tinkling laugh not much louder than the spoon stirring and was gone again.

She poured herself a second cup and sipped it. Bishop of Matabeleland. And these old people from wide spaces sat trapped in this field with the trailers; their daughter stuck in London in a place too small to hold a trunk, while inside it

really were keys to the kingdom: at least to an advance in the
high six figures from any publisher in New York.

She lifted out the second bundle of files.

WSC: Minutes, Personal for Memoirs.

She should have remembered that Churchill was a writer. More, that like herself, he was a correspondent. That
covering war from Afghanistan to the sands of Alamagordo
had been his consuming passion. And here in the hell of
1940, when he didn't even know that there'd be an English-
speaking world alive to read it, the old son of a bitch was still
setting aside copy ready to drop into print on V-E Day.

And his faithful girl Friday with *her* copy was staying one
jump ahead for when the great day came. The minutes were
numbered rather than dated for each year. She picked up
Number 6/43.

WSC MEM. PRIVATE. TOP SECRET. WSC ONLY.
25 Aug. 43 *Lake of the Snows, Que. Midnight.*
Present: WSC and Mack K.

King again. The notes, although transcribed back from
the shorthand were still partially abbreviated in a Churchillian
code. Occasionally the carbon was smudged.

"Torch":
WSC: Explain great success. Reviewed again aid obt
from Dieppe. Inval prep for Overlord.

    Mack K: Reiterate Canada gov't having gr troub
with Dieppe to Parl and peop. Partic Queb, etc.

    WSC: Dieppe *vital* in making Germ believe
cross Chann atck impos. Secret war will win for us
in end etc. Intell more powerful than divns men,
etc.

    Mack K: Agreed. But Forces at hand more than
know, etc. Divine Prov, etc.

    WSC: Div Prov *and* Uncle Joe! Hinge of ~~pin~~
fate, etc. Gr Brit and Can must be hinge between
Russ enig and Amer. Dearly *loves* Amer. Blood ties,
etc. But too *gabby*! Fears safety Red Rose/Tube
Alloys etc after *Southern Cross* affair. Too soon to
tell etc. One more month if fish has the bait etc.

Hopes for big fish in morn Gen Brooke two five-
pounders, etc.

If the fish has the bait.

The feeling from the first mention on the radio, from the
vault in Ottawa, from the Public Records room in London,
was with her now. She was quite certain. She opened file
number 7/43.

The entries for the last two weeks of September were
occupied completely with Salerno, the capture of the Italian
fleet, biting into Italy, returning to Britain by battleship
Renown. The first four days of October revealed endless
wrangles with Allies over the preparations for Overlord, and
events involving long-forgotten names: the resignation of
Admiral Pound; the death of Kingsley Wood, Chancellor of
the Exchequer; his replacement by John Anderson—senior
representative on Tube Alloys.

Always Tube Alloys. She stopped to stretch, to shake out
the tension. If the log had been correct, the fifth was the day
before The Day. The man with the cigar stared over her
shoulder.

Again she was flabbergasted by the European sense of
time. The entry for the fifth covered negotiations with Portugal
for the use of the Azores. The treaty in question went back
six hundred years—to 1373. Its age had also fascinated the
historian in Churchill.

She turned the page.

Oct. 6:
PLACE: WCR
TIME: 1330
   Topic: "J" requests release for operation Sugar
       Candy. Approval to proceed, granted. HM
       informed.
PLACE: The OP
TIME: 2130
   Topic: Discussions with "J."
Transcript:
"J":   Weather satis, no moon. Swed low risk.
WSC: Agreed. But v *high* risk Scylla N. Denm.
      Germ Mobil. Inspector Thompson: (Intercom),
      Captain Dexter from Ultra re Sugar Candy

op, etc. Has SLU pass—but no appt, etc.
"J":   v unfort case. Personal conn'n. Sensitive Amer
      link via Donovan.
WSC: Send in.
Capt. Dexter: Excuse etc. Scylla abort urgent.
"J":   Not poss. Rad silence with a/c.
Capt. Dexter: Call Swedes. Charybdis has transmit.
WSC: Jumbo—No treasure trove on this.

October 7:
PLACE: Annex.
TIME: 1100.
Present WSC, Mr. Attlee, Mr. Bevan.
 Topic: Coal Mine Nationalisation. . . .

So her father *had* seen a problem; *had* come to Churchill;
had spoken; had lost.

And Scylla too. But a war had been won and that was
Churchill's—and, presumably, her mother's—only aim: In
war, resolution.

And in peace. Resolution of this goddamn puzzle with so
fucking few pieces. What the hell was a Charybdis? If she had
paid more attention to Radcliffe first-year English she might
recall. But endless Homeric literature and its attachments
was why she had left Radcliffe for Bennington. The classics
always got the hero stuck between a rock and a hard place,
she remembered. And always for thoroughly stupid reasons.
Welcome to the club.

The tea was cold and she was keeping an old man from
his chair and his paper. Halfway back to London, passing a
small Jag being driven too slowly, she realized that she'd
forgotten to look for anything on Harry Oakes. Coming off the
M40 at Uxbridge with the Jag in close behind her, she
thought that she was being followed.

11

The church, left to the ecclesiastic between weddings and parliamentary ceremonies, was hollow and waiting. An earnest young man perched on a wooden ladder was setting hymn numbers on the boards. He said, "Good morning," as though it might not be.

"Hi." She never knew how to address these rankless, sexless men. "I was hoping to find the gentleman I spoke to last week."

"Mr. Mellows?"

"I didn't catch—"

"Glasses and fairish hair?"

She nodded.

"Yes, that would be Mr. Mellows. I'm following him. Can I help?"

"Following?"

"He's gone on diocesanal staff—as principal private secretary."

"It must have been kind of sudden," she said. "He didn't mention it on Friday."

"I rather think the appointment *was* sudden. Certainly, *I* was not expecting a move so soon—although this is a *marvelously* rich opportunity." The replacement climbed down from his perch. "Have you seen our glass? Created for Ferdinand and Isabella—"

At the office she called *The Times*.

"I thought you'd give me a buzz last night," Alleyn said. "Trip worth it?"

"I guess it was," she said slowly. "Yes, it was—because my father did get to see Churchill. But the conversation was censored and the woman's away. I never seem to catch ahold

81

of a thread that hasn't been cut—like this priest." She told him about Mellows.

"He'll be at Lambeth," said Alleyn. "Church HQ. Just across the river, next to the County Hall. You can walk it—use the Lambeth Bridge."

But Mr. Mellows was not at Lambeth. Gone with his bishop, the secretary said, to a Commonwealth conference in Canberra for four weeks.

She felt that she was fighting a ten-legged crab that danced sideways as she advanced, always one dimension out of phase. An ambulance roared by, bell ringing. Cancer the crab! The sexton at Saint Margaret's. Somewhere in her notes she had the name.

The ambulance screeched into the forecourt of a large building across the street and braked to a halt. She waited for the light and walked over to it. Even without red crosses the building was unmistakably a hospital.

The sexton's name was Johnson—and for the first time luck was halfway with her. To the left of the ambulance, attendants were moving a stretcher at the double through an entrance marked: Emergency—St. Thomas's—Admissions.

Inside it, she found the usual mixture of relief and apprehension mixed with the professionals' impartiality.

"Yes?" The woman behind the desk was impartial to a fault.

"I want to know if you have a patient named Johnson, please?"

"Male or female?"

"Male."

"Initial?"

"I wouldn't know. He's old."

"You're not the Press?" Terror of shock-horror probes convulsed the institutional face.

"He's just a friend of my folks."

"Oh." Human interest was abandoned with relief. The woman spun a card file. "Not registered. Records—across the hall. Next!"

Records, divorced from the living present, was on indefinite tea break. She picked up an old copy of the *Daily Mail* and looked for the crossword. It had been cut out. She put it down. Records came back. "Yes?"

She asked again for a Mr. Johnson from Saint Margaret's Church, who'd been a patient, she thought.

"Recently?"

"This month, for sure."

"We're going on the computer—I'll have to cross-check. Just a minute."

The whole clerical world was moving house for the machines.

"Yes," said Records. "From Saint Margaret's. He was with us."

"With us" must mean another broken thread. "He's dead?"

"Dead?" As though the hospital had never seen death. "Oh no. We show him discharged to own care last Friday."

"Do you have an address?"

"Yes—oh, that's unusual—it's City. Very rare nowadays. 12A, Milk Street Mews."

Outside the hospital she double-checked her notes again. Friday had been the day of the church parade. The day Mellows had put old Johnson at death's door.

The contrast—between the reality of Britain, and what she had expected—was nowhere greater than here, in the City: the Empire's true heart, its monument to Trade. There might still be offices like Leofric's in their old buildings with old retainers, but they were being dwarfed by the high rises climbing on their backs, climbing even on the shoulders of Saint Paul's, and along the streets between the buildings the working masses thronged in platform wedgies and Jagger haircuts. But where were the brollies and bowlers? The reverence for the past, the sense of heritage? Leofric had told her Londoners never had one—had invented the fast buck, the hustle. He must be right.

She turned off Cheapside into Milk Street and then, halfway along, right again into a mews backing onto Wood Street. Number 12A was an island of the old, with a green-painted door and a boot scraper outside it and a hitching post set in cobbles and a list of company names on brass plates. The interior of the building was a mirror of her uncle's: a black-and-white inlaid floor; turned stair newels; and bouncing down the stairs a large, comfortably fed old lech eyeing her breasts. "Lost?"

"I'm at the address I was given but I think they've made a goof. I'm looking for a Mr. Johnson."

"And quite right too," the lecher said expansively. "Old Johnson's our 'looker after.' Once we've all gone home he has the place quite to himself. Whole City for that matter. His rooms are behind the stairs and down a step."

She thanked him.

"Not at all, not at all. 'Goof'—I must remember that."

Below stairs had no brass plaques. A small, once-white card browning at the edges like parchment was held in a metal holder. "C. Johnson" was drawn thinly in Olde English script. There was no bell. She knocked on the door. Twice. It opened.

"Are you? . . ."

"Johnson? I am." The voice was soft and hoarse. A white scarf partially hid the blue marks of the radiation treatment on the throat. He was waiting for her to go on.

"You're the—sexton—I think it's called? You work at Saint Margaret's?"

"It's not *work*, young woman. But I've been there forty-three years—at Saint Margaret's. And that's a long time. You can see a lot in forty-three years."

"Yes," she said. "I guess you can."

"You don't need to guess. It's a *fact*. Now, what can I do for you?"

She wished Fadiman were here to share the old man's pedantry. "I'm a reporter," she said. "There's a memorial to my mother in your church—over by the big door on the side."

"The East Chancel? Our Lady Mary? Your mum? Well, well." Mr. Johnson opened the door wider and tipped his head to one side, like a sparrow, to look up at her. Then he nodded. "You'd better come in and have tea. I'm not supposed to have it myself but the day a person can't have tea's a poor lookout, isn't it?"

"I guess—I'm sure—it is."

Mr. Johnson smiled at her. "You come in and sit down. Our Lady Mary, well, well."

His accent—a cross between Coombes's cockney and Spoonfield's phony major—must be the product of a London birth and forty-three years of the Messrs. Mellows.

She watched him cross the tiny room to an even tinier

kitchen and get down a cup and she thought, *Christ,* I can't drink out of a cup of a man who has cancer!

"This mug over here is mine," Mr. Johnson said. "My special. No need to worry."

With the sword above his head, he knew and cared for her. She had to look away. Mr. Johnson produced a biscuit tin with a picture on its lid of George the Sixth and his Queen at their coronation. "That must be worth a dollar nowadays," she said.

"And that's a fact. I collect 'em, the Royals." He pointed at a mantel over a small, black iron, gas grate. "There's Her Majesty, and Her uncle Edward, and his father, George, and *his* father—Edward again. And here's the old Queen. I've seen all of 'em."

"At their coronations?"

"Well not the old lady, now. That's her Diamond Jubilee. Nor the Duke of Windsor—but I've been as close to him as me and you now. And shook his hand. He would have been all right, no matter what they say."

"You're a great royalist, Mr. Johnson?"

"Now, I wouldn't say that. They have their place and we have ours. London's seen them come and go. And lose a head."

"And a throne."

"That too."

They looked together at the unseated eighth Edward on his painted metal box. "That's rare, that is," said Mr. Johnson. "Seeing's how he never got there—to wear that crown."

"I guess it is." But this time Mr. Johnson just smiled and sipped a sparrow sip of tea. "I was asking at the church," she said, "about the flower being left for my mother."

"Oh, yes. Many of our regulars have their own deliveries. Mind you, hers is a little different, like. Being just the one flower—the red rose. And every year. That shows feeling that does. Shows that someone thought out something special. I said that to Mr. Mellows, just last week."

"But I thought you were in hospital last week?"

"I was."

"And Mr. Mellows came to see you?"

"A going-away visit you might call it. Nice, though. Most of your new young curates wouldn't bother. But it's all changed now, hasn't it?—wanting to be like the ordinary bloke—swearing on the telly, and trendy clothes, and no

collar. If they don't want the collar why do they join up?" His
hoarseness had increased with the effort. He took another sip
out of his King Edward mug. She could see that it hurt him.

"I've tired you," she said.

"Not you. You're a treat, you are. It's been a bit downhill
lately—in that hospital. And missing the Opening. First
Opening I've missed in twenty years."

"Opening?"

"The House. They're all our people, the M.P.s—even if a
lot aren't churchgoers regular anymore—particularly Labour.
Mind you, I've voted Labour myself all my life. Wouldn't
have been in that hospital now without it and the National
Health, and that's a fact."

"Well," she said, "I was there for you—at the Opening.
Just at the tail end."

"For the recessional? *Were* you?" The old strained face
took on an alertness, a strength from before illness. "Did they
come out to 'Valiant'?" he asked eagerly.

She smiled and shrugged.

"My favorite of all of 'em, 'Valiant' is. You *must* know
it—'He who would valiant be'?" His eyes looked pleadingly
to her for confirmation. To her alarm, he wheezed in a deep
breath and began to sing.

If that was the word for this tortured, rasping noise.

> *"He who would valiant be*
> *'Gainst all disaster*
> *Let him in constancy*
> *Follow the Master. . . ."*

She shook her head, hoping he would stop, feeling the
soreness in her own throat. Yet somehow the voice had
rallied. Under the hoarseness was an effort at pitch, a semblance of tune.

> *"There's no discouragement*
> *Shall make him once relent,*
> *His first avowed intent*
> *To be a pilgrim."*

"Yes," she said gently, "that was it."

For the first time the nodding face had the glow of a

living man, and she thought of him as a man—not as a subject. "It would be," he said, "old 427."

"Like your M.P.s, Mr. Johnson, I've got to tell you I'm not a churchgoer."

"But you're a reporter? You write things, eh? You must know the hymns." He stopped for a breath. "Oh," he said, "they *really* knew how to write—chaps like that Bunyan. Now, you've read the *Progress*?"

"I should have in college—"

"Well you can't go through life without old Pilgrim! '*As I walked through the wilderness of this world*—' 'This world—' that's what he says. Why, Pilgrim's been there before all of us—and he's shown there's a way through and out of the shadow. I'm not much of a religious man myself—now that'll surprise you, me working in a church—but it's not the religious part. It's like a marvelous play, isn't it? If you forget that a lot of the cast aren't much good as actors. But as the colors, and the light through the windows, and the processions—and the recessions—and the words and music—" He coughed, and slapped a hand against his chest. Hard. "Well, where else could you see all that? *And* for free?"

"You couldn't," she said. "And that's a fact."

The coughing was giving him real pain. She passed him his mug.

"I'm all right, don't fuss." The cough backed down, he sipped again. "Finding out about your mother after all these years—Pilgrim would like that." He stood up. "Yes, he would." He crossed to the other side of the room where a small table held an alarm clock and an old radio on one of the Royal biscuit boxes. He reached behind it. "It's not new," he said. "It wasn't new when *I* got it and it's gone as rough a way as I have from the looks of it, but it's all there—*and* with the pictures. I always liked the pictures. So you take it—with no more said, then." He pressed a book into her hands. It was covered in brown calf, but nicked by so many fingernails that it had scaled like fishskin. All that remained of the embossing were furrowed lines in the leather. He put a little dark-red book on top of it. "And a *Hymns Ancient and Modern*—they don't use *that* neither, with all these reforms. Now you tell me about the ceremony. Did you see any Royals? Or the Prime Minister?"

"Yes," she said. "I saw him. And the Speakers in their robes—the Lord High whatever—"

"The Chancellor—well of course you did that, with our Lady Mary being your Mum and all. And what did he say to *you*?"

She'd kept him too long at too great an emotional pressure. "No," she said. "The Lord Chancellor didn't speak to us—just to the Prime Minister."

"And you didn't tell him about your Mum—after all these years? He would have wanted to know!"

"I guess you're right," she said, because what was the point? Let him wander on with Pilgrim. She held her presents tightly. "Thank you for the books. Really."

"But his Lordship—" old age couldn't be diverted, "he'd *want* to know—there's not a doubt—" The cough was clawing at the throat again. "In the first years—before the florists took over, I spoke to him, often."

"With Lord Piers? The rose for my mother comes from Piers?"

The coughing was shaking the old man in his chair. He fought it to a gasping draw.

"And that's a *fact*."

12

"Roger, I don't get it. The whole deal with the priest makes no sense."

"That he forgot to ask your old boy about the flowers?" Alleyn turned a wry face. "Doesn't surprise me—I hate visiting bloody hospitals. I can never think of a word to say."

"But Mellows never mentioned a visit. From my notes, he said Johnson was goddamn near dead!" She threw the notebook on the cluttered table. "It pisses me off—the fruity little bastard must have *known* he was being transferred or promoted or whatever, when he spoke to me."

"Perhaps. But you know big organizations and sudden moves—Reuter's sending you to Montreal. How's the trial, by the way? Squashed yet?"

"Still percolating. But I'll skip before I pay a Jesus nickel. Trespassing!"

"I believe you!" Alleyn said, laughing. "God knows, I believe you! What's the next step?"

"I want to see Piers."

"The Keeper of the Royal Conscience and Ecclesiastic Peace. You'll have to catch the bugger at the House of Lords—between kissing babies and dishing out jobs for the bishops—" Alleyn stopped.

"And jobs for the Mellowses?" she asked.

"I'll have a permit for you," said Leofric on the phone. "Do you want me to send Piers a note on your behalf?"

"It's kind, but I'll start cold, as we say. Where do I go?"

"Saint Stephen's Porch—that's on the Old Palace Yard side, just south of Saint Margaret's."

"I know where that is."

"Good." The house sits at two-thirty—what day is it?"

"Wednesday."

"Ah. Then it'll be three o'clock tomorrow. You sit in the Strangers' Gallery. Did you try for a press ticket?"

"I never thought of it. Why?"

"They're in front of the Strangers—bit better view. Doesn't really matter—you'll be asleep five minutes after Piers plonks on his Woolsack."

"You've lost me again," she said. "Why does he sit on a sack?"

"To tell you the truth, my dear, damned if I know. These things rather keep going on their own momentum—we used to sell a lot of wool seven hundred years ago. You're all recovered from your time in the trenches?"

"Yes, thanks. I've still got to hack this goddamn summons."

"Summons—Good God, they haven't had the cheek! Well at least I can deal with that. I'm lunching Chantley today. I'll get him to call one of his Home Office people."

"That I would be grateful for," she said. "Has your chauffeur got over his shock yet?"

"He's been sleeping with the beast for the last two nights—" Leofric laughed. "It's made a full recovery. I'll send you the old bonnet emblem for a souvenir. Don't forget—Saint Stephen's. You go in at ten past the hour. I'll tell the staff to be nice to you. God bless."

The staff, a middle-aged man guiding her with a squint and a slightly bemused air, knew his subject but was easily sidetracked. They bogged down at some murals and whether the *Death of Nelson* by Bryce had preceded *Waterloo* by someone else. She nodded when it seemed necessary. Alleyn had been stating the obvious—that she would need a guide. Britain today was a nation of bureaucrats, not shopkeepers. Yet—like this visit—how smoothly bureaucracy could still be sidestepped if one knew the plays and where to make the end runs. . . .

With Hitler bombing the Commons and the ousted Lords having to slum it in the Sovereign's Robing Room for the Duration, the tour was over and she was into the Chamber itself. It was almost empty: row on row of red leather benches and not a coronet in view. Of the members present, most might have been in business, like her uncle. A few looked military. A handful of others were clearly up from the country. There was one woman. Everyone stood. A bishop droned opening encouragement.

"Tomorrow will be more interesting," said the guide without any great certainty. "The Speaker will be moving for Papers on the South African oil embargo—rise for his Lordship."

His Lordship was gowned again in black, over a black costume with silver buckled shoes. Watching the small procession she was back to graduation day at Bennington; the sudden hush from cynical fathers, mothers putting hands to throats as at a wedding. If you had a mother. Piers was passing right below her. A full wig covered his hair. The face under it was remarkably unlined for a man who must be well into his sixties. Not much emotion in the face, but this was not a place to show it. The balcony cut him off before she could see him on his Woolsack.

The standard of debate—on saving water rats from marshland drainage—beat the Senate and the SALT agreements all to hell.

A door opened above and behind her. She turned her head. A page in breeches stood at the top of the stairs.

"Mrs. Montigny?" She nodded. The page began to run down toward her, then stopped, and walked with processional calm the last few steps.

"His Lordship's compliments, madam," a speech from strict rehearsal, "but he regrets that his duties this afternoon preclude his meeting with you." As she'd expected, but still disappointing. The boy stretched out his hand with her note—and dropped it.

They bent forward at the same instant; heads bumped. The boy was crimson. "My fault," she said. "I haven't been here before. I guess I'll have to learn the ropes."

Her smile brought immense relief and then a momentary wide grin. "He wants your address and phone number, miss—I mean madam."

"That's okay," she said. By now they were conspirators against the weight of convention. She wrote the information on the back of the note. The only other people in the gallery, a stout couple carrying a lot of wool and leather and a book on British mammals, remained engrossed in the debate. She got up to leave and could see Piers again. He was just turning his head to one of the advocates. But she knew he had been looking at her.

A woman's training is to know that.

Tremblay's parcel was waiting with a letter at the head porter's desk in Rodney House. It had been opened and resealed by Customs.

Hi Jane:
　　Harry Oakes. A real sweetheart. More about him in English Canada than with us. I had a guy in Toronto dig through the *Star*'s files—also the old *Telegram*. Not difficult; there was paper rationing. I had no clue Oakes's holdings were so huge. How did you know he visited High River? Why would anyone invite the son of a bitch?
　　　　　　　Affectuesement,
　　　　　　　Skinny

Most of the information was backup, but there were parochial illuminations: Even by 1943 Canadian morality was still outraged by the tax-evading change of citizenship. Canadian morality made no mention of King's renegging on the Senate seat.

A lengthy piece on the *Telegram*'s financial page listed Oakes's investments. The murder had upset some financial applecarts:

> Toronto trading was halted in shares of Consolidated Mining and Smelting, and E. B. Badger and Sons, Company. Rumors that both Oakes and Swedish interests had been seeking secondary extraction of zinc from previously worthless tailings at Warfield, two miles from Trail, were denied.

> The SEC had also suspended trading on the Big Board. Company spokesmen for Consolidated Mining in New York had been "unavailable for comment...."

She sorted through the names and dates and checked them against her lists. Finding Oakes at High River was a shot in the dark from Mackenzie King. Perhaps if she knocked on wood the diaries could do it twice. She went over the extracts yet again. *One knock for yes*—and there it was.

If Hitler was to be misled about the atom, said the final entry on her mother, then somehow a flower must do it. She called Washington, but Fadiman was out. She asked his secretary to put in a Freedom of Information search on the name Tube Alloys.

She sent a wire to Tremblay to ask about *Red Rose*.

13

There are, in cities the size and age of London, two ways of finding anonymity, of hiding from the light. Drunks, dropouts, and petty thieves can follow Mao's maxim: Be just one of the fish in the sea of working faces. But for the face which can't hide from its money or rank, the sensible way, the best way, is to live in a building like Albany. Discreetly, quietly, in the best of taste in the heart of town; with no names on the doors and a porter trained for life to catch an accent, a posture, any pattern of behavior that belongs to the peasant schools outside. And to chuck it back.

The first screen, one of those ridiculous things which mean so little and so much in Britain, is the name: Albany. Not Albany House like Burlington House, and never "the" Albany. Just, as it shows on its letterhead, Albany, Piccadilly—residential chambers for bachelor gentlemen, and now because of the distemper of the times, women. If you must have directions, and to ask will weed you out, we're across from Hatchards, the bookshop. Books and their writers have featured prominently at Albany: Byron, Bulwer-Lytton, Macaulay. Graham Greene. Politicians have liked to hide there too—from Gladstone playing after dark at reform of whores to Edward Heath playing the piano. And just a few doors past Mr. Heath, in A16, her mother's suitor, Geoffrey Piers.

"In the Mansion, madam," said the porter. "The old house—through the Arcade. His Lordship is expecting you."

A hotel smell very slightly tinged with damp reminded her of the basement of the red-brick bungalow by the trailers. Was nothing dry in this country? A hint of chamber music sifted through one of the nondescript black doors. Number A16's was freshly painted and had no door knocker. An old brass bell push was set into the frame, but the button itself was new and there was no sound when she pushed it. Without the newness of the button, a Regency dandy, sedan-chaired, scented kerchief to the nose, servants in livery front and back, might pass at any moment.

"Do come in."

Piers opening the door himself was a first surprise. The apartment's interior was the second: polished bent steel frames, smoked-glass tabletops, built-in's of pale ash, a picture she thought was a Picasso. There were no comfortably embroidered cushion covers from old purses. The apartment's owner was not a comfortable man.

Without his wig, Piers' hair was almost black, swept back and down to the right. The sideburns, cut to the edges of the eye, were too silver to be natural. The eyebrows too dark. But the effect, as he intended, was hypnotic and striking. A face for television.

"This is really good of you," she said. "I was expecting ten minutes in a cell at the Tower—with aides to catch the misquotes."

The smile, over the slightly melting chin, almost reached the eyes. "I seldom have to worry about being misquoted, Mrs. Montigny. One should be able to handle one's own affairs, don't you think?" Piers closed the door behind her. "May I take your coat?"

"No old retainers, either?"

"I wish I had. Only people like your grandfather can still have men like Kendall. There is a state apartment in the House with rather a fine view of the river, but the tourists have made life there somewhat exposed, as it were." He gestured at a buffet through an arch. "I do have a housekeeper, but she has a flat of her own, and grandchildren, and telly. As a matter of fact I do almost no entertaining—one's official life is so full of overcoursed affairs." Piers stopped abruptly in the arch. "Your uncle tried to tell me, but I'm afraid I was not prepared—"

"Prepared?"

"How like your mother you are."

Despite the protestations, there was nothing unprepared in his laying grandfather, Kendall, mother, on her: intimations of just how *well* we old boys—and girls—know each other.

"From her portrait," she said, "my mother had a much better nose—and her hair was lighter than mine."

"I'm surprised you aren't as gray as a badger after some of the squeaks you've had. Being caught between juntas isn't my idea of earning a living. Whiskey?"

"Fine. So you've been speaking to Leofric?"

"At the club—just today, as a matter of fact—he was with John Chantley sorting out your fight with the army. I told Chantley, if I were in your shoes I'd have slapped in a countersuit by this time. Of course, the thing's done with—I hope you'll take my apology as that of Her Majesty's Government?" Now even the eyes smiled.

"It must have been a mistake," she said, "missing one of your vital signs."

"I had exactly the same trouble with your level crossings. We're used to gates. I never knew when the train was coming." Piers handed her a glass. "One can't help noticing that we are rather skirting the business of names. Do please use Geoffrey."

"Jane," she said. "My biggest hangup over here—after roadsigns—is titles. An American accent just won't hack 'My Lord,' not even Douglas Fairbank's accent!"

Piers laughed with a deprecating sincerity for just the right amount of time, and raised his glass. "I absolutely agree. The damn things are millstones—to any sort of progress in this country. Your good health."

As Alleyn said, the rank was easy to deprecate as long as one had it, but no man with this consciousness of image, of appearance, would really give it up.

"About your mother," Piers jumped, without preamble. "I'm not *quite* sure I see what you're after. Finding motives or a state of mind after such an interval—"

"Seems pointless?"

"Oh, no. That's too strong. But *upsetting*, perhaps—rather than soothing? And as to *why* she did it, surely as a war correspondent, you—"

"No way. In Vietnam, Sinai—in any straight-out, bombs-falling, shells-shooting deal you always know it's going to be the other guy. Although the other day with the Germans—"

"Yes," said Piers, casually, "the Germans?"

"Word association, I guess. Wehrmacht, Gestapo. I was

talking about it with my Washington editor before I left. And the odds for those women—"

"Were those of the men in the bomber fleets."

"But they were in groups, with fighters, guns." The judicial head was poised to listen politely to the woman's point of view, but the politician's eyebrows and the corner of the mouth had dismissed the argument—were *humoring* her! She changed the subject. "When did you first meet Scylla?"

"How curious, to use 'Scylla'—she was Mary, naturally, to me. We must have met once or twice as children: my people knew her—your—people, do you see? I suppose seventeen would be the first memorable occasion. But then the seventeenth summer has to be memorable, doesn't it?" The head tipped back theatrically. "It's an age which puts the girl light-years ahead in experience. To me she was, quite simply, a mystical creature—always winning steeplechases!" Again the deprecating laugh. "If I do say so, some of them against damn rugged competition."

"A mystical tomboy?"

Piers made a sharp movement with his hand. "I've given you the wrong impression. Simply that if she rode, she did it first-class. But dancing would be the same thing. Or school—not many girls in her group got Double Firsts at Cambridge—not in the thirties, I'll tell you! Her interests were—" The jurist's head searched the air for the right word. "Eclectic. Amazingly eclectic. A photographic memory helped, but with languages and mathematics, she must have been carrying twice my load."

"Before you joined the Duke of Windsor, did you propose to her?"

"Good heavens, no!" Piers was out of his chair. "Do excuse me. I must see that my housekeeper has left things functioning. If you'd like to touch up, there's a mirror around to the left."

There was more to her father in her reflection than just a bent nose. A width to her brow, a general largeness of bone. Her mother must have been three sizes smaller. What would it have been like to grow up in the shadow of the perfection Piers described? She felt a sudden rush of affection for the unremarkable but steady kindness of her stepmother. Strange how loss could still stab if you came back to it without warning.

Why was Piers single? Career? The love of his life denied? Not for her mother—not with that reaction. Gay, maybe? But she had no sense of that—and the message usually came through: The feeling that you didn't have to worry if your leg was crossed too high; that no bells need ring if a hand landed on the inside of your arm. For that matter, she said to the mirror, perhaps the guy *was* married—you haven't asked.

Piers had the lids off the serving dishes, two candles lit, jazz piano playing quietly through a corner speaker. Gay, hell!—the stage was set for an attack! "A game broth, my dear. Mackerel, a light curry of some leftover duck." She doubted the duck had been left for long. "Or cold beef if you'd rather." Piers picked up a bottle wrapped in white linen. "My woman's covered the label, do you care about these things?"

"To be blunt, the wine bit leaves me cold."

"Bluntness is one of your considerable strengths." Piers smiled. "And after the scandals from Bordeaux, I think I agree with you." When they were seated he said, "You will have researched your subject, but I'm curious that you should mention the Duke of Windsor."

"It came up in conversation with someone else. Naturally I'm interested—all Americans are—"

"In 'the woman I love'!" There was a bitterness.

"That's one part of it, sure, but I'm more intrigued by his differences—the splits in his personality. From what I've read, the Duke never showed the same face to two people. He could seem a spoiled kid or have total self-discipline. One guy will say he was too stupid to express a coherent thought, another that he gave a brilliant appraisal of the French Army before the fall of France. He was a bigot—but he prepared a sandwich for a black boy with his own hands. A coward—"

"No!" Piers was suddenly vehement. "Not a coward. With the rest—like most of us he was a mixture. But not on courage. He took foolish risks. I can tell you that he damn near got us *all* caught in France. He was convinced that he was the Flying Dutchman—cursed and impervious to harm."

"And did he think that about the Duchess?"

"She was his Achilles heel—even though he insisted on the *Excalibur*—an American ship—to get us out of the Lisbon rat's nest, he worried all the way across about German torpedoes."

"And German kidnapping?"

Piers dismissed it. "HRH never took that seriously for a moment."

"But he asked for police protection in the Bahamas?"

"Oh," her host had his back to her at the sideboard, "it may have been mentioned, to Monckton or Fruity Metcalfe—but again, only in case there might be an attempt of some sort against the Duchess. And that wouldn't have had to be German—feelings ran incredibly high. And of course there never was an attack. Life in the Bahamas was altogether too much of a backwater. One felt very useless at times. . . ."

Piers took her plate.

"But it would have made things easier," she said, "for the Nazis if they could have had a tame king after the invasion?"

"*If* they could have invaded! But in fact, as we now know, there was never a chance. Nor the slightest possibility that the Duke could have been coerced."

"And yet he sent a telegram to the German ambassador in Lisbon—which clearly seems to be asking for instructions."

"It was *not* clear!" Piers looked sharply at her, "No supporting evidence has *ever* been found in the German files to support that allegation."

"Found—or released?"

The pauses were getting longer. "You may rest assured," said Piers, "that the Government are *completely* satisfied as to the Duke's loyalty. I'm not quite sure how we got to this subject from your mother."

"Because I think they all come together over Harry Oakes."

She could never prove that some invisible barrier had been struck. No eyelid twitched, no finger tapped, no knee jerked. Piers' voice, when he finally spoke, stayed even. But there was simply a sense—what the crazies called an "aura."

"Oakes? Harry Oakes? Why on earth do you think there was connection between that affair and Mary?"

"She was a courier and she was in the Bahamas within hours of Oakes's death."

Another demitasse was filled. Then, "We're moving into a rather sensitive area, Jane." In spite of the urged informality at the start, it was the first time he had used her name.

"I got that—from the warnings."

"Warnings?" If the lift to the voice was faked, Piers was a hell of an actor.

"A Colonel Smythe from some Foreign Office department—I guess we can both figure which one."

"They put fishing lines in all sorts of odd places—like those salmon rods with little bells on. Your inquiries about the Duke may have set one of them off."

Piers had paused in front of a glass case holding what looked like two small plates, one scarlet and one green. "Patents of the Great Seal—you might be interested. One feels that they do rather reflect our history: the close, if somewhat undefined, relationship of the country to the Crown."

One side of the seals showed the monarch seated on her throne, the reverse showed her on horseback. "Are they wax?" she asked.

"Nowadays, a form of plastic. Without special rules they could be stamped out in millions. And special rules, I suppose, are really what I'm trying to put across, Jane. I feel that I should emphasize to you that the separation of the Royal *Family*—as distinct from the Crown—the Family's separation from politics is absolutely *essential* to the orderly functioning of this country." Piers stoppered the decanter, "A second rule might be that we also try to respect privacy: perhaps in greater measure than you're used to on your side of the Atlantic."

"Smythe already ran that by me."

"I mustn't flog a dead horse then." Once more Piers was almost paternal. "What you may *not* know, however, is that in this Jubilee year the Palace wishes to make amends to the Duchess."

"Forty years—she must be thrilled!"

"Many would agree. But you can surely see that it would be most unfortunate if new mud were to be stirred at this, of all times."

"That certainly isn't my intention."

"*No?*" tapping the case of seals sharply. "Then where's the line to be drawn? In your head? Won't there be a book, interviews, installments in the papers?"

The jazz record had ended, was clicking to itself in the corner. One of the candles guttered and died as though the force of Piers' questions had blown it out.

"Is this another kind of D Notice?"

"Of course not. Forgive me." Piers stood up, flicking a crumb from a lapel of black wool, smooth as velvet. "I only mention the Palace by way of advice."

Advice again in velvet: one short step from a mailed fist. A time for caution. "This thing *is* personal," she said. "I can promise you that. And I'm prepared to submit copy pre-publication U.K. But I'm going to continue."

"I wouldn't have expected otherwise." Piers was smiling again, eyes and all. "And I'm quite sure that we can reach accommodation—in fact, I can tell you we will! I want to help. I hope you believe that."

She smiled back. "To the extent of further interviews?"

"Certainly. There are some areas I should like to discuss with colleagues first, of course."

"Of course."

Piers took her hand lightly. "Before the most recent emancipation of women I should have felt free to tell you how very attractive your 'ensemble' makes you, Jane. You share the Duchess's American trait of 'Just the right touch.'"

"Thank you, Geoffrey." With the slightly archaic verbal pass any threat of an attack was over. She stood inside the door fastening the buckle on her coat. "I have to tell *you* that *I* was really touched—that you still send the flower."

"Flower?"

"To Scylla—to my mother. The one red rose on her memorial."

"But I don't," he said.

14

There was no answer at the painted door with the fading parchment calling card. She went back up the half flight to the ground floor and the first of the varnished doors with the brass plaques. A girl sat inside the door typing.

"Mr. Johnson?" said the girl. "Oh, the old boy downstairs. I think he's in hospital again. There was an ambulance. Yesterday? No, the day before. He's a funny old duck."

"Yes," she said, "he is."

"Sorry I can't help. Try the hospitals. I hope he's all right."

Admissions at Saint Thomas's spun the card file. "See Special Discharge, second on the right."

Special Discharge. Another institutional euphemism for a final solution. "I'm very sorry," said the woman. "Last night—a massive coronary. Perhaps it was just as well—I see he had C.A., larynx."

"Were there relatives?"

"None listed. Just a church for final arrangements on release."

"Saint Margaret's?"

"That's it. Will they be taking his effects as well?"

"I don't know," she said. "But I guess not."

"No," said the woman. "I suppose they wouldn't have room. It'll end up with the Public Trustees."

Would they have room at Saint Margaret's, a church of fashion, for one old theatergoer to lie among the fashionable urns and Latin mottoes? Would he make it in the guidebooks, this solitary pilgrim?

"This afternoon," said the new young curate when she phoned. "The funeral will be at two o'clock before the House sits. Some of our members always like to attend when one of our servants passes. We *are* the—"

"Parish church—I know. Thank you."

A priest, an organist, an old woman who might have been a char in a large-brimmed hat twenty years out of date, a handful of M.P.'s and herself. A few words about life and service, challenges and satisfactions. And then an ending. "... His favorite hymn. Number four hundred and twenty-seven...."

"It's like a marvelous play" with a shaft of late-spring sunlight through our Isabella's window to make a catafalque of a simple coffin. The dust caught in the light fell as gold powder on the lid. Fell as dust to dust....

Six men in dark jackets moved into the light.

And as the organ thunders not every old theatergoer has members of Parliament, representatives of the common people, for his pall.

> *No foes shall stay his might*
> *Though he with giants fight:*
> *He will make good his right*
> *To be a pilgrim . . .*

A long fight to get democracy this far on its journey. The six men in dark jackets showed no politics as they took their places left and right and grasped the handles.

> *Then fancies flee away!*
> *I'll fear not what men say.*
> *I'll labour night and day*
> *To be a pilgrim. . . .*

* * *

"I'm sorry, those files have gone to Kew," said the clerk at the PRO. "You'll have to make an application there. Do you know the way?" She shook her head. "I'll give you a brochure and a map. If you go by train, you leave from Waterloo and then you walk via Kew Bridge and the Towpath—or you could go via Kew Bridge, Kew Road—"

"I'll drive."

"Oh!" The clerk seemed totally nonplussed. "Oh. Well take the A205 South Circular."

After the Gothic tower above the Searchers' Entrance on Chancery Lane, the great white concrete whale squatting in a grassy field at Kew held no sense of mystery, but its tinted glass and modern line made a suitable home for the computer.

At first glance it reminded her of the Archives in Ottawa. Inside, looking at the round tub chairs and plant pots of blackly shiny plastic she realized it was more nearly Piers' apartment.

She presented her ticket to a girl at a desk surrounded by bar graphs and strip lighting. Numbers were punched into a terminal.

"Your ticket's not current."

"That's crazy. I only got it three weeks ago."

The girl shrugged helplessly. "It happens all the time. We're just going computer. I'll try again." The machine digested its information. "I'm sorry. You'll just have to make another application. Would you like a card?"

She took it, filled it in, and handed it back. Hostility was pointless: "Only following orders" was the order of the age.

"We're running behind with our processing," said the girl. "Check back in a couple of days."

Cursing, she drove back to town and called *The Times* but Mr. Alleyn was still on the Continent. A wipeout of the day was only averted by a large packet from Fadiman waiting at her desk. Despite the "No Dutiable Value," Customs had been at this too.

> Hi Janey:
>
> Herewith two thousand Jesus pages of *Tube Alloys*—romantically rechristened *S 1* in Washington.
>
> There's a synthesis, the Smyth report, at the beginning. I've circled a couple of sections to help out. Okay—so you'll do your own goddamn digging! I know, I *know!*
>
> Take care,
> Fadiman

She missed him. Missed working on the same wavelength with the same words. Missed stopping at the deli beside the trick shop to buy him a Reuben's sandwich: missed watching him eat it.

She took the parcel home and read the note again. Colonel Smythe and a Smyth report. Just one of those wartime things, just one of those crazy things. . . .

She picked up a massive first volume.

Introduction and Statement of the Problem and Administrative History up to 1941. . . . "The Plutonium Production Problem as of February 1943. General Discussion of the Separation of Isotopes, Separation by Gaseous Diffusion, Electromagnetic Separation . . ." She shook her head and made coffee.

At the back of the report a series of addenda covered auxiliary projects: The Silver Program, Operation Peppermint, Land Acquisition at Oak Ridge, Construction of the Clinton Pile, the Hanford Pile, Project Trinity, Project Alberta. . . .

Alberta! That least was a geographical link with the ranch at High River. But the report, in the first person, dealt with history, not geography. History later than 1941.

CONSTRUCTION ON TINIAN AND THE FAT MAN TESTS—HIROSHIMA AND NAGASAKI

The cloud was observed by our aircraft as far away as three hundred and sixty-three nautical miles . . . the higher part of the cloud had a bluish tint . . . the lower part which appeared to be largely smoke and dust was a brownish yellow . . . because of the dense smoke it was impossible to determine the magnitude of the fires . . . one observer commented it was so solid one could walk on it. Analysis of the photographs indicated the area of total destruction was about 60 percent of the area of the city. . . .

What was that in people, in grandfathers, in kids?

The report was concerned with the workingman.

. . . in view of the difficulties encountered, the Performance of Commander Ashworth and Pilot Sweeney and the crew of the combat airplanes was of a high order. The performance of the military and technical group at the base in Tinian was outstanding, and all concerned should feel a deep satisfaction in the success of the operations. . . .

From *Tube Alloys*, to *S 1*, to a column of dust three miles wide and ten miles high. To a job well done.

She made herself a ham and lettuce sandwich from a loaf of dark brown Hovis bread. Even if she had the fortitude and the technical interest, the report would take weeks of reading.

She flicked through the pages of Fadiman's marks.

THE P9 PROJECT (HEAVY WATER)— DECISION FOR TRIAL PLANT.

. . . for production of heavy water at an estimated rate of about 0.5 tons per month, by the "hydrogen-exchange" process, using natural water from the Columbia River, and the hydrogen already in production at that plant. To implement this decision, contracts were made, on behalf of the Government with the Consolidated Mining and Smelting Company (for development, design, and construction) and the E. B. Badger and Sons Company (for engineering and design of an "exchange unit") . . . arrangements were made for the U.S. Government to lease six parcels of land from the Consolidated Mining and Smelting Company. . . .

Which had all stopped trading when an old man got four prong holes in the head and died.

In the morning she telephoned the Records Office at Kew. Her application had still not been processed. "Well, I should say, it has been processed," said the girl, "it just hasn't been approved by Mr. Wilkins. But it's on his desk. I'm sure it will be out this afternoon."

But Mr. Wilkins was still sitting on it when she met Alleyn for lunch at the Popinjay next door to the *Express* on the following day.

"Three days? My dear Jane, *nothing* in this country—"

"That's not the point—blaming a screwup on changing offices is just bullshit. I already *had* a goddamn ticket, approved, signed, sealed—whatever."

"Give thanks you aren't in the hands of our tax people." Alleyn lifted drinks off a tray. "How was dinner—did Piers make a pass?"

She shook her head. "Has he a reputation for it? I wondered—but I couldn't put a label on him. At first I figured he might be gay—"

"A long and glorious tradition in our Public Life—but now you don't think so? More woman's intuition?"

"Maybe. It's hard to say just what Piers is. One minute he's sleek as his furniture. The next, he's mentally dressed up in those robes and seals as the heart of old England."

"Again, that doesn't make him unique. The reverse. What about the flower?"

"He denied it."

"Denied?" Alleyn looked at her. "No flower—what did your old sexton say about that?"

"He died three days ago of a massive coronary. I went to his funeral. And there was no autopsy. I checked."

"Doesn't have to be. That's at the discretion of the hospital board." Alleyn drained his beer. "It's tough, but the old boy was probably gaga."

"The 'old boy' was right on, Roger! I phoned the flower shop. I phoned fifty fucking flower shops. This one does flowers for the Palace, the Lord Mayor, up the Life Guards' horses' asses, you name it. The kid on the phone tells me they've been sending one rose for thirty years. It was just canceled. By his Lordship. And when I go around in person, a clown in black striped pants scraping the floor says 'No, madam, a mistake, madam.' Rally round the flag. There's no kid, no flower, no order. *Why, Roger?*"

Alleyn stared at the tabletop. "Irrational, I agree."

"That's *all*? Aren't you the guy who's up on tribal customs?"

"Jane, the man's too keen a mind, too much the judge, too shrewd a politician."

"Yeah?" The calm dismissal in the British balance of the speech was infuriating. "Well one of our Washington customs is that politicians drop the shrewd when they're scared shitless. Why didn't that asshole Nixon burn his goddamn tapes?" Alleyn's mouth opened. "And for *Christ's* sake don't tell me again it can't fucking happen *here!*"

"No, Jane, I won't. If something started ticking under a bed in the palace or Number 10, I think it would be all too easy." Alleyn took the new round of drinks, paid for it, and pushed a glass across the table to her. "But I think it would have to be a very big bomb."

"Oh it was, old boy. It made a bang three miles wide and ten miles high. And I think Harry Oakes, the Duke of Windsor's pal, tried to sell it to the beastly Hun."

But Alleyn, his finger stirring round and round the edge of his glass, ignored her melodrama.

"*Well?*" She wanted to chop his long stiff English neck. "*Come on?*"

"I'm prepared to help you take things a step further," Alleyn said at last. "But I don't think you'll get your license back. As Chancellor, Piers runs the PRO."

15

Even reporters, cynics at large, have their shibboleths, their touchstones, their place of the grail. A place where the soul of the fourth estate forgets the gossip columns, the nude of the week, the scoop of what the minister saw—or did. Papers like the *Post* of Washington, the *Glove & Mail* of Toronto, *The Guardian*—once of Manchester—form the outer wall defending this wistful news-world integrity. The Keep—perhaps Pentagon, to bring things up-to-date—is in New York recording all the news the family sees fit to print. But for any reporters manning the battlements for a last semblance of free speech, the sanctum, the mystic heart of the castle, still lies in London: at *The Times*.

Walking with Alleyn to Grays Inn Road, she felt a junior-prom excitement, imagined turrets and spires, scribes and inkwells, Pepys and Johnson scrapping in a corner—but the Times Building, when she saw it, looked like an empty concrete wine rack. The building of *The Sunday Times* beside it looked like nothing at all—half-a-dozen stories that could have been the accounting headquarters of a utility company. Only the stoplight at the corner attempted to bring back the past by mating itself with a truncated Victorian light standard: a heavy casting of bulbous wreaths overlayered by years and rings of black and white paint.

"We left romance behind," Alleyn said, "when we moved from the old Blackfriars spot at Printing House Square. I want you to meet a chap from Aunty: TV—BBC One." He opened a door. "I'm afraid that after Washington you'll find my cell a cubbyhole."

"After Washington, it looks great. Thompson could buy and sell Reuter— Oh, hi."

"Hullo." A cherub run to seed had jumped up and stuck out a freckled hand. The freckles on the first two fingers were almost invisible in nicotine. A tooth was missing in the smile. The eyes were green and shrewd. A dozen nicknames sprang to mind.

"Adam Cushman," said Alleyn.

"Jane Montigny." She released the hand. Cushman stuck it in a sagging corduroy pocket and brought out a packet of cigarettes and lit one from the stub in the ashtray. Alleyn closed the door.

"Adam lives on dirt," he said. "You have a prey in common."

"Piers?" she asked and Cushman nodded. "From what angle?"

"So far, only financial." The little man said it with such regret that she had to laugh. "I think His Lordship, while voting the party line on Supertax, failed to declare offshore income. We know the bugger got deep in the sticky in the early fifties—the family place at Anstiebury was on the block. Somehow he got the necessary to spring it loose."

The Picasso seemed evidence of the fact.

"My interest," said Alleyn, "is that Adam's got Piers holding a very large block of Distillers'—liquor shares."

"Booze? What's wrong with that?"

"Babies without arms and legs," said Cushman.

"Thalidomide? You really think Piers has helped them to stall the Courts on *that*?"

"I hope so." Cushman's accent was from an unidentifiable central region. The cable-knit sweater under the jacket was riddled with holes from falling ash. She couldn't see him as an interviewer—perhaps as "voice-over." "I like *your* interest," he said to her, "because it's from such a totally different direction. We could get his nuts in the wringer both ways."

"I figured I had the personal vendetta."

"Piers' forces of the law have just nailed Adam's favorite bookseller," said Alleyn. "One of the dirtiest."

Cushman was unabashed. "I buy direct from the Yard now."

They broke for lunch and crossed the road to the cafeteria in the parent building. A defiant edition of the *Daily Mail* was being hustled on the corner as they stopped for the Victorian traffic light. She saw the word "novelist" above a photograph that seemed familiar. Alleyn looked more closely. "Obit—Dennis Wheatley's dead."

"Must have been a good age," said Cushman.

"Eighty. And still working."

"We should be so lucky," she said. "What did he write?"

"*The Ravishing of Lady Mary Ware.*" Cushman relished the words. "Kinky—sex, Napoleon, and the Iron Duke."

Alleyn bought a copy of the competition and tucked it under his arm. "Wheatley was really known for thrillers—more on our side than yours. I'd forgotten he did a war stint with SOE."

"SOE?" she asked.

"Special Operations Executive. All the superhush games—deception on the grand scale. Your namesake, Monty's Double. *The Man Who Never Was*—Wheatley must have been right at home there. His first big smash, prewar, used the same actuality gimmick: clues in an envelope, police reports, specks of blood, strands of hair. Match and solve. Do-it-yourself detection. I see the publisher thinks its time has come again."

"They'll have to stuff the bloody envelopes in Taiwan if they want to make a profit these days." Cushman commandeered a table. "What's the name?"

Alleyn skimmed the column. "*Murder Off Miami.*"

She remembered the solitary woman among the faces looking at the Faun, the names beside the X's: Derek, Noël, Dennis W. This dead face had been thirty-five years younger then.

And Harry Oakes had just become the title of a book.

Always make an index. Fadiman's first advice. But even with the list it took her two hours to link Violet B, the lone woman sitting beside Wheatley in the picture, with Captain Barham, the FANY woman mentioned by Leofric as looking after Mary. She gave the name and the acronyms to Spoonfield and Coombes.

Two weeks passed and two planes made the biggest crash in history at Tenerife. Williams sent her for the story. When she landed, the horror was still on the runway. She and the others who knew there would be a bigger crash next time, wrote their words, watched five hundred and eighty-two wooden boxes loaded out, got drunk, and flew home in planes identical to the wreckage left behind. Life went on. The density of Jubilee bunting in London's streets increased. A giant "pearly" crown had been erected on the school facing Dolphin Square.

She stood in the kitchenette about to light the burner. The explosion lifted the stove off the floor and set it back. She hadn't turned the valve. She stared without comprehension. The match burned her thumb and finger. There was no smell of gas. The picture on the wall above the couch had fallen. So had the lamps.

Now there was a smell. Dusty, thick, acrid, stabbing at the eyes. Sounds were starting. Someone coughed in the hall, a moan through the open window. Already a high-low warbling of sirens racing with rising Doppler. Women screaming, men shouting. Something falling with a metallic crash. The fire alarm started in the hall. She double-checked the stove, threw the bulk of her notes lying on the table into her briefcase, grabbed her shoulder bag, went back to the dresser drawer for her passports, wondered what would be destroyed if the fire reached her flat. Halfway along the hall she realized that it would be the orchard photo of her mother and herself. *Don't sit under the apple tree with anyone else but me....*

There was no risk of fire. The alarm had been triggered by the shock. Except for a few of the closer windows, blown in by the blast, the damage was in the street. Her own window had been closest of all. If it had not been opened—she tried not to think of that.

The car that had carried the bomb was in three pieces—crude thirds of the blackened shell lying against the curb; against another car across the street. On the corpse in front of her.

The mouth that had grinned when it passed her in the hall, the roguish eyes of seventeen, the blond hair—all were unblemished, at peace upon the pavement. The blood, already starting to coagulate, filled a depression in the stone and ran under the metal hiding the crushed parts of a boy's body once so frankly shown off by white-and-green nylon jackknifing from a diving board.

Have they no shame? Alleyn had asked her as this boy ran by them. *There's a God who cares*, she had answered back.

But shame and caring had no meaning in a Tenerife world of random violence and nonpersons. Nor had God.

Activity now. A mother found a son, a father stood beside a wife. A policeman foolishly strained himself lifting off the metal. Someone with too much imagination vomited into the pool of blood. For someone else with even more, Ireland had taken another step toward the light.

Police and army antiterror squads sealed Chichester Street and began checking the remaining cars along the curb for nothing. "An hour earlier," said one of the troops looking across at the glass-fronted school, "the fuckers could really celebrate!..."

After thirty minutes the residents were allowed back into the building.

She picked up the picture and the lamps. The car had been outside *her* window. And she had *not* got lost on Salisbury Plain. She was as responsible as fate for the blond boy's death.

No matter how hard she tried, her hand would not stop shaking. She drank brandy, and blasphemed without meaning in the empty room.

The papers in the morning told her the boy was a Richard Herdenfeld, Jr., from Wallace, Idaho; a trumpet player and basketball star touring Britain with the Wallace High School Band. This was the band's return visit to London—their last day in Britain before flying back to the United States. Two other bombs had destroyed a pub and a baby.

On television, a spokesman for the persecuted in Dublin explained patiently that the action was required to effect the release of associates awaiting trial for earlier bombings. This objective, he said, had been expressed in triplicate by letter to the Attorney General, the Home Secretary, and the Lord Chancellor in advance of the attack.

The Attorney General and Home Secretary, on holiday in Spain, were unavailable for rebuttal. The Lord Chancellor stated for them that British justice—for which he was proud to be responsible—could never be influenced by threats or bombs and that he would make a further announcement shortly.

The call came as she was watching Piers take charge.

"I've found 'er."

"What?" she said. "Who is this?"

"Coombes. I've found your shrinking violet. She's not in the easiest spot to get info on these days, Mrs. Monteen. Not out of White'all." The screen roared its approval for some item of the news.

"Hold it, I can't hear." She shut off the set. "Did you say, Ireland?"

"*Inyanga*—a place in Rhodesia. Mean anything?"

"No."

"Well that's it. Oh yes—and she's changed her name, gone double-barrelled. Barham-Vrisser now. Must of got married when she went out. Real mess there, eh?"

"I guess I'll be able to tell you when I get back," she said.

Williams was sympathetic but harassed. "*Two weeks*— Christ, woman, you've seen the bloody bunting out there, and the fucking Jubilee's still a month away—*What is it?*" as the intercom buzzed again. "Hold a minute! Look, Jane, I *can't*. You can *see* how it is—"

"I could do a front-line eyewitness."

"Love, Harris is already *in* Salisbury—and bloody good. *Oh, Jesus!*"

She took her resignation up to the girl under the portrait on the seventh floor. She had a feeling that Paul Julius would have followed the hunch with her. "I'll pick up the severance check when I get back," she told the girl.

With her decision, spring came to London: a first real warmth in the sun brought out blossom in the parks and shirt-sleeves and dresses on the sidewalks. The flowering trees made her think of her grandfather. She should pay a second visit—at ninety-one how many springs were left? She walked for an hour. Through Saint James's Park past Saint James's Palace, then across the Mall into Green Park, up to Hyde Park Corner—deserted of orators and freaks—then into Hyde Park itself. She sat on the grass beside the Serpentine and watched the birds. A pair of barn swallows, brilliant in first color, swooped across the turf. One stopped with micro- scopic speed in front of her, caught a moth with a sharp clear snap of its beak, then was gone in a rolling flash of blue and buff.

She felt the same sense of control of her life. The foreign tours had put money in the bank, she knew her skills, could count on her experience. She got up and folowed the Ring to Victoria Gate and called a cab.

The phone was ringing as she got in the door. "Montreal, Mr. Tremblay calling. Will you accept the charge?"

"Sure," she said. "Go ahead."

"Hi, Jane." Tremblay's voice was here and there, drowned out by traffic.

"Skinny—this is a bad line. Has Ma Bell cut you off?"

"A call box. Can you hear at all?"

"Just go slow. What's the score?"

"The Mounties are reading my mail."

"You're kidding." And how stupid that sounded. "I mean how do you know, Skinny? Is it like this D-Notice crap over here?"

"If it was official, I wouldn't know—but there's going to be a Royal Commission into RCMP dirty tricks. It turns out the bastards have been opening mail for years! Four attorneys general all screaming like crazy they don't know. But these clowns have to give everything a name, right? This one will be *Operation Cathedral*."

"With God on our side, who needs a judge's order?"

Tremblay laughed, only slightly. "Jane, the pricks just started to look at *my* mail *this* year. February."

After a long pause she said, "You're calling from the street. Have they got at the phones too?"

"You guess. I'm telling you, Jane, it makes you feel sick. I mean, sure we're cynics—but not *all* the time eh? Not here?"

"The whole world over, Skinny. They'll save us in spite of ourselves."

"Then there isn't much point, darling."

And of course there wasn't.

"In the memo I saw, the bastards were real proud," said Tremblay. "How neat they were with letters. The fuckers don't have to be so careful with parcels. They can blame Customs."

A mechanical sweeper in the street caught the last

glinting shards of glass from the bombing. She saw Fadiman's ripped package on her desk. The sunlight seemed once again misplaced.

"Jane, I just figured you should know. What you're digging at—the word must really be around."

"Thanks, Skinny."

"Sure. Oh yeah—your *Red Rose*. Nothing. But the day after my inquiry at the Archives the Cabinet slammed the lid on the Gouzenko papers for another thirty years."

She went down to the Arcade for her copy of *The Times*. The letterhead caught her eye. She had never noticed the clock before, nor the legend: *Times Past—Times Future*.

One man had his eye to the future. Geoffrey Piers announced to a waiting world that after a suitable interval for family arrangements, he would be renouncing his title.

THE COUNTRY OF SKULLS

16

Rhodesia, April 1977

Independence, like conscience, has a price. The Cape Verde Islanders accommodated both by building a runway to keep the modified 747's of South African Airways out of the water—and out of Black Africa. With the cost of conscience at thirteen thousand dollars a bump, the airline—more responsive to the black and red of bottom lines than the black and white of politics—would gladly have taken her to Madrid (tower on strike), or the Canary Islands (radar unserviceable). The Ilha do Sal won by default.

Content not to be pushing her luck again with the controllers of Tenerife, she stared at the refueling drones pouring their extra gallops into the rogue queen's special tanks. A steward arrived with a menu after takeoff. She accepted the airline's trilingual word that because of galley space and sanctions, the food supply was limited, and ordered the *ligte ete*—a light meal in Afrikaans. York ham, chicken glazed with stuffed tomatoes and fresh asparagus tips, strawberry cheesecake, arrived. Glazed and bloated like the chicken, she dozed. Slept.

She woke with a flash of rising sun reflected from the ground.

"Kunini River," said the English–South African architect in the seat beside her. "Our boundary with Angola. We keep to the safe side now the Commies are in."

"Will we see the Falls?"

117

"Tew high. Yew may catch Kariba Dam at the other end. Yew're not a tewrist?"

"Because I haven't got a camera?"

The architect shook his head. "Yew don't see many women alone on this leg. Not these days. Going the other way, on the chicken run, yiss."

Yiss. The sibilant snake intonation of southern Africa. A black man in the seat ahead looked from a business diary to a Rolex and tightened his mouth. Civilization brings time the taskmaster, and a gift of Williams' twisted gut. Her ears popped for descent. A grayish patch showed briefly from the lake but the dam was obscured by clouds. Now there were farms with irrigated grass and fence lines: close-cropped on one side, full growth the other. White houses far apart. Twelve hours was a long time.

"Temperature is twenty-five Celsius—thank yew for flying South Afreecan," and she was in the Dark Continent on a crisp bright day at an airport like any other. But with a strange order of priorities.

"Pornographic films, magazines, or any other prohibited works?"

"No."

"Nature of biznisss?"

Williams in the office had prepared her. *For Christ's sake, don't say press.*

"Tourist."

She was not prepared for the official to be black—nor for his next question.

"Separate stamp?"

She shrugged. "Sorry?"

The official knew it was a game, and smiled; smacked the stamp on a separate sheet of paper, just the right size, and slipped it in her passport. "Welcome to Rhodesia."

Her traveling partner joined her at the gate. "The other new blacks won't let in a Rhodesian stamp. No one wants formalities to get in the way of a tourist quid. Going into Salisbury?"

She was expecting the strangeness of Asia but it was the valley country of California lifted to four thousand feet with the air filtered clean, the freeways emptied, Chicano bodies exchanged for black. Citrus groves stretched for miles in perfect grids. For a moment, as the limousine swept abruptly off the carriageway, she thought of Ottawa, and then she saw the width of Cecil Rhodes's double ox-span streets. Small caars were parked diagonally down the centers.

"Monomatapa Hotel," said the driver and she was back in the anonymity of the international travel industry.

She bathed, washed underwear and hair, and slept for four hours. A male hotel operator placed the call. "Trunk occupied, madam, I'll call yew back."

Next to the phone, a Bible and a copy of *Focus on Rhodesia*, a Government propaganda sheet, brought messages of unswerving faith in a better life—a little later on.

She walked to the window and looked at Salisbury's trees stretching below her. She recognized palms, the rest were green and numerous. Directly underneath her window a swimming pool on a lower roof held a girl floating on an air mattress. A boy appeared seal-like beside it. A smell of exploded car seemed to fill the room. She turned on the television to drive it out.

The sound preceded a black-and-white picture. ". . . RTV welcomes you to a new broadcasting day with our opening address by the Reverend January Ramakwebana." A shining face as round as its glasses beamed at her and recited the Lord's Prayer and spoke happily of lions and lambs. The Reverend January gave the whole thing a zoological emphasis. Allegorical meaning was provided by a smoothly white announcer trying to lose his accent in a BBC diction. Adam Cushman would have collapsed.

"Authorities report that all things look jolly good for the Whitsun weekend coming up. Hotels in the Kariba district and the Highlands are pretty well booked solid so you'll have to look lively there. Troutbeck's chock-a-block." The announcer produced a sportsman's grin. "Naturally, two-way convoys will be running between most major towns. If you use the northern roads, particularly Lupane to Victoria Falls, check with the police for any unusual activity. Now, a brief news report."

The news showed just how unusual some of the activity could be. The car smell tried to come back stronger than ever. The phone rang.

"Inyanga," said the operator. "Go ahead, please."

"Hullo?" said a voice. "Who is it?"

"My name's Jane Montigny. My mother was Lady Mary Dexter—I guess you knew her as Arbright—"

"*Oh, my dear. . . .*"

Perhaps this was the wrong way. Perhaps, as Williams at the office had said bluntly, she was nuts to piss away the money on a wild-goose chase half around the globe. For a woman who might be mad herself, or invalid, or simply unwilling to talk. But after Tremblay's Operation Cathedral, letters and telegrams were wrong too. Long-distance warning time allowed stories to be revised: old boy—and old girl—nets to be reactivated.

"I've come quite a ways—"

"Yes," the voice cut in. "You *have*. And I'm *very* glad. Are you visiting friends in Salisbury?"

"You're the only reason I'm here."

"I see." Again a pause, shorter this time. Then briskly, "I think you should fly. I'd collect you myself but I've had to give it up." A slightly disappointed laugh. "Call Harry Rogers at Air East. He's a small show, but he'll bring you to the farm in his sleep. Some of them are rather stupid at the moment. And allow a full day. It's always wise. Let's say tomorrow. If there's a problem call me. All right?"

She thought back to the interminable briefings with the twelve-page Op Orders to line up a photo opportunity of a tamed village or a bombed Buddha. This woman too old to fly would have stood Saigon Command on its ear.

"All right," she said.

"You're traveling light?"

"Just one bag. But I've brought a sweater."

"Yes." The voice was pleased. "You sound like her daughter. Tomorrow then. Good-bye."

Harry Rogers was at a place called Wankie and would call her on return. She went down to the pool and swam sixty lengths to lay the ghost of Dolphin Square. In the late afternoon she crossed the street to see where Cecil Rhodes had raised the flag, and to walk in his gardens along paths laid out to match its patterns. Then she went back to the hotel and had a long gin and tonic. Harry Rogers' call paged her in the bar.

"Booked solid, man," said Harry Rogers. "All thiss bloody army. Where is it yew want?"

"Inyanga. A ranch outside it somewhere. Barham-Vrisser—"

"Vi Vrisser?"

"She gave me your name."

"Yew're on! I like to make it early. Can yew be here by eight."

"That's early?"

Harry Rogers laughed. "Siix, then. The Terrs'll reely be tits up!"

Back in her room, the television showed the Cartwright brothers of *Bonanza* holding a ranch against impossible Indian odds. The episode was four years late.

She left the hotel at five. The black clerk taking her credit card at the desk called a black doorman who summoned a black rixi driver who waved at a black policeman and broke the white speed limits on the empty road. The rixi, a tiny Renault with direct dash-mounted gears, gave the skittish feel of a motorcycle sidecar.

The driver chattered and grinned her past the Lotteries Hall and the Floral Clock and Laxman Shoe Service— Receiving Depots in all Suburbs. A. Ratanje, Repairer.

"Oh yass. Very good mon," said the rixi driver, perhaps related to A. Ratanje.

Harry Rogers was in the little brothers' compound across the field from the 747's. He was arguing with the army by way of a black sergeant who'd been up all night and was tired of civilians. Some form of compromise was being reached.

"All right then," said Harry Rogers. "I'll *do* the fucking Chipinga drop. But yew just have those bush bastards cleared out. I'm not having any more fucking holes in the Otter."

The sergeant spat and waved two soldiers forward with a trolley.

"I'm Jane Montigny," she said.

"Bloody KitKat bars." Harry Rogers looked disgustedly at one of the cartons. "Give us your bag."

"I can handle it."

"Good. Yew flown in things like thiss before?"

"Cessna, Piper, Grumman American—"

"Friend of Vi's. Why'd I ask? Strap up."

The Tower and Control Net were already working hard with innumerable small aircraft, helicopters, two Buffaloes in army drab. Not all carrying KitKat bars. The chopper gunships carried death. The Otter was fourth on the taxi strip. Number three cleared. The Tower held them for British Airways 351 from Joburg, then they were loose.

"First visit?" Harry Rogers asked, over the engine noise. She nodded. "Right, man. I'll go at a thousand so yew can get a boo. Yew're a flier eh?"

"Just for pleasure. How did you know?"

Harry Rogers cut back on the pitch. "Watching your feet."

"The Otter's a long way from home," she said.

"De Havilland and the Canadians reely know bush-flying. Besides," waving at the propellers, "I like looking at two fans."

She stared down. "You've got bush, okay."

Harry Rogers nodded. "This run's High Veld pritty well all the way. Not much color in the Dry." He touched the rudder and steadied the heading in one-four-zero.

"How long?"

"Hour and a half to Chipinga. Two hundred kilometers back north to Inyanga. Say another hour—if the bloody army pongos don't fart around tew much."

"Unloading the KitKat?"

"Right on!" Harry Rogers grinned and lit a cigarette. "Want to drive?"

"Sure. You've taken out the dual control?"

"Can't afford to waste a paying body. Here's the important bits." Her pilot ran his hand across the panel overhead, calling out name and function. She changed to the left-hand seat. The plane dipped to port. She corrected. Harry Rogers nodded. "Yew've got it, man. I'm going back to count the candy."

She flew on smoothly. The country was a bluish-gray brown, largely flat. Occasionally farms with irrigation broke green and smooth in the bush. Twice she thought she saw dots that might be game. Harry Rogers came back and sat in the right seat.

"No herds of elephants," she said.

"Wrong side of the country. The best is Chirundu up in the Zambezi Valley—if yew can dodge the walking handbags and the blood budgies."

She smiled helplessly. "Snakes?"

"Crocs and mosquitoes. There's good eland near Melsetter,

though. Yew might spot something there later. I'll take her now to get us over the Wedza."

An irregular line of hills folded up out of the bush to the southeast, flattened below them as they skimmed the tops at a few hundred feet, then dropped away again. A splash of blue appeared in the trees. Two shapes moved shadows away from it. "Rhino," said Harry Rogers. "They like the reservoirs. We'll follow the Sabi all the way down the gorge now." A scarcely visible slit in the bush widened to a considerable riverbed, only a third filled, waiting for the rains. Once or twice dirt roads ended abruptly on either side.

"Drift crossings," said Harry Rogers. "The only way for the settlers." And for a Daimler fording that other Salisbury Plain half a world away. A suspension bridge leaped up to horseshoe the river with nationalist pride. "Third largest in the world—"

"Birchenough Field." The radio crackled for the first time. *"Come in, Otter."* A small airport with two light aircraft and a quonset hut slipped beneath them.

Harry Rogers acknowledged the call with casual informality. "Hiya, Birchenough."

"Catch any floppies, Harry?" asked the radio, hopefully.

"Nope. Terrs are all still bye-byes, man."

"Drop the bastards in the slot if they wake up," urged the radio. "Cheerio, Harry."

They followed a paved road completely clear of traffic. At one point, an army truck sat on a track beside the paving. "Waiting for a convoy," said Harry Rogers. "There's Chipinga. See the tea plantations?"

On the far side of a square mile of glossy green segmented by red-dirt roads an airstrip identical to the one by the bridge had a limp windsock and a small Shell avgas tanker waiting beside the runway. Harry Rogers snapped his fingers forward, the Otter gave a slight chir-*umph* of rubber touching down and they coasted in.

"Nice," she said.

"For an old bloke. We'll be a minit. If yew want the loo she's in the hangar round the back. Girls and boys together—don't be shy."

To her surprise the air was cool. A band of thin mist to the east obscured the sun. She found the toilets—as Harry Rogers said: share and share alike. But there were still two doors. One was marked African. She used the unmarked door.

When she got back to the aircraft Harry Rogers was arguing with another sergeant—white this time and about twenty. The sergeant, with Selous Scouts on his shoulder badges, had the cocky look of a man who had killed recently. She had seen a hundred like the man before: West Point honchos whirlybirding through the Delta marking villages for life and death. Here a gook, there a gook. Balancing the body count for the computers: all yellow faces were the same. Now the faces were black.

"Only if I get a bloody fill, then, man," said Rogers. The sergeant nodded tersely for a bad bargain, and waved the tanker over. They stood upwind while the driver filled the tanks. The soldiers drove off across the strip. One of the Africans in the back of the vehicle was attacking a KitKat bar. He gave them broad grin and a salute. The wrapper fluttered to the ground.

They climbed back into the Otter. The tower said, "See yew, Harry." The mist dropped behind them. They set a course of north.

"Does the army give you a hard time?"

"Just right." Harry Rogers flipped up his sunglasses and rubbed the bridge of his nose. "With rationing I'd be tight for fuel. This way I get bags of it." He grinned sideways with white teeth in a leather face. "No point in giving them the match though, right, man?"

The aircraft rocked a little for the first time. Some higher cloud formed to the northeast. "There really *is* a war on?"

Harry Rogers stuck out his right arm. "Wog land, ten kilos—Mozambique. If we were on the ground, we'd be worrying." He brought his hand back and dropped it on the rifle beside the door. "Can yew handle a gat?"

"Yes. But not against—"

What? Blacks, Africans, gooks, floppies? Men?

"Don't sweat it. Vi's on the leading edge and never seen a Terr. The Wombles scare 'em off." From Harry Rogers' roar of laughter, Wombles were apparently hilarious.

"What are they?" she asked.

"Wombles? Old service hands," said Harry Rogers. "Haven't seen the quarterdeck for a hundred years. The army gives them batons, for Christ's sake. Yew known Vi Vrisser long?"

"No. She knew my mother in the war."

Harry Rogers listened with interest to the saga. "My view, aristocrats are like blacks—it's instinct. They don't feel pain the same way as us. 'Over the top' and all that crap, they're bred to it. Service is ingrained in aristocrats like sex. A dust-up or a piece of tail—they rise on heat to both as they would to a good pork pie. Instinct," Harry Rogers said again. "Women like Vi act the hero as easily as they shit—*hey! There yew go!*" His arm jabbed down. "*Eland!*"

In a savanna clearing, large brown shapes separated like a shoal of fish as the aircraft shadow passed above them. On the edge of the clearing half-a-dozen thatched kraal huts formed a postcard circle setting. Wisps of smoke came from the holes in the centers of each thatch. Children looked up and waved. The bush closed in again.

Harry Rogers coughed.

The sound was out of place. Infirm, frail. The wheezing cough of an old playgoer ending his tether in a London room of Royal biscuit tins.

"Take it, man," said Harry Rogers.

The blood was forming a fine and bubbling mist around his mouth: his left hand clutched the center of his chest.

"*Take it!*"

She took it. The carburetors coughed with Harry Rogers.

17

The air whistled through the small hole in the door panel. All the controls responded. Harry Rogers, dragged dead weight into the right seat, whispered, "West, go west. Umtali Road." His eyes closed.

She came around to two-seven-zero.

Seven hundred feet on the altimeter. Her first instinct

was to go higher but that would waste valuable forward distance. Like her pilot, the coughing engine might die at any moment. She held level at six fifty. Harry Rogers seemed to nod. The hills dropped away, the instrument showed true height above the ground increasing.

"*Call,*" whispered Harry Rogers.

Radio. How goddamn stupid not to think! "*Mayday, Mayday, over.*"

"Umtali Field—who are you, Mayday?" The immediate response astonished her. "*Who are you, Mayday?*"

Her mind had blanked. Call signs, air line, all wiped out. The port engine coughed. Stopped. *Holy Christ!* "Harry Rogers," she said. "Umtali Field, this is Harry Rogers' Otter."

"You've changed, Harry." The radio voice held out a hand. "Now steady, Otter. Tell me where you are, girl. Slowly now."

"My position unknown but I'm about ten minutes north of Chipinga. Present heading due west. Looking for a road."

"That'll be right. Are you still in the hills? Over."

"A big valley's just opening now."

"Have you power? Over."

"Starboard only. And intermittent."

The voice didn't like the word. "Are you a pilot? Over."

"Yes."

Her lifeline's radio procedure lapsed briefly. "Thank Christ! Is Rogers hit?"

"A bad chest wound. My fuel dropping sharply also."

"All right, Otter. Did you go to auto feather on failure? Over."

"Yes."

"Let's see if we can get you going, port side, then. The fuel shut off lever's on the pedestal."

"Got it. Over."

"Good, Otter. Throw it. That'll give us cross-feed."

"Done. Over."

"Fine, Otter. Now close the valve and I'll run you through a flash-up. Use your battery start and get the generator to twelve percent."

She found the switches, carried out the drill, tried not to see the froth dribbling down Harry Rogers' chin.

"Okay, Umtali."

"Good girl. Now, throttle to ground idle, prop levers ahead at max rpm. Over."

The engine housing shuddered briefly. She tried again. "Nothing, Umtali."

"That's okay, girl. We only need one. You'll see the road any minute."

She wanted it as much as the voice. "I can see a flash of water through the bush. And some hills beyond that."

"Good. Good. Wait." He must be looking at a chart. "Right. The hills will be Mapanda Range, you're north of Hot Springs. You should be at the road now. Are you sure you can't—"

"I've got it, Umtali! An intersection. Another paved road comes in from—*My starboard engine's going*—"

"Not to worry, girl." The calm voice was with her instantly. "Like a breeze now to bring old Otter down on the road. Come to north heading."

"Is there any traffic?" Imagination brought loaded tractor trailers around the bend at seventy.

"Convoys north and south, but we're talking to them. No problem. Have you brought Otter in before? Over."

"No."

"Not to worry," said the voice again. But this time as much for its own benefit, she thought. "Altitude now? Over."

"Five hundred. There's a creek here. The road curves."

"It's all right. You're all right. You'll have two clear kilometers any second. Stay centered on the line. There's a power grid to your right, that's east."

"Got it. Okay, the road's straight." *Over the hump*. She took a second to glance beside her. Rogers' face was the white of near death from exsanguination. The engine died before him.

"*Umtali! My power's gone*."

"It's all glide path now, girl. You're fixed gear so no problem there. Are your stick and pedals all right? Over."

"Heavy."

"Yes. But they're working. Can you tell wind?"

"Light."

"That's great. Altitude?"

"One hundred. Coming in now."

"Super, super. I'm right with you."

"Fifty feet."

"Super. Super."

"I'm down."

But now the radio was silent. The air stopped streaming through the hole.

"Umtali. I'm down!"

"Yes . . . good girl . . . are you armed? Over."

Only the slight rasp of Harry Rogers' breath broke a perfect stillness. There was a strong smell of fuel. The bush shimmered slightly in a heat that was near tropical. The change of elevation from Chipinga must be a thousand feet. The cane plantation to the south had become a wilderness. A large hill stood out immediately to the east. The empty road ran out of sight behind a curve half a mile to both north and south. A training camp example for an ambush.

The strain had returned to her controller's voice. For the first time she noticed how much less harsh his accent was. "Otter—I say again—are you armed?"

"Umtali, I have a rifle."

"Good. Stay in the aircraft. Don't present a target. Get down on the floor. Over."

"Roger," she said, to keep him happy. She looked for a first-aid kit and discovered it on the right-hand side hidden by the army boxes. She opened it and found pressure pads and bandages. She studied Rogers. The bullet entry was on the lower-left chest, traveling upward. Miraculously, no major arteries seemed cut, but the shirt was already stuck to the flesh. The exit wound on his back was hidden by the seat. She decided not to move him again, but to apply the pad to the front and strap the bandages tight across the body and around behind the seat so that he sat like a mummy in a chair. She could not risk giving him fluid but wiped his lips with tea from the Thermos. His eyes stayed shut.

"Otter, this is Umtali. PATU with you very soon. Can you indicate your position when fired on? Over."

She saw the graceful shapes bounding across the grass of the savanna, the tiny bodies waving black hands and arms in greeting to the shadow from the sky. At a time and a place behind them she saw again the track with the other, lighter, Asian bodies running burning and screaming in the firestorm unleashed by the gunship in the Delta. One word, now, and another village would be saved by destruction.

"Sorry, Umtali."

"That's all right, girl." Was there disappointment in the voice? "Keep low."

She sat on the floor. It seemed indecent to let the strapped-in head of Harry Rogers be a target. Unbelievably a fly had already found an entry through the torn skin of the door and buzzed at Harry Rogers' mouth. The noise of the fly was louder now than Rogers' breathing. She took quick glances of the perimeter at frequent intervals.

Between glances, her mind, perversely free to wander in the confined quarters of the cockpit, brought back two soldiers trading hair-raisers in the hotel bar: You tell me your atrocity, I'll tell you mine. The tale of the two African girls was the clear winner—not because of the commonplace rape by the guerillas. Because of the gunpowder inserted and ignited.

She remembered her contempt for the bullshitting bastards swapping their good ol' boy white macho myths—*until they had swapped pictures*.

She checked the rifle magazine. Seven bullets. Six for outside . . .

"Otter, hang on, girl. Chopper has you visual. Over."

"Thanks, Umtali. *Thank you*."

What sort of bond was this?—with this voice that she would hear for the rest of her life? . . .

A noise louder than the fly. Two Alouettes whipped in around the curve, tornadoes of dust and leaves churning from the rotors, their skids almost breaking branches. Bursts of fire withering the bush in a circle around her as they made a cautionary housecleaning. A deerlike creature the size of a fox bolted across the road.

The radio crackled nonstop. One gunship kept up a constant circling. Men with leopard's paw badges on rolled sleeves ran toward her with a stretcher, portable transfusion kits slung across a shoulder. Rough tanned hands opened the cabin door. A ruddy farmer's face looked in.

"Christ, man! A lady driver!"

"Only just," she said. "I hope it's not too late for Harry Rogers."

She was White Womanhood incarnate. Rorke's Drift and the Great Trek and Mothering Sunday: All that was best of "our way" holding off the primitive dark blood pulse of Africa. The *Umtali Courier* took pictures, a lady in a flowered dress urged rest, an army surgeon expected hospital and a battery of tests.

"No way! I just want to see the guy who helped me down," she said to her farmer rescuer and was led in a gaggle across the tarmac to a flat-roofed, white-painted, cement-block building with a starfish antenna on the top.

Her farmer opened a door. A small office held a barograph and half-day weather maps, the radio, a desk mike. An anemometer and a book of call signs. An electric kettle and inevitable teapot. Equally inevitable, a pipe and pouch.

"Here's your girl, Bill," said her farmer.

The man behind the voice was short but not small. Wiry. Muscular brown arms in cut-off sleeves. A scar six inches long and a quarter wide ran down the left bicep. Irregular white stars of scar tissue straddled the main wound like eyelets in a shoe. He was partly bald and perhaps forty. His eyes were either gray or blue and steady enough to have brought her down. To do it again.

"Glad there are no scratches," he said.

"*Thank you.*"

"We've been through that." From the lines of the face, this smile was not given often, not wasted. A smile to be appreciated. Off the radio speech was still used sparingly, like the smile. "Muir. Bill Muir." A firm handshake, held for an extra moment.

"Jane Montigny."

"A cuppa?" pointing at the teapot.

"The best suggestion yet."

"Quite a crowd out there. You Candaian?"

"American—from New England, way back."

"Just wondered. Flying the Otter like that."

"It was my first time," she said. "And it flew itself."

"Perhaps not quite?" He looked straight at her.

Perhaps not quite. She nodded, said, "It takes two to tango," realized something might be happening between them in this back of beyond. That it would, if she could stay around.

"Umtali Field," she said. "I'll never forget it. Do you live here—your accent—"

"Doesn't sound as funny as the others?" The smile again.

"I didn't mean—"

"I trained at home—England. The colonial edges get brushed off. Where are you heading?"

"To Inyanga. I'm meeting a woman called Barham-Vrisser."

"Two of a kind. Are you stuck for a ride?"

"I guess maybe I am. I haven't had time to think."

"I'll take you."

"Okay." Help would not be offered, if not meant. *And she wanted him to help.* "When are you through?"

"Six hours is my part of the war effort. I was just quitting when you called."

"I'm glad you didn't," she said. "Don't forget your pipe."

"Not mine."

She let him take her arm without thinking about it.

Umtali, treed and ringed by hills, was midwestern in its cleanly modern churches, libraries, broad sweeps of lawn. The town center had a touch of Spanish Mission with a clock tower and red-tiled roofs, and a pillar-fronted Cecil Rhodes hotel waiting for a frontier shootout. Perhaps that was closer than this quiet plaza dreamt of: the hotel had been commandeered as an Army H.Q. The clock face was bisected at ten-twenty. Impossibly, all this had happened in four hours!

A "robot"—the Rhodesian version of the stoplight at *The Times*—halted the Land-Rover at an intersection marked Main Street and Victory Avenue. Umtali would have to have a Main Street. What midwestern town did not? The alignment of the clock and the names gave her a sense of déjà vu for diaries and vaults. Muir pulled into a diagonal parking space outside a police station on one corner.

"I'll just check the convoy times. Won't be a minute."

She sat in the car watching the colonial faces. The pace of life was slow. A bus originally painted green-and-yellow rocked past, jammed with Africans and slung with crates and coops of miscellaneous creatures waiting for a market and the pot, hinting at another life—another world. A radio in the bus blared Beatles music incongruously on steel drums.

Muir came back. He had the smallest trace of a limp. "The next run's at eleven-thirty— What about something to eat? I know Harry's early starts."

"I hope he makes it," she said.

"Yes." Speech clipped again. "Do you mind Woolworth's?"

"After this morning, I should complain?"

He smiled. Perhaps he smiled more often than she'd thought.

Woolworth's provided ham and eggs and not bad coffee. Blacks ate on either side of them at the counter. A black mother watched two small children try on sailor hats across the aisle. American sailor hats, presumably embargoed.

"Christ, I hate politics," she said.

"Is there an alternative?"

"I guess not." She pushed the plate away. "Maybe as a farmer you don't see as much of it as I do."

"I'm a lawyer," he said. "And a South African. I've seen politics."

She tried to place him in a corporate structure. He sensed it. "I wear a tie when I'm before the bench."

"Sorry. My father was a lawyer. I just couldn't see you in Wall Street."

"I wouldn't mind giving it a try—but only part time. That's one of the reasons I left the Cape."

Yes. He would have seen politics. Walking back to the Land-Rover, they passed a store, Kingston's, Booksellers and Stationers to the Nation. "I'd like to find a book on animals," she said.

The books sold to the nation were of itself: Row on row of Rhodesiana. *Umtali Yesterday and Today; Moodie the Man; Limpopo to Zambezi*. A new novel, *The Iron Trek*, had a pyramid display of hype, "The raw nerve of courage and daring, lives and loves superbly interwoven. . . ."

She took *Mammals of Rhodesia* to the clerk. "Have you got le Carré's new one?"

The girl shook her head apologetically. "We have *Tinker, Tailor* in paper."

On the way out, Muir said, "Hard-cover first runs from abroad take dollars better spent on Harmony Pills—ammunition. The Government have just packed in a drive for, I quote: 'brotherly love between men of good faith.'"

Harmony Pills for gooks and floppies. Like "pacification," the snap slang had a morbid obscenity.

"Come on," he said. "I'll show you the ideal. It's on our way—the convoy forms up at the Wise Owl Motel."

"For real?"

He laughed with her and reversed into Churchill Road. Mackenzie King, believer in signs and portents, would have died happy here. After that, names were alphabetical but at least mixed: Methuen and Murambi streets bounded a polo ground with two riders practising backhand shots. A helicopter, skimming across the pitch with a stretcher on the skids, brought the scoring up-to-date. It landed beside a hospital. "Would you call me about Harry Rogers?" she said. "When they know anything?"

He nodded. They turned on to a divided carriageway curving up through a cut in the hills.

"Christmas Pass," Muir said. "It doesn't look much now but for wagons she must have been a bugger. Rhodes came in near here—it's a historic spot. Used to be a busy one when Mozambique was open. The border crossing's just a couple of miles east of Umtali."

"Once the streets were paved with gold—"

"Too right! I'll tell you a story. The road to Penhalonga, just north of here, was to be made of mine rubble. Driving home one night, the civil engineer found to his horror the African crew had loaded the wrong pile. You can still pick up ore-bearing quartz beside the road. Or could. You'd be foolish to slow down now."

"Nothing really shows," she said, "but I guess there's nothing much untouched."

"And getting worse." He pulled the Rover under a sign saying Murahwa's Hill—National Trust. A statue was set in from the road and backed by trees. Frozen in bronze, two boys and a dog gazed past her at a view of the plains and hills of Africa. *A child, a dog, and an apple tree . . .*

But these children were older. Sandwich-lunched and water-bottled—off for a hike. One boy, dressed in shorts and jacket, jackknife on a bronze lanyard round a bronze waist, stood, the dog's face pressed fawning at his knee. Behind him, on his right side, the second boy knelt, his face like the dog's, stretching forward by the first boy's waist. He seemed to be thinking more of the ground immediately in front of him than the endless miles of veld. Even in bronze the boy was black.

"The standing figure is Fairbridge," said Muir. "His dream was for a partnership, character development for the underprivileged lads of all races."

"The white boy's burden."

"Easy to be glib nowadays. But he did try. He established a chain of farms throughout the Commonwealth, the Fairbridge Schools."

Which said it all. The helping hand. God's white finger stretched out to the black and brown Adams below him. Always below him.

"I didn't mean to be a knee-jerk liberal," she said. "But I think the artist's swallowed the colonial bit down pat. The relationship was always symbiotic—never equal."

"Perspectives change." Muir led her round behind the statue.

Now the dog was leaping, eager for a chase, and the African's back was bare, muscled, the spine showing. He was on one knee. His right hand was held as though bound behind him. But the left arm, raised behind the white boy's tailored shoulder, and the left hand—which from the front appeared raised in greeting—seemed now only halfway through a movement. Seemed frozen only for a moment in a curve that was going to pitch the standing boy before it, out and down into the valley.

"In Delhi," said Muir, "you pass rows of marble bases left from toppled viceroys. I often wonder what will happen to this statue."

18

"Don't aim—*shoot*! If it's an oxygen waster in the bush yew may scare the black bastard off. We go as fast as the slowest car. Renault and Fiat in the middle. Rover, yew tuck in behind. Sergeant's going to pass out a Ruger Mini to anyone without." The very young lieutenant put his bullhorn down beside her. "Short-barrel shotguns are even better," he added conversationally. "The Mini's killing power's not tew hot. Thet's why your cheps didn't like it in 'Nam." The lieutenant climbed into a Toyota half-ton and drove up the road.

"I'm afraid they thrive on it," said Muir. "On the sense of once more being on the Trek, of settlers once more under siege."

The sense was reinforced by the covered-wagon super-structure on the Toyota: roll bars and corrugated metal to take the vehicle over safely once the vee plates underneath the chassis deflected a land mine's initial blast. With these covered wagons Umtali moved farther west. Became a Salt Lake City with its separated Mormon life: its Israeli mission to make the desert bloom.

The black trooper on the first of the two Toyotas, bringing up the rear, swung a machine gun in a testing curve. He waved up to the head of the column. A white boy with a strap around his arm waved back. "University kids," said Muir. "Filling in. Here we go."

The Fiat could keep up sixty on the flat. On the hills, half that. On the worst hill the convoy crawled to twenty-five, and her hand was not the only one to sweat.

"But there's very little risk," Muir said. "Not on a surface like this. The terrorists like one car alone on a dirt

135

road. The favorite dodge is to disguise the mine with dung."

But the road to Hué had been paved with all the right intentions....

The convoy drove in and out of Penhalonga, where the streets were paved with gold, and north again toward *Inyanga, 117 Km.* Every few kilometers they passed a military vehicle like the one she had spotted from the air.

"Those guys aren't old Wombles," she said. "How do the government find the man power?"

"Eighty percent's African—but you're right. That's why they have to recruit a peg-leg air force vet like me. It wasn't too heavy when it was just these border areas—a breeze when the Portuguese were still there—but now there are raids fifty miles from Salisbury and the terrorists have access to Russian weapons. It's only a matter of time until they'll be shoving something a damn sight heavier than bullets up at aircraft. If they ever go for the communication links you can close the shop. Thank God they aren't that sophisticated."

"Yet," she said.

"Yet."

They drove another kilometer. "Bill, you've left South Africa, but aren't the numbers the same?"

"The numbers," Muir said, "are much worse in Rhodesia. There will have to be accommodation here, and every white knows it. In South, half the Europeans don't believe that compromise will really have to be reached. Certainly not this year or next year."

"And the other half?"

"The Boers will die first."

Two vultures flapped scraggy red necks out of a thorn tree.

"Black and white's just camouflage, Jane. It's *all* tribal. Five years ago you could drive with impunity in Mozambique, and the Umtali middle managers and their wives would nip down to Lourenço Marques for a dirty weekend and a fling at roulette—"

"On a diet of *Bonanza* and that bookstore, I'd get out and play too!"

He didn't smile. "The real game was played the minute one got past Forbes Post. The Portuguese never had the cash to throw away on tarmac and white lines. Two cars can't pass abreast—someone has to climb the shoulder—"

"Chicken of the road. *American Graffiti*." She had to explain the ground rules of a teenage Saturday night as she remembered them from 1959.

"Here," said Muir, "the rules are simpler: Don't move until you see the color of the skin. If white sees white, both slow down and ease over. White sees black, black moves. Brown sees black, black moves. Brown sees brown, both stop and have a hell of an argument. Black sees black—a head-on! When white goes from Rhodesia, Jane, and there are no painted lines on the road, that's the way it will be here."

The convoy slowed to pass through a hamlet. The Juliasdale Market (Pvt.) Ltd, faced the street with a display of plastic leopard skins, UDI flags, mock Zulu spears and shields. An African in tribal dress and old running shoes squatted beside them. She tried to square that with the suburban, country-club signs of order: Montclair Hotel, Montclair Golf Course, Claremont Orchards.

Signs, like statues, could topple overnight.

"Will you stay?" she asked. "If the lines go?"

"I think this is only my halfway house. But then I'm lucky. I've got very little here that could be expropriated. After my wife died—"

"I'm sorry."

"Five years ago. Coming home from the New Year's break at her family's place near Howick. A new road, but it drops fifteen hundred feet coming down the escarpment from Hilton into Pieter Maritzburg. Too steep for full loads but the mineowners won't short-ship the trucks. The man couldn't help it. A white driver would never have seen the inside of the court. . . ."

"Or in Alabama," she said. "Without one hell of a fight from the NAACP."

"Still? Well, after that I sold up down South, got most of my money out. Come to that, the new Zimbabwe will need lawyers worse than ever to sort out the mess. Africans are natural jurists, they love litigation. Not following our quaint customs, of course, but the principle of hearings and weighing in judgment is as old as time here. That's their problem: 'Time,' in quotes. If I go out to get the first examination for discovery—say for a child-custody case—the village will expect me to take a week for a thirty-minute appointment! Not

only that, they'll all know what the judgment and sentence
are to be before the whole thing—"

BANG.

The Fiat swerved hard right into the oncoming lane.
Brakes screeched. A burst of automatic fire from the rear
Toyota ripped tracers in the dust. Muir flung the wheel left
and accelerated. Her hand went up involuntarily. Something
black and solid slammed their windshield.

"Blowout!" Muir was pulling back on the pavement.
"Can't stop. One of the trucks will stay with them."

A glimpse of frightened faces flat against the Fiat windows. Two children, a mother. Father running a hand through
his hair.

"Without lines, Bill, kids are where the track gets really
rough."

"You have some?" glancing quickly across at her. She
shook her head. "Always time."

"Not much," she said.

An armored truck raced south with reinforcements. Another convoy followed half a mile behind. Muir looked at his
watch. "That's it for today—nothing moves after half past two.
Do you know Lady Vrisser well?"

"I didn't even know she has a title. I've seen her face in a
thirty-five-year-old picture. She knew my mother. It wouldn't
make much sense to you."

"It might," he said.

The Holiday Hotel at the end of the run was West-
County-England thatched and plastered. A tea garden with
wood and canvas chairs set around tables on a lawn screened
behind a low wall offered Real Devonshire Cream: $1.50.
Three women sat at one of the tables. They ignored the
arrival of the convoy.

She walked across to the hotel veranda. A huge and
solitary African stood beside the steps. "Miss Montinay?" The
man moved forward.

"Yes."

"I am Jonathan. From Chiumbwa." The African held out
a heavy-knuckled hand. She shook it. One of the women at
the tea table stared. "Have you luggage, missis?"

"In the Land-Rover," she said. "I'll get it."

But the African swung a long black arm high over her

head, plucked the case out of the backseat, and walked with a relaxed stride across the parking lot.

"Self-assured fellow." Muir looked after him. Then at her. "Jane, I'd like to go along."

How easy to say, yes. Please! Hold the hand of this stranger in a paradise decomposing by the month. See me safe to the door....

She shook her head. "It isn't reverse chauvinism, Bill. Just that if this Lady Vrisser figures I'm okay—"

"I understand." But she wasn't sure that he did. "If I give in on this one," he said, "will you call me before you leave Rhodesia, tell me how things went?"

"Sure." She kissed him. The type of kiss she gave as rarely as his smile. "That was a bad fifteen minutes in the Otter."

"It's an ill wind— Take care, girl."

The man, Jonathan, was waiting beside an old Willys four-wheel-drive shooting brake cum station wagon: long-bodied and high off the ground. Coachwork of wood faded white outlined the panels. A plate at the back urged Caution, Left-Hand Drive. Gun cases built in long before the present crisis straddled both sides of the hood over the front wheels. The cases were empty. Muir waved—a short, controlled gesture. All three of the women at the table picked that up.

Jonathan turned the vehicle east to *Troutbeck 14 Km—World's View, 22 Km.* The gears were rough and the transmission whined. They left the paving. She looked for dung. The land was high and open. There were no farms or ranches. Twice they passed a crowded trailer park set among tall thin pines and guarded by the army. She thought of Colonel Dodgeson and his bullet-scarred tiger skin. Beyond the second park the road was flanked by long low stone walls tumbling down into clumps of red-hot poker plants.

"Nyangwe," Jonathan pointed at the ruins. "From the old, old days. And over there is Mount Inyangani, the highest mountain in Zimbabwe-Rhodesia." The mountain was a round-shouldered hill rising higher than the range beside it but not spectacular in relation to their present elevation. His words made more of an impression.

"Zimbabwe?" she said. "You think independence is coming, then, Jonathan?"

"Of course, missis. Don't you?"

She nodded, but his frank opinion was outside her African experience. "You're not afraid of terrorists here?" she asked. "You have no guns."

Jonathan tipped his head back and rolled his eyes in exaggerated apprehension. "*Me*, missis, I would have three *machine* guns! But Ladeevriss—oh, mon!" He roared with laughter. Violet B, the young woman with the lustrous hair in the picture would not match with Ladeevriss, matriarch of these far-flung hills.

"*Hang on, missis.*"

The road was torn up for repairs. A yellow grader sat abandoned for the unsafe hours. The Willys bumped ferociously up onto the left-hand verge. Jonathan engaged the front transmission. The protesting whine grew louder.

"Mines, missis," anticipating her question. Now there was nothing happy-go-lucky in his concentration. Two yards from the wheels a gorge dropped fifteen hundred feet to a silver ribbon of water winding through forest. A solitary eagle with a matching silver head floated with them for a quarter of a mile. The gap closed, bird and river disappeared. The bush was thick again, not tropical but still primeval. Once, a huge boar face with yellowed tusks stared out. The muscles on her African driver's neck were tense. Despite a sign, Construction Ending, Resume Speed, Jonathan stayed up on the shoulder. Expecting the double bluff, she thought. Shrewd.

But on both sides. A guerrilla mind that could master double bluffs might go for the communications sooner than even Muir might think.

Muir. Surely he was only another war-zone reaction? Her reflex response to a helping hand in a sea of strangers? She remembered looking at the hand as it gripped the steering wheel of the Land-Rover. As it relaxed for a moment on his thigh. A man's thigh. A man of intelligence, awareness, humor. A man who could talk of love without Alleyn's crutch of pipe or studied nonchalance. A South African man who stayed fair-minded in the face of death ending a marriage and a holiday of endless summer in Natal, where the schools of Harder and Yellow Tail and Kinklip swam unimpeded through shark nets to the shore. . . .

A truck driven by a black.

The Willys bumped back on the road. Civilization returned

with a store and a tennis court. Another hundred yards and she saw that the court was for a different game. The steel mesh stood ten feet high, twenty-five feet from the building, with lights at the corners, locked gates at the front, double barbs of wire as a trip line.

A frenzied German shepherd dog ran inside the wire. Would his barking deflect a mortar shell fired from the bush? A mile past the store the Troutbeck Inn, turreted and gabled, accepted the army but refused latecomers and a fence: Wire would be obscene in these surroundings. A fisherman in an army jacket snapped a gossamer line onto a stream beside the inn.

"I love that, missis," said the African beside her.

"Water?"

"Fly fishin'. Fan*ta*stic, mon."

"I guess," she said. "I've never tried."

"They don't have *fly fishin'* in America?" Faith in the rainbow land was shattered.

"Oh sure," she said. "All kinds. How much farther?"

Reaction and exhaustion had found its way with the dust into every crack of her skin.

"Soon, missis, soon. We on Chiumbwa now."

But African time, as Muir had told her, has its own measure. They climbed another five hundred feet. Dazed, she watched bush become tea plantation, tea become coffee. Saw stands of temperate pines and weeping cedars begin to share the hillside with the tropic natives, and small alpine meadows of soft grass support flocks of strangely patterned sheep and goats beside a waterfall floating a veil past ferns and moss. . . .

A change in the tires' rhythm woke her.

A stone bridge was carrying the Willys across a gorge toward a giant tree wrapped in vines guarding a last curve. Beyond the curve was a house. Outside it, in a garden filled with every kind of scent and color, a woman stood looking at a statue in the center of a pool.

A statue of a faun.

19

She had come across the world to get this woman's words about her mother! And yet, for almost three farming days— and four fireside evenings—she talked instead to Violet Vrisser about subjects utterly unrelated to her mission to Africa. She talked about her life, about a woman's way in the world of politics and sudden death, about her once-and-failed marriage, about Muir, about a gift of *Pilgrim's Progress*. About the terrible ways in which children died in places like Beirut and Vietnam and London.

And Violet Barham-Vrisser for some reason understands her—because she listens; conducts the business of seven thousand acres; drives her in the Willys from the orange groves in the valley through the plantations and dairy meadows high above it; shows her the Africa of the white man's dream, tells her of the Africa of the white man's making, prophesies to her the Africa of the white man's passing. Of her own passing.

"I know it's a wasted gesture, Jane, but the farm proper will become a cooperative for the present families. Most of them have squatted here for so long that they think it's theirs anyway."

"Why wasted?"

"If the country goes black like Kenya the estate will be forcibly acquired by one of the new elite. If not, and we stay, the land will be so fractioned by succession to every bastard son that it will drop to a bare subsistence level. That's why I want these upper four thousand acres to pass to the nation and become part of the Park before I go. Before *we* go."

The thatch of the house roof showed as a pale leaf in the

green sea of vegetation far below them. "I think of Kashmir, Vriss. Without the houseboats on the lake. It's a jewel."

"Rhodes said the same thing to my grandfather." Violet Vrisser stretched an arm eastward across the valley. "Rhodes had already bought the hundred thousand acres of World's View next door, but this was the jewel, he said, the place the waters rose—he would give *anything*!" Violet Vrisser laughed. "God knows, he could afford it, even then. But my grandfather was a great gambler—although religious too, in that nonconforming, unregimented way that so many of those exploratory English were—and he said to Rhodes, 'God brought me to this piece of Eden, we'll let five cards straight see if He meant it.' My grandfather dealt the hand on this very rock and drew a royal flush in hearts. Rhodes wrote across the cards, 'The price of Eden.' They're framed somewhere in the house. We must look them out when we go back. Did you have an interesting time with Jonathan this morning?"

"Tremendous! He was kind of edgy while we were close to the river, but it was worth it. We saw a blue duiker, which he says is rare, and one of those cats like a lynx."

"Caracal. You were lucky!"

"I guess. Jonathan's a fascinating guy. I mean he comes right out for independence. 'The land is *ours*,' he says with that enormous conviction that raises goosebumps, and then he pulls back and throws it all away with a shrug. 'But the land goes down the hole if the whites leave, missis. Just wind blowin' on burnt-out grass.' And he gives you these Zambian horror stories of no transport, no oil, no tires, no salt. 'And bribes just to shake your father's hands, missis.' Mozambique he won't even talk about. 'Jungle,' he says. Jesus—if I put that on the wire CORE would burn the Press Building."

Violet Vrisser smiled wryly. "One hand could hold the people who can read this continent correctly. Jonathan is unique in many ways."

"But not popular? That's just a guess—but in the village, when he tells them to do something, they hop, but then they look at him afterward behind his back, and it's not friendly."

"You're quite right. Partly it's education—he went four years past standard six, and agricultural college on top of that—but mostly, as everywhere else, it's the tribal mix-up.

Rhodesia's main groups are Mashonas—pastoral like the Kikuyu in Kenya—and Matabele from the old Zulu-warrior stock. That's bad enough, but Jonathan's neither. I took him in after his Portuguese-African father was killed in a beer drink-up. To my people—even after thirty years—he's a foreign boss boy. You talked about your time in Ireland—it makes as much sense I suppose. He's a simply outstanding manager."

"And concerned about you, Vriss—about the risks you take. I would have to say he has a point, the bush on the far bank is perfect cover. If there are terrorists in this area—"

"*If?* Dear Jane—of *course* they're out there. I could count half a dozen lads from my own village who've gone over in the last year. But they don't have to hide in the bush, they can walk up the garden path—they know where I'll be. I don't leave a light on in an empty room or play musical bedrooms to confuse my houseboys." Violet Vrisser reached across and held her arm. "You mean well and so does Jonathan—and God knows, the local PATU never stop hounding me! I've put in the Agricalert button to keep them happy—it plugs us in directly to the police station at Inyanga—but what else, in God's name, do they expect me to *do?* Sit out my life in a damned concentration camp of wire and dogs like Johnson's store? After what I've seen at Belsen. At Ravensbrück . . ."

The names were carried away by the wind, carried like carrion in the claws of the silver headed fish eagle floating past.

"Was Scylla at Ravensbrück?"

"Scylla." Violet Vrisser stroked the hair which had gleamed like hand-rubbed chestnut in the photograph and was now thatch-gray. "I've often wondered if that name didn't damn her from the start."

"I don't know the myths."

"One used to learn them in the old days—instead of psychology, no doubt—we drew on them for the codes. If we'd stayed strictly alphabetical in the choice of names, Mary would have been Sappho, but she turned that down for its lesbian connotations. God—what irony! From the Freudian side, Scylla's was the story which was really nasty.

"Scylla," said Violet Vrisser almost by schoolgirl rote, "was a sea nymph, and daughter of all sorts of possible gods. Glaucus, one of the minor echelon, was smitten but she wouldn't have him and he appealed to Circe—you can see that Glaucus wasn't bright because Circe, as always insanely jealous, poisoned Scylla's bath. But not to kill her." Violet Vrisser stared out across her valley, and her voice was not a schoolgirl's. "Not to kill her. The fates in myth have to be worse than death. Circe chained Scylla to a cliff. Her upper body and her face remained beautiful, but below the waist she was hideously transformed with a belt of heads of frightful dogs constantly grasping and rending the bodies of passing sailors. Ulysses sacrificed half a dozen to her rather than lose the ship. Eventually, to end her torment, Scylla broke her chains and cast herself into the sea to become the famous rock beside the maelstrom."

A rock and a hard place. Some rock, some place, as Churchill might have said. The odyssey of wartime life and death seemed inseparable from myth.

"The family thinks she took a pill, Vriss, and went to sleep. Did you tell them that?"

"Samuel Butler," Violet Vrisser said inconsequently, half to herself, "wrote a book to show that the *Odyssey* was the work of a woman . . . but yes, I told all the families that, Jane. Being 'put to sleep' is such a beautifully Anglo-Saxon euphemism, isn't it? So much less bloody than 'destroyed.'"

A flash of scarlet plunged into a thicket of Munondo trees. "Purple-crested lourie," said Violet Vrisser with the reflex of the inveterate birdwatcher. "The facts were set down in my report. It was classified, but any of the relatives could have asked to see it. I don't recall that any did. I can't blame them—because my girls *were* destroyed, Jane. A few with phenol at Natzweiler, but most with hands behind the back and a shot through the neck at the base of the skull. I saw two of the skulls. The butcher bastards had saved them! *Filed them*—filed them on a shelf with the other office records. The rest of the evidence went up in smoke. . . ."

Violet Vrisser's eyes seemed to be looking for it in this empty air. "All I hear from the PATU is atrocity—African or Asian Stone Age barbarism. Good God, Europe could teach them! A hundred and fifty years ago, the peasant mass of Europe couldn't read, couldn't write, couldn't add. Only three hundred years ago we burned witches and kept Guy Fawkes alive to see his guts ripped out. Stone Age! Our Terrs are late Stuarts in their barbarity—associates of Isaac

Newton and Pitt. Men right on the edge of the Age of Reason."

Men who built and decorated Saint Margaret's Church for its society weddings. In that perspective, William Flower's grotesquely spurting, severed hand was less than a stone's throw from the Victorian Eric of *Little by Little*. From the Teutonic destruction of her mother.

"Was Scylla shot?"

"Yes," said Violet Barham-Vrisser.

But after fifteen years of interviews, microscopic pauses can loom large as full stops on a page. Can hold information as dense as microdots. As secret.

"Vriss," she said slowly, "be frank. If you don't want me to push—if there's still a hang-up with security—"

"Security?"

"For the British Government."

"I despise the British Government." The bitter edge would cut through flesh and blood. "Not England—never England. And certainly not the Queen, poor woman. Good God, how sick she must be of the whole postwar pack. At least to begin with, one gave Labour the benefit of the doubt for idealogical myopia. That went in Biafra after the Arabs squeezed and Nigeria had the oil. But the tragedy is that it should never have happened *here*. My husband killed himself telling them, Whitehall, that there must be some way stations on the ladder, some resting places for the pressures to equalize. But even after all the shambles of East Africa and the Gold Coast—I can't *tell* you what they're like, Jane. You have to see them at the conferences. The Foreign Office types who 'know our Africans,' and bring along the tame black one from the London School of Economics who wouldn't be caught dead actually coming back to live. And always the Top Man, the political head of the team, standing in the middle of the group pictures with his arms around the black shoulders while he gets his M.P.s riding changed at Home from Putney or Notting Hill to somewhere safer. And then the communiqués and the tributes to the democratic vision of the elder statesmen in Nairobi and next door, sitting on their piles of bones. And after the communiqué, the postconference gin-up with the old hands, and the jokes about bush babies still rockabyeing in their treetops. That hypocrisy was what killed my husband. If he'd lived, and been P.M. instead of that dreadful Todd, hankey-pankeying his Mission girls..."

A pair of the louries cocked their heads to one side, as though considering that prospect. "It would probably have made no difference. The woolly thinkers still like Todd." Violet Vrisser stood up and brushed her slacks. "Come on, it gets cool as soon as the sun moves behind Inyangani." The louries shrieked and flipped away.

The fish eagle went with them, drifting slowly past the peak as she followed Violet Vrisser down the track toward the Willys. "That peak is what Rhodes *really* wanted, Jane. On another day we'll go across. Do you mind if we pass the dairy on our way home? My best Guernsey has mastitis."

How did one measure the distance from Ravensbrück to this dairy? Was it the distance to Conrad's heart of darkness?

Jonathan informed them that the vet had irrigated, injected, and departed with his bag of modern tricks. "Old Shillin' just makin' sure, Ladeevriss."

Old Shilling—so old that his skin had grown too loose for his skull—sat on the ground beside the tethered Guernsey. A crude circle of sticks and feathers were laid out around her hindquarters. Old Shilling crooned in a tuneless chant. The cow listened with liquid eyes, then urinated into the circle of charms. Old Shilling stopped chanting to stare at his glistening-wet black leg.

Jonathan snapped his fingers and a boy led the cow inside the dairy. Old Shilling gathered up his feathers and departed like the vet.

"Does that help?" she asked.

"It helps Old Shillin', missis." Jonathan looked at the retreating old black back and offered explanation. "The cow gets better, he take all the credit. The cow does not get better—" the huge black hands spread wide expressing Hobson's choice. "If the vet doctor can't fix, who blame Old Shillin'?" He followed the cow into the barn.

"Old Shilling's the *nn'anga* at Chiumbwa," said Violet Vrisser. "Part patriarch, part witch doctor. And although Jonathan would die rather than admit it, sometimes the old boy's mysteriously right about cattle. Cows are the lifeblood of these people: currency, *lobolo* to buy wives, food, and drink." The Willys turned into the Main House compound with its garden of flowers. A shadow fell all the way across the garden and onto the roof.

"That's an incredible tree," she said. "Is it a redwood?"

"A Nyasaland mahogany. I have an ongoing fight with the forestry people about its height. They insist on giving 'Rhodesia's tallest' to one in the Chirinda Forest by Chipinga. Probably just as well—I couldn't stand the hordes coming for a gawk. Do you want to wash before tea?"

The bathroom, a sepulcher of white tile with fixtures pedestaled and claw-footed that had come with the grandfather and Cecil Rhodes, reminded her again of the visit to Dorset. The pleasant surprise of hot water was a second link to Britain: like Dolphin Square and its central heating from the Battersea Power Station across the Thames, the hot water at Chiumbwa came from a forty-gallon boiler outside the house. The boiler was stoked by a kitchen boy almost as ancient as Old Schilling.

In the drawing room Chimgeru, the houseboy, was unloading the contents of a trolley onto warming plates raised on a metal hob beside the fire. Violet Vrisser and hundreds of glass eyes watched him.

"Vriss," she said, "just how many goddamn trophies *are* there in this house?"

"It is rather a museum. You don't shoot?"

"On a range. In real life I'm with the baby seals."

"Killing to get feathers for a hat was always frightful—and so much has gone now—but killing cleanly, and not to excess?" The flickering eyes on the walls seemed equally uncertain. Perhaps to them a bullet was preferable to rending teeth.

"Have you ever shot a man, Vriss?"

The eyes waited.

"I shot a Vichy French policeman in March of 1941. At close range."

"Was it like shooting anything else?"

A log exploded. The shower of sparks was picked up by all the eyes. "No, it was quite, quite different. But if I had done it again, it might not have been. And if I had done it a hundred times, I'm sure it would not have been. When I interrogated the staff at Ravensbrück, when I heard how they rocked their nailed boots back and forth on my girls' bare feet, I tried to remember that."

The fire crouched down into a small red heap and pulsed like a wounded heart in all the eyes. "So many of my girls were so afraid of the *little* things. Marjorie, who smuggled a tartan ribbon through three camps and wore it on the final morning was terrified of pigs. Alice, of landing in nettles. And Noor Khan—Noor Khan was terrified most of all of the effect of her own dark Indian skin. Schwarzhuber, the Second-in-Command who'd kept her naked, chained hand to foot for months, wept in front of me about Noor Khan. Why didn't the Gestapo do it themselves, he asked me? And then his Germanic sense of jurisdiction answered, but of course: chain of command. 'You couldn't run a place like this,' he said, 'a place of such complexity, without chain of command.'

"*I remember that chain,*" says Violet Vrisser to the eyes. "Every rattle, every link: Suhren, the Commandant. Schwarzhuber, the lackey. Corporal Schult and Private Schenk, the killers. The good soldiers, Schult and Schenk. And the professional man, Dr. Trommer, so punctilious in recording cause of death as shrapnel from an air raid. And Zappe, who stood there laughing as my girls knelt hand in hand. Zappe, you're dead, girls. . . . And Herta Oberhauser for the woman's touch, the only female defendant at the Doctors' trial, how could I ever forget the woman's touch. . . ."

Chimgeru spreads hot butter on the crumpets, cracks the tops on eggs, pours tea into Doulton cups with English roses on the sides.

"Your mother and I held cups just like those," said Lady Violet Barham-Vrisser, once nearly wife of a prime minister. "The first time we ever met, in a tent on the lawn at Buckingham Palace, when we thought the worst death you could die was curtsying to old Queen Mary, frozen like a centerpiece of ice behind the King."

"Wasn't she always afraid he was going to stutter?"

"Our man was still father George—the one who looked like the Tsar. A terrible waste of time, Presenting, but like Old Shilling, we all have our tribal customs."

Tribal custom. From Langley and its daffodils, to Dorset, to Albany, to Old Shilling: To Natzweiler and a command in chains. But for any tribal custom, Alleyn had said, you need an interpreter, a guide. A flare in the fire burnished Violet Vrisser's waiting face with the patina of the copper rings on Old Shilling's legs.

"The Faun, Vriss," she said. "What was the meaning of the Faun?"

20

"The meaning of the Faun?" said Violet Vrisser. "I'm not sure any of us really knew—John Bevan just brought it in."

"Bevan—not the coalminer with the eyebrows?"

"Aneurin?—Good God, no! Although I suppose we did have rather a plethora of Bevins and Bevans—but Ernie and Aneurin were sons of the people. Our man, John, came from old banking and the Dukes of Buccleuch and was a damned cold fish. He took over LCS after his predecessor's stomach couldn't stand the slaughter at Dieppe. John's stomach never had a problem. You could sense that as soon as you met him." Violet Vrisser smiled. "And I must tell you about that first meeting, Jane. The Committee, you see, before taking anyone on used to have a vetting session at Bevan's club, Brooks's—the absolute essence of British masculinity."

"The Rideau in Ottawa—no girls allowed?"

"Exactly. And they'd never *had* the problem of a woman on LCS before. My dear, you would have roared! All these brilliant men dropping the entire war for half a day to wrestle this ridiculous problem. They must have a pope of Clubland who mediates these things, because eventually I was summoned to the sanctum and there they all were like a group of Spanish Inquisitors huddled under Spencer Perceval's portrait. One of them told me later that they felt equally awkward, but for a moment it was rather much." Violet Vrisser paused to remember just how much, for a young woman to walk in alone like that. "I'm quite sure John Bevan picked the spot deliberately."

"Why?"

"British history—I'll explain. You see, while the Faun, as Bevan put it, was meant to symbolize the whimsical spirit of mischief in the forest, LCS was much, much darker. After the image of Jael, the woman in the song of Deborah who sleeps with Sisera and then drives a tent peg through his head." Violet Vrisser stared at the fire as though she saw it happening. "Well, the Faun may have kept our minds turning out the petty-nuisance stuff—keeping Hitler on the hop like a blue-arsed fly, someone said. But Jael, and her spirit of guile and deception—a spirit utterly free of *any* restraint in pursuit of its objective—that was what Churchill saw when he produced her as the code name for SOE. That was what Churchill *demanded* when he bellowed the name.

"'Set Europe *ablaze* with it!'"

Violet Vrisser stabbed savagely at the fire with a poker.

"*That* was how Churchill passed the torch, Jane. And that was how one felt as a new recruit receiving it. I suppose I still feel a little of that, you know, even today."

Feel the heat of that flame of Resistance passing hand to hand under a picture in an old boys' club.

"One realized later," said Violet Vrisser, replacing the poker gently on its hook, "why Bevan made us stand under it. That picture of Spencer Perceval was a message straight from Jael's dark side. Perceval, you see, was the only British Prime Minister ever to be assassinated."

Ghosts of Perceval and Hitler seemed as phantom as all the other myths which ran through these worn-out wartime tales: tales that should be of no consequence except to old Womble soldiers reliving old horrors of the best times before they fade away.

But neither the image of Smythe or Piers, jumping from a quick study of her notes, seemed ready for fading yet. Nor was Violet Vrisser's memory, now thoroughly warmed up.

"Your mother and I fell into the underworld together— although of course we didn't know it—two years before the war: half a dozen years after we came out—"

"Out?"

"Presentation at Court, dear, old Queen Mary and the curtsying. Most of our contemporaries married right after it but we'd gone a long way on with education. Mary through a second degree at Cambridge, and on my side there had been family delusions about medicine at Edinburgh." Violet Vrisser smiled again. "Even *that* was considered the forefront of your women's lib, Jane, in my parents' set."

"Did you get your M.D.?"

"I got the marks but I never really wanted it—the doctoring—and you must have that. And, if things had stayed more normal—because we'd just come down from university for the year, so that would have been June, June of thirty-seven, when this typically naval man came to see me, right out of the blue: Would I like a holiday through Europe at the government's expense? He laid it out as though it were rather what we'd call now a public-relations tour, and I thought, Why on earth not?—and then he mentioned that Mary was already on and that clinched it. And what a marvelous trip it was, being swept off one's girlish feet by all these gorgeous father figures in their primes. Looking back, it seems to have been an endless round of flowers and waltzing uniforms—but overripe. When you think what was about to happen in Europe, almost putrid in its excess."

"Like the wreaths at a Mafia don's funeral."

"Dining at Karin Hall—Göring's Valhalla—was like being stuck right inside the damned hearse! I remember I got an awful attack of the giggles because we'd met up with Unity Mitford and every time she and the ponderous Göring would go sloe-eyed at each other, Mary would start humming 'Three little maids...' from G and S. One of those quite absurd things but it kept us in stitches all the way to Berchtesgaden."

Where three little maids visit a mad Mikado. And now only one was left to tell the tale.

"We spent a whole day in the aerie, and it was an anticlimax. We'd all expected Göring-plus, but lunch was so bank-manager *suburban*. The salts and peppers were bloated silver pheasants on little wheels that trundled around the table, and Hitler was captivated—he didn't eat a thing himself—playing with these damned birds. He's push them back and forth to the people on each side of him, Unity and your mother, or across the table to me, and all the time telling funny stories with odd punch lines. The punch lines never seemed to match, but of course the Germans made him out as Charlie Chaplin. So did Unity. And Eva Braun—when she wasn't jumping up to snap pictures—would simply smile this porcelain little smile and catch the birds before they fell off the table when he pushed them too hard. The rest of the time she just stared at the view. Of course that was quite beyond description."

As was the man himself: this mock Charlie, this man with the mustache playing mein gracious host to his three little English maids on the roof of Europe; watching, like the eagle this afternoon, the tiny mice running and playing with no hope of escape.

"I remember," said Violet Vrisser, "once some salt spilled out of one of the pheasants and Mary and Hitler both threw it over their shoulders at the same moment. For a girl who liked science she was oddly superstitious. In the afternoon, we played Ping-Pong with Speer and some Nordic gods brought in from the SS barracks on the estate, and then there was more food—plates and plates of tortes and pastries stuffed with cream, and Göring and the ghastly dull Bormann shoveling it in while Hitler held a cup like a Deportment course at Cheltenham College— Did you endure those dreadful things at school?"

"We called them 'Going to Gracious'—I don't see Adolf in that picture."

"No. You couldn't imagine it. His Viennese side, perhaps. Odd you know, the Austrians with only a tenth of the greater German population made up nearly half the Nazi membership. As though they had to out-Roman the Romans. Anyway, after tea there was the business side—Goebbels and Speer were both trotted out to emphasize the Aryan bonds with England and tell us how *well* they'd all got on with Edward—he'd visited a month or two before—and didn't we agree that our common culture made us all a happy family."

"Do you speak German?"

"Yes, but not as well as your mother. There were a lot of questions then about English politicians—I don't think Hitler had met Chamberlain yet but he did a devastating impression. And he had another of Goebbels, complete with limp, that was dead on. The dwarf was furious, you could sense that, but giggling and applauding like the rest of us."

"The giggling, I get," she said, "but what the hell could three girls—"

"Tell him that would be useful? Absolutely nothing! Only the sort of gossip that goes the society rounds at a low level, but I can tell you they lapped it up! You'd mention some minor idiosyncrasy of a man like Eden, and Hitler would say delightedly to Winnifred Wagner—she was English too— 'Effeminacy, you see, you *see*!' and the entourage would all nod. The opinion of experts—if ever there was a group who could authenticate degeneracy that was it! Not that I'm implying poor Eden should be tarred with that brush. Really, it was enough just to mention the names—all the Nazis had a frightful inferiority complex. Hitler was simply captivated by Mary's link with Windsor—"

"She *knew* Windsor?"

"I don't mean they were intimate—Edward always went for the safety of married women—but he certainly liked your mother's company, her marvelous sense of humor. Until Mrs. Simpson cut it off Mary was often invited to Fort Belvedere, his retreat, and damn few were—men *or* women! Mary charmed him as she charmed them all. With Hitler, of course, there was his thing for blondes, nothing could have been more Aryan to look at than your mother. . . ."

Violet Vrisser fell silent and stared into the fire. The houseboy creaked in to collect the tea things on the tray as the Austrian girls in their pinafores and white caps must have done at that other tea party above the clouds. She asked Violet Vrisser how it ended—the day at Berchtesgaden.

"Like wet fireworks. Unity had stalked off in a real huff about Mary—*I* think that's when Mitford started to go strange—so there were only the two of us left to go to their vast evening meal. It was set up on buffet tables with room for dancing in between. I suppose I must be one of the few women left who can admit to having danced with Hitler, and he was charming as a partner, absolutely charming. Smart as a whip, amazingly informed, creative—there was a flower growing on the terrace and he drew me a little sketch on the back of the menu—I have that somewhere. And his eyes—that brilliant, electric blue—were kind, deep, warm, unwaveringly steady; not shifty as they were when he dealt with English men.

"And then the music ended—there was a small orchestra, picked from his SS regimental band—and Goebbels took a moment to come up and ask if Hitler had signed a minute or something that had been left on his desk that afternoon. Hitler said, absolutely calm, 'Minute? No, there was no minute?' and Goebbels hadn't said another word, not a word, but he'd started to open his mouth, and *the* most extraordinary shift I've ever seen in my *life!* I was watching Hitler, and this frozen wall came down behind his eyes and his cheeks grew stiff—white—and he said in this flat, deadly voice, '*How dare you!*' and just walked out of the room leaving the lot of us there. Except his dog, and Goebbels who ran—literally ran—out after him, game leg and all. That anecdote fascinated Churchill more than anything else. We must have had to trot it out a dozen times."

The names dropped from the conversation as casually as rain, as casually as the stars in a 'Gee There' movie: Gee there's Goebbels; gee there's Churchill. Violet Vrisser with a life spent behind the movie set didn't seem to notice.

"You know, the oddest thing—before we left, Hitler sent a personal note, through Goebbels, with his *regrets*, pressure of business et cetera. That would be worth a quid or two now, wouldn't it? Is that clock right, Jane?"

"By my watch, three minutes slow."

"My goodness, what an elaborate beast!" said her hostess, leaning over. "A real lifesaver— 'All dancing, all singing' as we used to say. Jap I suppose. This grandfather of mine always kept perfect time but my clock man was killed a year ago. Doing a repair at the Mission. A Dutch chap, awfully nice. Extraordinary how the Japs have taken over so much of the world." Violet Vrisser stood up and stretched. "I think I'll have my lie-down. We could go on after dinner if you like." She paused at the door. "Funny how things come back. I didn't think I could remember a quarter of all that, and yet now I see it like a picture. I really must be getting old. Like Shilling."

"Your reflexes are still better, Vriss. You'd move your leg."

A shout of laughter followed the gray hair down the hall.

Tea, lie-down: the rituals of this end of Violet Vrisser's isolated life were now as fixed as the seasons' mark upon her farm. After her rest, the *Inkosikazi*, the mistress of Chiumbwa, pays a visit of inspection to her cool, southern hemisphere, south-facing kitchen with the polished red quarry-tile floor and the old flat-irons resting on their faces on an even older "Dick King" wood stove that had been wrestled across the mountains before the road through Christmas Pass became a pushover.

Violet Vrisser asks a question, "*Kapisa, upfu hwei?*"

Kapisa, the cookboy, waves a knife at greens soaking in a galvanized-iron sink, and plays out the circle game with patient exasperation: he must have flour because the vegetables are not enough without the fish, and the fish must have batter and the batter must have flour—"which I asked you for three days before I went to visit my second wife's eldest daughter, *Inkosikazi*...."

Before dinner, which continues exactly as Kapisa has intended, Violet Vrisser mixes a drink in the drawing room under the glass eyes: two ounces gin, one of sweet vermouth, a large dash of bitters; making everything that was right about a martini completely wrong.

And then through supper Violet Vrisser's cheeks are a little flushed.

After supper, as on all the days she eats alone, Violet Vrisser reads her papers: a two-day-old copy of the Salisbury *Mail*, or a ten-day-old air-expressed *Observer*, or a six-week-old *Country Life*.

"Your crash landing made the weekly roundup, Jane. I must say I do *miss* flying."

"Vriss, come on! I've seen you shoot the eye out of a bug. Why quit?"

"It's not really age. The maintenance was getting more and more of a grind, and then when the shortages really hit five years ago, it was just simpler to let the aircraft go. Like mustard powder, and Scotch, and olives for the gin. The sanction squeeze is deceptive at Chiumbwa, we're so self-sufficient, but if you were at a house in Bambe Zonke—that's Graball, the African's name for Salis—"

Jonathan burst into the drawing room.

"ZANLA, Ladeevriss! They have taken the children from Old Shillin's houses." For the first time she was aware of sweat on an African face. "Maybe seven children, maybe eight."

"How many Terrs, Jonathan?" Violet Vrisser's right hand stroked the cover of a *Country Life* where sheep might safely graze in a Somerset meadow.

"Three. Maybe four."

"Are they on foot?"

"Yes, Ladeevriss. But the boys are frightened to be trackin' in the dark."

Violet Vrisser, nearly seventy, stood up a little stiffly and dropped her paper sheep. She walked out into the hall and took packs of .303 cartridges from a cabinet. "Bring the Enfields," she said.

Jonathan lifted down two rifles from the rack beside the door. "Do I press the Alert, Ladeevriss?"

"No. If the Terrs hear the helicopters they may do something stupid in desperation. Jane—"

"I'll come."

Violet Vrisser nodded.

The wheels of the Willys ripped the edge of the lawn to make the turn by the giant mahogany, then careened downhill toward the small white huts in the working center of the farm. A shape sprawled beside the road. Three women huddled by it, hands across their mouths. Wails of "*Twuno, twuno*" came through the hands.

Jonathan snapped a question impatiently at one of the women.

"*Yambuka, Jonathan*," with rolling eyes.

"They believin' the children already taken across the river, Ladeevriss."

"Find out."

The flattened accelerator left the eyes in billowing dust.

Violet Vrisser opened a packet of shells, and prepared her gun. The *click-click* of the bolt action mirrored the African speech in the village.

The road ran through maize plants taller than a man. The high beams made the stalks rows of pale palisades. Twice, red eyes shone through the palisades like those in the heads watching the fire in the drawing room. Jonathan slowed. A small white sailor-style hat, a ghost from Woolworth's counter at Umtali, lay in the road. The lights went out. The maize stalks blackened to iron bars. The Willys growled softly to itself, the wheels made no noise on the cushioning dust. An Enfield's wicked snout was cradled on Violet Vrisser's arm.

"*Headlights!*"

A quail covey of frozen figures at two hundred paces. A black stick pointing at the Willys. A flash. A whipping Enfield *crack* beside her in the car. A body leaped up, staggered back, collapsed into the maize stalks. A shattering of glass.

"*Damn, damn, damn.*" Violet Vrisser dropped her Enfield and held her arm.

Another stick—probably Chinese—pointed death toward the Willys. Fired. The bullet ricocheted off her door. She grabbed up Violet Vrisser's gun. A second guerrilla was leaping for the river. A third swung his killer stick—but away from the Willys; at the little huddle on the bank. The death stick chattered at the children. One fell. Two.

She was out. Running down the floodlit track toward the children, feeling rage she could not speak, screaming words she could not hear. A face playing a pawn's politics with kids' lives turned his death stick on her. She stopped; an oblate silhouetted head was centered in her sights; she squeezed the trigger; the head snapped right.

Something horrible flew away into the night.

In the river, at the limit of the headlight's reach, flailing arms stroked for the shelter of the trees. She aimed, steadied. Could not shoot. Beside her, Jonathan's arm was up, up, then a whistling silver flash from a machete. Four fingers were gone like minnows, black-blood diluted in the stream. The truncated arm of a new martyr splashed out of sight.

On the bank, a child with no stomach was dead. One with bullets—probably Russian—in the leg began to cry. Jonathan lifted it as lightly as a twig and set it in the car. Violet Vrisser had wrapped a handkerchief around her arm.

The night smelled of blood.

At the village, the wailing mothers seemed only half-glad to see their children back.

In her room, sky-high on three scarce double whiskies and adrenaline, she could not sleep. Violet Vrisser was right. Shooting men was not like shooting anything else. Not, at least, for the first time.

"The people are afraid," Jonathan reported at breakfast the next morning. "Afraid of the *ngozi* of the dead men. I have told them the live Terrs never comin' back twice when they are beaten, but you know how it is, Ladeevriss. The PATU have taken the child to Inyanga in the jeep and three soldiers will stay for tonight. How is your arm, *Inkosikazi?*"

"Only a scratch, Jonathan, but thank you. Order a new headlight for the Willys." Violet Vrisser waited until the big man left the room. "*Damn and blast!*"

"Problem?"

"The *ngozi* business. A *ngozi* is a spirit of a person who died with a grievance, and it wanders around, looking for redress like the ghost of Jacob Marley looking for Scrooge. If that damned Shilling's decided a Terr's *ngozi* has settled in at Chiumbwa, every minor disaster of stupidity and inefficiency will get blamed on it for months! And there's bugger all mortal man can do!" Violet Vrisser stared ruefully at the bandage. "They'll look at this and say it's already started. Perhaps you'd better pour the coffee, Jane."

The memory of the vampire piece flying from the head was too fresh, the tiny figure with the spilled purple sausage guts too terrible. She passed the cups without reply; without the light touch these people loved to save for the special occasions when Saint Paul's rocked in the bombs or the band tuned up on the *Titanic*. The ten-year-old chant she had heard all night refused to leave her head. *Hey, hey, LBJ. How many kids did you kill to-day?*

"Why is it always the kids, Vriss? Why, every time, is it old men's politics wiping out kids?"

"I don't think it is, Jane." Violet Vrisser finished her egg and set her fork exactly in the center of her plate. "Except for Gandhi, these postwar struggles are the mad passion of the young out to prove their manhood—the failed young, one might add."

It was too broad, too predictably reactionary, too oblivious of the guiding hands of all the Uncle Ho's. And then she saw again the butcher faces at the places where the murders happened: the mindless childmen's faces of My Lai, of the camps in Gaza, of both sides of the barrier in Derry, of the zealots of Cambodia herding the hospital beds through the streets of Phnom Penh. Of last night.

"Mugabe's a typical example," said Violet Vrisser. "The ZANLA leader—although after his operation for postsyphilitic cancer in a Mission hospital I'm told he hasn't much manhood left to defend."

The wound in all the wars that dared not speak its name. *Emasculation*. And by a white man. What, in Christ's name, must that do to a black man's head? Violet Vrisser's concern was general, not specific.

"One often wondered what effect illness had on the leaders. In LCS we knew just how ill they were. Roosevelt especially, but Churchill's pneumonia and depression too. Hitler was mainly rumor. Except for his mental state—and we had Walter Langer's incredible analysis for OSS to help us there. Your mother and I were two of the hundreds Langer questioned in assembling the profile."

It was her own state of mind that alarmed her, not Hitler's. She forced herself to eat a small piece of a breakfast roll baked by Kapisa that morning; forced herself to extend the conversation, to listen to Violet Vrisser go back to Edinburgh for her finals and "a sort of two-year odyssey around the world with a rather foolishly wonderful young man." Around the world in ten times eighty days. And nights. You forgot, looking at the old, that there had to be nights.

"He was killed at Singapore," said Violet Vrisser, ending a chapter. "Your mother, though, with her golden hair of the chosen people, went back to Germany twice. The last time was over the brink—she was still in Berlin after the Declaration—but Hitler sent her home with a special pass and a soothing word for the Government. She went straight into Menzies' circle. She was one of the few—not the pilots, but those who'd seen the real inner workings of the Reich. The separations of the yellow stars at the railway stations, the old men in beards and bandaged heads. She came back dedicated, that's all one can say. Still the marvelously warm, funny girl, but with this absolute belief that the Teutonic 'Spirit of the Ring,' as she called it, had to be beaten back into the cave and buried in the rocks. With that sort of imagery and conviction you can see why Churchill liked her."

She could see that. See this flaxen embodiment of Nazi myth vowing to stamp it out. "What I can't see is a child, Vriss. Why, for God's sake, right then? Just accident?"

"Absolutely not! We put only forty women into Europe but we had three thousand in the FANY at home: manning the secret staffs at Bletchley and London. Well, I mean! Exceptional girls like you or your mother locked up with equally attractive male agents in safe houses and isolated training camps. We couldn't afford accidents. We had our own tame gynecologist for abortions— You don't approve, Jane?"

"I don't like it, who does? But I accept it." The houseboy stacked the empty plates. The trolley clattered off along the hall. "It was the bit about me. Putting me in that kind of group with her."

Violet Vrisser looked at her across the table, cleared and polished. It was a look carried in her head since the secret treasure trunk of Cynthia Dodgeson had been opened. A look that saw secrets of the heart.

"My dear," said Violet Barham-Vrisser gently, "I think you should lay that burden down. That pilgrim's pack of self-doubt on your back. I recruited every one of our forty girls, and I watched them train and I said good-bye to them, and when it was over, one way or another, I brought them home." The bandaged arm was stretched across the table. "You are everything we could have needed. Everything, dear Jane, your mother would have wanted. Believe it."

Believe it.

She looked down at these two hands upon the table, the hands of women that shot men's heads apart and never trembled.

The hands of women that knew so many answers. Women who had never borne children.

"No," she said. "If it wasn't an accident that Scylla got pregnant, then we're *not* the same." Because the old bastards in their bunkers would never manipulate *her* with Old Glory and Our Way. Never splay *her* on her back to conceive for the land we love, never get *her* to squat to drop a baby in an English country garden as quickly as any good or floppy bitch that hid wide-eyed behind a third world hedge as the boys went marching by. "If *I* had it, they'd never get me to just *dump* it!"

She pushed blindly from the table and its reflections past and present. Stood at the leaded window carried like the stove across the mountains. Stared through the panes at Eden planted in the wilderness. Watched the flowers blur and wobble in the uneven glass. Felt an arm around her shoulder, a kiss on the cheek, a trace of scent from flowers far away and long ago.

Violet Vrisser opened the window. Fresh air with the smells of a new day drowned out a faded past. Without the distortion of the glass the perennials in the borders stood in clear sharp lines against the backing of the grass. A bird with stilt legs and swept-back brown-white wings lifted from the grass with a cry of *keeep keeep keeep*.

"Our *dikkop*," said Violet Vrisser. "The Cape plover. Like all plovers she nests on the ground without protection.

All she can do for her young is to draw the fire, drag a wing, feign weakness. If necessary, give her life. But still she breeds. Survival of the species may be manipulation, Jane, but it's not manmade. It's the world as it is. Do you ride?"

"Ride?" Her mind was still caught in the garden, trapped with the image of a bird and its trailing wing. With the world as it is.

"Horses, dear."

"I can't do the Hyde Park up-down bit, but I can hang on."

"Yes." Violet Vrisser had made these decisions about women before. "Yes, I am sure you can."

21

For a novice and a woman with a wounded arm the ride up Inyangani was no trot on London's Rotten Row. The western side was steep, dry, outcropped with basalt from before time; the lush Eden of the eastern slope replaced with scrub wild pear and wattle. The horses made a steady upward plod, took flank-heaving pauses, hunched forward with their shoulders, and went on. Rounding a corner at the top of the steepest section yet, her horse, a brown part-Arab gelding, shied violently. An evil slither in the rocks raised a flat triangulated head.

"Horned viper," said Violet Vrisser. "Not a problem unless he's startled. Ah, good. Moses' Rock—we're almost there."

They had to be. A shoulder of the mountain, smoothed by the wind to the texture of an old duke's face, reared vertically two hundred feet and hung out into space across the trail. The horses plodded on toward a shadow line running top to bottom down the center of the face. At a hundred yards the shadow became a split just one-horse wide. She followed Violet Vrisser through. They lost the sunlight. And now the impossibly balanced rock was not smooth, but scratched. Scratched by hands of the past, crude etchings of bison and elephant pursued foxes, and strange hydraheaded human figures pursued them.

They came out of the cut in the rock to a level place the size and flatness of two tennis courts, quarried from the hill, so that it was bounded on three sides. The hunted figures pursued each other around the quarry to the mouth of a cave. Opposite the cave the open edge of the court dropped away forever. Beyond the drop, Africa stretched farther than that.

They dismounted. She helped Violet Vrisser tie a halter rope across the exit gap and released the horses to crop at thin brown grass. Their riders dumped packs and saddles on the ground, drank coffee, stared without words at the panorama before them.

Violet Vrisser finished her coffee, leaned back against her saddle, crossed her feet. "I shall be buried here, Jane. I've made it a condition of my will."

Africa, like this quarry, was a trap for wishful thinkers: Following Cecil Rhodes's example to the grave was the thing for all good "Africa hands" to do—but in an Africa free to ignore Muir's white lines on the roads who would follow the directions on an old white woman's piece of paper?

She wished Muir was here to see the view. To sit on the African grass and explain things to her. *To lie on the grass. . . .*

"Before we ran out of breath on the way up," said Violet Vrisser. "Oh, I'm sorry. Had you dozed off?"

"The altitude, I guess." She snapped in a new cassette and put the recorder in the shade of a rock. "All awake now. Go ahead."

"On the way up you were asking about Geoffrey Piers: Was he a 'spook'?"

"Right."

"Such a good word. Well, he was. As a matter of fact, we ran him as a double. The Germans had marked him as a sympathizer from Cliveden, and when he went with Windsor on the German trip after the abdication, they made overtures. 'Made' isn't quite right; 'renewed' would be better—there had been several tries while Edward was actually King. Saxe-Coburg, Windsor's second cousin was the front, but Goebbels was the orchestrator. The clever little snake—it was

Goebbels' game from the first time they pushed Wallis as a
Royal Highness—refusal to grant the HRH was the very thing
that had driven Windsor to the wall with the British Government. After that, the visits to the Dresden china factories
were gilding the lily. Windsor was already Heil Hitlering
back in the streets."

"Was he really sucked in?"

"Then, it seemed black and white that he was. Now, one
sees all the grays. I mean, there it was in front of him:
Germany reduced, to Germany resplendent, in only five
years. A whole people with a sense of purpose, health, and
vigor against what? Russia clawing at itself flat on its back.
America fighting fear with Fireside Chats, and England—
well, *look* at England! Chamberlain and the dole and all the
bills from the first war unpaid. Windsor saw Germany and
saw solutions—or at least thought he did—and who else even
had that? A single will had *done* it in Germany, why not one
man on a horse for Britain? Was he wrong? Churchill did
exactly that in war three years later."

"But Windsor must have seen the other side. The side
my mother saw. The bearded faces with the broken heads and
yellow stars?"

Violet Vrisser snapped a stalk of grass. "Mary's term-
mates at Cambridge wouldn't fight against it, nor would your
America First crowd. It was easy not to look under the
stones. And with Windsor, the thugs kept away you know.
The hard line, direct stuff all went to Piers via Ley—he was
the treasure who pushed Hitler to use nerve gas in forty-four.
Ley transmuted all Saxe-Coburg's hints of a golden future
into leaden reality. Ley, Göring, Speer, what a pack they
were! 'The animals that could talk,' Mary called them. Piers
oiled his way like a house on fire with the lot."

Violet Vrisser gave her little snorting laugh, "Actually,
the oil may have caught us Hess. The first person Hess asked
for after Winston was his 'so good friend' Piers—who would
have made a first-class reporter, Jane. He got all the meetings
and conversations down near verbatim for old Admiral Smith-
Cumming; I read it years later. There was an hilarious account
of Göring, medaled and corseted top to toe locked in an
Elizabeth Arden Massage Machine."

Close your eyes and the fat man in the white suit was
standing in the field with the horses: buttocks and belly and

gross parts jiggling in time with his medals. "But where was Piers' doubling?" she asked. "Reporting is playing things straight."

"That came a little later—and I didn't mean to pinch a nerve, dear." A small sardonic smile came and went for the integrity of reporters everywhere. "A damn good thing for him that he *did* play it straight. After the fall of France, when Canaris tried to stop things from becoming completely Wagnerian, he gave us Piers' name as one of the offerings. A very unsung hero, Canaris." The chewed stalk dropped to the ground. "But Piers muffed his chance to be a hero—that's why I find your story about the flower so extraordinary. Talking up a 'good war' for politics, I suppose."

"From the way he covered tracks, more like a guilt."

Violet Vrisser nodded slowly. "He might feel a bit of that—over Nassau. But there was no hint when I met him—"

"You sound surprised?"

"Just that I'd quite forgotten he was out here—on the first team after Labour got back in, the middle sixties. He was already playing best fella with 'my African brothers' but he still stayed at Government House—not at a hotel with the Mission. A real hare-and-hounds man all his life."

One of the horses looked up as though catching an echo of the chase. "Nassau, Vriss—the Bahamas—is that where Scylla started?"

"Started?" Violet Vrisser watched the horse scratch its face against one leg, exposing yellow teeth. "It's catching water in one's hand to say where any of these things *started*, Jane. But I think you could say that Mary's—your mother's— big run really kicked off in Washington because Mrs. Simpson, as was, had had a toothache."

"A toothache."

"Give the devil her due, an impacted wisdom tooth— and this is 1940, by the way, three years before Nassau *and* before SOE was really off the ground so I'm fitting part of the puzzle by hindsight—but it was the first sign since he left Lisbon that they were still after Windsor's heart and mind."

"The Germans?"

"Yes. No doubt it was partly just to stir the pot. I'm sure the Abwehr knew there was a tremendous amount of Whitehall backbiting because Windsor was visiting the United States at all. After he saw Roosevelt in *private*—well! Halifax was packed off as ambassador *bang!*" Violet Vrisser slapped a saddle blanket. A cloud of dust exploded.

"The Duke wanted the job?"

"The man wanted *anything* except to be stuck in the back of beyond, but he couldn't stay in Washington as a 'guest after the wedding,' and the Duchess recovering from her dental operation wouldn't go near Government House while it was being redone, so they both leaped at the chance to delay the return with a sea voyage."

"Wenner-Gren's *Southern Cross?*"

"Is this old hat?"

"I did some research into the Harry Oakes case."

"Did you?" Violet Vrisser gave a shrewd look. "Then you know that Oakes was on his way back with them? No? Well he was. He'd been looking at his uranium mine—a place called Pitchblende. And uniquely important because it was the only mine we had. Piers' report of Wenner-Gren's immediate interest in *that* subject is what rang the bells in London. The Swede was considered totally amoral about anything that even sniffed of armaments."

Piers again. Round and round the garden with all the king's men. All the ex-king's men.

"You're saying the British Government had the Duke of Windsor under close surveillance through Piers?"

Violet Vrisser had picked another piece of grass and stroked it gently across the leather of the saddle. "It sounds Shakespearean and War of the Roses, Jane, but Fifth Column was on everyone's mind. And you must remember that the monarch is privy to a great deal of the secret world—the Intelligence world—from the choice of its Chief—"

"I didn't know that!"

"Government prefers these things to remain in the shade, dear—but if you think about it, there has to be a court of last resort, doesn't there? In case a bad apple gets to the top of the political side of the tree. And the monarch, as in the present case, by simply being there, by seeing prime ministers in and prime ministers out—Well after a while damn few secrets are hidden, I should say."

"But Edward wasn't around long enough to pick up much, was he?"

Violet Vrisser shrugged. "Who knows? Those were delicate times. Certainly Wenner-Gren's third officer made no bones at all about making contact. Mind you, a Swede could do that—pass along the Nazis' hope that Piers would ask the Duke to keep in touch, see things from both sides, remind Winston Churchill and King George that Bolshevism was the real enemy—month after month like dripping water but all pretty harmless stuff."

"What stopped it being harmless?"

"New Year's Day 1943. The Swede came up to Piers on the Princess Golf Course—Freeport—and asked point-blank whether the Duke approved of programs that breached the Geneva Convention. Programs called Manhattan and Chicago!"

"*Jesus!*"

"Exactly. The sky fell in. Arthur Compton and Fermi had just done their chain reaction thing on the football field in Chicago—I remember that vividly because Churchill put on the memo: 'What a marvellous Xmas present.'

"Which seems horribly ironic now, but what choice did we have? None. Only to go full steam with Tube Alloys–Manhattan and try to make Hitler believe in his guts that the whole atom thing was useless. You can't get from hindsight, Jane, how hopeless it looked and how terrified we were, but to us Stalingrad and Alamein seemed only nibbles at the Beanstalk. The Nazi war machine was still the giant. We *knew* they had the rockets and heavy water. It appeared absolutely inevitable that they'd pull the whole lot back from Norway inside Fortress Europe, mobilize full-strength—which they never had by our standards—and having poured all their resources of slave labor into some underground fastness come bursting out with the bomb stuck on a V2 like a head on a pike."

Like the heads of martyrs stuck carnivorously on a frieze in a Christian church in London: Deterrence, then and now.

"We had to counter it. The round robin in LCS went on for days! The art of the first move—deny, confirm, deny *to* confirm—was arcane, but the facts were crystal. Despite all our frontal assaults on the installations at Norsk they were still going ahead with heavy water, and they still had Bohr, the man who knew about it, in the net in Denmark. And every dambusting effort we made to get at either, simply reinforced the Germans' sense of their value. We finally threw it back to the boffins—the scientists—on your side, in

America: Einstein, Oppenheimer, Teller, Szilard—all the funny
names that became household words. Their answer was that
we could live with Jerry drinking heavy water but we *had* to
have the stuff in Bohr's head.

"So it was one of those things where you twist a strip of
paper and get an endless loop: If we grab Bohr, it shows that
he must have something to say—but we must grab Bohr. And
then John Bevan's Second in Command—usually rather a dry
old stick—said very quietly, 'The jewels are always paste.'
And we all looked at him and he said, 'In Victorian detective
yarns, after the villains nab the jewels they always leave a set
of paste. Scotland Yard and the owners never know. We
should get Bohr, but discredit his work. There must be a
weak link.'

"He was right. There always is. And the weak link in the
bomb was the trigger mechanism—getting the two halves of
the uranium orange like *that!*" Violet Vrisser clapped her
hands violently together. "But the weak link with the *Germans* was Hitler's mind, because we knew that all really
major Intelligence evaluations went to him for final judgment. After that, it was a witches' brew: flashes of genius,
intuition, astrology—"

"Old Shilling and his feathers."

Violet Vrisser smiled. "The trick in any magic, Jane dear,
is arranging the feathers in the right circle. For this operation
we called the circle "Sugar Candy,' and it was in three parts:
first, feed information revealing a fundamental flaw with the
bomb's construction; second, grab Bohr; third, replace him
with fudged papers."

"Authentic 'fudging' would be the toughest part, I guess?"

Violet Vrisser shook her head. "In 1943, both sides were
predisposed to failure—the scientists were satisfied about
dotting the technical i's convincingly. It was the psychology
wizards' bit that was tricky—the mind-to-mind stuff. They
started from the premise that Hitler was moth to a flame for
one-man bands and magic names—that in geopolitics he saw
only individuals, that he put all his trust in princes."

"Kissinger's life story."

"Granted—but Washington's decisions are made only
after almost interminable conferences and group discussions.
With Hitler it really *was* as quick as grabbing a feather on the
wind—it's all in Langer's work: When Hitler thought England,

it was Churchill; Italy, Il Duce—and if there was a touch of Jew in the association the fascination was fatal.

"Well, with that, we really didn't even have to think: An Einstein letter to Roosevelt began the bomb, another letter could seem to end it. The *crucial* question was how and where did we let the information out? Because to believe such a letter Hitler had to have it in his hands, had to imagine to himself an old Jew writing it, signing it. Had to visualize his other hated 'near Jew' in the White House reading it. The process had to happen. But there was no chance whatever that the Abwehr or the SD would buy a document fed directly from London or Washington—Canaris and Himmler knew our home spy net was shut tight. Nor was it feasible to wash a second Floating Major up on a beach as we had for the Torch landings in North Africa—an Einstein letter would never go to a theater commander. The problem began to seem insuperable."

"Or time for the inevitable breakthrough."

Violet Vrisser nodded. "But isn't it odd how it always takes that last *excruciating* inch to squeeze it out? In this case Wheatley had taken the Langer work home to read it again, and in the morning he tossed it on the table by the Faun and said, 'Trust in the princes—feed the letter through Windsor'. And it was exactly right—because Hitler did still trust Windsor. Did still believe that the British Government would drag the man back to London if brother George and the princesses disappeared under the rubble—and by God," said Violet Vrisser, "with nine hits on the Palace they almost *did* disappear. Hitler's madness was never without method."

Method in the madness. What could seem more methodical, more plausible to Hitler than for Churchill—staunch supporter of Edward through the abdication—to brief a king-in-waiting by dropping the Einstein letter on a plate in the Bahamas, where a neutral Swede could pick it up and run it home?

"A while back, you mentioned the Wars of the Roses, Vriss. Was Edward the Red Rose?"

"You have done your digging." Violet Vrisser wore her appraising look again. "We had names for all of them, and yes, Windsor was red. His brother, the new King, naturally had to be White."

"Naturally?"

"He'd been the Duke of York, dear." Which was apparently sufficient historic explanation. "So—all we needed now for this Bahamas run was our courier. The choice of your mother for royal courier was the wizards' crowning touch."

The wizards who thirty years before MacLuhan knew that the *person* of the messenger—female, Aryan, aristocrat, like the silver pheasants once touched by the very hand of Adolf Hitler—was in his eyes, the message itself. Not the actuality of a letter sent from Washington to Nassau on the day following Fadiman's last fireworks holiday at home: the fifth of July.

"We thought for a bad moment that Lisbon had got wind—a sabotage threat stuck Mary in Bermuda for half a day—but she eventually got through to Oakes Field, where Piers met her. A cool moment, I imagine, because we hadn't told her he was on the team and she'd once turned him down flat for his pro-Nazi—"

"I asked him that straight out. *He denied proposing!*"

"I can't imagine why," said Violet Vrisser. "It was common knowledge in our set after the 1937 tour. The male ego's slow to heal I suppose—because there was more than politics in her rejection."

"I wondered if he was gay?"

"Jolly enough at a party—"

"I mean homosexual."

"Oh, *queer*! Possibly—most of the male courtiers are, you know. Victoria brought that in after an episode with one of her daughters. But how can one say? God knows, he was sleek. 'A lounge lizard for Craven A and Brylcreem,' Mary called him. 'A very little dab is too damn much.' But the Duke doted. You can understand it. After all, Piers and Gray Phillips—the senior equerry—were the only links left from the old days at Court and the weekends at Belvedere. And unlike Hitler, they remembered all the punch lines of the society jokes; they knew all the names and the dirt on the politicians and the generals. If the Duke couldn't talk to them, who else was there?" Violet Vrisser considered her own question. "Mary must have brought back a bit of those days with her."

"How about the Duchess in all this?"

"Her gracious charming self—with that delicate trace of 'slit your gizzard if you get too near, *dear*,' as Mary went in to show the Duke the letter." Violet Vrisser laughed, not kindly. "Windsor's reaction to Einstein's news and signature was typically profound: 'Damned dons,' he said to Piers, 'can't make the damned thing *pop!*' As though it was a chemistry stink gone wrong—but then he had second thoughts on the real implications. 'Damn bloody Oakes,' he said. 'My shares will come an *awful* cropper, Geoffie.'

"And that," said Violet Vrisser, "was when Piers began to turn the horse. Tons of sympathy for Master, and an extra ultradry martini, but 'fair play on the field, sir. Old Harry will be smashed much worse, sir. Pity one couldn't drop a word, sir . . .'"

A beetle with brilliant coral carapace had landed on the saddle pack. A lizard with humped shoulders materialized from grass and air; a thin black lariat of tongue whipped out; the lizard rolled one eye. The African late afternoon slept on.

"One must *be* fair," continued Violet Vrisser. "The last thing Windsor could have imagined out of all this was violent death. Nor did Mary. The final mechanics of making contact with the other side are always tricky, but having Piers pass the good word to Oakes would seem the perfectly natural move to Berlin."

Helping an old friend profit from national adversity. What top Nazi wouldn't instantly buy that?

"Piers told Mary he had set up the letter drop in Windsor's yacht, the *Gemini*. She'd been squeezed out of an active life by the fuel shortage—like my poor aircraft—and was parked alongside the Front Street seawall as a very private floating bar."

With only a quartermaster-nightwatchman left on board this Hollywood set waiting for its Mata Hari and the pieces of the puzzle to fit. A puzzle which she was now sure had been assembled under the hand of Wheatley, writer of yarns, of *Murder Off Miami* that revolved around a yacht; a hammered, bashed-in head; a pair of Florida detectives and a host of clues meticulously crafted to take the flat feet in the wrong direction.

"The plot for Mary—or nowadays," said Violet Vrisser, "I suppose you'd call it 'the scenario'—was straightforward. Piers removes the quartermaster. With our Guy Fawkes handbag we go girlishly aboard—"

"Guy Fawkes what?"

"The courier's satchel. It was chained to the wrist and rather sensitively wired up with amatol."

"She was 'girlishly' wired to a bomb?"

"One gets used to these things, dear. So—we go aboard with Harry. We have a drink. Have two. Giggle a little. We mention the letter—*in strictest confidence*—to Harry. Have another drink, receive compliments about our beauty. We weaken and let Harry *see* the letter with the great man's signature—"

"Let Harry take a picture of it?"

Violet Vrisser nodded. "With help from Piers. Who got the quartermaster ashore all right, but then there was a snag—in the most literal sense. Oakes had already been boozing some RAF grass widows at Westbourne and when he got down to the seawall he tried to climb on the wrong ship—*Southern Cross* was tied up in front—and he caught his trousers on the gangway. All very sordid and drunken. Give Piers credit—he jumped right into his royal-flunky act, said he'd stay to smooth things over with the Swedes, if Oakes's pal Christie would sort Harry out and deliver him safely to the right address."

And then drive off, leaving a pissed old toad son of a bitch with his hopes up and his pants half down with Scylla, her mother, Lady Mary Dexter.

"One has to feel *some* sympathy for the man, Jane. Alone with a damned attractive, apparently half-stewed young woman. Wife and kiddies on Cape Cod. Saloon doors to a private deck of a Royal yacht. For a brief moment of the tropic night Harry Oakes must have been Bogart in Casablanca—and tip or no tip, his damned uranium shares *were* going to come an awful cropper in the morning. Good heavens!" Violet Vrisser looked suddenly at the sky. "I've almost left it too late! Leave the packs, Jane. *Quickly now!*"

Without wings where was there to go? But Violet Vrisser's march across the grass toward the cave was not haphazard. Nor, she now realized, was the placement of the pair of giant mammoths on guard beside it, etched heads up, ears flapped back, tusks touching above the arch. Nor were the rocks, at first sight seemingly dropped beside the entrance as the earth shrugged in its sleep. There was an imposed order in the animal figures, in the massive blocks, in the great slabs of slate placed as steps between them.

The steps led upward through a herringbone stone wall familiar from postcards of Zimbabwe. Violet Vrisser stood at the top.

"*Hurry, Jane!*"

She jumped the last three steps. Behind the herringbone wall there seemed to be a platform on a fill of rubble. The thin sound of water fell in the dark.

"Face outward!" She turned back to the light. "Now wait," said Violet Vrisser. "Just wait!"

The blue mouth of the cave grew paler, whiter, brighter. Unbearably bright. Became, even through sunglasses, impossible to view.

"*Turn!*"

The eyes on the walls behind them were liquid amber, skins rich deep-brown, hooves a gleaming polished black. Wounds bleeding scarlet. These animals were *alive*, racing undimmed across the barrier of time to escape the hunting figures with the spears. Odd, angular, leaping figures old beyond belief, but men. The figures of men. The animals escaping from the spears raced into the arms of a shape beside a pool. The sun moved its light farther up the wall. The shape became a goddess kneeling, ten feet high, with a two-foot head sweeping in concave planes to a long and graceful neck. The belly and breasts beneath the neck were swollen, fecund. A ring of gray rocks sat on the floor of the cave, circling the goddess. The sun moved again. The rocks became men's skulls. Row upon row, upon row of skulls.

"My God," she said. "My God."

"There are more," said Violet Vrisser. "The platform is built on them and I've found pieces in the ground outside— Lord knows how old they are! Leakey wanted all his life to see this place, but I couldn't bear to think of it dug up and torn apart."

The spirits from the skulls neither approved nor disapproved. They waited. The sense of their waiting made the ghosts of five centuries in a Dorset abbey, of a millennium at Westminster, flicker as a page in your Domesday Book.

Sunset. The light went out. The animals retreated to

prehistory. The skulls became as dark as Africa beyond the cliff, as dark as the void itself.

Violet Vrisser touched a match to kindling in a depression of the platform. When light was ordered from the darkness had it flickered here? How many flickerings had there been, how many fires? And who, or what, sat round them?

Not Violet Vrisser's late husband. "James thought the place barbaric. He's with his people in Saint Mary's Cathedral in Salisbury. I'm afraid I think bones are bones. Ah, good, that's going. Would you mind?"

She helped fetch a canteen kit, frying pan, and food from a pack; hung water from the pool in a pot on a spit across the flame.

"Thank you, dear, I can manage now. Where were we?"

Against this backdrop, events in the Bahamas faded from significance as swiftly as the colors on the walls.

"Oakes was playing Bogart."

"Oh yes. Oakes. He was loathsome and crude but he had that *something* that excites women, that indecipherable component of the self-made man—like Beaverbrook. Like your Kennedy woman's Greek." "Greek" had a ring to it that Violet Vrisser never used on her Africans. "And it's always the most unlikely Bogarts who try to be the heroes."

Violet Vrisser stirred a pancake mixture with her good hand and remembered more of those heroic times. "Mary had got herself safely through the first round of drinks but the atmosphere was difficult, because the last thing Oakes needed was more fuel, and Piers—who should have been with her to make three a crowd with his witty banter—was still stuck next door with the Swedes. And then the show went off the rails. Mary said the opposition was extraordinarily quick. One moment she just had Oakes to worry about, slobbering on her arm—the next, two of Berlin's boys in black rubber suits were dripping salt water on the carpet."

"Nazis!—"

"I very much doubt they were Germans, dear. War or peace, the Caribbean always has talented nasty people ready to work for the high bid. And this pair had talent. The Guy Fawkes couldn't be torn off without an awful mess, so they simply went straight to work on *Oakes*—with the first tool at hand: the flame of the cabin table lighter, one of those things with the fluid under pressure."

"Christ."

"Yes. Not a nice spot. But I'm afraid that the torture of third parties is generally effective in producing the results. For Mary it must have been particularly horrible. Here she'd been given the answer to our prayers—some hoods that actually want nothing more from life than to deliver our bogus bloody letter to the Reich Chancellery by *hand*—but how is she to let them have it? *When* is she to let them have it? Too soon? Not genuine. Too long? —Well how long *can* you watch an old man being grilled like that?"

How long can you watch a little girl run down a napalmed track with her skin in tarred knot strips. How do you help her? How do you touch her?

"I don't know," she said.

"I don't either, Jane. But somehow your mother drew a line and the hoods accepted it. She deactivated the circuit, unlocked the chain, passed the Guy Fawkes over. There was no more nonsense. Not with professionals. They took the bag and started back for the ship's side, and then he went for them—"

"Oakes?"

"Poor dumb, maddened Oakes." Violet Vrisser sighed. "Who was *not* professional, but quite brave. They put him down hard—against a grappling anchor."

An anchor with four prongs to make four holes, and after that all the ex-king's horses couldn't put Harry Oakes or his Humpty-Dumpty shares back on the Big Board. Nor could the ex-king's man.

"Did Piers finally show up?" she asked.

"In time to catch the fading sound of a launch roaring through the night to any one of seven hundred outer islands. Mary would have been better off without him. He saw the blood, and the body, and he came apart. The very opposite of Oakes's reaction. That's one of the troubles on a first-time run—you never know how people will play if it's bad."

"But it fits, right?"

"Fits, Jane?"

"Isn't there a pattern—with all these instant denials? The flower, the proposal? Any threat against the outer image of his robes and seals and the guy crumples."

"Perhaps." Violet Vrisser thought about it. "Perhaps. Mind you, he's much older now, and at the top of the legal tree he has to be supercareful on the human side—so many judges caught in brothels or lace corsets in the last few years. I must admit that afterward, when I heard, I wasn't really surprised that he crumpled, as you put it, but for Mary, faced with the housekeeping, it really *was* unfair. Oakes dead—or as close as she could tell—no pulse, and these really horrible holes in the head. And now Piers trying to be sick— Ah, good, the first one's done. If you'll just hold the pan again?"

Violet Vrisser left the war long enough to roll a thin pancake expertly into a tube, sprinkle it with lemon juice and coarse brown sugar and place it on an enameled plate. "If I do say so, not too bad for one hand."

"Incredible! But the story, this whole place is incredible. You really stay up here *alone?*"

"The first time was difficult—a test of a sort, like one's first jump. But it seemed absurd to allow them," indicating the darkness behind her, "to exert a living force. You'll laugh, Jane, but I was actually more leery of bats."

In the presence of the skulls and the ghost of Harry Oakes, she felt no urge to laugh. The stone goddess staring at her, as she ate a delicate crêpe in this hole in the rocks, obviously never had.

"This coincidence with Piers," she said. "You didn't query his timing? Maybe he was doing some 'doubling' on his own? Maybe he set the Germans up?"

"In war all things are possible, Jane, but in the immediate aftermath, all one's attention was on Mary. I mean, the hounds had run her into a hell of a spot—where could she possibly go to ground?"

If an answer was expected she didn't have it. In these barbaric surroundings this old woman's spontaneous *Country Life* allusion to a pink-coated, view-holloing, county hunt cantering after the corpse of Harry Oakes was too grotesque for words.

"Government House!" said Violet Vrisser, responding to herself. "And when Mary told Piers that, he really did vomit! But she was absolutely right: the grounds were sewn tight by the Highlanders; the communication link was there for traffic to Whitehall; an army surgeon could check on Oakes. And God bless her, she did it! Got Piers to drag Christie back in from Westbourne with his car—a wagon like the Willys—to get Oakes loaded, and one-fifteen Bahamas time, they set off. Down Front Street, across Dawson Square—and then, just as she thought she could breathe, the net damn near split wide open: Erskine-Lindop, the district commissioner, recognized the car and wanted a chin wag."

Violet Vrisser poured strong tea into two mugs. "Mary bluffed him through. Smiles and pats and 'all these awful chaps, Commissioner, are half seas over,' and she had them past the gates and tossed the thing across to us. The message came through on a one-time pad with *Flash* precedence at five in the morning, Greenwich time—hand in hand with Flag Office West Indies' signal that *Southern Cross* had cleared Nassau Boom Control for Bimini. She actually ran straight for Kiel. We brought Piers and Mary out together in a Sunderland an hour later."

And left the rest of the "housekeeping" to Jael, to "our way"—to Whatley's way—of doing things.

" 'We'll have to complete it so that it appears bizarre,' Wheatley said. And *I* said, '*Bizarre*, Dennis! For the love of God, it's bizarre enough!' And he said, 'It's Caribbean, Vi. We should tie the burns into voodoo ritual, more evidence of fire, chicken heads—the Camerons' Specials can run that for us.'

"I remember, all the clocks up on the wall for the different war zones ticked for rather a long time after that, and then John Bevan said, 'Well, as long as the man's *dead*.' Which really didn't help, because no one was absolutely certain that he *was*—yet—and if he wasn't . . ."

The blank eyes of the skulls dismissed that alternative with the shrug of Violet Vrisser's shadow.

She stood up and walked to the entrance. The stars flickered with a Bahamian tropical brilliance. One of the horses still cropped quietly at the grass. She turned back into the cave. Violet Vrisser sat beside the fire, eating. Behind Violet Vrisser, the stomach and thighs of the goddess reflected the fire with dull gloss. The skulls' eyes reflected nothing.

"And you people *sat* there, and put an innocent son of a bitch on trial for his *life*, and you didn't feel a fucking *thing*?"

A soft hollow puffing sound of air as though all the skulls were laughing. And then the thin sound of an African voice crying in the wilderness.

"*Inkosikazi!*"

"Oh dear," said Violet Vrisser very quietly.

"*Inkosikazi. Inkosikazi Vriss.*" The horses neighed back the panic in the call. Hooves hit against rock. Blackly silhouetted by her fire Violet Vrisser moved to face the outside world.

"*Mukati mhako, Sixpence Hwata?*"

A second silhouette, slim, African, terrified by everything in the night, came out of it. A boy's breath puffed short white clouds like the steam from the pot over the fire. Like the laugh of a skull.

"*Jonathan tambira, Inkosikazi! Jonathan futa!*"

22

The horses, more terrified even than the messenger of shadows innumerable and perhaps deadly, lurched downhill. There was no moon. The wind gusted with increasing strength from the southeast. "*Guti* weather," said Violet Vrisser. "Can that Jap watch of yours see in the dark, Jane?"

She pressed the small button on the side. "Ten-thirty. What does the kid mean, Jonathan's gone? Over the border?"

"Never!" But under its conviction Violet Vrisser's voice knew more of African alternatives than it would say.

You tell me your atrocity, I'll tell you mine....

With each foot of lower altitude the bush thickened invisibly around them. Night noises screamed and shrieked in agony and triumph. Every nerve end in her neck shrieked back. Imagined vipers the size of pythons dropped from trees, fanged mouths tore guts. The damp air carried a vague smell of rot. A branch crashed across the path in front of them sending Sixpence Hwata's horse rearing. Its eyes were white even by starlight. So were Sixpence Hwata's.

"Brave boy." Violet Vrisser patted the shoulder of both horse and rider and moved to take the lead. "It took immense courage for Sixpence to find us. My Africans won't normally touch the cave even in daylight." A brief flare of the flashlight showed a division in the path at a huge baobab with Popeye arms, pointed out that morning on the fringes of the coffee plantings. Its thousand years of growth had made it ancient then. Now, against the age of skulls, it was a sapling. The horses bent to the right. The wind drooped. Silence. An unnatural silence. No lights showed from the village houses. Swapped pictures of man-to-man obscenity beat out natural night-fears of the forest. She forced her mind to keep the red Agricalert button beside the glass eyes in the house as a beacon.

The horse's neck had straightened. She was no longer leaning back away from its shoulders. The path was level and the night smelled safe with nicotiana from the garden. Sixpence Hwata vanished with the horses through the gate into the stable yard. A chink of light showed from the kitchen window. Inside the kitchen a Kapisa with worried face broke into a huge grin and rushed mugs of steaming chocolate at them.

Violet Vrisser, who should have been wiped flat with exhaustion, smiled, said, "Telephone first, Kapisa," and lifted the receiver in the hall. A clock ticked. Tocked. Brought back the comfort of Leofric's office. Violet Vrisser hung up the phone. The small red eye of the Alert was dead. "The lines are gone, Jane."

Go for the communications ... and close the shop ...

Muir's words. And now, with an irrational speed that overwhelmed her, she knew she *wanted* Muir. And wanted to get out of Africa, get out of the news world, out of real life—and unreal deaths. Wanted to retire with a virtual stranger to a Walden Pond in Maine and raise his children and bake him bread organically with the ecology freaks.

Had she left it all too late?

A distant boom sounded in the valley. "Thunder?" The old Africa hand showed surprise. "That's unusual for May."

The useless knowledge acquired in ten years' search for truth behind the lines enabled her to say, "It's a mortar, Vriss. Eighty-one millimeter."

A flash of manmade lightning struck the giant mahogany and lit the flowers in the garden. Kapisa dropped Violet Vrisser's mug of chocolate on the floor.

The windows were shuttered and barred on the inside. The front door, cut in half, Dutch-fashion and made of ironwood three inches thick held with heavy, drop-forged bolts, should stop a rebel AK47. Two automatic FN rifles provided by the army were ready to respond. In the hall behind them, Kapisa had filled saucepans, tubs, crocks, anything that would hold water. Kapisa could barely hold his own. His eyes looked with constant longing at the way of last resort: a wine cellar built into the hill behind the house.

"Thank God for my grandfather's expensive tastes," said Violet Vrissér. "The Terrs are awfully slow, Jane. Would they have to be on this side of the river to hit the tree?"

"I think so. Maybe they've jammed the tube."

"God willing! The army certainly doesn't have a high opinion. I'm afraid we shall soon see." A long sigh. Sitting in her chair with the lion's head arms and lion's paw feet, waiting for tomorrow's Africa behind her ironwood door, Violet Vrisser was only another immobile animal shadow in her darkened hall. The clock ticked.

"It might pass the time to talk, Vriss."

"Can you work your machine in this blackout?"

"It's on battery."

Another long pause. "Blackout. How that takes one back. Everything in war is so incongruous."

"It describes my parents."

"Jane, dear, you do put an *edge* on things. Incongruous surely means mismatched, out of keeping. They weren't out of keeping one bit! Mary needed his laconic, calm view of life. I liked him enormously—although I was astonished that he was a lawyer, he was much more like a planter, someone used to the seasons and taking his movements from them. But my goodness, couldn't he move when he wanted—when he'd fixed his mind! Of course, time changes shape under pressure—isn't that what Einstein said?—but they'd only been together five days!"

"This is the trip through France after the collapse?"

"Yes."

"I guess there were no letters from Hitler that time?"

Violet Vrisser gave a small snort of a laugh. "With her handbag stuffed full of the Château Vignolle crypto wheels? Oh no. There were no more gifts from Hitler." But once again, she sensed there was a hole, something missing, something left unsaid. Violet Vrisser closed it over.

"I met your father for the first time when they got back from France—and wasn't that a saga!"

"Catching the last boat out."

"If you know it, you mustn't let an old woman ramble."

"Vriss, that's *all* I know!"

"I see. Well the point was that they didn't catch it. They'd been waiting in Brittany to come off—in a ship driven by Mountbatten, of all people. Not his immortal *Kelly*, she was in drydock being sewn up, but the Admiralty had lent him another destroyer in the meantime—I forget, some sort of weapon name. Only a footnote anyway, because that one got torpedoed under him as well on the run in."

"While my parents were still on the beach?"

"Oh yes. Stukas screaming down, roiling smoke, all the Pathé news-film stuff. But if one was *there*—" The mechanical note dropped out of the storytelling. "With the refugees and the blood on the shingle and the wind getting up for one of those vicious June blows that almost scuppered us on D day. And no way home . . . well, the hind-sighters can say what they like, Jane, but the Dunkirks didn't *have* to go in our favor. I think there is a god of battles—and your mother knew it! Because in all that mess your father found them a fishing smack—"

"And her god of battles brought them through the storm."

"You're quite right," but Violet Vrisser's tone was not one of acceptance. "Our generation can't have an *Iliad*. All our sagas have become clichés . . . but when the naval people went down to meet the boat in Plymouth, they were gaga with admiration for your father."

"He loved to sail."

And yet in all those Poynter's Corners Sundays in Jane's Fancy out at sea; all those "gaga" father-daughter hours of instruction, of companionship, of mugs of hot chocolate just like these; in all the hours never a hint of Drake and Plymouth Ho. Of another woman in the crew.

"Plymouth had been terribly battered by Göring but I'd squeezed rooms for your parents at a pub and we went along, and in one of those odd meetings that seemed to happen so often in those first two *bad* years, Mountbatten was there at the same time—after this torpedoing fiasco. Feeling it pretty hard, because the talk and the envy—his German-background nonsense—was still very close to the surface. And he did show a lot of color, even as only a four-ring Captain—where he was convinced he'd stick forever."

"And you told him to deep-six his pack of self-doubt."

Violet Vrisser's laugh rolled the glass eyes in their plaster sockets. "I did *not*! Mary might have, because to her, through Edward and Belvedere, at that time he was still Dickie—not Lord Louis, the god with Burma and royal matchmaking under his jeweled belt. So there we sat. With the gale howling through bombed-out Plymouth, your mother and Dexter high as kites after clearing the wall, Mountbatten staring at the coal fire and seeing two ships lost and a father kicked out in the first war, and me, in my FANY suit, somewhere in the middle. Emotionally as well.

"Mary began to talk about the trip and Mountbatten liked that—he always gobbled up these commando special-ops things—and we got through a couple of bottles of this wine they'd brought back, and then they said with luck they were going to get married. And I know I thought, *Crikey!* because her mother, your grandmother, was very heavy on the class game rules. And the wind blew, rather like tonight, and Mountbatten looked at his glass, and the fire, and them, and he said, 'Don't wait for luck to be your anchor. Luck can come and it may hold for you for a lifetime, or it may break out and let go in an instant, we never know. We never know!' And then he stood up and flashed that incredible smile that went with the rake of the cap and said to the two of them, '*This* is your instant, people. Don't wait for all the trimmings at Saint Margaret's—you bloody *do* it!' And they did, at the registry office in Marylebone with me and your uncle to witness it."

Mary and I were rather close. . . .

She could hear the Harrovian voice, see the long face behind the desk with the carriage clock ticking as this clock ticked behind her now in a black passage half a world apart.

"Leofric said my parents were happy, Vriss."

"Happy?" The shade of Violet Vrisser considered the word. "I can only tell you that Mary was lit up when she was with your father. That everything was heightened as though she'd touched one of those electrical fun-fair things with all the volts that make your hair stand straight out and you think you're breathing and burning like a flame in pure oxygen. . . ."

Until the flame was snuffed. *Zapped*. Transposed by a bullet in the neck from a clear white light to a jack-o'-lantern skull with two black holes for eyes.

"Did my father read your report?"

"I gave it to him."

Violet Vrisser's head made an impression of movement in the dark. "With her Cross, and her ribbon, and citation. I collected them myself from the other George—the one who stuttered." Violet Vrisser's sigh was very tired, very old. "I'm afraid your father wouldn't see me."

"Why?"

Ticktock, ticktock, marking time that changes under pressure.

"*Why, Vriss?*"

"In the cave, Jane, you asked me another question— whether we felt guilt for letting de Marigny stand trial for Oakes's death when he was innocent."

"I don't—"

"See a relationship? No, I suppose not. But on our wall at the head of the round table we had a plaque—a tract—like one of those 'Pray with me and bless this house' things, all roses and folded hands. But ours was harsher. It was a quotation from the front of the *Soldier's Pocketbook for Field Service*, and written by Garnet Wolseley, then C in C. Wolseley said,"—and once more Violet Vrisser's voice had the dryness and emotion of dust—"he said, 'We—the British— will keep hammering along with the conviction that honesty is the best policy, that truth always wins in the long run.' And then Wolseley added, 'These pretty sentiments do well for a child's copy book, but the man who acts on them had better sheathe his sword forever.' Your father, Jane, had read the plaque. He refused to believe a word I said."

Behind them, Kapisa shuffled in the dark and hit a bowl. The pad of his feet flopped in spilled water. The wind, tired of listening outside the house, rose again, stronger than before, and bit angrily at the thatch.

"When you ask your questions, Jane, especially in Britain, remember, as you're waiting for the answers, that while the people and the organizations change, the plaque and the spirit of Jael are still there; that like Christopher Robin's bears they're still waiting too under the pavements of Whitehall. Waiting for anyone to step on the lines, and not the squares. Jane, dear, are you quite, quite sure you want me to tell you the rest of circle *Sugar Candy?*"

"Yes," she said, "tell me the rest."

The wind, cynical as her father, drew in its breath.

"Very well. The counterfeit Einstein letter on the bomb's weak link was in Berlin—by mid-September all our Intelligence signs read that. Repairs in the Norsk heavy-water plant at Rjukan had been halted for six weeks. The project leaders from Norway, and the Collège de France in Paris, and the experimental pile at Hechingen near Stuttgart had been hauled back to Berlin for a conference. All their top atom people were in on it: men like Diebner and Bothe—I'm afraid I forget the other names—"

"Your memory's unreal!"

"There had to be *some* reason for LCS taking on a woman, dear," Violet Vrisser said dryly. "We were told to play the Bohr business for the first week in October. There were to be two runs. The first would get Bohr from Denmark via Sweden into Britain. The second run, Mary's run, would drop our boffins' fudged notes in Bohr's laboratory.... I remember she came down from London in the Austin, and after she'd done her costume change to make her one of the crowd in Denmark—and *I'd* done my doublecheck for any tickets to the Palladium left over in the pockets, and *she'd* put on her Guy Fawkes bag—we still had half an hour to kill. Rather a difficult half hour. Just time for some tea, I think I said...."

A lady's time for a trace of never-never land to block the reality of a purse of high-explosive on a lady's wrist.

"Mary joked about Piers' reaction to the bag—"

"*Piers?* He was in on this part *too?*"

"Just a paper watchdog. After Nassau he fell into his proper niche in Whitehall. With anything politically sensitive the mandarins insisted on having a dog of their own along until the documents got off the ground. I wish you could have seen Mary do Piers on the drive down—the tip of the head, the cigarette, but every second watching this amatol sack of snakes on the seat between them. We *laughed....*"

Laughed like two girls without cares in the world. *Laughed until the boys were ready with the moonflight on the field.*

"We walked the Guy Fawkes out to the aircraft together, and I helped her up and she said, 'Watch my proper handbag for me, Vi—just till I get back.' I probably managed something clever in reply—I hadn't found the snapshot yet—and then I closed the plywood door and watched the matchstick Lysander, pitch-black, take her out and all I could think was, my feet are freezing in these heavy bloody socks and she can't even go with *stockings*. I felt—well I can't tell you how I felt, but it was your own gut churning and dragging and bouncing across that grass and lurching through the air. 'It would be funny, Vi,' she used to say, 'if I didn't hit it *every* time! And if my damned stomach didn't ache so much,' because something the men never even imagined, Jane, was that the moon dictated the time of the month for more than just the flights." Violet Vrisser switched abruptly to a professional point of interest. "Would the Pill have helped us there?"

"It trades one anxiety for another—it doesn't fix the mood swings." Her own mood was a mixture she could not define; nor her true feelings for the woman in the aircraft or this one on the ground. "Were these jumps always in the dark?" she asked.

"No. In the early days going to France we went blacked-out because we were afraid moonlight would give aid and comfort to the enemy, but our losses were too high. And anyway, we found that, like the Africans, the Germans weren't good at night. Night belonged to the Resistance. It was simply damnable bad luck that Mary's drop happened to coincide with the SS's abortive roundup of the Danish Jews. Old King Christian-Frederick had stood Himmler off so well for so long. . . ."

A moment of silence for the singular courage of the Danes.

"But we should still have been all right, because Bohr worked from his home in the country, one of those typically Hanseatic cottages—and Rozental, Bohr's right hand, had already got the original of the papers from the old boy before he left for Sweden. Like a man shooting his best dog, Rozental said, Bohr giving up those pages! Although I'd bet a fiver he forgot it a minute later. Bohr was the original absent-minded—"

Only half her senses noticed that Violet Vrisser had stopped talking.

Because when the night snakes slithered from the trees of her subconscious, this was the noise they made. This sound of heavy sacks dragging on the ground, one coil pulling another up behind it, pausing, dragging again, the gravel of the drive cracking and scattering. Then nothing. The coils had found the softly slippery comfort of the grass beside the house.

Thump.

"Jane, take the automatic!"

She swung open the two small shutters, lay on her stomach, her eyes level with the narrow oblong window to the right of the door. Violet Vrisser sat in her lion chair, the barrels of her shotgun tight against the diamond panes of the glass on the left.

Thump.

The second step of the veranda. Four more to go. She fitted the butt of the FN rifle against her shoulder, rested the barrel on the ledge, slid back the arming lever. The veranda was marginally grayer than the blackness of the hall.

Thump.

What would happen to the leaded glass when the guns exploded? How did you jump to the void of a black night? How did you live with the word *Gestapo*?

A sound now from the veranda to which she knew the answer. Breath and blood. At the lower pane, level with her eyes, some essence of horror gleamed indistinct, not black, not really white.

"*Ladeevriss.*"

"Dear Christ!" Lady Violet Barham-Vrisser could read her Africa in the dark. "Jane, be ready. I'm going to unbar the door."

You could never be ready. The photographs in government reports and propaganda might show it, but they were miniaturized, yesterday's news. The caved row on row of skulls might show it, but they were dry and dead.

Jonathan, of Chiumbwa, and before that of Mozambique, was alive, life-size, and in the low paraffin illumination from the Tilly lamp, very much in color. The colors of a charnel house. The colors of a child's riddle: *What's black and white and red all over?*

An African without his lips. Without his face.

The vomit was halfway up her throat. Violet Vrisser closed the door. "I have morphine in my cabinet. Kapisa! Water, towels! *Nokukurumidza!*"

Quickly, Kapisa, for Christ's sake, quickly, so that we can cover this dreadful head trying to speak through its clotted ghastly white-and-red gorilla grin.

"Easy, Jonathan." His head, cradled in her hands, stuck to her fingers. "Easy, Ladeevriss be back." Talking childlike to this giant whose strength was as the strength of ten. Who must have cralwed with ten men's strength from the heart of darkness to get here. How much blood did ten men have? How much must he have lost?

"He mustn't lose more," said Violet Vrisser. "*Steady.* Steady." As though comforting her horses.

The injection slipped in its tranquillity; the tension in the muscled shoulders on her crouched thighs melted to the flab that precedes and follows death. She eased him onto cushions laid on the floor. Violet Vrisser placed dampened pressure cloths across the wound.

Two shells exploded without warning into the hill behind the house.

A flash from the gorge. A third shell fell, still overranging.

"Jane, give them a burst from the FN."

The noise, held in by the veranda and the hall hammered her head from side to side. The tracer swarmed down the valley and flickered out among the trees. Jonathan moaned. Behind him Kapisa huddled, teeth chattering. Violet Vrisser lifted the phone again.

"Damn. *Damn!* Time, Jane?"

"One-thirty."

"I had a radio," said Violet Vrisser, "with the aircraft, but I let it go. My dear, I am so *bloody* sorry—"

"No draft, remember—I volunteered. I just hope you're right about the night-fighting."

"Oh yes. The African's nothing like your Viet Cong."

Who crept on his little cat feet among the kids from Chicago and Des Moines to kill the black boy from Atlanta standing beside the pot-smoking girl in the fatigues who was covering it all for thrills. The black boy's death giving her thrills enough for a life time. *Or just until the next time?*

The night stayed silent, the wind and the attackers all

resting for a minute from their labors. For five minutes? Ten?

"Thirty minutes," said Violet Vrisser, "for Bohr. For that stupid old man."

This extraordinary old *woman's* casual dismissal of the immediate horror of the present for the remote dead past, astonished her. Repelled her?

"Vriss," she said. "Jonathan has no *face!*"

"And we can do no more for him." Which should be obvious to you, said Violet Vrisser's aristocrat's voice. "They think we're mad, you know, the Africans. Pretending to ourselves death isn't here and then dying of fright each day to find it around the corner. They send along these awful things like Jonathan to shock us. Not themselves. After thirty thousand years of hunting, sliced flesh has lost its shock for them."

"You *can't* believe the 'no feelings' crap?"

"Of course not, Jane, and of course the African mother weeps for her butchered baby. But if the *nn'anga* says making soup from a child will break the drought or bring black rule to Zimbabwe? Western mothers offer up whole generations to military service."

"But the *nn'angas*—the witch doctors—the politicians are all *men.*"

"Oh, Jane, dear—Golda Meir was a grandmother! The tribe comes first."

The logic was as dry as dust and brown grass; as old as the scratched figures on the cave's walls.

"Go on about Bohr," she said. "I thought he was in Sweden."

"Bohr was in Sweden." Violet Vrisser now sounded impatient to get through it. "And the original copy of his notes was safely in a rowboat on its way across the Kattegat with Truelsen, our top Danish Toby—our link with their resistance: a quite splendid man. Everything was good. We got the word, sent back the signal to proceed. The reception group put out the marks. At 23:59:59 hours Mary dropped."

On the stroke of midnight. It would have to be at midnight to give Mackenzie King something to write home about to Mum. *The most propitious hour on the clock, Little Pat. . . .*

"She had a chap of Truelsen's with her after landing." Violet Vrisser's voice matched the wind outside, now sighing as through parachute silk. "She had a chap of Truelsen's, and the thing was," and Violet Vrisser repetitively spoke so softly—as though she might disturb Jonathan's nightmare morphine dreams, "the thing was, Truelsen's man said at the debriefing that even though it was a heavy force—squad cars, personnel carrier, searchlights—the Germans didn't really seem to know what they were looking for, and she could have got away to the canal at the back with him. But he said she just stood there in the doorway with the searchlight on her, stood there so they could see her handbag . . . she must have been so cold. So cold without stockings. . . ."

Violet Vrisser's voice ran out altogether. Behind her in the silence Jonathan made Harry Rogers' noises: noises now synonymous forever with Zimbabwe and Rhodesia.

"I want it all, Vriss."

"The details were in a Gestapo report filed at Shell House in Copenhagen. 'The agent, Scylla's, satchel was self-detonated at 06:00 hours—fortunately, however, the stolen documents were saved by containment within a stainless steel tube, and returned to the laboratory. There can be no doubt of their authenticity. . . .'"

After such a plover's run for England how could there be room for doubt?

"So she wasn't shot?"

"No. She wasn't shot." And Violet Vrisser's voice this time held nothing back. *Did it?*

"Vriss—"

"Yes, dear?" Violet Vrisser, sitting with her shotgun, seemed to be waiting for one last thing to go bump in the night.

"My father knew that the Germans had been tipped off. He knew while she was still in the air. So did Churchill. So did your Intelligence chief. Didn't *you?*"

"So Menzies knew?" Some questions, said Violet Vrisser's voice, aren't meant to be answered. "We used to pretend to ourselves, you know, that we controlled it, but I don't think any of us truly believed that. We realized Churchill's Russian enigma was really about us. By the end there were so many layers of cobwebs that even LCS couldn't find the spiders." A sigh filled the hall with the weight of years and tears. "Jael would have liked to go for that one last level of deception, that one last web: prove to Canaris that black which was white really *is* black. So they'll grab white."

"But a radio message was intercepted. Going out of Britain."

"Was there really?" Now Violet Vrisser seemed to take refuge in mechanics. "Cheltenham were very good—they could skewer a transmission anywhere in England in thirty minutes. I wonder who that was? By 1943, Double-Cross had every spy in the country."

"The call sign was Charybdis."

"It would have to be wouldn't it? The Odyssey's whirlpool dragging her down. How very—"

The small window erupted into Violet Vrisser's face.

Kapisa helped her drag Jonathan and Violet Vrisser along the hall and through the kitchen. The cellar was an adjunct of the kitchen and shared a common foundation wall and a massive door sheet-lined with zinc. The wine racks inside the door were almost empty. A handful of bottles with Paarl labels gathered dust. The racks linked her with the building of _The Times_, impossibly far away. She went back for the guns.

A shell landing just outside the veranda had caught the thatch. She dashed into the drawing room, threw open the shutter. Kapisa's pots and pans of water were barely adequate but the flames sizzled and went out. If the wind had gusted they would not. In the last flicker she saw the Willys standing in the drive, unscathed. The faun beyond it had suffered a direct hit.

Violet Vrisser was conscious. A god of battles had spared her sight, but a long gash ran across her forehead. Kapisa dabbed at it by the light of the Tilly lamp.

"Vriss, honey, I'm going for help."

"Yes." The voice was weakened, but still the voice of Control in London, the voice of coping with the blitz. "Yes, perhaps you should. Take one of the automatics for your run."

Both women knew what that meant.

She kissed Violet Vrisser's cold face, put the recorder in her shoulder bag and turned toward the door. The blackness beyond the cellar seemed deeper than all the empty eyes in all the dead skulls of Africa.

Violet Vrisser stretched a hand against the darkness. "Pilgrim's valley of the shadow's not out _there_, darling. Not when you jump, and not in the camps. It's inside us with

Giant Despair and all his Doubting Castles." The hand squeezed tight, "But Valiant-for-Truth is *real*, Jane," squeezed tighter, "Valiant-for-Truth is why the trumpets sound," and the pale face no longer shone copper like the rings on Old Shilling's legs: it shone white, clean, steady as the flame of a candle in pure air. *"Valiant-for-Truth is why the corporals cried at Ravensbrück."*

"And Jane," with the small, slightly ironic, now so familiar smile, "Unlike Butler, Bunyan wasn't 'liberated.' Valiant-for-Truth was obviously a woman!"

The Willys was tired. Three tries were needed to wake it up while the starter screamed loud as a hyena and she waited for the shells to fall. The engine shook, choked itself, shook again, then ran rough but steady. *The gears? Two-wheel drive or four-?* Whatever. *Lights?* No. No lights. Not yet. She let out the clutch. Began to move. To creep.

The flowers with their English perfumes faded with the smashed pieces of the faun, and the curve, and the blasted mahogany—no longer in the running for tallest in Rhodesia—on guard beside the bridge spanning the gorge. She turned downhill, leaving the raked gravel for the red dirt of the tea plantations. A burst of angry gold and fiery bees sprang at the Willys. She slammed her foot flat to the floor, fired a wild burst with the FN into the bushes, threw the lights on high. The Willys, rocking and swaying with shared rage, howled and screamed downhill. A black body standing in the road was hurled, or jumped, aside. A second burst of bees flew overhead. Then there was quiet. Just tree after tree passing with thoughts of a grandfather's arboretum, of prunus in the spring.

She checked the gauges. Everything worked. *Was a third of a tank of gas enough?* How many angels can dance on the head of a pin?

She came out through the columned entrance to Chiumbwa on two wheels, was going up like the Daimler, was going up. *Down.* Stupid bitch to chance it. She slowed to forty—still like rocketing on the washboard surface—dodged potholes when she could. Jonathan had used the shoulders here, but at night, at speed, their cure seemed worse than the disease. Adrenalin and the Willys howled, *Damn the mines, girl, damn King Solomon's goddamn mines....*

The mound of droppings, rounded and blood-black in the headlights, sat like a sand castle washed by the first wave.

She wrenched the wheel, but now it was useless. Within a second, she and the Willys would be flying like the silver-headed fish eagle smoothly through the night, up into the trees, as the droppings were squashed.

And left behind.

Ankle-deep in shit the Willys roared on.

"Thank you for helping to Build Rhodesia: Your Roads Department." Pitch in for Rhodesia and Washington, D.C., the lands of tricks and jokes. The Willys leaped back onto the asphalt with renewed vigor. Reflected eyes watched her from heads not yet on walls. The wind seemed gone for good. A cold mist wrapped angel hair around the lights. She slowed to thirty-five, to thirty. To twenty at a sudden curve.

The tree was beyond it, lying dead across the road.

She went through the motions, turned off the key, hit the pedal, grabbed the hand brake, swerved hard to the side. The Willys rammed its right-hand wheel at the log, ran for ten feet along it squealing pain and stinking rubber, and stopped.

She forgot the pythons and the AK47's waiting in the woods, forgot about Violet Vrisser, and her good and faithful servants, forgot about everything except feeling sorry for herself. Feeling tired, drained, exhausted. Feeling nothing. She cradled her head on her arms and sat. . . .

Moisture from condensation on the roof dripped on her face. The lights were dim on a dying battery. She opened the door and stepped down to check the damage.

Only the counterbalancing weight of the Willys, and her hand grabbing at the door handle, held her.

Somewhere underneath, far, far underneath, a river ran unconcerned. She dragged herself back into the vehicle, crawled shaking across the seat and out on the other side to the doubtful security of the road.

The gorge? *How far from safety was the fucking gorge?* Halfway? No, better—three-quarters. Just past the ruined walls with their first view of Inyangani—before she knew about its skulls—just past the walls. And walls led to trailer parks, and trailer parks the whole world over were guarded by old Womble colonels and the army.

She would walk. She found the flashlight, a heavy one

with a separate battery, and strapped it to her bag so that the weight was on her shoulder. She checked the laces on her boots, put a fresh clip in the FN, another in her pocket, took the gun in her right hand and climbed over the tree trunk.

The tree was lost to her in five paces.

In ten, she realized it might not have fallen in the wind.

The light was useless in the mist. A horrid shape reared out at her. Another tree. *She was off the road.* Behind her? In front? Don't panic. DON'T PANIC. Turn the light straight down, sweetheart. Tap the feet, Bojangles. Tap, tap. Tap, tap. Her toe found the edge of the pavement. By keeping the light on it she could follow the road. In Africa the roads are paved in ignorance with gold. *Follow the yellow brick road, follow the yellow brick road.* Where would it take her, who would she meet? *Dr. Montigny, I presume?*

She tripped and fell over a bush. The light went out. Came on. Shone straight up in the air, a beacon pointing nowhere, at no one. She had seen men like this in Vietnam, the walking wounded, the zombies. Punchy. Punched up and down by chemical highs and out-of-action lows. Dogfaces dog-tired.

Idiot! She should be following the *lines,* the white man's gift to good order and discipline. She picked herself up. Then the bag with the light. Then the gun. She followed her road. After ten minutes she knew something cunning followed *her.* Cunning because she couldn't see it, hiding in its African ghost's clothes in the mist. African ghosts. The *ngozi.* Sent by that goddamn ancient asshole Shilling. Tripping her, losing her, slowing her so they could catch her with their gunpowder. Laughing. Singing. Someone singing in her head, far away, far away, an old thin voice.

> *Who so beset him round*
> *With dismal stories,*
> *Do but themselves confound;*
> *His strength the more is.*

Her strength, you unliberated old bastard, Bunyan. HER *strength.* Now there was no fear. She was only choked up, pissed off, infuriated as she would be by a blood budgie biting at her face. She fired a burst of three rounds at the bush. The mist and vegetation grabbed the bullets with wet mouths so that the sound was *plop plop plop* not *crack crack crack*, but still loud enough to tell the *ngozis* to fuck off. How neat and smooth and black was the black ribbon of the asphalt. Like Jonathan's shoulder lifting the injured child in the maize field.

Her mind was suddenly clear. Dreams and goblin fancies from the world of Oz swept out. Fled away. She quickened her pace. Left right, left right, one two three four: One-two. THREE-FOUR!

Columns of invisible Marines marched with her, then a unit of black-and-yellow wasp-badged Air Cavalry relieving the Marines as they had at Hué and Khe San: the 1st Cav boys incredulous as their generals at seeing a twenty-seven-year-old white girl, a broad, *a fucking split-tail, man!* beside them. One-two. THREE-*FOUR!* She sang it with them in the mist. What else was there to sing? No Halls of Montezuma. No Battle Hymn of Victory. Not in 'Nam. Not here. Just a form of Montezuma's revenge aching in her gut from the pancakes.

The mist that swallowed the explosions gave up noise with equal softness: a purring, swishing of tires on dew wetness, and then two watery pale-moon eyes peering weepily through the grounded clouds.

And almost past her. Stanley and Livingstone would never meet!

"Hey. HEY!" Frantic waving of her flashlight, knowing it *was even weaker than the headlight.* "Stop. *Jesus Christ, you mother fuckers, STOP!"*

It stopped.

"Stand where yew are." A bullhorn ripped the fog apart. *"No tricks."* Boots slammed down on the asphalt. A second vehicle came in too fast behind, brakes squealed. Men from Inyanga or from Mars moved in a blur toward her.

"Thet's no language for—*My Christ*—look at the blood!" said one voice.

"Hullo, Otter," said another.

THE ALTAR
OF JAEL

23

Washington, May 1977

Her grandfather would like Arlington. Would like its trees, its vistas, its hints of Capability Brown in the designing hand. Was that Jefferson's hand? Had he sat as she did now, looking down the hill across the river, across dairy fields, planning the heart of a new nation? This heart interred all round her: two hundred years of blood nurturing these trees, this grass. And was it a cemetery's grass where Keats said no birds sang? Fadiman would know. When she met Fadiman. Because with two days home in Washington behind her she still put off that meeting. Put off anything with anyone—even the long-distance call to Muir about her change of plans.

Meeting or calling meant explaining. Explaining the *irrationality* of the change; describing the unreasoned panic that swept over her on the tarmac at Madrid en route to London when she finally saw the fine print in the Salisbury *Mail*.

And she couldn't explain it. What man would have understood it? Why, if she didn't take advantage of that jumbo of Pan Am's *right now*; didn't grab a seat at *any price*; didn't leave the astonished clerks to reroute the baggage somehow, *anyhow*; if she didn't find something she *knew* for her mind to hang on to—some familiar anchor as Mountbatten told her mother long ago, for luck to hang on to—she wouldn't make it.

So here she was: back with the familiarity of her home-base favorite places and her shoulder bag and this devastating sense of loss, staring for another uncounted time at the headline:

LADY VIOLET BARHAM-VRISSER DEAD. . . .

"Asphyxiated," Salisbury said. *Gassed*. When Chiumbwa, built by Violet Vrisser's grandfather on a bet, burned down around her ears. The newspaper photograph showed the bodies as she and Muir had found them apparently asleep on the floor of the wine cellar.

All my girls were put to sleep. . . .

A second photograph showed the mutilated body of Sixpence Hwata sprawled blocking the chimney of the air vent on the sod roof of the cellar.

"The funeral will be held at Saint Mary's Cathedral," Salisbury had also said, because "although Lady Barham-Vrisser had wished to be buried on her estate, a spokesman for the military authority in the region stated that with the uncertain situation, the remote grave site could not be considered secure. . . ."

Security. Another word that had become as ephemeral in her nonperson's world as the shades of the skulls in the cave. Or had security always been a trick? A Poynter's Corners, Norman Rockwell, Saturday-morning movie, make-believe illusion?

"Of course, dear," Violet Vrisser would have told her in that calm, sure voice she still heard so clearly. *"Because humanity in Rhodesia or Poynter's Corners is only a blink from the Stone Age anyway."*

Hearing that *ngozi* voice as she lay in the tear-blurred darkness of a hastily commandeered room at the Troutbeck Inn, she had finally understood why the woman called Scylla had left a child under an apple tree on her way to the last jump. Because security *is* luck. For either an aristocrat or a black, security is crossing one's fingers, watching the clock, tossing the salt, having a baby. Praying.

Pretending.

Pretending that if we drag our superstitious wings low enough the lightning won't strike; the night snakes and the gas ovens won't get us; the air-control computers won't fuck up in Tenerife; a bomb in a car won't kill a blond boy in the band from Wallace, Idaho. Falling in love won't end like last time. . . .

Love! Christ, love is the most ephemeral damned word of all. Love has to hang on filaments as light as the fisherman's line on that stream outside.

So how, she had asked the darkness, could love possibly have made it through the tears and blood of this terrorist war? How could it have got past the barbarous, Stone Age, New Age, mines and wire around Johnson's Store next door? How could she be so certain that it *was* love she felt for this latest war-zone man in bed beside her?

"You ask too many questions, girl."

She had stopped asking. Had grabbed Muir's back, had locked Muir's legs; had put all the overtrained fucking muscles through their paces one more time. . . .

She had not gone to Violet Vrisser's funeral. Or Harry Rogers'. Or any of the others. At that point she had left Zimbabwe-Rhodesia to its fate.

Muir would follow. He had promised that on the Inyanga airstrip in the morning after the night at the Troutbeck Inn. He would join her in London, but it would take him a week to get things squared.

"A week!" Knowing she was being female and unfair, but knowing too that time, as Einstein said, was different now. Luck could run out in a week.

If the Whitehall forces of "our way" chose to let it.

Because *that* was the message that changed her mind on the tarmac in Madrid. The knowledge, buried in the fine print of the turn of the *Mail's* story continued on page ten below a picture, that when the velvet gloves were off, and she was off home base, then "our way" could get her— anytime, anyplace. As it had got to the outlaw forces across the river on the day *before* her first arrival at Chiumbwa. The picture proved it.

The man in the picture was still tallish, still wore a hat, was still a perfect gent smiling benignly on his blacks. But the man had abandoned tweed for khaki, and the hand holding an AK47 up for appraisal by a keen Sandhurst eye, wore no glove of any sort.

"The British delegation for the back-stabbing ZANLA

talks," said Salisbury's caption with the innocent outrage of a colonial for fair play, *"was led by a Colonel Smythe...."*

No dikkop birds had sung in the smoking ruin of Chiumbwa, but hundreds of birds sang here, in Arlington, at eight o'clock on a May morning. An American Sunday morning when simple citizens worship any god still in his heaven or under his Camelot flame flickering in its granite circle.

The trick of any magic is arranging the right circle....

She walked on past the circle, past the crosses with their skulls invisibly row on row, until she was face to face again with the Marines raising their bronze flag at one of those places where the action was. Iwo Jima. One of those places which—after all the warlike hands behind the scenes in Washington and London stopped waving, and manipulating—had had to be taken by frontal assault.

By blood.

"Those were the days." One of the simple citizens turned from his study of the statue. Freed from his monitoring daffodils, Selbach had discarded the formality of the buttoned-up vest for a corduroy jacket with tabs and patches of synthetic suede to take him hunting on days off. "Overmagnified," continued Selbach, "but clear-cut: go out and take the opposition. Right, Mrs. Montigny?"

"This creeping-up bit—do you black-ops bastards all go to the same school?"

"Elements of style are universal—Fadiman must have told you that. You've really been moving around, Mrs. Montigny. Switching your plays. Or maybe the game is over? No one would blame you for that. This one never was a game you were equipped to win."

"What happened to the Girl Scouts defending our Constitution?"

"No chauvinism intended," said Selbach mildly. "I have some stuff at the office. Do you have wheels?"

"I'll take a cab."

"I'll call a car."

A miniaturized walkie-talkie produced a gray wraith at the cemetery gate to float her air-conditioned along the Potomac away from the city. She had a moment of sympathy for the deans of the Washington columns who had been hooked. It would be all too easy for a man in midlife crisis to get bought off by the smoothness of this helping hand; to expect the wraith to be at the door; to take advantage of the bus express lanes; to glide through the gate at Langley with scarcely a nod of the head from the guardians, human and otherwise. To rely completely on the touch of a button to pass the word as Alleyn had prophesied that all doors and hearts were to be open. Apparently open.

This time there was a proper office with a title on the door, DIRECTOR—NATO ONE, and a desk and photographs hinting at humanity hiding in spook's clothing. There were no flowers, but the jug of coffee was the same.

"Or maybe after your time with the Brits, it should be tea?" The on-off smile was unchanged as well.

"Coffee."

Selbach poured, then stirred, then pulled a picture from a bulky yellow file on his desk. "The guy on the right is Meyer Lansky."

The Mob's biggest barracuda discussing business with a lounge lizard before there was a trace of silver in the sleek black hair. A cigarette—a Craven A?—tapered from Piers' fingers. Both men were walking along a stone jetty with palm trees in the distance. "Florida," said Selbach. "There were several meetings through forty-one and forty-two. This is from Hoover's collection—you can keep it. Do you want a copy of Piers' party card?"

"His Nazi? . . ."

"We have that one in the original." Selbach allowed himself a full four-second smile with the next rabbit from the hat. "I was thinking about something from Moscow. Oh sure, Moscow's had his lordship in deep sleep since 1929. How about the name of his recruiter? One of those great Oxbridge fag don's names. Here we go—Myles Tenning."

There were moments in self-defense workouts that were like this. When your opponent had her thumb on your neck and you could see and hear but not move, not speak.

"You're saying, *why*? Right, Mrs. Montigny? Why is the asshole son of a bitch *giving* me this? Well, let me background it." Selbach appeared more interested in the Ultra-Suede edging on his cuff than her reaction. "The *Amos 'n' Andy* show up the road may want brotherly love in southern Africa, but we don't. It doesn't suit our purposes to have the Cubans run another Angola that close to the end zone."

More than the frank admission, it was the casually proprietorial "we" that chilled her to the bone. Despite all the hearings and all the firings, "we" would survive and function no matter how many heads were cut off.

"Now the Brit Cabinet, Mrs. Montigny, mainly because of your mother's old boyfriend, have been trying to push a deal with Rhodesia's Bobbsey twins—Nkomo and Mugabe: For wishful thinking about chrome downstream tomorrow, we give you boys Special Air support for the new Zimbabwe today. The hairy Left in the U.K. has had a hard-on for some 'progressive' action ever since Suez. The Cabinet is an even split right now. If Piers picks up the party leadership, they'll go the troop route."

"Then why don't you act? Give this crap on Piers to their Intelligence?"

When Selbach found things truly funny there was no smile at all. "Where do you think we got this, Mrs. Montigny? The Easter Bunny?"

Her mind had stopped working. She could see no pattern in his movement.

"You want to leak it through me?"

"That the Agency says there really has been a red under the British bed all these years? Mrs. Montigny, the next Labour Party convention at Blackpool would be a coronation!" For the first time Selbach looked pained. "You say 'act.' We used to 'act,' Mrs. Montigny—but you people in the press screwed that! If we can't hit that cocksucker Castro—" and in talk of assassination Selbach really came to life and slammed his hand down on the table—"if we can't hit *Castro*, or that ape Amin, you think Congress is going to let us take out a lovable old Limey in a wig and a granny dress?"

"But if the British know? . . ."

"Now there is a honey of a question. But let's take the 'if' out of it. The Brits, Mrs. Montigny, know all kinds of things. They know they had a red spy ring in the twenties bigger than Gouzenko. They know they had a couple of Benedict Arnolds digging in at the Foreign Office as early as 1937—shit! I'd give you three to one they even had the *names!*" Selbach formed an executive pyramid with his fingers and looked at her across the top. "The only way to run a railroad like ours, Mrs. Montigny, is to make the boardroom seem a bunch of fucking idiots. If the other side thinks they're up against Bobby Fischer we'd all have to work much harder."

"You don't have to sweat it," she said.

The pyramid collapsed abruptly but Selbach still pretended to be pleasant. To be helpful. "You know what I'm told is the biggest trouble with the Brits, Mrs. Montigny? I'm told those guys don't tell the truth. In fact I hear," and from the totally deadpan face Selbach found the trick of this joke as hilarious as Harry Rogers with his Wombles. "I hear that the Oriental Brits, Mrs. Montigny, *can lie with straight faces.*"

She got the punch line of the joke. She had to. It was her own, from the first call to Alleyn at Dolphin Square. Tap the *phones*, Bojangles. "You prick."

"A brave new world, Mrs. Montigny."

Where all the walls have ears. A man's world, she had told Alleyn. Was Alleyn part of it? Would being Mrs. Muir make it any different?

"The British won't rock the class-war boat for Piers," said Selbach. "Moscow keeps the marks on this one. The son of a bitch is the perfect sleeper."

A real hare-and-hounds man, Violet Vrisser called him. And it was now obvious that for the hunt masters here and in Whitehall—whether Piers was hare or hound, better the sleeper they knew, the sleeper that they could keep an eye on, blow the horn on if the trail grew too hot or too cold. And if Piers killed other creatures in his sleep—Harry Rogers, Violet Vrisser, Jonathan, and Sixpence—the shock, as any hunter knows, wears off after the first time.

She picked up the photograph of Meyer Lansky. "But if you give me this, with everything else I've gotten—we're not in the thirties, they can't block it out like the abdication. With satellite it will wash worldwide—"

"With Teddy and Mary Jo, Tricky and the Tapes, Margaret and Roddy—all the good stuff from your fellow 'professionals' at *People* mag and *Private Eye*. Well, Mrs. Montigny, even the *Eye* can't afford the price of the libel suits over there if they run with this one." He slid the file across the desk to her. "But don't take my word for it—ask Fadiman."

She opened the envelope and saw the contents.

There was no point in asking Fadiman. Fadiman, like Muir, would have to wait.

24

Case 1. *United States* v. *Brandt et al.*

The Doctors' Trial. Why must she reread it! *Why does the rest of the world forget?* Forget Dr. Karl Brandt, Adolf Hitler's personal physician and Reich Commissioner for Health. *Found guilty and hanged....*

"You okay?"

The stewardess was bending over her. "I'm fine." The report had wiped out the activity all round her on the aircraft: the sequence of takeoff, drinks, food, lights-out, movie. She was astonished to find herself hemmed in by ear-phoned zombies with tears pouring down their cheeks. On the silent screen a tow-haired moppet clutched the hand of a cauliflower-eared prize-fighter spread-eagled on a couch.

"He croaks," said the stewardess. "Sure I can't get you something?"

"Maybe a sandwich."

The stewardess moved away. A flood of tears. How would the zombies react to this *real* tearjerker on her knee? And she was the only one not crying....

After Brandt, the proceedings left room at the top for the missing Mengele, then ran down through the ranks past Dr. Trommer, who only watched the Zapping and signed the bills—Good-bye, Dr. Trommer—to the bottom of the list: the woman's place in any masculine order. The only woman: defendant Herta Oberhauser.

Deposition One: Report by Captain V. Barham FANY
Re Lady Mary Dexter (U.K.)

Scylla. Who, Violet Barham-Vrisser *now* admitted, although her Guy Fawkes handbag *had* exploded, had *not* died

204

in old Bohr's garden but had suffered a compound fracture to her left leg and been removed to the Military Hospital for Occupation Forces in Copenhagen.

> Where the record shows that Lady Dexter's initial treatment was of a high—indeed exemplary—standard. On the express orders of Central Command, Berlin, a specialist was brought in. . . .

But the hospital record doesn't show that despite repeated inquiries, no word of Lady Dexter gets passed to the Red Cross in Geneva, nor that once she can hop around she goes regularly to Shell House in Copenhagen for "prolonged, but correct, interrogation. . . ."

Prolonged but correct.
Did that mean she only heard the screams; only smelled the smells?

Mickey Mouse stuff. After D day we need *results!*

> Lady Dexter was therefore taken to Gestapo Special Centre at Aarhus University, where interrogation became more severe. . . .

Where the medical boys really have to start digging into their little black bag of tricks, says the Danish witness, Marksen.

> . . . Lady Dexter was placed on an operating table and informed by defendant *Gehren* that her leg would be rebroken surgically without anaesthetic. . . .

But Harry Rogers could have told them *that* wouldn't work. Aristocrats like Lady Dexter don't feel pain: they act the hero as easily as they shit. The boys that bring you Belsen are not impressed by aristocrats. Not at first.

> "On the night of September 20, 1944," writes Captain Violet Barham-Vrisser, "Lady Dexter was taken to Ravensbrück, where she was placed in the Medical Experimentation Centre under the direction of defendant *Oberhauser*. In the records of the Experimentation Centre, Lady Dexter is listed as Test Person 721 (TP 721). . . .

Test Person.

All the words in old Pilgrim's book couldn't describe "Test Person," or a "Test Person's" progress.

> Beginning in October, Lady Dexter was moved by the staff of the Experimentation Centre to Dachau and subjected to those activities which are the principal charges of Case 1 against defendant *Rascher.*
> *Example:* After witnessing the death of a TP by ice-water immersion, Lady Dexter would be placed in the tank but then removed.
> *Example:* After witnessing the death of a TP in the high-altitude decompression chamber, Lady Dexter would be placed in the chamber, and the vacuum pumps started. . . .

And for anyone who doesn't know the particularly disgusting effects on a TP of *that* attempt to make the lives of Luftwaffe pilots more bearable, read on through the testimony of witness Pacholegg.

The aircraft bounced through a thunderhead five miles over Iceland. Her stomach felt sorry for the Luftwaffe pilots.

"Do you want a discomfort bag?" The stewardess was back.

"No. I'll be fine. Really."

"You're sure?"

She nodded the girl away. You could be sure that the airline would have a euphemism for barf, but what *else* could you be sure of, after all this? Death and taxes? That was the inconceivable bit—using the modern mechanism of the tax man for actions as old as the skulls in the cave. The barbarism of men of reason, said Violet Vrisser. Men with death's heads on their uniforms.

> After each of these experiences at Dachau, Lady Dexter was interrogated by Gestapo witness *Zossler,* from defendant *Kaltenbrunner's* staff at Fürstenberg Castle. . . .

And still for nothing. Harry Rogers was a better judge of character than the Nazis. The visits to Dachau stop. The butcher of Fürstenberg Castle decides it's time for the woman's touch.

On November fifth, 1944, Lady Dexter was returned to defendant *Oberhauser's* charge at Ravensbrück and taken to the X-ray laboratory for the first experimental radiation treatment. . . .

Remember, remember the fifth of November. . . .
The boys in black never forgot it till the day they died. Zossler, the Gestapo man, told Violet Barham-Vrisser that. Both he and the guard, defendant Schwarzhuber, were deeply moved by Lady Dexter's aristocratic conduct and bearing.

Not Kaltenbrunner, now the new boss of the SD, visiting in person with personal instructions from Adolf Hitler on Lady Dexter's case. The hell of the New Order has no fury like the suburban host of a good luncheon, scorned. The Führer with his back to the rat hole was out for blood.

Treatment had been halted to attempt healing of the outer tissues but at the end of January 1945, it was recommenced. Dosage levels were increased. . . .

Because, says witness Zossler, SD HQ has new information *"from the most reliable source in Britain"* that Lady Dexter in her quiet, well-bred way is sitting—lying—on information of the gravest importance for defense of the Reich.

But you can't get blood from a stone, weeps Zossler, and on March the fifteenth at 0600 hours Lady Mary Dexter dies—from Allied shrapnel, says the death certificate. And who's to call it a lie when the evidence goes up in smoke from the mass crematorium?

The tax man.
You can't piss a good German taxpayer's money away like that! Not without something to *show* for it!
So with Teutonic thoroughness and obedience the records laboriously assembled by the lady doctor's Experimental Staff to show the effects of intense radiation on the human female ovarian cycle are retained, and filed. And are submitted,

writes Violet Barham-Vrisser, together with the photographs as Appendix One.

"*Lady Mary*," says her closest friend, underlining a summation to be used for the posthumous George Cross, "*died without disclosure.*"

Lady Mary was put to sleep in accordance with the highest traditions of her class and country: Lady Mary was *destroyed*, in silence.

The question still not fully answered as the warning lights came on for Heathrow was why had Selbach so frankly broken silence?

From a woman's intuition she now thought she knew the answer—and like the invisible stench of the terrible photographs face down inside her briefcase—was afraid of it.

25

London, June 1977

Heathrow, six days shy of a Jubilee, was bedlam. The Immigration line for the unwashed without a British parent stretched halfway around the terminal. She found her British passport and went to the Home gate.

Immigration, a man of forty with an adolescent's once-red hair straggling down his neck from underneath his cap, demolished the pretensions of a terrified couple from Ceylon.

"Next!"

Her name and passport number were punched into a machine.

"Passport invalid—revoked. Leave the line." A thumb jerked at a glass door. "Wait there."

She should have guessed that "our way" would have her number. She rummaged in her shoulder bag and produced her U.S. passport. Immigration glared at it. "I have a British mother and two grand—"

Immigration raised a hand for Security.

Fate stepped in with a hand of its own. The note delivered from Piers at the House of Lords fell out onto the counter. Immigration looked at the heading, at the signature of the Woolsack bastard who had just dropped her in the shit. "Do you *know* His Lordship, madam?"

"Buster," she said, "when I leave this line, Geoffrey Piers is the next Englishman I meet."

Customs, in an unexpected gesture, made up for Immigration's bad manners and bad breath by being on strike and she sailed through with the smiling faces. Signs as futile as those by the Washington trick shop implored them all to make a voluntary declaration.

Good humor was short-lived: outside the terminal transportation was nonexistent. Sex appeal eventually got her into a limousine with an Indian and a Frenchman who complained nonstop about accommodations throughout the journey into town. Passing Marble Arch, she realized that she had no accommodation of her own.

The woman at the desk at Dolphin Square was sympathetic but run off her feet. "We really owe you something for that awful bombing business, but you've *seen* the streets—"

"Anything would be okay—I'll share a bath." With sudden inspiration, she remembered the name-dropping effect of Piers' note. "Just till I meet my grandfather—the Duke of Dorset—"

The woman produced a key and a smile as a reward for good breeding. "I keep it for our sales reps. The room's on the top floor in the inside corner—and there's only a hot plate but it does have a bath."

From the corner room's small window she looked down again at the fishpool and the fountain and the rosebeds and the children sprawling on the lawns. It almost felt like home. But that was the trouble: the last place stayed in—*any*place stayed in—for a month, took on all the permanence of home. She would give up Walden Pond: *but she must have Muir.*

Instead, she called *The Times* and got Alleyn.

"Jane! My God, this is marvelous! Christ, you've had a

time out there. Where are you? What about digs?" She had never heard him so animated.

"I'm okay, Roger. When can we? . . . Just hold a minute." The woman from the desk was outside the door.

"I'm so sorry. After Reuter's couldn't give me an address, I should have sent it back, but I quite forgot. This letter came in for you a week ago."

The envelope, a pale-cream linen, was the kind bought most by those that can't afford it; the script was what old Harrington at Radcliffe used to call "*ostentatiously* cramped." The sender's name was Mrs. Whiteside. The phone was squawking at her.

"Hang in there a minute, Roger." Ripping the envelope she skipped to the bottom: *Cynthia Whiteside*.

Cynthia Dodgeson, the colonel's daughter and Churchill's missing girl Friday—now apologizing for her absence and offering to meet. "*Anxious* to meet! Vastly intrigued. . . ."

"Hi, Roger. Listen, can we get together maybe tomorrow when I'm back on your time?"

"Of course." But his disappointment was undisguised. Three weeks ago she would have been pleased. Now there was Muir and she was sorry.

The letter gave an address, 22 Campden Grove, but no telephone number and there was none in the book. She took a mini-cab, which was a mistake. The young driver was gabby, aggressively Jamaican, and unfamiliar with London. "I thought you guys had to take exams," she said as they circled filthy alleys behind Euston Street Station. The young Jamaican bawled for help at a regular-sized taxi stopped at a light beside them.

Various expressions passed across the elder cabbie's face. "Kensington," he said, "not bleeding Camden Town!" She tossed a bill into the front seat and scrambled out. The Jamaican stared after her, speechless for the first time.

Her new man reversed direction past the Post Office Tower and eventually emerged beside the Albert Memorial. Now the names had Kensington in them: Kensington Road, Kensington Church Street—then past Kensington Barracks to Campden Grove on the left.

She gave an extra pound as a tip. "You watch those bastards," the cabbie said enigmatically.

Number 22 was not in a grove but there were gardens visible behind it and window boxes to the street. She remembered that the colonel's brick cottage had had window boxes. This house had once been grand and a door with a fanlight of multicolored glass opened into a large hall. The sound of a piano and a girl singing came from somewhere. A plaque with an ornate medieval script said:

Mannering Music Academy — Private Instruction

At the top of the plaque an arrow cut from green cardboard pointed up the stairs to an engraved card of Mrs. Whiteside's. The stairs were very wide and the handrail very solid in beautifully turned mahogany, but the carpet was worn-out from all the singing and wrinkled as she walked on it. The singing grew louder and higher in pitch. Almost at a climax, it stopped. A male voice with a heavy accent shouted behind the door as she went by. Cyntha Whiteside's was the door beyond it at the far end of the hall. There was no bell. She knocked. The singing began again.

26

Cynthia Dodgeson was still there in Cynthia Whiteside's face—the thinness of the nose and the largeness of the teeth couldn't be disguised—but having sons had provided ballast, and the girl who'd looked as though she might blow away standing in the pictures of the past on the *Prince of Wales* and the *Hood* was firmly anchored to the present.

"Come in," Cynthia Whiteside said. "Come *in*. What an *extraordinary* surprise. I met your mother once, imagine that! Won't you have tea?" The voice was high-pitched like a schoolteacher under pressure and the upper-class accent made the voice a little piercing. Violet Vrisser's had been a comfortable voice. This one kept things slightly on edge.

Cynthia Whiteside gestured vaguely as they sat. "I'm sorry I'm so cramped but it is convenient. I get a lot of work, you see, from the colleges and the institute and I can have my music—one can walk to the Albert Hall. And the gardens. It's not like the country, but then just *look* what they've done to the country—you visited my parents. England is too *small.*"

"I guess you liked Canada?"

Cynthia Whiteside held the teapot and considered. "I think I did—yes, I did. Although I'm not sure that Montreal really is part of Canada—it's very *French,* isn't it? My son drove me to Toronto, where he has an office, but all the people there seemed to be Italians." The tea was poured. "But there is an *awful* lot of room. I enjoyed Washington."

"Your son drove you there as well?"

"Oh no, no. Years and years ago—in the war. And that's what you want to know about."

"People must bug you to death about Churchill—you must get bored telling it?"

"But I haven't," Cynthia Whiteside said obliquely. "Haven't told it, I mean. Someone after the war did want me to write a book—because some of the other girls had, and people like his policeman and his valet—but it seemed awfully *rude.* And then, of course, anything really interesting couldn't be talked about. Now, I don't think anybody still cares, do they? That's why I was so intrigued when Father told me about you—after so long, wanting to know about your mother. And those other marvelous women taking those awful chances. Although *he* used to joke with me—"

"He?"

There was only one god emphasized in Cynthia Whiteside's life. "Mr. Churchill—I know one should say, Sir Winston, but it's never sounded *right,* has it?"

"And what was this joke?"

"I don't really mean a joke—it wasn't exactly funny—but he'd chivy you along if you got too involved about the risks of things. 'Risk!' he'd growl, in that marvelous gravelly voice. 'Risk, Jumbo! Women accept childbirth, don't they?' And he'd do what I used to call his *wicked* look over the tops of his glasses. But I envied them, you know—those women—my sitting there just typing while they really *did* things. Important things against the Nazis."

Cynthia Whiteside pronounced it "Nah-zees" like her mentor.

"Did you get to type the speeches?"

"That was almost the very first thing, because I joined him in the same week as Dunkirk, and I left him on the day they dropped the bomb. In between—except for the first trip across in the *Prince of Wales* when he went to meet your man in the *Augusta* for the Atlantic Charter—I don't think I was away from him, or from work, for longer than twenty-four hours." The expression on Cynthia Whiteside's face was one of complete happiness. It clouded slightly. "I didn't get to type that—the *Charter*—which I would have rather liked. You know, the part—

> "The President of the United States of America and the Prime Minister, Mr. Churchill, representing His Majesty's Government in the United Kingdom, being met together, deem it right to make known certain common principles in the national policies of their respective countries on which they base their hopes for a better future for the world."

Cynthia Whiteside looked out at the little back gardens of Campden Grove. "It isn't what they thought it would be—the world—and for people like my parents and poor little Czechoslovakia it's really *dreadful*. But you know I think for our children it is better in some ways, don't you?"

"I guess. I don't have kids."

"Oh," said Cynthia Whiteside. "Shall you?"

And wasn't that the question to end all questions. The question to really take her time over. Just a little more time and the question would find an answer by itself.

"I hope so," she said. "Did you memorize *all* his speeches?"

Cynthia Whiteside laughed: a high, piping laugh like her mother's when she talked of Matabeleland. "Good heavens, no. But some of the phrases have sort of stuck. Do you know, I don't think I ever actually heard him speak—in public—I was always so busy. And, of course, that actor—the Winnie-the-Pooh man doing the things on the wireless didn't count—"

"Huh?"

"Didn't you know?" Cynthia Whiteside seemed genuinely surprised. "I thought it was common knowledge by now. I mean, *he* gave the speeches in the House—of course he did—and on the records after the war—"

"But the big ones on the radio were by a *stand-in?*" The words that lit up the world to fight and never surrender? The words that kept the workers like Violet Vrisser and her mother off the rocks? "They were read by a guy who played Winnie-the-Pooh?"

"I suppose I shouldn't have mentioned it," said Cynthia Whiteside apologetically. "It never really seemed to matter at the time. I mean, he was so busy—and they were *his* words and *his* thoughts, but it could make a difference . . . I do see that," the high-pitched voice trailed off. The weight of her idol's clay feet dragged Cynthia Whiteside's spirits down.

"How did you get started?"

"How did I come to join him, do you mean? By a fluke." Cynthia Whiteside revived as she described it. "I wanted to drive a tank, but I'd had rheumatic fever as a small girl and the doctors didn't know much in those days. You had to lie in bed for weeks and weeks not lifting a finger. Now, they'd have you running around a track three times a day! But after they turned me down I thought, Well, if I can't fight on the edges then I'll jolly well fight it from the center—and be a secretary to one of the bosses. Naturally I never dreamed—"

"Someone got sick, your father said?"

"A car accident, actually, and *he* needed two personal secretaries even when he was only at the Admiralty—to answer letters on his publishing, and business, and from private people—there were an enormous number even then. So I got in, and then another girl left to get married in one of those whirlwind war things, and Mrs. Hill—his senior secretary—wasn't up to traveling. I mean, the Lancasters and those old flying boats weren't exactly a honeymoon—not like our jets today, were they?"

She thought of Fadiman snooping through his honeymooners' luggage. "No," she said, "not exactly. So you started going on all the trips?"

"Oh yes. Washington, I told you that, and Quebec and Teheran—and *Casablanca*," bringing back departed shades of Harry Oakes and Humphrey Bogart. "I just gradually sort of got to the same position in the office world as his valet in the personal one. 'Jumbo,' he'd say, 'you keep all the socks and hankies and the cuff links of my paper war *copacetic*.' And he'd grin at that as he always did when he worked in one of his little 'Americanisms.'

"One of the other girls told me at the beginning that it was rude—the Jumbo thing—and I shouldn't let him do it. But you know I really didn't mind. And on the very first day I was simply scared to *death* anyway! My very first day . . ." And Cynthia Whiteside looked after it down the length of her small living room with its clutter of porcelain ornaments and reproductions of *The Blue Boy* and *The Laughing Cavalier*.

"I came in, I remember, with a new hairdo—you know the ones all piled up on the top of one's head, absolutely the latest fashion—and to keep it out of the typing—and he took one look at my ears as he passed me in the passage to the Annexe of Number 10, and said 'Hullo, Jumbo,' and it just stuck. And, of course," said Cynthia Whiteside going back a little, "after a year or so I *did* know how to keep his office cuff links 'copacetic,' so that when he shouted, 'Klop, Jumbo,' or 'My box, Jumbo,' I'd have it."

"What was this 'Klop'?"

"His paper punch. He was always losing it—in bed or in the White House, it didn't matter, shouting away in that ratty old dressing gown with the dragons. He really thought it was Chinese, that dressing gown, until Madame Chiang gave him the real thing in Cairo in 1944." Cynthia Whiteside stood up to brush a speck off the cheek of the *Cavalier*. "That's when he began to look at the other side of the war too, forty-four. You know, when you set off up the mountain you're so busy just *getting* to the top you have no time for wondering what you'll see or how you'll get down. But after D day he was *on* the top and he didn't like it. Because until then he'd been able to pretend it was a marriage of equals—the Empire, with you people—and the Empire wasn't imagination to him. It wasn't *funny*." Cynthia Whiteside looked accusingly at the picture. "He *believed*! I mean, he'd been there, hadn't he? India and the durbars and fighting the Dervishes—straight out of all the storybooks. But you Americans hadn't read them—or if you had, you didn't like the endings. And when he'd say, 'I've convinced Franklin about Suez, Jumbo,' I could have cried! Knowing that all the time someone like your man, Admiral King, was pouring vitriol in Roosevelt's ear."

"Churchill talked to you like that?"

"He had to talk to somebody didn't he, down there underground in the middle of the night? And somebody had to type up even the most secret stuff—sometimes it was really horrible to know it. I'd wander around the garden of Number 10 in my time off and think, I've got all these ghastly things in my head that no one knows about; and then I'd think of it from *his* side—actually having to *do* the things— like talk civilly to Stalin through the Warsaw horror when we just *knew* the Russians were going to sit there across the river and let the Jews go like rats in holes and we'd just lost eighty percent of another convoy for nothing. There were nights at the OP when he simply sat and stared for hours at his maps without a word."

"This OP?..."

"I'm sorry. There were so many initials, weren't there? These stand for the Other Place."

"Was this Chequers?"

"Oh no. The Germans knew all about Chequers, there was no security at Chequers at all. I mean, we used to say that's where he was, but for the superhush things we actually went to Ditchley Park—near Blenheim." Cynthia Whiteside smiled a little smile for the gullibility of Germans. "He was born at Blenheim, of course. Ditchley was almost as overwhelming—with footmen and five different echelons of maids—and because all the able-bodied had been called up, or pulled into the war industries, you'd find these incredibly old retainers who'd probably waited on Queen Victoria! But they were so marvelously loyal—the security was as absolute as you could ever get with human beings."

"And this was underground bunkers?"

"Quite the opposite—although, if you'd like, I can get you a chance to see all that? The WCR?" Cynthia Whiteside looked at her for confirmation.

"If it's a hassle?..."

"I should love to do it." The perfect secretary made a note on the cream linen paper. "So that I won't forget. No—the OP was completely different from the atmosphere in

London. We had a small room off the main library which was called Winston's Room with the special telephone and one of my silent typewriters so we could just walk through the door at any time and go to work. He used to go and stand by the window—one of those tall ones that come all the way down from a twelve-foot ceiling to the floor in a bay, but specially fitted with bombproof glass inches thick on the inside, so that it wasn't visible from the garden. And special blackout shields inside that again, and soundproofing in leather upholstery inside *that*, and on the back of the door! But he could go out and stand in the garden safely—so one didn't have to worry so much."

"And he met other people there?"

"Only not large groups. There wasn't the space."

"And you kept track of it all?"

Cynthia Whiteside nodded. "I had to be at the machine because I never knew when he would want to switch from shorthand to a typed transcript to see what they'd been talking about. It would all be done on tape now—and I must say," Cynthia Whiteside became professional: "*I* thought your Mr. Nixon had rather a good idea there. Tape recording would have saved an awful lot of work! One feels really frightfully sorry for that poor woman of his—Rose something?—being put on the spot like that for just doing her job. I'm sure *I* should have done exactly the same."

"I can't see Churchill letting his secretary carry the can?"

"No." Cynthia Whiteside said it quickly, but then she added, "Not for something personal. Mind you, if it was the war he could ask for any sacrifice, only you always simply knew that he would do it himself. Because he had—with some of those terrible decisions. Not the popular myths like allowing the destruction of Coventry, but the small-scale, individual cases. Like the betrayal of the entire Prosper network in France, where we knew in advance—" Cynthia Whiteside stopped.

The singing had started up again along the hall. The girl achieved a last crescendo and must have satisfied the task master. A door opened and closed. Footsteps hurried off toward the stairs. Inside the apartment, Cynthia Whiteside hid her confusion by fussing. She straightened a muslin curtain and opened a small window. Sounds came through it more appropriate to memories of war.

"That must be the Guards from the barracks rehearsing some of the odds and ends for the Colour Ceremony." A jug of china roses was lifted, puffed at for invisible dust, and set down. "This show for the Jubilee will be rather superspecial. I suppose you'll go?"

To a parade glorifying our way? Not while the photographs burned holes through the bottom of her briefcase.

"I'm sure you'd like it, there's usually a Cabinet person falling asleep or something." Cynthia Whiteside gave an almost nervous little laugh at her indiscretion. "I say, I am most *awfully* sorry—about your mother."

"Do you remember the night she went over? There was a meeting with the Intelligence boss—"

"Menzies, yes. And your father arrived." Cynthia Whiteside's voice had risen like the singer's and sounded more anxious than ever. "Your father had come over on a motorcycle—Bletchley and Ultra being only a stone's throw from the OP, the people at the gate thought it was a normal courier run. It was a horrible night, quite black and pouring wet. He was soaking." Cynthia Whiteside wrung her own hands in sudden anguish. "He really did feel it you know. He really *did*, Mr. Churchill, I mean. But to your father it must have seemed so awful, sitting there watching the hands on the clock and doing *nothing*, while she got closer and closer and we had those signals. Even General Menzies felt it and he was a very cool customer, 'But it *has* to go through,' Menzies said, 'there's nothing bigger.'"

Cynthia Whiteside stared toward the sounds of the troops coming through the window. "I suppose he was right about Tube Alloys and the bomb but I've often wondered whether every other life in 1944 and 1945 was wasted. Whether we couldn't simply have sat back and waited and dropped the awful thing on Germany... but not your mother—her death *wasn't* wasted! That's what *he* told your father... and showed him the photograph with that one devastating verse... the tears were pouring down his cheeks—"

"*It was a verse?*"

"Oh yes. Can I remember it? I wonder. Faith, I think?" Cynthia Whiteside dabbed at her own cheeks with a pink tissue as she thought. "No—I'm afraid it's gone. Isn't that too bad, I almost had it. But it was *frightfully* appropriate. Shall I go on?"

One more frightful adjective and she might throttle this old bitch. "Yes please," she said. "Do go on."

"Well, then Mr. Churchill even told your father *about* the bomb—that it probably would work and that we were crashing ahead full bore in his own country, in America. We didn't realize, you see, that it wasn't her mission that your father was so desperate about. He accepted that—"

"Accepted it?"

"That was the first, the only rule with Ultra: for any operation dependent on information received by an Ultra source, things *had* to proceed. It was just incredibly dreadful luck that your mother was part of one of them. Your father was such a calm man, and you could see that he was beside himself—trying desperately to hold things in and stay rational when he must have thought the whole world was mad. 'Goddamn it, sir,' he said in your American way, 'but Cheltenham has got the map coordinates. *They have the coordinates within a quarter mile!*' He pounded the leather top of the table right in front of Mr. Churchill!" Cynthia Whiteside was still appalled by that presumption. "*A quarter-mile!* So it *has* to be Anstiebury. We can't miss—we'd nail the bastard *cold!*" Cynthia Whiteside's little voice was almost laughable in its re-creation of the scene.

Almost laughable.

"I've always remembered that, because we used to visit the Roman camps with Father, and have picnics, and Anstiebury was his special favorite. It seemed such a wrong place to find a traitor—but then of course, they didn't. Find him, I mean." Cynthia Whiteside stared at the *Blue Boy* staring back. "That look was all General Menzies gave Mr. Churchill—just one of those looks. And your father left. . . ."

Cynthia Whiteside had at last run out of things to say.

Which no longer mattered. Because although her hunch had known it all along, the index resting on the photographs in the briefcase proved it. Geoffrey Piers was born, grew up, and entertained his party friends in his ancestral home at Anstiebury Camp.

27

She did not want to go back to fighting paper or the bureaucrats who cared for it, but now there was an added obligation to her father. The thread had to be followed to the needle. The bastard had to be really nailed cold. Cheltenham, she noted from her index, had been a college for young ladies: for three little maids teaching Hitler how to hold a teacup. But Cheltenham had also, Violet Vrisser said, been very good at pinning double-crossers to the map.

"They were shit hot, love," said Cushman at the BBC. "And still are. Although it's called GCHQ these days— Government Communications. They don't miss a dirty postcard. Computers are taping us now, I shouldn't wonder. Do you want their number?"

The nerve center's lines were all tied up: a temporary, rotating strike, a recording informed her. If she would just be patient, all would be well. . . .

"In the war?" GCHQ's operator made the word sound as remotely out of fashion as the Crimea. "Can I have your name?"

"Arbright," she said, for the part of the nerve center that tripped on names. "*Miss* Arbright. I'm writing a book on the wartime radio services."

"Oh," said the operator, "I think I'll give you to *Mr. Hincks.*"

Mr. Hincks had enjoyed the war. "I say, jolly good!" but he spoke in gibberish, "Dee-effing, eh? Huff-Duff or Muff-Duff?"

"You've got me."

"That's direction finding," said Mr. Hincks. "In dee-effing the logs were maintained by frequencies. Huff for high, muff for medium. For a spy, I think we could almost certainly say muff, don't you?"

The two sides of the Atlantic were obviously *not* yet speaking the same language. "I'll take your word for it," she said. "May I see them?"

"Oh we don't have them here any longer." Mr. Hincks gave a jolly laugh. "The logs, not the spies—they've all gone to Lambeth."

She associated Lambeth with archbishops and said so. Mr. Hincks found that delightful. "War records to an archbishop, oh *very* good! Very *good!* Shall I call ahead for you, Miss Arbright?"

She said yes please, and thanked him.

"Oh, not at all. Arbright. A famous name. Famous."

Having a duke for a grandfather was obviously the right key to tribal custom.

The taxi took her past so many points around the circle: Saint Margaret's, where the flower and old Johnson started; the PRO, where the paper war engulfed her; Lambeth Palace, where Mr. Mellows vanished in the pillow softness of his church; Saint Thomas's, of Records, where old Johnson ended. As the taxi stopped in front of two enormous guns, she felt not only history repeating; she felt the circle close. Standing between the guns was an old friend.

"Hi," she said. "You've left your Domesday Book."

"And *you* were looking for your mother, miss," said Sergeant Henry Hithertwaite. "Are you nearly home with that one?"

"Yes," she said, "I think I nearly am."

"Well that's grand. If you can keep a secret, miss—" Sergeant Hithertwaite cast a conspirator's glance at the steel mouths of the barrels, "I like it better here. I didn't mind being pulled out of Public Records—even if it was sudden—"

"Sudden?"

"Right after I met you, miss. But I never was one for books—and that's a *fact!* Did you forget something, miss?"

She shook her head. "Someone I liked used to say that. I want to look up some radio logs—"

"And you don't know where to start."

She smiled and shrugged. "So what's new?"

"Well, I don't know either but let's go inside and find

out." Sergeant Hithertwaite put a fatherly hand on her elbow. "A pity it's just papers, miss, because there's so much here that's *real*. These beauties," patting the barrels, "they're off your battleships, *Ramilles* and *Renown*, and we've got your gun which put out your first round in France in the First War, and your Spitfire and V2 from your Second."

Papers or planes, the jargon was the same. They passed through the doors of the portico.

"Our Dome," Sergeant Hithertwaite changed possessives, "was done by Smirke. You won't believe it, miss, but we used to be a madhouse, the Bethlehem Royal. Now, I'll leave you with our Doris at the desk. See me afterward if you have time and I'll take you round, miss. There's your uniforms of Monty and Lord Louis, and Hitler's will, and your Munich piece of paper. . . ."

All housed in a building for the criminally insane. Doris at the desk had her head on straight for the granddaughter of a duke.

"Cheltenham called about you, Miss Arbright. I've made out your ticket and the custodian has sorted the boxes for you for the years 1943 to 1945. All that material has just been moved to the side gallery beyond Air Warfare—go through the Dome and turn right. Room seventeen."

It was impossible not to get sidetracked by the human-interest side of war: by the size of a hat, the cloth of a coat, a piece of paper that might have been written at the Berchtes-gaden table with the silver pheasants. By a row of photographs on a gallery wall.

My girls were so afraid of all the little things. . . .

My girls.

Noor Khan with her dark, haunted eyes. The tartan-ribboned Marjorie—round and jolly, not patrician in the least—looked like a farm girl but was educated at Oxford and the Sorbonne and terrified of pigs. Alice of the stinging nettles. Eighteen pictures of hidden fears hanging on a wall.

What did Number Eighteen fear? Violet Vrisser had never told her that. . . .

The radio logs, in cardboard cartons tied with string, were labeled by their theater of operations. Three cartons placed separately on a table were marked "Transmissions—Home Regions: South, Central, Northern." She looked at her map of Britain and picked "Central."

The earliest records for 1939 and 1940 were the fattest and covered the shortest intervals. The logs shrank as the Double-Cross Committee ran the Germans out of spies. By the autumn of 1943 the entries were down to six a night and almost all were analyzed as "Own Forces, Operator Error." Occasionally an entry would be annotated "Undetermined." Once, a transmission was labeled "Active": three nights later, "Terminated."

Before the remarks column, reading across the page, there were divisions for "Time, Bearing Coordinates in Degrees (magnetic), Bearing Coordinates in Degrees (True)," "Geographical Location (British Isles)." Beside the location column was a final space. "Agent Code ID."

On the night of October fifth, a black Lysander night, Cheltenham says bearing 131 degrees; the Isle of Wight says 043; both stations call it Anstiebury. Both identify, Charybdis.

But she knew that. She turned to January 1945.

The pages were as white as they should be when the drifts lie deep and crisp and even. White and blank until January twenty-eighth, when not two, but three cross bearings skewer the snow around an Englishman's country house. Around a lounge lizard with a telegraph key turning the dogs loose on Scylla, the woman who rejected him.

No!

Not Scylla any longer. Not just a girl in a picture. *Her mother.* Her mother on the wall outside. Her mother having her guts corroded on the table. Her mother dying an agonizing death in silence for things she must believe in. *Must.*

In Room 17 of what was once a madhouse, she stared into her open briefcase. Tears like Churchill's rolled down her cheeks.

She made copies of the entries and signed out at the desk. Across from the desk a bronze head of Churchill regarded her with all the weight of the world on its missing shoulders.

"Wonder what the old boy's thinking, eh, miss?" Sergeant Hithertwaite patted the head affectionately. "Always loved his toy soldiers, didn't he? We've got them here, you know—just along in your Land Warfare? Did you finally get what you're after, miss?"

"Not quite," she said. "But I will, Sergeant. And that *is* a fact!"

But how much of her certainty was like the Ottawa drivers' wishful thinking? All the wheels moving but still slipping backward? Because the newspapers on sale by the guns showed Piers still driving forward; Piers still threatening to put the Irish Problem in its place: Piers now at odds of five to three for next P.M. if the present incumbent went. *And*, the papers said, Lord Piers was ready. Lord Piers had this day taken action by not only surrendering the Great Seal of England to the Queen, but by surrendering his title. His lordship, Geoffrey Piers, was this day just plain *Mister*!

28

The marquess, her uncle—said Leofric's city house-keeper—was at the Abbey for the weekend with Sir Rollo, her cousin, and the marchioness, her aunt, and they had all—upstairs and down—followed her African adventures in the papers and she must go down at once to help them prepare for the duke's ninety-second with the Jubilee bonfire and the Jubilee tree.

"Although with the holiday crowds I don't know about *driving*, madam," the housekeeper added cautiously. And after a little laugh together over her last drive through the army, "I've always thought the best way, madam, was the train. It's not an express—but none of them are expresses now, are they? All these Intercity's and HST's or whatever they call them and you can *never* get a porter—they just won't look at you—"

"Where do I take it?"

"Take, madam?"

"The train—where do I catch this train?"

"All the Exeter trains go from Paddington," said the housekeeper, "except ours." As though the train and its line belonged to the family: Perhaps at one time, they had. "Ours go from Waterloo every two hours and we get off at Sherborne—I'll call ahead and have Kendall send the car to meet you. There is a stop or two—perhaps I should make you some sandwiches, madam? I could deliver a hamper to the station in a taxi?"

This hospitality ensnared as swiftly as the CIA's. She declined with thanks—and then regretted it after a British Rail lunch. The housekeeper, right again about the porters, was wrong about the stops and it was late afternoon before she was reunited with her family.

Until she spoke, the aunt was a little like Violet Vrisser. She had Violet Vrisser's gray hair and lived for lost causes: at the present time, saving the rail line from the village of Maiden Newton, and putting the Liberal Party back in office. She absolutely *deplored* the press's disgraceful hounding of poor Jeremy Thorpe and the frightful ongoing ordeal for poor Jeremy's *mother!* The aunt seemed torn between deploring Jane herself for being in the press, and seeking her opinion on the reactionary bigots in Rhodesia.

"After the enormous strides by the Negro in your own country, Jane, you must have been appalled by those plantations. One feels so *helpless*—if only they'd picked a man like Todd when they had the chance. And where *is* Rollo?"

Her cousin—the "army man" next in line for the succession—was fishing, said Leofric, and the duke, tired from the excitement, had gone to bed: but with a ducal command that she was to come up immediately upon arrival.

Kendall, the butler, had her grandfather propped on pillows looking at the shadows falling across his park. "It'll be midsummer soon," said the duke. "I always like midsummer. It keeps the dark back a little longer. Leofric tells me you've done wonderful things, my dear, wonderful things."

"Not really, Grandfather," but the old man expected that and squeezed her hand very slightly in disbelief and closed his eyes. She tried gently to disengage.

The eyes opened and were suddenly lucid. 'I'm planting a *Sequoia prostrata* on the big day. A dwarf redwood—I chose it for you, my dear. American in origin, but bred out of the Botanical at Cambridge. It seemed fitting, rather fitting." The eyes closed again and this time he was asleep.

Through the window she could see Cousin Rollo casting a line onto the ornamental lake. The delicate tracery of the line and its ripples jabbed keenly of Jonathan and his incongruous love for fly fishing. She mentioned it to Leofric.

Her uncle nodded and watched his heir. "I'm sorry about my wife's politics. I don't argue with her about all that—one can't change things, so what's the point? There's no hope out there. No hope at all. We had so little time. When I think of Africa, I always think of the Romans, because it must have been like that when they were pulling back. Worse, in a way. I mean, after four hundred years when they left *us* we were almost as civilized as themselves. But I'm sure even if their best augur—like your man Shilling—had told our ancestors that the lights were going out and it was going to stay dark for six hundred years it wouldn't have changed things here, any more than it will there. You either stay, and take charge, or you don't. But you can't take charge everywhere outside the walls—you know that now, in America. You might want to, and it might well be best if you did, but you can't. Eventually things have to work themselves out."

"In Ireland as well?"

Leofric didn't answer. They left the duke's bedroom and walked along the hall between her ancestors. Again she felt as she had at Albany, that in these passages there was no way of telling time, that the Irish question might have been discussed here on a weekend by Churchill and Lloyd-George. Even fifty years before that, by Gladstone and Disraeli. They stopped beside the study door on the first landing. "Very *much* in Ireland," said Leofric. "Go along and meet Rollo. I have to do some telephoning but I'll be in here later if you want to talk."

Perhaps her thoughts of Jonathan came from the size: her cousin was a huge man in his forties, with iron-gray hair and a great square face. Where were all the chinless wonders of the British upper classes?

"I'll have him in the bag in just a second," said Rollo. "Would you get the creel—the wicker basket over there?"

She passed it to him. There were no speech impediments in this voice, no affectations of any sort. This voice said what was necessary and said it only once. This voice would whip the arrogance of a Colonel Smythe up, down, and sideways and go on eating breakfast.

"A pound," said Rollo. "Do you want him in the morning or shall I put him back?" The huge hand held the fish at the water's edge. The iridescent flanks made no attempt to twitch.

"Isn't he all hooked up?"

"The fly's barbless." Rollo removed a tiny black speck of bristled hairs from the trout's lower jaw.

"Let him go, I guess."

The fish waited for a moment to see if the gods were only toying, then swirled and was gone. A heron standing gauntly farther along the bank gave them a banker's stare for a giveaway.

"I nearly looked you up once." Rollo stuck the fly into a slice of cork and dismantled the fishing rod. "I was in Borneo and I saw your name on something in a magazine about relieving Hué. I wouldn't have allowed it, having a woman along on a show like that."

"It started when we got the vote," she said.

"I don't mean your female sensibilities." Rollo's voice, unlike the trout, refused to rise to the bait. "It's bad for the men. Inhibits them or makes 'em foolish. The press is a menace, male *or* female—"

"Peace or war?"

Rollo smiled a white square smile. "Politicians deserve anything they get. More power to you."

The sentiments seemed to disturb the heron's sense of order and it flapped away with a harsh screaming cry, its long legs trailing like those of a corpse across the water.

She stared out at the lake, at the island with its small white ruin that Mackenzie King would have sold a Senate seat to steal for Mum; she stared at the trees and gardens in all their acres rolling down from the great house. If *her* mother had been her uncle—a first son and not a daughter—would it all be hers now instead of Rollo's? Not in a man's world, sweetheart. But would she have *wanted it?* To be a Lady Jane? Was *that* why she had snapped at Alleyn?

"I guess you're polishing your armor for the big day?" she said to Rollo. "I saw one of your horses being brushed up on top of a roof yesterday in Kensington."

"It looks a little odd doesn't it? Knightsbridge new barracks are a far cry from Combermere down at Windsor. Combermere was condemned for human habitation in 1800. Of course," Rollo was totally impassive, "they've only troops there now. We got the horses out."

So there was a sense of humor.

"But I'm not really in that line of work, Jane, thumping around with five pounds of brass and silver on my head."

"You've quit the Life Guards?"

"One can't step down from the Tins—senior regiment, do you see—but we have a part of the Special Air and I slid across to that."

The Special Air Service: for whose secret ways in dirty places even Selbach had had a grudging admiration. Her bluff cousin with his open face looked like a man who had never heard, let alone kept, a secret.

"Keep going after Piers," he said as he left her outside Leofric's door. "The man butchered the old regiments when he reorganized at Defence. No sense of the value of tradition—he's a sod. See you at dinner. We don't dress."

Leofric's London office, she realized now, had been Leofric's country study moved to town. The two rooms were clones, even to the carriage clocks. "The man only made those two and one grandfather," said Leofric, "and then shot himself. Quite common with clockmakers, the complexity of the works drove them mad. Did Rollo take a fish?"

"He let it go. When you told me he was in the Guards, I figured a guy on horses not some kind of a commando."

"Horses?" Leofric smiled. "Rollo hates horses. Always has, much to the Duke's sorrow. He had to do his training with them—riding through the dustbin lids—but then he switched to tanks and later to the parachute business. Not every man's cup of tea but it makes him feel useful in peacetime. And I suppose it is. Although as you mentioned, the Irish thing's not nice. Fire that must be fought with fire never is. Now—sit and tell me."

She didn't tell him of impressions, she only told him facts—as though he were Fadiman assessing the weight of a story. But Fadiman would have shown surprise, annoyance: would have stood up, sat down, sworn, drunk coffee, smoked a pack of cigarettes—Marlboro's—a little sheepishly.

She got to Violet Vrisser's report.

"I read it, Jane."

She could only stare at him.

"I know," he said. "Perhaps if I'd told you..."

She would never have gone. And Harry Rogers might be

flying over floppies; and Violet Vrisser and Jonathan, and Kapisa and Sixpence Hwata might still be attending all their ordered routine tasks. Or they might not. Because war would still have come to Chiumbwa, if not last week, then next week: because Violet Vrisser would never have hidden behind the wire at Johnson's Store. And although she would now be spared this terrible daily sense of loss, she would never have known Violet Vrisser either.

"Then you saw the photographs?" she asked, still trying to hold it in.

"Photographs?" The long sympathetic face for the first time showed just a trace of apprehension.

"From Ravensbrück."

Now there was no answer.

She opened her briefcase. "You know what *gets* me, Leofric?" as she reached, without looking, beneath the papers, "what *really* gets me? That those fuckers, in the last month of the fucking war, when their fucking country had nothing to fucking eat—wasted money on *fucking color pictures!*"

The obscene language had not prepared him. The mouth squeezed until the lips vanished altogether; the hands resting on the table dug their blunt but well-kept nails right through the French polish of its surface.

"In Washington," she said, "the first time I saw these, I threw up."

Leofric turned the photographs face down. "What is it you want, Jane?"

"It's what I *don't* want! I don't want that son of a bitch to have another goddamn day in *any* office, Leofric. I don't want him kissing another fucking bishop or another baby. I want Piers *out!*"

"Only Piers, Jane?" Leofric inclined his head toward the walls of the study, and the arch of its window, and the scarcely visible arches of the ruins outside it; toward the countryside beyond the ruins, that rolled all the way to London. "Not the rest?"

"I can't get the rest," she said. "I can't get Churchill or Menzies, or any of those other bastards around the circle— *but I can get Piers.*"

Leofric stroked the backs of the photographs softly. "And why do you tell me, Jane?"

"Partly because you could do it *quickly*. If you got your act together, your old boy act, you could get the bastard out before he buys another vote. Christ, if the Queen says she won't meet him once a week, the fucker wouldn't even *try!*"

Leofric did not dispute that. "Partly?"

"I want to let that old guy upstairs plant his Jubilee tree without a scandal."

"Scandal, Jane? How could scandal possibly touch our family?"

"She was your *sister!* Doesn't an Englishman have to do something about *that?*"

"Even if it means tearing the body of his country? Is that what she would have wanted, Jane? Is that what she died for?"

Or just for the play part, the stained glass and the music and the carvings, and the marching bands and the medals and orders on the velvet cushions.

She turned the photographs face up. Atrocity up.

"Leofric, if this was for anything less than all the things you say you stand for—if she was gutted out just to save your tourist shell—*I'll blow the fucking thing wide open.*"

Leofric placed one set of the pictures gently, reverently, in his desk. "I shall go up to London with you on Monday morning. But, Jane, you won't be irrational? A small merchant banker can't promise miracles."

"Two days," she said. "Get him out before your Jubilee."

Leofric squeezed her hand. As a small merchant banker he knew when terms were nonnegotiable.

29

The *Times* office, she sensed at once, smelled more strongly of embarrassment than of Cushman's butted cigarette. Alleyn tried to disguise both by kissing her without the support of his pipe. She moved her head away abruptly.

"Don't snow me, Roger." The worst part of Selbach's trick-and-joke disclosures was the slime coating of suspicion they smeared on everyone they touched. Tremblay was right: it made her feel sick. "So the rats are quitting the ship before we even sail?"

"Jane," Alleyn was even more awkward, "there must have been rumors. There's already phenomenal pressure on my owners. With material that's the least bit 'iffy'—hearsay rather than documentary—"

She tossed the photograph of Piers and Lansky on the desk. "There ain't nothin' 'iffy' about that, honey."

A burning piece of ash fell unnoticed into a fold of Cushman's sweater. She told them Selbach's conversation. Both men were flabbergasted.

"*Cabinet!*" said Alleyn. "To know about Cabinet, the Yanks must have a minister breaking his oath on a full-time basis!"

"If the CIA has ears on the wall in Dolphin Square," she said, "why not Downing Street as well?"

And why not here? There was a long silence.

"*Christ!*" Cushman scrabbled frantically at his stomach to find the ash. The smoldering edges of the new hole melted into an old one beside it.

"Bugged or not," Alleyn continued, "I simply can't believe the present lot—even with Piers in charge—would pull a Suez in reverse. Dropping the Specials in against Rhodesian whites, I'm not sure what would happen if they *did!*"

"It wouldn't be a pushover," she said. "Those guys won't give up the country club at the first Union Jack. Adam, this Mob tie-in with Piers. Can the BBC use it?"

Cushman shrugged. "At the Beeb we don't even have the luxury of private owners, love. My little team effort on the drugs got squashed flat. If you could get things started on this with someone else, we can float the 'attributed to.'"

"The French are out," said Alleyn.

"She might try the Germans—we've still got the Thalidomide connection."

Alleyn clicked his heels. "Remember children, today ze Chermans are your *friendts*."

"I agree." Cushman exhaled heavily. "With anything that smells Nazi, it's asking a lot. The anti–Statute-of-Limitations crowd might get behind it, but they're more a lunatic fringe than the mainstream."

Alleyn sat on the corner of the desk in front of her, his stork's leg swinging just above the floor. "Jane, I told you when you started, it's very, very tricky in this country. We're only getting the drug thing aired because we're using the venue of the World Court—not our own. I don't see any way that you can get personal accusations into the open in Britain except through a straight-forward police charge—and you'll never get that. Not with hearsay on tape from dead witnesses."

"He's right, love." Cushman lit a fifth cigarette from the fourth. "You just have no idea of the weight of the Official Secrets Act! Short of a Guy Fawkes trial for a public murder, they can cloak anything—"

"But let's grant," Alleyn interrupted, "that the CIA is correct. That Piers *has* something treasonable on him, that he played for either side, left *or* right. Even both—Burgess and Philby were ardently pro-Nazi until Stalin turned them off in 1941—and say we could 'borrow' a copy of these files Washington says our SIS are sitting on, *strewth*—we'd be pinched ourselves before the word got set in print. The Establishment ranks would close like oysters, from the palace down. Jane, you'll have to go from your side—from the States. With your 'in' at Reuter's you must be halfway there?"

She shook her head. "The Press Association half on this side would never ride with it. They have too much tied up with their commercial wires—the big money hates hassle."

Cushman climbed down from his chair. "It's not all negative, love. I think we really can get heads rolling on this backstage Rhodesian thing. Enough to screw Piers for P.M. even if he does get the party nod in Blackpool, I shouldn't wonder."

"Wouldn't that be enough for your mother?" asked Alleyn. "After so long?"

The list was a whole lot longer than her mother. She stood up and walked across to the window. The Victorian traffic light had almost disappeared under an enormous Jubilee rosette.

"No," she said. "It would not."

Another of Cynthia Whiteside's extravagant envelopes waited for her at the desk at Dolphin Square. A second envelope, discreetly unobtrusive to the outside world held an invitation extended to her "by the Officer Commanding and Officers, London District, to attend The Colour Ceremony on the occasion of Her Majesty's Silver Jubilee."

Cynthia Whiteside's invitation was a folded, mimeographed map of the Whitehall area. "War Rooms—as Promised," was written across the top and some superimposed instructions followed an illegible signature underneath.

> *c/o 41, Sub-G*
> *Treasury Chambers*
> *Parliament Street*
> *For Mrs. CW and one.*

1. *Please assemble at: approx. 2 p.m., June 5.*

Further instructions about passes and holidays had been scratched out.

Below the scratching, the same indecipherable name had scrawled "Strongly advise carry a small torch!!" A hand-drawn arrow ran from "torch" up across the page to a building on the map marked "Treasury Chambers." A large "X" with ASSEMBLE HERE was printed underneath. Dots ran backward from the "X" along Great George Street to the Westminster tube station.

She dumped her briefcase on the bed—but accidentally upside down so that when she opened it the contents all fell out. The heaviest items, the recorder and cassettes, were on the bottom. The photographs, the lightest things with the heaviest weight, lay on top, staring mutely. She stuffed them in a drawer, then went to the john, came out, found her shoulder bag and flat shoes for walking, looked at her watch. There was nothing to do with her day but think, and thought was intolerable.

She headed for the hall, turned the door handle, and then with an impulse that she had long since ceased to question went back for the recorder and the photographs.

Intuition demanded that an old prime minister's ghost down there should see what it had done.

30

She arrived early underneath Big Ben and wandered for half an hour through the streets it dominated, beside the buildings with the names that tied everything together since her start in April: six weeks ago—a period now as remote as her mother's past. She moved slowly along Downing Street, Parliament Street, King Charles Street, and down the steps to Saint James's Park, where she had walked out on old Reuter and his pigeons.

She found the building where "X" marked the spot. The gray bureaucracy of Silver Jubilee Britain had turned the romance of Treasury Chambers to the dross of a Central Statistical Office.

"Oh, you're in *trousers*. I do wish *I* were." Cynthia Whiteside, voice even higher pitched than usual, hair escaping in the wind, seemed uncertain of it. "And I do hope we're not late. Mr. T.'s a dear but he does like one to be *punctual*—oh, good," as the clock struck twice above their heads, "we are!"

Mr. T. was not. A small office lined top to bottom, side to side, with card-index files at first glance gave no sign of him. "Although I think those *are* his glasses," said Cynthia Whiteside, a trifle anxiously. "Ah—a note. He's unexpectedly detained. Do I know the way?" Cynthia Whiteside gave a peal of laughter—a trifle forced—and shepherded her from the office like the girl guide at the Dorset abbey.

"One wouldn't want to go down without his blessing," said Cynthia Whiteside. "The Annexe papers are Mr. T.'s labor of love, no one else could have done it. But then this was *all* his idea, the tours of the War Rooms. For years and years they just sat here—even now I'm sure no more than a handful have been down. I haven't been myself since . . . goodness, I don't know! And now that it's all being passed over to the Imperial it will be run as just another fixed museum display. No touching, no sitting in the chairs. There won't be any sense of *being there*. You have flat shoes—that's good, it gets rather steep."

A set of stairs built like a ship's companionway led down in front of them. They descended it and then another. At the foot of the second flight a steel ladder marked Escape Hatch was stapled to the wall. The nautical atmosphere was reinforced by a massive watertight door held against a rubber seal by a wheel-control and heavy steel lugs.

"For gas," said Cynthia Whiteside, stepping over a high threshold and ducking at the same time, "it was an awful palaver getting *him* through all this on his bad days—his chest days. When the sailors had to hoist him up and down in his chair he looked just like an old Regency figure—until of course you saw the siren suit."

The door was on a hinge that lifted as it opened and automatically swung shut behind them, spinning the wheel and the lugs back into position. "Isn't that clever?" said Cynthia Whiteside. "Why don't they do something like that in lavatories do you suppose?"

Now they were in a passage so low that she had to keep her head down as they walked. Every three paces the roof was reinforced with massive oak beams and the walls were lit with small generator-fed blue and white lights that flickered down onto the linoleum. Air puffed weakly through punkah louvers on a nautical trunking.

"The lino's new!" Cynthia Whiteside's tone disapproved of any change in the rites. "That must have cost *pounds*! I mean the place is huge, you know. We had five hundred people here—and there are almost two hundred rooms! The passages run for miles and miles—I've no idea where actually. Some go under the river."

"And all this was done for the war?"

"Oh dear, no. Most of it was here already as wine cellars and crypts and things, one of them was Wren's, I think—at least they call it Wren's 'Bundles Room.'" Cynthia Whiteside gave a little laugh, "Bundles for Britain, you see?"

She smiled back but found the joke impenetrable.

"It was here," said Cynthia Whiteside, "but it wasn't tied together until Hitler was being really silly—over Danzig, was it?—and Maurice Hankey, who'd taken a good look at Number 10 and seen that a bomb would knock it down like the Red Queen's house of cards, on his own bat organized the Marines to jolly well get on and do the job. Day after day they'd march along with bits of wood and doors and things for 'maintainance,' in the charge of a Mr. Rance, until people just got used to them—'Rance's Grenadiers' they called them. I suppose in the phony days it must have all seemed rather funny."

They came to another of Mr. Rance's gas-tight doors.

"Once it was real, it wasn't funny at all. There would be a sentry at each one of these and we'd have to give a special knock and say the password and have our cards ready and they'd check you every time no matter who you were—except him of course. *He* didn't need a knock: you could hear the slippers a mile away, padding along to the Midnight Follies —the really hush-hush meetings. Could you do the door?"

She did the door. It closed behind them.

In silence that was absolute a sign still asked for QUIET PLEASE. A pigeonhole file still sorted messages as "Routine," "Secret," "Most Secret." Lights with single bulbs still hung from the oak ceilings on twisted cords and chains threading between snakes of plumbing; air pipes and knee beams still holding things up; tubes and wire baskets from department stores in the days before cash registers, bringing things down: "Messages, Home Forces," said a card on one of the baskets.

"The Lampson Tubes used to whistle night and day," Cynthia Whiteside said. "This is his War Room."

Even the most raw recruit must know that, as she looks at the chairs around the table, each with a name: Cripps, Attlee, Eden, Brooke. One chair, larger, with a rounded back and massive arms, had no name. The chair's back was to the *World on Mercator's Projection*. Half the world was red. Beside the unnamed chair, a blotter, a pen, a set of inkwells, a dispatch box open as though in use, an ashtray—but no cigar.

"He would *insist* on simply tossing the stubs over his shoulder." That untidiness still almost upset Cynthia Whiteside's tidy nature. Almost. "The sailors were always dashing to intercept the stubs before something quite vital went up in smoke. Mrs. Hill told me that Chamberlain read the Declaration from this room but then didn't use it very much. I used to think that it was as though the room knew it wasn't real, and that it was waiting down here, waiting for the phony war to end. Waiting for him. Waiting for it to really *matter.*"

In front of the chair with the rounded back, for those moments when things really mattered, was a written inscription: "We are not interested in the possibilities of defeat: they do not exist."

"Queen Victoria," said Cynthia Whiteside. "When Mr. T. gives the tour he says that he reads that phrase aloud and then he plays tape recordings of the speeches. It must be rather goosebumping with the V for Victory drum beating away—"

"Even if it's Winnie-the-Pooh?"

Cynthia Whiteside gave her a long, long look. "I think if you'd been here . . ."

Which was what all these bards of the wartime *Iliad* said. If you'd been here, under the clocks on the walls, with one now stuck forever at eleven—the time Chamberlain announced that Berchtesgaden Charlie wasn't joking anymore. Next to the clocks was a map of Anzio. Estimated losses for the landings were written in beside it. "Medium casualties."

Medium. . . .

"The one thing Mr. Rance couldn't get for the tables was that green cloth, you know for billiard tables? They got this from the London policemen's trousers. 'Stroke one of my tables and stroke a bobby's bum,' Mr. Rance used to say. . . ."

Cynthia Whiteside passed her hand across the cloth with a tiny hint of sensuality, and smiled, and moved through a low but ordinary doorway.

"*His bedroom.*"

A blue naval blanket, a blue cover on the bed. A heavy mahogany bed from a tree like Violet Vrisser's. A high headboard, armchairs, a desk with three labeled baskets: "Action This Day," "In Three Days," "Report Progress One Week!" More inkwells—how much writing had he done? A candle stopped at halfway down, a bell carafe of water with a glass. A prayer book like old Johnson's for inspiration, a paper punch: "*Klop, Jumbo!*"

"I can hear him, you know," said Cynthia Whiteside. "Quite, quite, clearly. Roaring for his effing boots," said Cynthia Whiteside, although the mother of two sons, blushed slightly as she had for the policemen's trousers. "You know, for weeks I thought he meant *flying* boots, because they were those fleece-lined zip-up ones. Inspector Thompson and his valet used to hide them so he couldn't go out and stand in the garden to watch the raids. I used to be terrified—even down here you could hear them crumping and the air would give that extra *whoosh* in the trunks and one of the Signals people would put up his umbrella and grin and you'd go on typing or coding or whatever it was. You always knew when it was really bad because the lights went completely out and we had to use the candles."

Beside the bed was a curtain. Cynthia Whiteside drew the curtain back and England ran floor to ceiling on a map behind it. Not an inch of coastline was without an annotation—a platoon could hold this cliff; tank barriers here; flaming oil on the waters there; positions for a division to stand for a last ditch south of London.

"We would have fought them in the fields and streets," said Cynthia Whiteside.

And under the streets?

"You know, you can't imagine but when France fell, and that was on a Saturday, I mean we just *knew* that they would be here on Monday—Nazi paratroopers in Saint James's to take the Palace. This enormous wooden rattle was to tell us that they had landed. I don't think anyone told us what came next— Now here's something that will interest you."

A tiny room, not much more than a broom closet.

"I think Mr. Rance did use it for brooms once, but what *I* remember it for is Mr. Roosevelt, because all the talking was from here. You can see the telephone inside. It was one of those scrambler ones—brown boxes we called them. I never had the least idea how they worked—I'm sure neither did *he*. The guts of it were under Selfridges, I think. You see the two clocks? He always sat with his back to the Washington one. I don't know why he hated your time so much."

"What did he sit on?" The cubicle was devoid of chairs.

"An Elsan—you know, one of those portable lavatory things. It was really rather funny because two sailors would carry it in—and you see the 'Vacant/Engaged' latch?—he'd slide that over and the poor troops would hang around outside for *two hours* before the latch moved back. They must have thought he was most shockingly bunged up! There was a story about the Elsans—that the RAF used to drop them on the bunker in Berlin, and Hitler actually complained about it through the Swiss. This is the Map Room."

With two rows of desks, and banks of old-fashioned

phones: white, black, one red—the colors of Africa. One map
had air raids, fighter dispositions; another had convoy routes,
U-boat–sortie channels, all the important naval actions of the
war. The last map had the turning points on land, the high-
water marks at Stalingrad and Alamein—Burma of Lord Louis—
before the hinge of fate swung shut like the gas-tight doors
and the waves washed back across the map and along the Elbe
and down into the rat hole of the other bunker in Berlin.

"There was a small map room next to this one, behind
that wall, and do you know, people worked in it right through
the war and never had an inkling we were here, and they'd
been phoning us reports—*right through the war!*" Yet from
Cynthia Whiteside's face those long darkest days when it
really mattered, hadn't lasted long enough. "I was with him
on V-E night, you know," and Cynthia Whiteside's voice
dropped its anxious affectations, became soft and almost
crooning, "and we stood on the balcony up above us at the
Annexe, and oh my goodness how we cheered, and cried,
and they—all those thousands and thousands cheered and he
stood there with the cigar and grinned and grinned, and
started us off on Hope and Glory... oh my goodness..."

Cynthia Whiteside dabbed at her eyes with a small
lace-trimmed handkerchief. They walked back to the first
main room. "That was *his* finest hour—not the beginning and
not the parade at the very end, because after V-E it was
Potsdam and never knowing when 'Mr. Mouse'—as he called
Attlee—would get that extra vote and let 'six years of hope
deferred' have its way. Which it did—he was right on that
too." And Cynthia Whiteside's voice was once more partisan.
"From the first result in the Midlands it never varied,
although *we* didn't think it was possible, not to throw him out
like that. I mean, I know now it's fashionable to say he was all
wrong for peace—but it *wasn't* peace then, was it? Still as
close to war as shooting with the Russians, and then straight
into Korea. Anyway, he knew by just after lunch and we
made the arrangements at the Palace and off he went with his
cigar and his hat, stumping out of the door of Number 10
because we weren't down here by then, not anymore..."

Cynthia Whiteside took a last look around the rooms and
the memories.

"As brave as a lion, with the rest of us crying and the
telephone never stopped ringing and all the telegrams poured

in for days and days from all over the world, and then he left for the holiday in Italy, where General Alexander used to go. And he sent us that lovely wedding present—you probably saw it in my room, the picture of the wall and the garden and the pond at Chartwell? And all built with his own hands. . . ."

To build up. To tear down. A time to hate. She found it impossible to hate him. Winnie-the-Pooh may have read his speeches, but she believed his tears.

Cynthia Whiteside was walking out of the War Rooms now, along a passage that opened into a large space lined with triple-tiered bunks. There were folding wooden chairs and trestle tables and a rack of magazines: *Picture Post, Woman's Life*—on paper that was thin and transparent and rationed in December 1944. On one of the tables was a tattered songbook. "Bless 'Em All," "RUN, RABBITT,—RUN!" "When the Lights Go on Again. . . ."

All over the world? Selbach was at least partly right. The lights might be on, but there weren't many places that governments couldn't arbitrarily switch them out. Or burn what was being read.

"We had a little library in here. This was Q Dorm for the switchboard girls from FANY. At first there weren't enough spaces and to sleep you'd have to 'hot bunk' or use bits of cardboard on the floor, but naturally no one *minded*," said Cynthia Whiteside in the glow of time and distance. "Oh, we used to have such times in here. Such sing-songs—"

And Cynthia Whiteside, as carried away as old Johnson by her theatrical surroundings, launched into a high thin soprano:

Run, Rabbit,–Run, Rabbit,–run, run, run.
Run, Rabbit,–Run, Rabbit,–run, run, run.
  Bang, bang, bang, bang, goes the farmer's gun,
Run, Rabbit,–Run, Rabbit,–run, run, run.
Run, Rabbit,–Run, Rabbit,–run, run, run.
  Don't give the farmer his fun, fun, fun.
  He'll get by–without his rabbit-pie.
So, Run, Rabbit,–Run, Rabbit,–run, run, run.

"Flanagan and Allan." Cynthia Whiteside said the names with reverence as though the lyricists were Bunyan and Wesley, and closed the songbook gently. "And after the sing-songs we watched pictures—all the ones with the floods of tears, *Mrs. Miniver* and *White Cliffs*. Why on earth we wanted to watch that I can't imagine now. Of course we laughed a lot too, Laurel and Hardy and *The Great Dictator* with Charlie Chaplin."

On the wall above the songbook, fate, or someone with a taste for irony, had hung a picture calendar showing an artist's impression of the new cathedral for ravished Coventry. The calendar beneath the picture marked off another good year for Jael: 1956.

"Mr. T. told me the Rooms were started up again for Suez. I suppose for Eden it was rather like going back to the nursery for tea, when you knew where everything was, and it was all comfy laps and a fire and Nanny to cope with the crisis—but then," mused Cynthia Whiteside, wistfully, "the trouble with Suez was that poor Eden didn't *have* Nanny anymore, did he?"

They came to a doorway even lower than the rest and blocked down its center by a pipe. "*He* had an awful time squeezing past that," said Cynthia Whiteside. "That's why he so seldom came in here. Mind you, very few people did. It was rather the end of the line, this room. I don't think any of us really wanted to know what they were really doing in here. Please," Cynthia Whiteside seemed once again a touch embarrassed, "do go along in. You won't mind if I leave you?... Just for a moment? Taken short...."

She didn't mind.

She was glad of the silence. Glad to *be* alone for a moment in this extraordinary dim room, where the ideas started. Just for a moment, to let imagination bring all the photo people back as well. Violet Vrisser there, by the left and the edge of an invisible map. Bevan, the deception master at the head of the table—Wheatley in that seat beside him dreaming up death plots for his novels that mirrored life. The table itself, so lustrous in the picture, mirrored nothing. Layered by a fine screen of dust it absorbed the gloom, so that the object at its center was as shrouded as the skull goddess in the cave.

By reflex, she ran a hand across the table, turned on a light.

Thirty-four years since the camera caught its likeness, the Faun, bronze representative of Jael, danced again in the sheen of the liberated wood.

There would be no seal for good housekeeping here but

she felt obsessively compelled to wipe clean the remainder of
the table. She lifted the Faun, blew the dust off its metallic
skin. Set it gently back.

She read the words of General Wolseley on the plaque,
heard footsteps coming back along the passage and a wheeze
of breath squeezed out by the post bisecting the doorway;
sensed as the voice spoke that the plaque was suddenly
brighter from a flicker of the blue lights. That the lights made
the air as blue as the Forum in Montreal.

"Mrs. Montigny," said Mr. Geoffrey Piers, "we must
talk."

31

Piers picked the chair beneath the plaque. The manner
was as suave, the demarcation between black and silver in
the hair as crisp, the tailoring as perfect as at Albany two
months ago. But like the crazy cracking of the glaze of a china
plate under too much heat, there were also tiny signs of
pressure. The way the right index finger stroked beneath the
corner of the eye, then dropped to scratch at the crease in
the pin-striped trouser leg. The constant tremor in the gleaming
shoe at the end of the leg, so nonchalantly crossed. The way
the left hand, working in opposition to the right, constantly
returned to the knot of the old school tie.

"Mrs. Montigny, please—do sit."

She took Violet Vrisser's chair, which put the Faun
between them as referee. In this dim blue light Piers looked
his age. Had he worn makeup for the dinner in his apartment? By the end, Nixon—a jaundiced Californian ghost in
winter Washington—had never gone anywhere without Max
Factor. She realized abruptly that Cynthia Whiteside and her
war stories had also become ghosts.

"Was it rigged?" she asked Piers. "This whole deal?"

"Rigged?" The theatrical eyebrows lifted in a classic manner. "Ah, arranged. After a fashion, Mrs. Montigny. It was, one might say, only this afternoon that Mrs. Whiteside *fully* understood that there still are—that there still *have* to be—areas of silence in national life. And with that understanding Mrs. Whiteside has most generously surrendered her private papers to the archives. Mrs. Whiteside," Piers allowed himself a small, political smile, "from her war experience, knows as well as anyone the absurdity of your American phrase, 'open government.'"

Her foot touched her bag leaning against the leg of her chair. Under the guise of reaching for a Kleenex she switched on the recorder.

Piers was gesturing around the room.

"Do you know, although indirectly all this has been my bailiwick, I've never been down here? As Chancellor there are such a multitude of odd departmental nooks and crannies that one never does quite know all of them. For example, I hadn't realized with quite what single-mindedness *you* were proceeding, Mrs. Montigny, until I chanced upon your inquiry at the hospital—when the estate of the churchwarden from Saint Margaret's came through to the Public Trustee."

Fingers in all sorts of pies, Alleyn had told her. "A real Jack Horner," she said to Piers.

An inclination of the head. "Your search seemed to me then to be single-minded almost to the point of *neurosis*. Neurosis, I should explain, my dear, in an advanced form requires my wearing another hat: as the Court of Protection—for those certified incurably insane." A smile again, this time for a finely judicial joke. "Certification in such circumstances is non-appealable."

He was relaxing, she noticed. The flow of language putting him deeper in his chair, making the gestures fuller, more expansive, the foot no longer tapping but resting firmly on the floor. "With such Jubilee celebration in the air, I should like to reach agreement quickly, Mrs. Montigny. I understand that we shall be guests together at the Colour—no doubt you have a new hat of your own for the occasion?" The smile now was chauvinistically expansive.

"Not yet."

"I always think the hats are one of the glories of the season." Compliments concluded, Piers leaned forward to talk business. "Mrs. Montigny, the first lesson of jurisprudence—brought home to me with great force at Nuremberg—is that contests such as ours are always *what* the terms of settlement will be: not whether—"

"*You were at Nuremberg?*"

"Not in judgment, Mrs. Montigny." Generations of the right breeding produced a deprecating laugh. "As what you would call a junior counsel—to Hartley Shawcross. I had resumed a legal career in 1944, the year in which I joined the Labour Party, as a matter of fact—but you encourage me to digress: from Nuremberg, I understood that there is always accommodation, Mrs. Montigny. Naturally, not for the handful at the top—there had to be a ritual offering, they all understood that—but for the rest, from Speer downward through the ranks it was remarkable how tacitly both sides realised the necessity for give-and-take."

A real hare-and-hounds man. Berlin and Moscow side by side were difficult enough but Nuremberg was too much. She could no longer keep track of which parties, which people, which events he had been party *to*. Our side, their side—always the winning side. The lounge-lizard bastard sitting sleekly on the winning side of the dock watching his old animal buddies drop through the trap: The Leys, the Kaltenbrunners, the medicine men like Dr. Brandt. "The animals that could talk," her mother had called them.

This son of a bitch in front of her could talk the legs off the whole zoo.

"I left the trials after Göring cheated us. The seat had opened at Anstiebury and I realized that there could be no possibility of the troops returning after this war as they had after the first one: to Depression without jobs; to the lockstep of wealth and privilege." Piers switched smoothly from polemics to conversation. "Careers are always a series of accidents, of timing, are they not? The party had few people of my background immediately after the war—most members of my class had been backing the wrong horse." Piers shook his head at memories and classmates, then set the black-and-silver wing of hair in place with a patting hand.

"Which party, *Geoffie*."

"I beg your pardon?" The urged use of first names from Albany must have been abandoned with his makeup. The Windsor name had thrown the lizard calm off balance. The foot began to tap again.

"I have you recruited on vacation, in August 1929—a professor called Myles Tenning? Would that be right?"

"Old Tenning?" But the laugh had lost all mellowness. "A *very* frail reed. My good woman, your Congress in its idiocy may still get effect from a waving of red flags, but I assure you that in this country undergraduate Communist flirtations rate a little lower than pinching policemen's helmets. In the early thirties, if one had a conscience, one *had* to lean to the left."

"But you were being a Nazi then, Geoffie, remember? With your old buddy, the Duke? Surely 'one leaned to the right' to be a Nazi?"

"Don't be snide with me! You know damned well my overtures to the Germans were not from personal conviction."

"That I believe!" She produced the shot of Lansky. "So let's talk about convictions. You're the lawyer, could you get one on this? Or is there a statute of limitations over here on murder?"

The blue-white lights stopped flickering. The Faun stopped its dancing: frozen as Piers' face.

"What *are* you talking about?"

"Harry Oakes."

"*Lunacy!*"

"Neurosis, sweetheart." Her smile was not answered. "What a gas, Geoffie, if that unidentified thumbprint lifted by the Miami cops matches the one you've just made on this table."

The thumb jerked back.

"And that's only the first question, honey. How about depositions from defectors with your name in the slot? How about your Moscow Party number—"

"Oh please! Spare us hyperbole. Your readers have the minds of gnats!" Piers dismissed them with a snap of the fingers. "And as for tele*vision*—" The shrug was his court-room finest.

"That's right," she said, "morons. But you know what? The weirdest thing with TV—the morons watching never remember the *answers*. They only remember the questions. And pictures."

The eyebrows arched, the wide mouth with thin lips that lived only for words turned down.

"*Pictures!*" Piers' disdain for his visual electorate was too great for words.

"Of a Test Person." She took the photographs of her mother's naked body from her bag and put them on the table beside the Faun. Her mother's Judas gagged, and closed his eyes.

"There are moments," Geoffrey Piers used the voice that had moved for mercy at the bar of the highest tribunals in the land, "moments in a nation's life more important than *any* individual. Moments when duty requires—"

"A Charybdis."

And now that he knew that she knew, Piers stopped the con. He looked without blinking at the dreadful pictures, he looked at her, and he said nothing.

"You figure the British people are ready to follow my mother down the whirlpool?" she asked. "Ready to be sucked in by a triple-crosser? By a guy who burned a woman's guts out to let Hitler have the bomb?"

"Hitler?"

Perhaps, the tone in Piers' voice now said, perhaps there *might* have been a man called Hitler once, a paperhanger of no breeding, who dabbled, as Langer showed, politically and sexually in shit. And perhaps there had been an Allied struggle to clean up the filth, but thirty-two years later Piers' voice and conscience could scarcely remember it.

"The atomic development, and all this," the graceful hands, used to a prosecution's tricks, flicked at the photographs, "this was far too late to have had the slightest effect on the war."

"Then why the fuck did you do it?"

"Dear lady, the question you so succinctly phrase is surely: Why did the British Government of the Day *permit it*?"

Dear lady. The eyes looking at her now saw her as neither. They watched her as she wrestled with the implications of his question and they saw her as American, as female: as strictly second-rate.

"Oh, the naïveté of your new world, *Mrs.* Montigny. The signals were not for Nazi Germany. Germany was *dead.* Do you think that men like Churchill and Menzies, and John Bevan, men suckled on history, were going to give the *United States* hegemony of the world? But what do you people know of history or dialectic?" The tone was of absolute disgust. "*Nothing!* America's is the most ignorant ruling class the world has ever known. Untutored by the past, undisciplined in the present. You will lose the future. Well let me tell you the history you lack, *Mrs.* Montigny. The Pax Britannica did not keep the peace for a hundred years because Britain was *supreme*. Peace was preserved because Britain was the *balance* between opposing forces."

Piers swiveled in his chair to face the map behind him. The chair itself was equidistant between the postwar giants, and small enough to hide Great Britain.

"But in 1945," said Piers, "Britain was *not* great, and not a balance. Britain was collapsed from a tree to a nut—and frozen out of bomb development. No atomic weapons would be held in British hands: once Churchill was chucked out, no money would be squeezed from British voters to buy or build one. And Churchill knew he would *be* out. The man was a Neanderthal in social thought, but a genius in politics and power. Unlike your present fundamentalist petty bourgeois in the White House preaching in that awful voice—unlike the haberdasher, Truman, at the time—Churchill knew that the world *needs* division between heaven and hell: the world *wants it*. American wheels of technology have to turn—the Soviet structure would be gone like smoke without an external threat."

She stroked the Faun's bronze back. "Are you saying this bunch down here tipped off the Russians—through you? That Churchill *knew* that?"

Piers talked around the question. "This bunch, and their cryptographic staff were the one British achievement of the last war that deserved to win. Ironically, you in the Press accept that. Year after year each new revelation that Alamein or D day was the work of mirrors is puffed by the Press into a celebration of genius! Proof that the rabble of a 'Free World' *have* to win."

"The wartime Intelligence people *were* brilliant—too bad you haven't had them since." She turned the Faun toward her. "I don't believe they told the reds—"

Was the Faun smirking?

"No," said Piers, "of course *you* wouldn't believe it." And the "you" was every reporter who had ever given any official a hard time. "*You never have! Not once!* Not from the beginning with the scientists, Nunn-May in Ottawa, Fuchs here. Not when Pontecorvo gave tritium away as the fusion trigger. Not through all the tatty, sordid little spies escaping. Not when the drunken Donald Maclean was put on the Combined Policy Committee and able to feed from the Manhattan Project *from the first day*. Not even when Philby—who, I might add, was given to M15 by Krivitsky's defection in 1937—not even when Philby, three decades later, was so glaringly allowed to run away.

"Oh, you were not alone in your credulity. Your American political ignoramuses sacked the OSS and sat on the empty nest; fibbed like grammar-school children about the bomb to Stalin—who already knew, of course; refused Churchill's suggestion to take Berlin—as *he* was sure you would, so that the Russians got the atom people and laboratories there—and at Leipzig. And while all this happened, *Mrs*. Montigny— while you reporters howled through the years about the value to the boorish Russians of the fourth man, the fifth man, the *twenty-fifth utterly unimportant little man*—through all this time not *one* of you hacks in the Free Press, the Inquiring Press, the Western Intellectual press has ever asked the only significant question: *How?*

"How is it, *Mrs*. Montigny—and again I use your own finely chosen words—how is it that 'this bunch down here,' the same brilliant minds that went to school with all the little runaway men, how is it that the John Bevans of this country could be devious beyond Machiavelli's imaginings against the Germans, but since 1945 against Moscow have been so incredibly, so *unbelievably* dim?"

The recorder clicked off at her feet.

As with Harry Rogers' gurgled breathing in the cockpit, the sound of something electronic once more working underground, was wrong. Misplaced.

"What was that?" asked Geoffrey Piers.

"Tape, sweetheart."

"*Tape?*"

The elegant pattern of the face disintegrated all at once.

"Mrs. Whiteside figures tape's a labor saver," she said. "What do *you* think, Geoffie? Will hearing this one help the party at the polls?"

Piers' chair fell backward on the Persian rug. He started toward her around the table. She grabbed up the shoulder bag and moved easily away. Piers moved again with a crabwise sidle. The breathing was fast, labored, the face flushed. He tried to reverse direction quickly and tripped over the chair. She began to laugh. The bastard was no crab. He was ludicrous, a circus bear. Round and round the table like a circus bear. *One step, one step* . . . run the tape and tickle one of Christopher Robin's old-boy bears dancing under Whitehall in the phony world of Winnie-the-Pooh.

"Oh yeah," she said. "While I remember, there's no 'accommodation' over this one, Geoffie. No 'old boy' give and take. *The Times* and my uncle, and your 'Aunty' BBC, already have the works."

The bear stopped dancing: rested its forearms on the table, dripped sweat, and panted as it stared at her. But it no longer seemed afraid. Like Churchill, who got Jael's Britain a bomb of her own to play with in spite of everything, the bear was a master on its own ground.

"You stupid woman!"

Piers was gone down the passage. She heard him collide with a gasp into the support bisecting the door, and then his footsteps fading away. *You stupid woman*. She collapsed laughing into a chair beside the Faun. "Oh Faun, baby, doesn't that just say it all?"

The Faun was mute. As though from centuries of randy dancing, it knew what women were good for.

For Violet Vrisser's sake she straightened the chairs and the rumpled carpet, gathered her bag and found her eyes looking at Wolesley's plaque.

Honesty, the general reminded her, *is not the best policy for British winners. Truth does not always win in the long run.*

She heard the thudding shudder of a door. She began to run, herself.

32

The big ship's door into the War Room was shut tight.

She grabbed the wheel in the center and wrenched it counter-clockwise. It moved half an inch and stopped immovably. Clockwise. Back. Clockwise again. Nothing.

It was quiet in the War Room. The ventilation from the trunking had died away. Only the noise of her own breathing broke the postwar peace.

A generator somewhere was dying too: the blue and white lights dimming; the signs for "Action This Day" and "Vacant/Engaged" becoming indistinguishable from the names disappearing on all the maps. As dead and gone. Tobruk, Singapore, Bataan: all fortresses for one last stand. Futile last stands.

This flylike dashing around the room—this crashing over obstacles from door to map to chair, to door again—was panic. It had to stop. *"Well stop it then, bitch!"* Her shouted words echoed back from the passages. She stood and listened to them. Took three deep breaths. Three more.

The flashlight! She had the flashlight—the English "torch" purchased at an "ironmonger's" because it was so strongly recommended by Mr. T. Had that unseen public servant been in on it, too? Had Mr. T. laughed behind a smooth civil-service hand at the presumption that challenged Jael in her own lair?

She switched the light off. Not one candlepower of its batteries must be squandered. She needed no light to think. Sit and think with logic and rationality.

It was her own fault. She herself had pointed out to Violet Vrisser that the man did dumb things—irrational, silly schoolgirl things—in tight corners. That he went for blind denials and posturings of innocence that would have drawn detentions and a hundred lines in any elementary school.

So, for the moment he was gone. But only for the moment—he would be back, for sure. She must just sit here quietly in the great man's chair and wait for contact with the enemy to be made. What was the time? The eleventh hour, said the hands that stayed with the wartime legends on the Chamberlain clock. Her watch with its Japanese cleverness said three minutes after three on Sunday afternoon, the fifth of June, 1977.

The fifth of June. Tomorrow, one day later and thirty-three years gone, Jesus, this room must have waited! Waited for God to get back in His heaven and order the weather so that the invasion fleets could sail and embark on the creation of a new earth. How the phones must have been ringing then, with all the ships at sea. Fifteen after three. Twelve minutes. This was not going to be easy. *"Call you asshole! CALL!"*

Cool it, she told the echo. Spend the time usefully. Guess which phone he'll use—be ready, minimize delay. She let the flashlight pick the phones out: green, white, black, and red. Eeny meeny miney—send out a Smythe to catch a nigger boy Jonathan by the toe. "The *toe?*" the Smythe would say. "*In Africa, old man? By the balls, old boy!* Floppies are like *fish,* old trout, don't feel a thing. Buggers make soup out of babies to make it *rain....*"

The phone's ringing. THE PHONE'S RINGING. *Oh Jesus, keep ringing, phone!* Green, white, black, red? Hullo, hullo? *No answer.* Why are you playing these games, God? *Keep ringing.*

All the lines were dead but a phone *was* ringing. She shone her light again. "*The possibilities of defeat do not exist*" said Victoria Regina. And there it was! A wall unit with a crank handle and a small winking amber bulb. She grabbed it up.

"Mrs. Montigny?" As though she were at Albany with the ghostly footmen passing by.

"*Yes?*" fumbling frantically with her other hand to find the suction cup to stick the mike to the receiver.

"Mrs. Montigny—"

And it was done! *We've got the fucker, sweetheart,* she said to her recorder.

"Mrs. Montigny, I'm afraid I shall want *that* first. All your tape recording."

"It's in my apartment. I would—"

"*Mrs.* Montigny," the voice no longer hid its obvious contempt. Without having to make eye contact the voice could use verbal skills honed by its lifetime of woolsacks and the bench. "Mrs. Montigny, I already *have* the warrant for your flat, and I shall only state this once—pay close attention. These War Rooms will be closed for six weeks for transition to the Museum—do you understand me? *Six weeks of total isolation.* You would be dead, one would imagine, in ten days. And should you have thoughts of your family's assistance, abandon them. The P.M. and the Leader have both been briefed by Century House. There will be no calls for inquiries of any sort in this affair. Now, tell me, are *all* your papers in your flat with the recordings? Did you leave any materials with the detection firm?"

The Firm. Langley. "The CIA," she said. "The Agency has copies of everything."

"In Washington? Oh, good." The voice was genuinely relieved. "Good!"

"What the fuck do you mean, GOOD?"

Hopeless! She *must* keep control, not scream at him, and cry, and pound her tiny newsperson's fist against the wall.

"Washington will be the *last* to upset applecarts, Mrs. Montigny. Your NSA is very unhappy with Langley at the moment, *very* unhappy—NSA's adage being always far better the devil one *knows*. And they know *me*, my dear—with all my warts. We are comfortable with each other."

And wasn't that the message she had had from Selbach in his office? Certainly in all the congressional screaming for Langley heads, the blue-suited eminences of National Security—the *real* back-room boys—slipped around the capital unscathed. Happy to let the rubes think they were drawing blood. Equally happy, without doubt, to let the Reds think they had the next top dog of the United Kingdom in their Kremlin pockets. A once-united kingdom. Now, like Churchill's metaphorical shell, devolving in all directions, but even so, the heart and mind of a British prime minister with his nuclear toys would still be a royal flush for Russia.

Royal! A royal flush in hearts was the hand that had beaten Cecil Rhodes for his jewel in the crown of Africa.

"Will you be 'comfortable,'" she asked Piers, "when *she* knows?"

"I beg your pardon?" But the voice spoke from habit, not politeness. "What do you mean?"

"Leofric has an appointment for an audience—isn't that what you call it? Can you see meeting *her* once a week for your prime minister's gabfest at the Palace after she sees those pictures?"

A sudden hissing intake of breath along the line.

Oh Jesus. She was needling again. When she should be pleading, crawling, offering him body and soul. Swearing to lie splayed on her back for him as she had sworn to Violet Vrisser she never would. *Backwards, my lord,* if she had to. *Doggies—hands and knees, Geoffrey darling,* if that kink was what the old perv wanted. *A blow job, baby* transatlantic version, if that would get him back here in the flesh to let her grab at something.

She offered it all into the receiver. *"Okay, Geoffrey, honey? Okay? OKAY?"*

Her passion was wasted. There was no heavy breathing

on the line. No sound at all. And the amber light beside her had gone out.

So had hope. Piers, she knew now, would not be back.

But with a woman's trust in the irrational she would allow him one hour. So she sat in Churchill's chair in total darkness—but knowing the light was there when she needed it: and that made the difference, knowing it was there.

She made plans. Extremely simple plans, because the range of options, of contingencies that could be planned *for,* was now itself so simple. First: a note written on one of the sheets of paper marked "PM File/WCR," to advise anyone who came, of her intentions. She placed the note in the basket marked "Action This Day."

Oh God, make that come true. . . .

She had no food and no water. Water was more important than food in these situations. She had been told that years ago on a survival course at Camp Pendleton for a happy few of the Press. Fewer, by the end of it, when all the beer bellies and martini hounds had dropped out leaving one woman and half a dozen men—among them Mr. Montigny. Sitting here in the dark, the memories of moments with Mr. Montigny were not all bad. Mr. Montigny had a Hardy boy's enthusiasm on the job and in the sack, and he worshipped her, but he wanted to live in Seattle, near his mother. . . .

So. No food, no water. Two batteries of light. Air? Even without fresh ventilation, air would be no problem. Dehydration would be the problem. Every minute not spent actively searching for release was a minute closer to death. Every minute wasted in sleep—forget sleep. There would be an eternity for sleep.

What if there was no way out?

There had to be a way out. Cynthia Whiteside, true daughter of Jael, said the tunnels ran for miles under the pavements with the lines and squares. . . .*Forty-five minutes gone.* She picked up the telephone and cranked the handle. Not a flicker from the amber bulb.

Her stomach cramped. It was inevitable that that would happen—the frosting on the cake. She found a Midol in her bag and swallowed it dry. There was no point in wasting the last fifteen minutes of the promised hour.

She put the bag on her shoulder, switched on the flashlight and walked back along the passage toward the

dormitory with the ghostly girls' voices singing of their London
Pride—when the lights go on again. Singing, *Run, Rabbit,—
Run!* She forced herself *not* to run. The beam flickered across
the dingy whitewash on the walls flushing out spiders' webs and
beetles. *There were so many layers of cobwebs at the end,* said
Violet Vrisser, *that even Jael couldn't find the spider....*

She came to Jael's room. The beam shone past the post
blocking off the door, over the polished surface of the table.
Over the Faun. If anything knew how to dance its way out of
the webs, the Faun would. She picked it up.

"Where to?" she asked it.

The Faun's horny little beard pointed up and to the
right. She shone the light in that direction. The torch picked
up an arrow in the passage marked, Escape Route Fox.

33

Escape Route Fox brought her in five minutes to another
sign:

AT SOUND OF RATTLE—GAS IMMINENT
AT BELL—ALL CLEAR

Beside the sign was one of the vertical escape ladders.
Thank you God. Thank you. Ignoring the voice of conscience
crying hypocrite for the prayers, she set the shoulder bag at
the foot of the ladder and began the climb.

The God of Jael's battles is not mocked. The ladder was
closed off by a steel hatch. The hatch was padlocked.

From the foot of the ladder, the passage stretched nearly
out of the beam's reach to a sharp bend. The flashlight *must*
be saved. She would use it to pick out the next bend, or
ladder, or pipe—the next milestone—and go blind in between. She turned off the light and began to move forward
with her shoulder against the wall.

It was slow. The mind knew there was nothing in the way, no yawning pits, but it refused to let the body take chances. Her steps were hesitant. Her free hand scrabbled at the vacant dark. At a sudden niche in the wall she lurched a foot to the right with a missed heartbeat.

She turned on the light. A poster glued to another of the ship's doors informed her that "Careless Talk Costs Lives." The door was closed.

"Is this the end?" she asked the Faun but, as though perversely obeying orders, the statuette maintained its customary silence. A stronger voice inside her head spoke up. "Take the plunge, girl. Try the wheel, girl. *Try it!"*

The door was unlocked and swung easily of its own weight. Beyond the door, no money had been wasted on linoleum for the stone floor, and the roof changed from wood to brick and curved like a true tunnel down to meet the walls. The passage was narrower and ran beyond the limits of the light. How far was that? Fifty feet? Fifty paces? She picked a rust-colored spot on the wall, put out the light, and began to count. She counted aloud and by "three," her voice echoed back to her so that there was always someone following that many paces behind her in the dark. Her shoulder already felt bruised from bumping against the walls.

Fifty! Snap the light on—off. Fifty paces more. And more, and more. The fucking tunnel ran without end. She lost track of the fifties and changed sides so that her other shoulder did the work.

Another depression in the wall, but there was no fooling the shoulder this time. She leaned a little farther into the niche.

And fell in a heap.

The clatter of her shoulder bag hitting the flagstones beside her echoed and reechoed and died away. She sat on the floor. Her heart raced. Her wrist ached. She ignored the wrist. The fall could have been a broken *head*!

The passage had come to a sharp "Y." There were no signs or arrows but one side went up and the other went down, and that left her no choice: Up is where the light is. She got up and plodded ahead, counting the steps to the next magic moment with the flashlight: Forty-seven, don't cheat; forty-eight, *why not?*; forty-nine, switch *on!*

The monster tried to bite the torch.

She screamed. Threw her arm up with the shoulder bag to ward off the gaping flaming mouth and devil's horns.

The Squanderbug
alias
HITLER'S PAL

With a ring of swastikas round his neck. Wanted for sabotage, the poster said, and known to be at large in the Kingdom with a tempting leer and a flattering manner. A perfect campaign poster for Geoffrey Piers! She almost laughed, but knew that if she started she would never stop. The tunnel passage beyond the Squanderbug opened into a cellar with rusting iron racks and shackles for casks or drums. *Roll Out the Barrel....*

Once she got past the racks, there was no barrel of fun. The floor of the passage dropped, and kept dropping, with the temperature. Dehydration was no longer a problem. Water ran down the bricks and gathered in depressions on the floor. One trickle was large enough to fall in the blackness with the sound from the cave of the skulls. Her feet became soaked, then chilled. Imagining the skulls racked grinning up around her, she shivered violently and then wasted the light by leaving it on to scare away the skulls. The tunnel had arrived at a four-way fork, a perfect cross. *A double-cross?* There was nothing to choose between the entrances. She stood in the dark to think for a moment and was swept by terror that she couldn't tell which passage she had come down but when she turned the light on the wet prints of her feet still stretched behind her.

Eeeny meeny miney....

She took the left front fork. But now height was added to the obstacles of wet and dark. Forced to move in a continuous three-quarter crouch, and terrified of smashing her head she had to use the light more often. It only took thirty paces now to reach the end of the light. For one set of thirty paces of disgusting smell the whole tunnel was awash knee-deep. Dehydration, hell! She was about to drown in shit!

And then it moved. Rumbled. Shook. All the walls shaking and roaring and *she knew the river was coming in on her to sweep her along the passage, to jam her against the ceiling, to crush her....*

The roaring died away with a rhythmical abatement, underground. *Underground*. THE TUBE! The subway of civilization and helping hands waiting to take her aboard! But the next time she heard it the roaring was weaker, and the next it was gone. And she had to rest. Had to. In a relatively dry cellar with three doorways, she sat—collapsed—against a wall.

The place had a musty smell to it. Was this where Wren's Bundles lived? His documents and notes for rebuilding London after its first ordeal by fire?

Bundles and bundling. The words brought back stories from her girlhood of a New England morality before *American Graffiti* and the backseats of cars. The good old days when sleeping with a bolster and parental wishful thinking stopped boys' hanky-panky with the girls. If Todd had used a bolster in his Baptist Mission would he still be bossing Zimbabwe-Rhodesia? Who gave a fuck? Who cared? Who was left in her *own* life to care? . . .

Oh Muir, baby, where are you when I really *need you?*

But in the darkness she had lost his face! She could see only the scarlet-crested louries in the jacaranda trees outside the hotel window; could bring back only a frantic heel-drumming moment with some man who helped her drive out the pictures of gassed Violet Vrisser and her black boys who had all the attributes of men. . . .

With one hand between her thighs and one across her breasts she rocked in the darkness crooning *Muir, baby, Muir, baby* . . .

The rats watched her. Two rats with two rats' tails and four bright eyes mesmerized by the crooning or the sudden brilliance of the light. She was not afraid of rats. All rats—Vietnamese rats or Lebanese rats or Irish rats or Rhodesian rats—were gray at night. And might be food. Had been food, you fuckers, she told the rats, in half those places: done to a turn over fuel-drum fires in shell-case cook pots.

"Pack it in!" she screamed at the rats. *"Pack it in, you fucking bastards."*

The rats recoiled and ran squealing up the passage. How long had she been here? Eleven o'clock again, an hour to midnight: Mackenzie King's witching hour when Little Pat spoke to Mum and rats turned to horses and took gowned Cinderella to the ball. Or was that ass-backward? *Was it the hour when the rats turned on Cinderella, tore her gown to rags, began to eat her female flesh?* . . .

A faint skittering like the voices of *ngozis* came back to her. So she had not lost the ghosts in Zimbabwe-Rhodesia after all. She got to her feet and set off after the rats. The light was only good for twenty paces now.

Three hours later the light went out.

She had thought the road through the mid-night bush of Africa was dark. It could not have been brighter, she realized now, if its surface *had* been paved with gold. *This*—the absence of light—was DARK!

Furious with herself for "buying British," she banged the "torch" frantically on the floor; shrieked at it, cried on it; and when it would not come on she stood with her back to the tunnel wall, rigored fingers locked in the ledges of the bricks. Chained like Scylla with paralyzing fear to the cliff wall of the brick.

Run, Scylla,–run, mocked the *ngozi* wartime voices, *get those lights on again.* . . .

The lights would not go on again down here. All the sing-songs in the world would not bring them on again because Jael and her Faun had danced circles around Winnie-the-Pooh. The next time a boozy bear's voice urged Englishmen to fight the bastards on the beaches, that was all there would be. The sea and the beach. No lights, no fields, no streets. No historically romantic place to demand Action This Day. Just a hole, half a mile deep and as wide as greater London, and no nightingales would sing over the wastes of Berkeley Square: not for a half life of ten thousand years.

Could she smash her head against the bricks and end the singing?

But the thought of that darkness was worse than this. The darkness of blood and brain on brick was absolute. This other darkness was only as though she chose to close her eyes. And if she closed them, it wasn't dark at all. There was all the light and color of a lifetime stored behind them. All the friendships and the friends' faces, and all the feelings, just as Violet Vrisser told her. *You see,* said Violet Vrisser right beside her, *there's no valley of the shadow, Jane darling, if you close your eyes.*

Her fingers released the ledges in the bricks. She placed

one hand against them, put one straight out in front of her. She did as she was told.

Violet Vrisser led her forward, and when Violet Vrisser— because she *was* almost seventy—got tired, Muir took over, with a face that she could see again and an arm around her shoulder and a *"Come on, Otter, come on, girl,"* and twice when she stumbled there was Fadiman smashing his lunch bag with a bang and a *"Wise up, Janey, Holy Christ!"*

But when there were the worst moments, when the tunnels widened or divided and there was nothing for the hands to cling to and the water reached above her knees, all those helpful friends and faces left, and were replaced by the photographic face of a woman her own age, with her own gray eyes and her own fair hair.

And when the water washed around her waist, numbing and freezing, the photograph became a real woman lying on a table. A woman of her flesh, and her blood, and her sex, ravaged on a steel table. But the woman's gray eyes weren't closed like hers. They were wide open, unblinking, staring at the beast's skull-head leering from its shield of lead. And the eyes stay wide open as the beast drops the skull slowly, focuses its vision, shifts minutely left or right, and spits an invisible X-ray breath into the ring of pustulent, encrusted holes on the purple inflammation of the shaved belly. And only her mother's hands twisting the skin off their wrists in the leather bracelets show what the beast's breath does.

You stupid WOMAN.

This was what Piers had meant. In the face of the beast to stay silent, for Piers and Winnie-the-Pooh. For men's little-boy games.

No longer! she told the Faun. Unlike her mother, *she* would not be ruled by thirty years of silence, and she would not die here in these tunnels. She would get out and show the world, worldwide, the *Thing* that Geoffrey Piers—that Jael—was.

Still working out the details with the Faun, she opened her eyes and walked up out of the water into the darkness.

But by seven the next morning her rabbit's flesh had weakened. Had smashed into too many walls, so that when it heard the shooting noises the flesh had no courage left and in trying to keep running tripped once too often, and lay on the stone floor listening to the shots sound closer and to the contents of the shoulder bag rolling off into the dark.

Bang, bang, bang, bang, goes the farmer's gun. . . .

Something made a metallic clang.

Her rabbit mind wondered idly whether it was the useless light or the recorder that had clanged? But no, they were still with her, beside the bag. It was the Faun. *The Faun had left her!*

What talisman of security remained to save her life?

Her miraculous Japanese watch—a real life-saver Violet Vrisser had called it—and with its tiny light, following a flagstone crack at a time, she crawled across the floor to find the wall. Then along it. One foot, two foot, three.

The little bronze face winked at her. Like Harry Oakes at Swastika the Faun had struck gold. Or rather iron—iron that the Einsteins and the Bohrs said could be turned to gold with a little faith in physics. The Faun lay against the foot of one of the steel escape ladders.

She stood, and now for perverse reasons of its own, the tunnel which had made her crouch for miles, was high. Higher than a hand above her head. So a hand at a time, a rung at a time, she climbed. How many steps had Jonathan forced himself to climb to Violet Vrisser's veranda? Was it four, was it five?

Six.

At number six her free hand felt the hatch. She scrunched her head into her shoulders, climbed to seven, looped an arm over the top rung, raised the other arm with the Japanese watch until it was an inch from the hatch's surface, found the circular outer edge. Counting the rivets, she followed it round. First, the cross-hatching of the casting. Now a weld, now a hinge. Twenty more rivets. The second hinge. Her woman's arms were tiring, were going to give up the ghost.

"No, you BASTARD!"

And at that surprising show of strength the spirits pulled back like vultures in a tree to watch her count the remaining rivets; to come to the last weld for the hasp. An empty hasp that had no padlock.

With the force of all the ghosts behind her she threw open the hatch.

THE SOUND OF TRUMPETS

34

LIGHT. Faint and dirty yellow from a thin crack under a door, but after the blackness seeming brilliant as the sun pouring through our Isabella's window at Saint Margaret's Church.

But before she could reach the light she must return to the blackness for the tape.

Even with the lid off the tunnel and the end in sight, she found it almost impossible to force herself down there, to grope for her bag, to make sure that the recorder was inside it. Two rungs back up the ladder she remembered the Faun, and hung, racked with futile indecision: take him, drop him? But he had not only danced her through the darkness, she needed his help with the final wrinkles of the plan....

The shooting again. The farmer sounded almost behind her now, firing in continuous bursts. Galvanized, she grabbed the statuette, scrabbled with a frantic haste for a last time through the hatch, ran up the short passage to the door.

Locked!

She pounded on the door with both fists, kicked at it with both feet. Screamed at it.

The door opened.

Blinded by the light, she saw the small figure only as a triangular shape—the king of the Golden River from the fairy story. Stunned by the shock she blurted something about the farmer and his gun.

"Guns?" said the king, shutting off the firing noises by shutting the door behind her, "Oh—you want the *range!*" In ordinary light levels the king became a crabbed little clerk

263

with disheveled gray ringlets to his shoulders. "That's the next floor down." He peered at her more closely with a paper fighter's concern, and pointed at a sign. "But ladies' hours are only one till three."

Like an ad for Barnum's circus, a painted hand on a board stuck an index finger at Civil Service Rifle Range—Members Only.

"And the sergeant major's fussy about dress," said the king-clerk. "He won't approve. There's a lavatory up the stairs."

She thanked him for the tip. And at the same time realized it was all familiar—the smell of damp paper, and the worn stairs and the chipped paint. The circle had returned her to the PRO. The washroom was beside the iron portcullis locking in your Domesday Book.

How could she look so normal?

She should have aged like Rip Van Winkle, should be bruised, torn, have hair in rats' tails after living with the rats, but even with the black rings under her eyes she looked no worse than someone back from an all-night party, needing only a hair of the dog to pick herself up and get to the office. Except for her clothes: the sergeant major would definitely *not* approve. Christ, the English!

There was no soap in the dispenser and no hot water but there were some Stone Age Kotexes piled up with paper towels in a corner and she made emergency repairs, brushed and straightened what she could, then rummaged through her shoulder bag for lipstick.

The tube was full of water!

Her wallet, all the contents of her shoulder bag were soaking wet. *The photographs were soaking wet.* It took a while to sink in. To grasp that the pictures didn't matter. Leofric had his own pictures.

It was the tape that mattered.

She examined the Philips recorder. Even the Dutch hadn't made a machine that could keep the English wet out. The ruined cassette of Piers' admissions dribbled a last indignity down her jacket.

But the Faun apparently didn't care. Sitting through the cab ride to Dolphin Square the Faun looked perkier than ever: With one more bridge washed out, there was less chance of her turning back. She paid off the cab with soggy bills, and then could hardly walk through the door. The party *had* been rough. Aches and stiffnesses grabbed at every muscle, every joint. Five years ago she would have smoked one. Her mind, numbed with fatigue, moved as slowly as though it *was* half-stoned. Only as her hand was opening the door to her room did her mind ask what might be inside.

Normality.

Nothing torn apart, no bras and panties lasciviously strewn out of the chest or her suitcases. The suitcases themselves were still neatly in the closet, their contents even more neatly packed. But everything significant was gone. All the other cassettes, the notes from Selbach, the shot of Lansky. The only record of Violet Vrisser's final conversation. And, with a petty mistrust that infuriated her, old Johnson's *Pilgrim's Progress*.

In the tiny bathroom even a box of tampons had been opened, emptied, and then carefully restocked. She put the Faun down next to the box; threw off her clothes; ran a hot, hot bath; climbed into it. . . .

The water was tepid, almost cold. *Noon!* With so much to do, how *could* she have let herself fall asleep? Christ, there was a trick-shop joke: to survive the tunnel and drown in the tub. She dried, gulped a No-Doz and called Leofric at his office; then at his home. But the marquess, her uncle, his secretary and housekeeper both told her, was out and had left no message. "Faun," she said, as she hung up, "we're on our own, sweetheart—all systems go!"

With her mind now locked to the big decision, it was hard to concentrate on little things. Waiting in the street for another cab she realized she had no idea where to go for the right clothes. A passing double-decker bus with billboard placards on its sides made a suggestion.

"Harrods," she told the taxi driver.

And Harrods *was* the right choice. Harrods was used to last-minute returns from distant places, and invitations for great occasions; was used to Esteemed Custom and the inconvenience of cash. Harrods did inquire—because times unfortunately had changed—whether Madam had a reference, but when Madam has a marquess *and* a duke and an air of knowing her own mind and getting what she wants, all dress-rack doors were opened, and the saleswoman, free for once

of having to lie about round pegs matching square holes, luxuri-
ated in Madam's perfect fit—Madam's perfect American legs.

They worried instead about form—about color. "Not
pink perhaps, with Madam's skin? From California? No? Ah,
Africa." But displaying no greater surprise at one than at the
other. More concerned by far about the weather. "Not Queen's
weather at all, Madam—perhaps more white? But with the
green motif, quite so." And we must hope against hope, must
we not, that all's well for the big day tomorrow? That all goes
as planned. But just in case—because the English weather is
as undependable as Jael—"Madam should have the matching
coat, because even though the look is linen it's totally synthetic and suitable for anything!"

And now it was time for Madam's hat.

"A hat?"

*The glory of the season, the bastard said. All their great
occasions had* My Fair Lady *hats.*

"Sure," she said. "We've got to have a hat."

But it took hard digging until Harrods was satisfied that,
"We can exactly do the green once more, and for the shoes.
Heels *are* rising again. Madam, with her height, will certain-
ly stand out in a crowd."

The saleswoman stood back herself in admiration.

"Quite stunning! And Madam's choice of the umbrella—
more a parasol, actually—is a complete match for the pattern!
And white gloves, of course?"

"Of course," she said. *Her hands must be white. Spotless.*

Now there was only the matter of a bag. For Madam's
powder. For Madam's tissue of lace.

"A larger bag?" For the first time Harrods was momen-
tarily perplexed. "Ah. One that could hang from Madam's
shoulder? That could accommodate an object as large as, say,
a camera? With one of those long lenses?"

"Exactly right."

But the bag—if Madam insisted on fabric—was a problem.

And Madam did insist. Madam was adamant. No way
Madam would go with leather! Because dark leather, even
the finest crocodile and calf, stood out too fucking much in a
crowd!

"Too ostentatious? Yes. Madam is quite right, it should
be something that would blend—be practically *invisible*, in fact."

But there was nothing in fabric that came close and while one could certainly be made, even Harrods—even for a marquess and a duke—couldn't whip it up by morning.

And then they found it—a bag in pure white kid the texture of an old duke's cheek; the texture of rock worn by the winds of Africa since man first went to hunt. "And if Madam would attach the scarf, with its touch of color, to the buckle, like *this*—and look in the glass?"

Madam looked in the glass—and saw that it was good.

"Not good, Madam. *Perfect!*"

Which it was. Because in the old days, on the greatest of State occasions, when Piers' predecessors like Thomas More went out with the Seal of England to play for the highest stakes, they left all embroidery behind and carried the Seal's heavy metal alloy in a Spartan-plain, white kidskin bag. . . .

Outside the store, the Harrods doorman seeing all the boxes knew that it was perfect too, and good for a fat tip, and hailed a cab and had Madam in it in a trice with the boxes neatly stacked. And then asked for Madam's elegant address.

The doorman and the driver exchanged glances at an East End street but if Madam wanted some slum-screwing in the afternoon that was her affair—and probably with a black. You just couldn't tell these days. You watch those bastards!

"Wait," she told the taxi driver.

She took one of the Harrods boxes with her and walked up the flight of dingy stairs to the rippled glass door. The "Spoonfield" lettering by now was almost off the track.

The major was alone inside the door and pleased— indeed, delighted—to see a valued client: Perhaps by now, a friend? And what slight service might he be permitted to perform?

"I want a gun," she said. "A handgun. Something heavy. And one clip."

All pretense dropped from the major's accent and his eyes.

"That'll cost!" said Spoonfield. "When do you want it?"

"Now." She took out her sodden wallet. "How much?"

"Ah, Madam." Once Spoonfield knew the nature of the play he put himself back in the act. "To you, I know, this is a trifle, but in this country there are, I am afraid, obstacles erected by the law." She put two hundred half-drowned

Yankee dollars on the desk. Spoonfield shook his head doubtfully. "A transaction of this nature—to acquire something 'heavy,' as you put it, requires some finesse."

She added ten more tens.

"A forty-five would fit the bill," said Spoonfield, "and by chance I have one, Madam. Old cavalry job—had to shoot more than one good ride with it, too." With the same sleight of hand from their first transaction, the weapon was produced and lay beside the money like a waiting alligator on a sandbank. "Empty a nag's brain box clean as church on Sunday morning with this chap—however"—a mottled hand with a whiskey tremor stroked the notes—"it requires this quantity in sterling, Madam."

"*Pounds!*"

"The old ammo, you see, Madam." The major, as anxious as Harrods to close a deal, was genuinely apologetic. "Smith and Wesson still churn the stuff out, all right, but it's the license problem. Just a scrap of paper, I know, and only good for five hundred rounds a year, but that's bureaucracy, Madam! In the old days, with one's Commission," Spoonfield had the grace to look away, "but now that one's no longer Active—"

"Okay. What else have you got?"

The major gave a deep, deep sigh "The Mauser's been with me since Berlin. Flesh of my flesh, Madam, the Mauser. Bloody Huns—driving up the Rhine a chap couldn't get one of the buggers out from a rock to tell the way, and now look at 'em! *Look* at 'em, Madam! Damned Mercedes, stinking like tractors. Plumb awful car. Plumb awful."

"How much for the Mauser?"

"It hasn't got a silencer." Spoonfield's boozer's eyes had narrowed.

"I don't want it silent."

"Another fifty."

"Get it."

Resting beside the bulk of the .45, the Mauser was a Doberman, all whip steel and teeth. With a very large mouth.

"Nine millimeter, this chap," said Spoonfield. "You'll hear him bark all right! More African fun and games, Madam? Saw your bit in the papers. Still some sport out there, eh? Not like bloody Ireland." Spoonfield found a clip and put it beside the gun. "This wouldn't *be* an Irish do?"

"No." The Mauser fitted neatly in the Harrods bag.

"Just wondered. People doing rum things about the Irish these days. Vendettas—chaps get caught in the cross-firing with vendettas. Do you know the Mauser, Madam?"

She cleared the action, checked the pin, inspected the butt chamber and the barrel. "It needs cleaning."

"Ah!" said Spoonfield.

"I'll buy some oil." She took a ten back from the pile of bills and put the pistol in her workday shoulder bag. As Spoonfield closed the gun cupboard, she saw that there were two more Mausers in it. She wondered if the major had ever seen Berlin.

The Faun, prancing beside the gun on the dresser in her room, seemed even randier than usual: as though the glistening oil on the Mauser's metal parts excited it.

She washed her hands carefully, unpacked the Harrods boxes and hung the contents in the closet. She tried again to contact Leofric. Without success.

The No-Doz had worn off and she was ready to drop. She set her alarm for eight next morning, took the phone from the hook, and slept.

35

London, Jubilee Day

The nightmares only started as she was waking up. Recurring, terrible, slow-motion, close-up images of disintegrating heads, exploding heads. Heads cracking open in Dallas sunshine, in African night.

Why must it be murder? she asked the Faun. Why not a leaf from Piers' bête noire, the Irish? Why not a kneecap? The Faun's hindquarters gave that suggestion the derision it deserved. She stared at the now wrinkled photographs again.

For all her working life she had witnessed assassinations, executions, murders, and had tried to draw lines between them. Were there differences? *Or were she and Violet Vrisser murderers already for the maize field?* Surely the deaths of children and of mothers allowed a Biblical eye for an eye, a time to hate. . . .

Cut through the semantics and call it murder—the first of its kind in Britain since Spencer Perceval: Jael's example to the boys of LCS, hanging on the wall of their old boys' club. Could even a trial for *that* sort of politically violent death in broad daylight in front of millions be hushed by their Official Secrets Act? Will I, she asked the Faun, end up like the other old boys' playthings in the museum, in a place for the insane? Certified by Piers' replacement as non-appealably nuts?

There was no answer from the statuette. She made coffee, boiled an egg, made toast, then threw all but the coffee in the garbage. She put the phone back on the hook. Hoping for something mindless—*Bugs Bunny Meets the Road Runner*—she turned on the box, but the screen by now was solid Jubilee: BBC at its most High-Church, every voice taken out of the closet and brushed up for the greatest state occasion since the coronation. The Faun's graphically sculptured sexual parts were superimposed from the dresser mirror over the images of old ladies waiting on curbs, and little girls with posies and hats of Union Jacks.

The Independent channel at least allowed a break for news. Spectacle and ceremony it said, tongue locked in cheek, were not confined to Britain. A clip from Plains showed a Georgia wedding in white at a motel with a plastic London Bridge spanning the swimming pool and two mechanical plastic swans passing beneath it. The guest of honor, blood brother of her Head of State, poured champagne mixed with beer onto the clockwork swans and clowned through a swan dive to tumultuous applause. Tricks and jokes again.

The television tricked her by cutting back to a serious item in the news. "A principal secretary for Sir Winston Churchill died late last night after being struck by a vehicle on the street outside her home." A man was helping police with their inquiries. . . .

Had Cynthia Dodgeson Whiteside been able to die happy; to go thinking she still played the game for *him?*

And had the news been passed to a brick bungalow with white-painted lintels and a Womble Colonel for whom children at the end made all the difference? She felt desperately saddened for the colonel.

Nothing made a difference. Or if it did, it was most certainly not whether a Kennedy or a Violet Vrisser or a Cynthia Dodgeson Whiteside lived or died. The Piers on both sides of the Atlantic picked up the pieces and played on indestructibly; crooks turned by time and the attention span of their gnatlike public into statesmen, grand old men.

Well not this one, baby, she told the Faun. Not Hitler's pal the Squanderbug.

The Faun appeared to watch the Mauser keenly as it slipped into the white kid bag.

The screen now showed two children climbing Queen Victoria. The queen, not easily defeated or amused, seemed to be waiting for the next act. She hung the white bag on a door handle and turned off the television. The bedroom had a theater hush before the curtain-up.

Leofric, finally ringing on the phone, destroyed it.

"Jane! Your line's been engaged for hours!"

"I left it off the hook. Did you make it to the palace? Does she know?"

"Not exactly—but I can tell you that Violet Barham-Vrisser had many friends. Smythe is already out."

So that was fine. She had given the old boys time and their time was up: exhausted as their own blue blood. If there was to be action this day, she would take it.

"I just heard about the Whiteside woman, Leofric. Any guesses who could help the cops *most* with their goddamn inquiries on that one?"

"Jane—" you had to give the breeding credit for patience, for *manners*, because his tone was still so goddamn *fair*, "Jane, you must believe me—appropriate measures *will* be taken."

"Leofric," she said, "I don't have the smallest doubt about it."

"Good." Although his voice did not sound certain. "I'll have the car around at ten, to collect you for the Trooping."

"You don't have to bother, I can make it on my own."

"Of course I'll bother." And Leofric's voice now was its most kindly, its most truly avuncular, "In fact, I insist."

Nine-thirty: time for the players, as Violet Vrisser would say, to get in costume. To become one of the aristocrats' crowd.

She took the contents of the Harrods boxes from the closet and laid them on the bed. She should have eaten something, her goddamn gut-ache was worse. She dug through her neatly ransacked suitcase to find underwear.

It would have to be fresh. Even for an orphan, instinct from timeless generations of mothers cautioning daughters to wear fresh drawers against the chance of catastrophe and accidental sight by strangers, dictated that. And if she were with her favorite things at home in Sutter's Lane it could have been something special—the apricot silk teddy step-ins, hand-embroidered in Hong Kong and too impractical to wear. *She might have worn them for Muir. . . .*

She stared at her naked body as she had in Montreal. A body exercised year in and year out: a body all the ads for all the spas said anyone could have.

For what?

To be admired night and morning by its own eyes? To be kept quiet with its own hands? To be given when it got desperate for one-night stands to crazy guys in crazy places? And for how long—ten years? Until she was forty-seven? *Fifty-seven?*

No matter how special the lingerie or the occasion, the clock ran out past fifty-seven. . . .

Holy Christ! She was crying over frills and lace and, when it came to the crunch of those Gestapo boots, her own mother had not even been able to wear stockings!

She grabbed the first clean pair of cotton briefs and dressed.

The double-decker bus was right. Harrods had done the job. At least on the surface she had never looked better. Five minutes to ten. She put on the hat. Took lipstick, comb, and Tampax from her workhorse bag and put them in beside the Mauser. She put the new, white—immaculately white—bag on her shoulder, said, "So long, Faun."

She was suddenly sick to death of it.

Her last thought, as she closed the door, was for her old shoulder bag. It had been to all the crazy places except this one. And if that was not a commentary on her life—that she missed a fucking handbag!

The woman at the desk congratulated her on her appearance, and then turned the knife. "There was a message last night—did you get it?"

"No."

"I know it was here somewhere—oh yes—a cable. From a Mr. Muir?"

Mackenzie King and Little Pat would go ape at the timing of this one.

DON'T GO OFF ANY DEEP ENDS, OTTER, DARLING.
ARRIVING HEARTHROW, NOON TOMORROW.

Which was today.

She held the cable in her hand and thought of his: "gentle hands," her old duke-grandfather would call them—but they had steel in the fingers when they held the reins. She thought of the fingers. The first time they touched her arm in the control room at Umtali; when they met her in the mist; how they held her, standing in the ashes at Chiumbwa; how they inflamed her in the darkness of the Troutbeck Inn.

Muir or mother . . .

She crumpled the cable, dropped it on the desk, and walked out of the lobby with its jarring purple counter and maroon carpet and deep-pink ceiling and its faint atmosphere of chlorine mixed with wine; walked past the vaguely Southern columns of the portico, down the steps, along the path of the Italianate box garden and the fishpool, between the two neat rows of chestnut trees. There were no people in the garden or the street. The Jubilee had taken all the people. *The whole world is watching the parade.*

Which was what she wanted.

36

London had buried itself in bunting; its ancient buildings were completely hidden by rosettes, streamers, flags; portraits of the Royals in flowers, petals, paper, metal, pop-bottle caps, feathers, pearly buttons. The Daimler, plain and black in all the color, waited like a hearse at the curb.

"Jane."

For a long moment as he looked at her, she thought it was Leofric's turn to cry.

"Something wrong with the dress?"

"No, no. You look gorgeous. But the green of the scarf, do you see, was Mary's color."

Did these things happen by accident? Was it in the genes? Embedded in memory from the portrait at the abbey? By accident or design, it was appropriate. The chauffeur closed the door.

The Daimler's ride was smoother than the Willys but the crowds, ten-deep, flashing past the windows reminded her of the maize field. The pictures of the woman whose day this was, reminded her of Violet Vrisser.

"London is doing her proud, Jane."

"But you didn't tell her about Piers?"

"My dear," Leofric turned back from the window, "give her a sporting chance. Not at *this* moment, not at such a *special* time."

Run, Rabbit,–Run. Give the beast a sporting chance. For Leofric's class and generation it was still *how* one played. And that was why Piers beat them. Piers didn't give a shit about the rules: Piers tied the goddamn rabbit down. . . .

Unnoticed as she mused, the Daimler had left Grosvenor Road following the Thames, and Saint Margaret's with its plaques conferred for duty and with honor, and had arrived at Whitehall and the outer gate of the Horse Guards yard: where it came to a silken halt beside a Rolls.

A Guardsman in khaki had his hand out. "Pass, please."

The chauffeur produced a card. The soldier saluted, stamped his foot, then bellowed at Leofric: "Sorry, *sir!* Bomb scare, *sir!* Even an Ivory can't go through today, *sir!* If you don't mind, *sir!*"

They disembarked. The shouting soldier put a rope barrier across behind the Daimler. The crowd was fifty feet away.

"What's an Ivory?" she asked.

"It lets the holder pass through the low arch, below the clock tower," said Leofric. "It's a little special—the monarch, members of the family, not too many others. Not Geoffrey Piers, for example."

And *that* satisfies them! The bastard can get to sit in Downing Street, but he won't have a fucking *Ivory.* Washington, where everything of power could be reduced to a purely financial price, had a hick simplicity and comfort.

"The bombing was at Westminster," Leofric said as they walked through to the stands. "The car of one of the more outspoken anti-Irish members. We expected a terrorist flurry for the occasion. No one hurt, thank God. I'm afraid, Jane, we'll be meeting rather a lot of people. It's what one might call a social day. I hope you—"

"Won't be 'irrational' and let you down?"

"You're an absurd girl." Leofric took her arm. "I was *going* to say, I hope you will endure the day—and won't mind if I play the guide. That statue over there is Garnet Wolseley, by the way, from—"

"I know about the General," she said. "I think someone's waving at us."

"Ah, so they are. Let me take your card."

The smiles and nods, the "This is my niece—yes, Mary's girl," began. The overtures were nearly all initiated by others. Leofric must be even further up the social tree than she had thought. They came out of the shadow of the arch into sunlight that was faint but quite warm. A shaft of the sunlight struck a memorial on the far side of the vast parade square.

"Your grandfather attended the unveiling," said Leofric. "In the twenties."

"He was an army man? He looks so tiny now."

"The Duke had the squadron of the Blues that went over with the Composite Regiment under Bingham in 1915. Bingham was the chap who wouldn't let any of his officers have a medical, because he knew the doctors would chuck *him* out first. Father only lasted through the Mad Gallop at Ypres. Hit in both legs—that's why he's so bent. Lucky really. The Composite were ground down from three hundred and fifty to sixty-three—all ranks. Machine guns against horses—the military mind! Rollo's happy at it though. He'll be with us by the way." Leofric dropped it casually, "Rather a busman's holiday."

Her Harrods shoes were scrunching slightly. There was sand on the paving. *Give me the old soft shoe, that old soft shoe....* Leofric in his ritual dance was touching bases all the way along the front row of the stands. Another sentry ahead of them was checking invitations.

Was about to look in a woman's handbag?

Security hadn't crossed her mind—there were too many thousands—but the woman was rummaging in her purse. The sentry waited. Bits of tissue floated out over the edge.

She felt the white kid bag under her arm swelling like a balloon. What for Chrissakes would she say?

Leofric was holding out their cards, was nodding at the guard. The soldier was smiling, picking up the other woman's dropped coins.

And they were past. The stands were almost full. Why *was* Leofric so privileged—allowed to drive so close? Family? But there were thirty dukes or more. Maybe his banking was not so minor? Then if he *had* power, why hadn't he *acted*? Instead of getting misty-eyed about the color of his murdered sister's dress....

Colors. Black and red. Scarlet to hide the blood. The troops, half-hidden under their bearskins, stood immobile as the lead of Churchill's toys.

"Glad it's not too hot for them," said Leofric. "Ah, here's Rollo."

In a suit—but her cousin might as well be in a uniform. The carriage, the shoulders, the flicking eyes taking in the territory marked him unmistakably a soldier.

The crowd gasped. A man without her cousin's years of training and condition fell face-first, full-length onto the square. The bearskin rolled a foot ahead of the man as though his head had snapped off at the neck. Two stretcher-bearers ran out to take the body.

"It's the toes," said Rollo. "The damn fools won't wriggle their bloody toes. That's all it takes to keep the damned blood flowing."

She straightened the strap of the Mauser's bag upon her shoulder.

"PARADE!"

Sword and bayonet points flashed diamond sparks: an electrical relay, *click* passed down the ranks. The space for the fallen man was gone.

"PARADE!"

White gloves like her own, whipped up, down, up. Jesus Christ—until this moment the toy men had actually been *relaxed!* She had the sense that if there was a false start now, if one foot moved too soon, the whole scarlet mass would click, would sweep inexorably forward over the markers, over the guide ropes, over the stands and the spectators, over the wall of the Horse Guards, over the clock tower with its ivory arch. Would sweep until three hundred and fifty men were ground to sixty-three.

To one last man arriving late under the clock.

Piers.

And, as in Ottawa, when she had looked for the first time at the diaries, the hour hand was hidden at five minutes to eleven. Mackenzie King was right. Things did happen for a purpose.

Piers was walking up through the stands, smiling, a word to left and right: at this last minute, still collecting votes.

"PARADE!"

The clock was striking, tolling for us all. For Mother, daughter, Queen, and traitor.

"ROYAL SALUTE . . . pre-ZENT . . . ARMS!"

My country 'tis of thee, sweet land of liberty . . .sung in Poynter's Corners Junior High, at Radcliffe and Bennington; sung until the lumps in the throats of the fifties became giggles and jeers in the sixties, and then the seventies' bored resentment of empty gestures. . . .

The image of the woman frozen in scarlet wax and a million biscuit box-top pictures, had come to life; had ridden her horse out from the reverse of the Great Seal in Piers' glass case on to this square.

The black horse carried the woman sidesaddle across the

stands in front of these thousands, *tens of thousands*. What did they expect from her, from her gestures, from her tense cheeks beginning to show her age, from her salute to the boys in their leaden ranks with the huge band blaring?

And after twenty-five years of it, what did the woman think? Was there power in it for a woman? "I raise my hand and the multitudes bow down" . . . the Kodaks click. . . .

Piers had seen her.

The signs of disintegration in his face had gone no further. His face was also frozen. As rigid as all the queen's horses waiting for their moment in the royal sun.

"COLOUR PARTY WILL ADVANCE!"

Leofric was *talking* to the cocksucker! *Smiling* at him! Enjoying an old boys' joke at the girls' expense. She touched the bag. *Enjoy, baby, enjoy, enjoy.*

"BY THE CENTER . . . QUICK . . . *MARCH!*"

The rolling and roaring of the drums drowned out whatever Piers was saying. The woman on the black horse had come to a halt at the ivory arch. A wisp of hair teased underneath the hat and produced a tiny flicker of a woman's annoyance for its being out of place when all the rest was in such perfect step.

Left right left across the square, and she realized that the boys at Khe Sanh and at Hué had been strolling, *loping* in comparison with this. Left and right across the square, swords up, swords *down!*

With a health unto her Majesty . . .

Her left hand found the flap of the white bag with its Harrods touch of color from the scarf.

Some talk of Alexander, and some of Hercules. . . .

The bag was opened.

Of Hector and Lysander . . .

But not of women. And not of the Lysander that carried a woman without stockings into her pitch-black night.

There was no Cleopatra in the marching songs of the boys, no Boadicea—not even an old gray widow of Windsor who left statues to be toppled in India and Rhodesia and Ireland and Quebec. . . .

Her hand was on the Mauser.

Oh Muir, baby, if you could see me now!

Piers was turning away from Leofric. The eyes flicked across the woman on parade. *Stupid woman*. Riding the black horse, holding the heartstrings. But not the power strings. Men hold the power strings, and men pull them under the Whitehall streets with their lines and squares...

Of all the World's Great Heroes....

Her finger slipped through the trigger guard. Piers stood in front of her. Piers looked right at her. Piers smiled.

There's none that can compare—

Her hand could not move.

Her arm could not move.

Cousin Rollo's Grenadier grip on her wrist had the inexorable finality of his marching men. And Piers was turning, leaving, moving down a step, and another, and away to a seat upholstered in pink velvet.

"Not *here*, Jane," said Leofric on her other side pretending that he cared. "Not *now*."

Not ever.

She was as powerless to act as the woman on horseback.

"QUEEN'S TROOP WILL ADVANCE...."

The horses and the scarlet ranks, in twos and fours pass by; march and countermarch; wheel turn-and-turn-about while Cousin Rollo tells her the significance of buttons on the jackets, of Battle Honors, of the Farrier bringing up the rear with his headsman's ax for the horses fallen in battle. Putting England's faithful animal servants to sleep with an ax— because no *animal* in England must ever suffer.

"COLOUR WILL RETIRE!"

The clock struck one and the show was over, the woman on the black horse gone for lunch to a Jubilee banquet at Westminster to which all old boys were invited.

"I *have* to go," said Leofric, passing back the empty bag. "If you wish to appear ridiculous you may sit out in the car—with Rollo."

So they lunch with the lord mayor where, as Cynthia Whiteside has foretold, a minister of the crown snores while they wish more health unto Her Majesty and Rollo, a lord-in-waiting, stands oblivious of stares outside the ladies' until she comes out. And tries to be *nice* to her, to chat to her while the salt is passed. Not in pheasants on little wheels this time.

"You've got the goddamn gun," she said. "And I'm not going to throw myself under a train for you fuckers. Arrest me, or just let me take off."

But Rollo, determined to keep it all in the family,

behaves toward her as another uncle, not a cousin, and shakes his head sadly, knowing it's a man's job to look after her, if she won't look after herself.

"You can leave tomorrow," said Leofric. "Your grandfather's lighting the Jubilee bonfire down at the abbey as our part of the chain. You surely can't deny him that?"

She could deny them *everything*!

She sat, like one of the airline zombies, sullen and furious through the glorious afternoon with its endless round of introductions to faces flushed with English color and Jubilee booze. The same English circle dancing in lockstep from event to Jubilee event. Locked in it with the woman now off her horse but still smiling—God knows how.

But when the woman stood in front of her and mentioned Violet Vrisser, there was no smile. There was instead a pressure from the woman's hand and an expression in the woman's eyes which Violet Vrisser—expert at these tribal customs—could have interpreted. An expression which might be saying that there *was* power in it for a woman: Power of choice if she found a rotten apple at the top of her tree. She believed now that this woman might find it—*There are damn few secrets*, Vilet Vrisser had said. But would the woman choose—would she *exercise* her choice—when her special day was done?

And how would you know it if she had?

The woman who appointed chiefs of Intelligence and watched prime ministers come and prime ministers go, smiled at Geoffrey Piers and walked from the room leaving no way of telling. . . .

She couldn't stand another *minute* of being locked into this dance; locked in it with that prick who must have bought enough votes to be new boss three times over.

But apparently not. For electoral insurance, to secure a "comfortable" margin, Geoffie Piers states that he also will be lighting bonfires with his villagers.

"And leaving soon," he says to one and all, because even though dark in June is not till ten, with this traffic on the roads it will take hours. In fact—as Big Ben rings them out—he should start now.

At which, Cousin Rollo says to Leofric, "We should be moving too, Father. I'll drive."

A CHARIOT
OF FIRE

37

The new *Mr.* Piers did not own a Rolls or a Daimler.
Piers kept democracy happy with one of the people's cars
from British Leyland, a Jaguar, "An XJ-S," said Rollo. "Proto-
type, brand-new." Which Piers democratically drives himself
after a final wave of pig-skinned hands at a last pair of London
votes oohing and aahing at his silvered hair.

They deserved each other. Smythe at least was right
about that. The silent-majority assholes that voted them in
deserved what they got.

"Leofric," she said. "Just listen—please! I couldn't care
less about the goddamn bonfire, just let me out at Dolphin
Square. My guy has arrived from Rhodesia. For Christ's
sake—look, Leofric, *I want a chance...*."

But Leofric, still playing uncle knows best, says firmly,
"These occasions don't happen often, my dear." And Cousin
Rollo locks the Daimler's doors from the driver's seat.

"The Southern route, Rollo." Leofric slid shut the glass
divider. Her cousin's shoulders obscured the road in front.
She didn't care. Not about him, not about their destination.
Not even about Piers—*no,* that wasn't true! *Would never be
true.* But the moment and the heat for it had passed. Once,
she thought she caught glimpses of the white Jaguar fishing
its way through the density of Jubilee traffic crawling out of
town. She had no idea where they were.

"Croydon," said Leofric. "I must tell you, Jane, SIS
informs me that your notes and tapes both here and in
Washington have been destroyed. I suppose you would have
used that gun?"

"Yes." But she would never know. She remembered the way her hand had frozen by the river. Maybe Violet Vrisser was wrong. Maybe it would not have been easier a second time. Even on Piers.

This was bank-clerk country. Houses, behind discreet quantities of bunting, of a kind Hitler would have loved. "Redhill." Leofric took a thin calculator-clock from a small leather case and set it on the walnut writing shelf in front of him. Traffic was still extremely heavy. She pushed the Harrods hat onto the wide window ledge behind her and lay back into the exquisite softness of the seat. If she could take anything out of this goddamn country, it would be the Daimler. She saw a touch of white again.

Even with Piers' sportscar maneuverability they had gained a little on the Jaguar. There were fewer vehicles between them and more trees between the houses. "Reigate," said Leofric. "Your mother and I often traveled this road."

"Spare me the 'rather close' crap."

Leofric, ignoring that, leaned back into the seat beside her so that their heads were close—yet miles apart. "I drove them both down from Marylebone after the wedding. And I took you up this way to join your father when you were to leave. He didn't really want you then, I'm afraid. He near as damn it left you with us. Living with a ghost, rather. Looking at you and thinking of her—this is Dorking."

Red brick in curves, small factories. Sun and light both very low. Rollo took the Daimler into a traffic circle and came out of it heading closer to due south. When the road straightened briefly, the Jaguar was right in front.

"I never thought of it like that," she said. "Never ever."

"I'm glad, my dear. A child shouldn't."

The Daimler was running through England now, through England's fields with cows and cow parsley and brier hedges of English rose and occasional rabbits in between.

"And I'm sure," continued Leofric, "that your father must have been glad too, in the long haul."

Was Cousin Rollo affected by this reminiscing?

Did he give a damn? It was impossible to tell from the Guardsman's shoulders. The Daimler was still silent but there was a cutting edge to the swish of the tires, a definite sense that a machine was working.

Working a little harder.

And although its color was no longer white in the dusk, the Jaguar was more often visible than not. They ran through two villages in short order. "Holmwood and Coldharbour," Leofric returned to a favorite theme. "All Roman settlements here. The Romans were admirable in so many respects. But unimaginative. It was good for them and bad for them at the same time. You mustn't think, Jane" —and Leofric's head turned on the soft glove leather of the seat cushion so that his eyes looked into hers,—"you mustn't think, that with our phlegmatic ways, *we* are unimaginative. The photographs went to the Palace yesterday. This last village is Leith Hill."

Last? Why last? There were miles to go before they could all sleep in Dorset. So the woman had seen the pictures before she went out to ride her horse for all the people, and had still smiled to all of them. And to Piers. The apples could hang safely on the tree. This country was too old for moral outrage. "England Can Take It" those posters said down there in Churchill's underworld. *England was welcome to it!* She wanted only to go home. With Muir.

"Chaucer would have come this way," said Leofric, "making for Canterbury. Do you know Chaucer? Not well? Your mother was very fond. She used to say he gave her roots. These were the last miles of England that Mary saw. . . ."

Rollo switched on the Daimler's lights. The English countryside backed off and became black. The Roman road became straight.

Straight was not enough! This road could have cut Death Valley. Intuition, never needing reasons, raised hackles on her neck—because this Pilgrim's road was uncompromising, undeviating. *This road allowed no inch for human error.*

"Stane Street, they called it. The underpinnings are solidly Roman. If you scratch the surface you can find them. It must be very nearly time for the first bonfire. Don't you find *that* imaginative, Jane? A chain of fires running down the spine of England? And do you know what *I* always felt were Churchill's finest words?" Leofric spoke them in a Harrovian lisp that seemed no longer quaint or funny. "A spirit ran through our Island that was *sublime!*"

Two red eyes had come down from Violet Vrisser's walls to become the rearlights of the Jaguar. The eyes stayed steady at a distance of one mile. The Daimler followed the eyes at one hundred miles an hour.

"There are moments that *are* sublime in a nation's history, Jane—but not many. There can't be many. And the people that make those moments are only men—yes, and once or twice, like our first Elizabeth, women—but not Christs, not perfect."

Leofric tapped the glass behind his son's shoulder. Rollo's silhouette sat even straighter in the seat. The red eyes of the Jaguar, hidden by his bulk, went out.

"Anstiebury," said Leofric. "Jane, I should like to check the time. Would you push the button on the clock? Yes—that small one on the top."

She reached without question toward the walnut writing shelf; toward the green fluorescent digits on the clock's face.

Only as her hand was half across the gap did her brain record that she could already see the figures.

And so could he.

Her finger froze. She must stop this clock.

But on the new-age watches there are no spiritualist hands to hold the hours or make fresh starts: digital time never freezes; we cannot stop the clock.

She stared at the random bingo numbers counting: 10:13:13.

Counting to infinity for African children lying on a riverbank; for a blond boy bleeding in a street; for five hundred corpses on concrete at Tenerife; for skulls and tears in the ashes of Ravensbrück.

In the automatic counting of the clock, she understood the reason for those killers' tears.

The corporals had cried for a woman called Scylla at Ravensbrück because they knew it does not *have* to be easier the next time.

"No," she said.

She would not do The Firm's Manchurian work for them. In memory of her mother, there would not be a next time.

But the English gentleman beside her ignored a lady's wishes. Leofric's hand pressed hers implacably down upon the trigger of the clock.

The dusk twilight of a June in England lit ten ways to Christmas as the Jaguar exploded.

She followed Leofric through the smoke to the thing lying on the road. The line between black and silver in its hair was gone. So was the hair. So were the legs up to the waist.

The thing twitched.

Her uncle, a small merchant banker, touched the thing with his foot, and said to his Guardsman son who kept the line secure, "An Irish problem, Rollo. Make the call."

She could not look death in the face any longer. She began to shudder. She felt Leofric take her arm and lead her—as our way expects a gentleman to lead a lady—away from the unpleasantness.

"Oh yes," he said as they walked back to the car. "Something for you—rather an old friend, I think."

She felt again the fish-scaled calfskin that had first been offered by an old man waiting for the play to end; heard the cracked voice whispering Pilgrim's starting line: *"As I walked through the wilderness of this world...."*

I met a man with a book, the Pilgrim said.

"Perhaps its many associations will help you to take that chance tomorrow with your South African, my dear Jane. I do hope so. And I do hope that you'll give it a *proper* chance. That from here on in your life you won't travel quite so light of people who care for you. I've allowed myself the liberty of putting in an inscription."

She held the book up to the Daimler's cabin lamp, opened the scarred cover, read the words inscribed on the oiled paper of the flyleaf: words once written for a daughter by a mother dragging a wing into a dark, dark land.

She read her mother's words until the skeleton of the Jaguar was black and the clouded sky of Britain was closed by night above her head.

"But the stars, Jane, do you see—" said the patient man who must have been closer to her mother than she would ever have believed, *"the stars, like faith and courage, have not all gone out...."*

Away across the fields, with their Domesday ghosts, a new flame flickered, caught, held. Blazed. In tribute to her latest daughter a backbone of fire ran end to end of Jael's small island. Ran for a brief postwar moment with a spirit for its confused and independent people that was, perhaps, sublime.

ABOUT THE AUTHOR

DAVID GURR was born in London and emigrated to Canada in his youth. He served as an officer in the Canadian navy for sixteen years. Since then he has been a designer and builder of houses, and is now devoting his full time to writing. His first novel was *Troika*. Mr. Gurr lives with his wife and three children outside of Victoria, British Columbia.

The new national bestseller by the author of
THE SHOES OF THE FISHERMAN

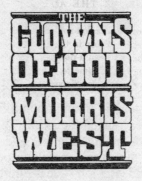

THE CLOWNS OF GOD

MORRIS WEST

A beloved Pontiff prepares to make public his startling vision: Death and destruction will end the world—not in some far-off future, but at any moment! Terrified his pronouncement will spread panic, Vatican Cardinals imprison him in a monastery. Is the Pope a madman—as they believe—or is he telling the truth? One man sets out on an incredible quest to find out—while terrorists and politicians use every deadly and unholy power to stop him.

(#20662-1 • $3.95)

Read THE CLOWNS OF GOD, on sale April 15, 1982 wherever Bantam Books are sold or order directly from Bantam by including $1.00 for postage and handling and sending a check to Bantam Books, Dept. CG, 414 East Golf Road, Des Plaines, Illinois, 60016. Allow 4–6 weeks for delivery. This offer expires 11/82.